THEATER
IN THE
AMERICAS

A Series from
Southern
Illinois
University
Press
ROBERT A.
SCHANKE
Series Editor

Composing Ourselves

Composing Ourselves

The Little Theatre Movement and the American Audience

Dorothy Chansky

Southern Illinois University Press - Carbondale

Copyright © 2004 by the Board of Trustees,
Southern Illinois University
Paperback edition 2005
All rights reserved
Printed in the United States of America
08 07 06 05   4 3 2 1
Library of Congress Cataloging-in-Publication Data

Chansky, Dorothy.
    Composing ourselves : the Little Theatre movement and the Ameri-
can audience / Dorothy Chansky.
       p. cm. — (Theater in the Americas)
Includes bibliographical references and index.
1. Little theater movement—United States. 2. Theater audiences—United
States. I. Title. II. Series.
PN2267 .C45 2004
792.02'23'0973—dc22
ISBN 0-8093-2574-8 (cloth : alk. paper)
ISBN 0-8093-2649-3 (pbk. : alk. paper)   2003020682

Printed on recycled paper.♻

The paper used in this publication meets the minimum requirements of
American National Standard for Information Sciences—Permanence of
Paper for Printed Library Materials, ANSI Z39.48-1992.♾

In memory of my father, George H. Chansky (1922–1993)

Contents

Illustrations

Acknowledgments

The support of many people and institutions has helped make this book possible. Foremost, I want to thank J. Ellen Gainor and Rachel Shteir, who read and commented on every chapter. Their insights and challenges were invaluable. Robert Schanke has been an astute and caring series editor. His energy and attention to detail continue to inspire.

My interest in the Little Theatre movement was initially sparked and encouraged by Brooks McNamara. Others who were influential at the early stages of the work—Marvin Carlson, Peggy Phelan, Ann Douglas, and Susan Bennett—asked tough questions at all the right junctures. The College of William and Mary provided generous institutional support in the form of two Summer Research Grants. These enabled me to travel for archival research and to devote two uninterrupted summers to writing. Barbara Watkinson, Dean of the Faculty of Arts and Sciences, provided funding for the index.

To paraphrase Blanche Dubois, I have always depended on the kindness of librarians. Research at the Lincoln Center branch of the New York Public Library was indispensable for this project and was facilitated by a number of staff members over the years, but Daniel Patrie and Kevin Winkler consistently worked with me, helping with an array of delicate scrapbooks and always creating the sense that I was a research VIP. At the Harvard Theatre Collection, Brian Benoit and Annette Fern made me feel as though they were my personal librarians. That these four people probably manage to make every researcher feel like the most important reader on the premises only increases my respect for them. It is also a pleasure to acknowledge the Dallas Public Library and Robert Eason for access to materials on the Dallas Little Theatre. Robert's own master's thesis was about the DLT and he was able to point me to useful items in the library's holdings. On my second visit to Dallas, I was allowed to work "backstage" in the stacks instead of having to request items a few at a time. Although most of the DLT collection is catalogued in a very user-friendly way, one drawer held unsorted miscellany. It was there that I found the photograph of the cast of "The No 'Count Boy." Geraldine Duclow at the Free Library of Philadelphia's Theatre Collection guided me to materials on that city's Little Theatre work and steered me to the delicious George Bernard Shaw letter quoted in chapter 2. Betty Fitzgerald, the Rhode Island Collection librarian at the Providence Public Library, helped track an early article by George Pierce Baker. Eleanor Buzalsky found and photocopied materials at the Gallatin County Historical Society and Pioneer Museum in Bozeman, Montana. Angela Schiwi at the Vancouver City Archives was helpful with locating material about the Vancouver Little Theatre. Grace L. Ward at the Detroit Public Library was a gracious e-mail correspondent and provided me with photocopies of the library's materials on the Detroit Little Theatre. Ellen Nelson at the Cape Ann Historical Association in Gloucester, Massachusetts, located materials about the Gloucester Little Theatre. Cheryl Greer of the Curtis Theater Collection at the University of Pittsburgh found and photocopied material about the Pitt Players. Anna Litten at the Emerson College Library perused and discussed with me a noncirculating thesis. I thank the staffs of the Newberry Library, the Chicago Historical Society, and the Southern Historical Collection and the North Carolina Collection at the University of North Carolina at Chapel Hill. Keith Longiotti went out of his way to help with photos from the North Carolina Collection. Librarians at New York University's Elmer Holmes Bobst Library and the College of William and Mary's Swem Library were indispensable. At Swem, I am especially grateful to Bettina J. Manzo and to the interlibrary loan staff. David Herzel at the University of New Mexico Fine Arts Library is an indefatigable and unflappable research librarian and did more than anyone else to get me up to speed on electronic resources.

Professional librarians were not the only ones to assist me with archival materials. My mother, Edna Agranovitch Chansky, was on-site in Massachusetts and gathered much data for me at the Cape Ann Historical Society. Mary Naish located clippings for me in Cincinnati. I am grateful to Sydney Grosberg Ronga for accessing and photocopying materials at the Missouri Historical Society Library and Collections Center in

St. Louis. Terry Brino-Dean photocopied portions of a noncirculating master's thesis to which he had ready access when I did not. Terry was also a valuable interlocutor about the Drama League of America.

Libraries and archives do not tell everything about "how I got that story." A network of devoted friends and fellow scholars read parts of this work as it progressed and they stimulated my thinking with their questions, challenges, and suggestions. I thank Lindsay Allen, Noreen Barnes, Ann Beck, Terry A. Bennett, Frances Brantley, Liz Cerubino-Hess, Edward B. Chansky, Elizabeth Drorbaugh, Robin Truth Goodman, Carolyn Hailey, James Harding, Linda Howell, John Istel, Shannon Jackson, David Krasner, Gail Lippincott, Paul D. Naish, Marcia Noe, Shane Phelan, Paige Reynolds, Cindy Rosenthal, DeAnna Toten Beard, Shari Troy, and Stacy Wolf. All either read parts of the manuscript and commented, heard sections of it in the form of conference papers and responded, or served as sounding boards as I sifted through ideas. Several suggested readings I would not otherwise have found. I thank Don Wilmeth for discovering an error in the original edition that has been corrected in this paperback edition. I am also grateful to Cheryl Black, Brook Davis, Alex Fraser, Betsy Gibson, Rob Marx, John Hutchins, Meredith Miller, and William C. O'Neil for assistance with some illustrations and citations. Last but not least, David N. Tabakin of William and Mary's information technology department was indispensable in the preparation of the manuscript.

Parts of this book have appeared previously in different form: Part of chapter 3 was first published as "The 47 Workshop and the 48 States: George Pierce Baker and the American Theatre Audience" in *Theatre History Studies* 18 (135–146). An earlier version of another part of the same chapter was first published as "*Theatre Arts Monthly* and the Construction of the Modern American Theatre Audience" in *The Journal of American Theatre and Drama* 10 (51–75). Part of chapter 5 was first published as "Alice Gerstenberg and the 'Experimental' Trap" in *Midwestern Miscellany* 30:1 (21–34). A section of chapter 6 was first published as "The Quest for Self in Others: Race, Authenticity, and 'Folk Plays'" in *Theatre Symposium* 11 (7–17). My editors and readers have worked with concern and integrity; any errors are mine.

Composing Ourselves

Little Theatre and Audience Construction

A Modern(ist) Project

The drama, it needs scarcely be remarked, involves nothing more nor less than a series of tacit agreements between actors and audience. . . . This tacit conspiracy, if originally carried out in the proper spirit, becomes in course of time a totally unconscious process in the mind of the spectator.

> —Archibald Henderson, "The Evolution of Dramatic Technique"

The 1996 film *Looking for Richard* documents the work of Al Pacino and a group of devoted actors as they put together a production of *Richard III.* Their goal was to show contemporary spectators that this play, the most popular of Shakespeare's opus on the nineteenth-century American stage, still reeked of passion, intrigue, and stageworthiness. That the project reached its widest audience as a film says much about the entertainment and performance climate in which the company was doing its looking (and producing).[1] Pacino's undertaking was unremarkable to the extent it depended on two longstanding American ideas about theatre and theatregoing: first, that Shakespeare is simultaneously "good for you" and difficult; second that schoolchildren need and deserve to be instructed in the salutary effects of theatre.[2] Indeed, many of the audiences the camera picked up included young students. But the most unexamined idea of all—arguably the idea on which the project was predicated—was conveyed by a rather remarkable source. Pacino interviewed an African American man who was missing several front teeth and created the impression of being homeless. The interviewee was, nonetheless, fully possessed of a belief in the uplifting work that theatre does and of the idea that the realm of self-expression via drama was a—and his—spiritual home.

Composing Ourselves is an investigation of the work, thinking, and institutional development in early-twentieth-century American culture that forged both Pacino's interviewee's expressed ideology and an infrastructure to disseminate it. That these ideas needed to be forged at all may seem strange to theatre lovers or to those who assume that because theatre is a longstanding element of human activity, its uses and value have simply been handed down. The American belief that theatre is spiritually and emotionally fulfilling, socially elevating, of civic importance, a site for assaying social change, and an enriching locus of cultural capital originated in the early decades of the twentieth century. Film killed the theatrical "road," simultaneously capturing most of its audiences and creating a vast new public for dramatic entertainment. "Without competition from commercial producers," notes Paul DiMaggio, "those who would elevate theater to art inherited the stage by default."[3] These inheritors included writers, various kinds of activists, university professors and other educators, clubwomen, settlement workers, artists, and social elites seeking outlets for self-expression. In their hands, American theatre "became an image of reform, struggling against a conservative corporate society. . . . [L]ive theatre persists because it offers an alternative image of society to an audience that desires one."[4] In this analysis, Douglas McDermott names the ethos undergirding the creation of a new outlook towards theatre; he also indicates broadly how and where it continues to have valence.

The collective name for the activities of these theatre reformers is the Little Theatre movement. This book is predicated on the idea that this movement is best understood as a national, multipronged phenomenon, and not just the work of well-known experimenters. Little Theatre workers came from many parts of the country and worked with diverse populations on widely varying kinds of stages and projects. Little Theatre offered Americans the option of a revised contract between audiences and theatre endeavors. Producing, financing, distribution of productions and texts, dramaturgy, training, education, criticism, scenic and lighting design, and advertising all acquired many of the features that are so entrenched in noncommercial theatre today that they seem natural to us. It was the Little Theatre movement that generated the college theatre major, the inclusion of theatre in secondary school curriculums, and prototypes for nonprofit producing. While it is possible to view activities in universities as separate from, for example, independent Little Theatre work and to separate these from the work undertaken in publishing serious theatre publications, I want to argue that the overlap of personnel, scripts, and widely circulated ideas about production and scenography represents one movement with action on multiple fronts.

Little Theatre undertakings were among many national reform projects, as Americans in all parts of the country sought political and social changes in the years from roughly 1890 into the 1920s. Treating the activities of so many kinds of reformers—even just the diverse theatre reformers—as a movement points to a conundrum for anyone who examines Progressive Era activism. A movement is typically a collectivity with continuity, some coherence, and particular goals regarding either promoting or resisting change, but Progressivism "lacked unanimity or purpose either on a programmatic or on a philosophical level."[5] Like other reform activities in the era, the Little Theatre movement had contradictory strains; it included forward-looking activism and modernist aesthetics as well as skepticism, nativism, elitism, and nostalgia, sometimes within the same production company or publication. Coalitions and alliances shifted; ambivalence, paradox, opportunism, and mixed values appear everywhere in Little Theatre writing. Most Little Theatre workers assumed that their middle-class, Protestant heritage was a standard by which all culture could be measured, yet even here, geography played a role in how they staged their aesthetic interventions and whom they invited to participate. Peter Filene's conclusion that "progressives espoused, at best, a heterogeneous ideology"[6] does not foreclose an examination of that ideology. Rather, it suggests to me that a continual back-and-forth between forest and trees is the only way to appreciate the details and passions of Little Theatre activities while also contextualizing them and assessing them in the aggregate. One of the themes of this book is that while all Little Theatre work was about improving American entertainment and American life—a notion that depends on specific ideas of what is and isn't worthwhile—efforts were neither consistent nor congruent in their day and are selectively recalled and invoked in the present. Since I believe that the Little Theatre movement was a founding period for many ideas that Americans today accept about theatre, I want to keep returning to the contradictions and ironies that emerged in the first part of the last century and whose legacies continue to challenge us today.

What did emerge got its start in the 1910s when small numbers of Americans in many parts of the country began to found theatre groups in a spirit of anticommercialism. Unashamedly amateur, although not always without professional ambitions, these practitioners and advocates sought to develop an American audience for serious theatre, simultaneously developing such theatre itself by writing and mounting plays in what might now be called "alternative spaces." The theatre they refuted was primarily a large network of touring shows from New York (as well as the New York productions themselves) that included melodrama, light comedy, musicals, occasional Shakespearean revivals showcasing star actors, and euphemistic realism, a style in which images of urban existence, recognizable social types, real places, or social problems are depicted, but in such a way as to avoid, for the most part, creating images that are too harsh or disturbing to mainstream sensibilities.[7] All genres for the most part used pictorialist scenography and musical accompaniment. The influence of this aesthetic package was substantial; touring shows reached all but the smallest towns, and ticket prices were often affordable for most except the poorest Americans. A major objection to these shows, which were produced and sent on the road by a cartel of New York producers, was that, besides being intellectually thin or downright frivolous—which not everyone resented—they were, in their touring incarnations, shoddily produced and sometimes falsely advertised as being original New York productions, which irritated even nonidealists.[8]

Little Theatre reformers found this package mindless, bloated, and detrimental to psychic well-being. They thought theatre could offer its participants and audiences a chance to explore social issues and to resist the numbing lure of predictably scripted spectacle shows. They believed that on a personal and also a collective level, Little Theatre could improve American society. Little Theatre reformers looked to European models, inspired by the plays and organizational structure of England's Independent Theatre, Dublin's Irish Players, the Moscow Art Theatre, the Freie Bühne, and the Théâtre Libre and the design and directing work of Adolph Appia, Gordon Craig, Konstantin Stanislavski, and Max Reinhardt. They also encouraged new work by American playwrights, often members of their own new companies. Little Theatre activists founded journals; renovated buildings; wrote plays and manifestos; taught playwriting; and produced, publicized, and acted in plays. They also worked with children, college students, new immigrants, and rural citizens who had little or no previous theatre experience, towards facilitating self-expression via dramatic work (endeavors addressed in chapters 2 and 5). The best-known Little Theatres include the Provincetown Players, the Washington Square Players, the Detroit Arts and Crafts Theatre, the Chicago Little Theatre; the Neighborhood Playhouse, which was affiliated with the Henry Street Settlement; and Jane Addams's Hull-House, which was known for its reformist theatre activities with immigrant populations. Philadelphia's Plays and Players, New Orleans's Petit Théâtre du Vieux Carré, The Pasadena Playhouse, and the Cleveland Playhouse were all founded as part of the Little Theatre movement in the 1910s and still exist in some form. Between 1912 and 1916, sixty-three organizations calling themselves Little Theatres sprang up in the United States.[9] By 1926, a writer for *Variety* claimed there were 5,000.[10] Little Theatre work became accepted by universities, high schools, and civic groups. Although many of the groups existing before the war dissolved, some held on or regrouped, and many more were created during the 1920s.

The work of the 1920s Little Theatres is less well known and is commonly regarded by historians as less glamorous than much of the work of the 1910s. Certainly this decade saw the creation of texts and productions that experimented in many aesthetic styles; the 1920s were the years when Little Theatre gained institutional stability. I want to argue here, however, that only the full arc of the work within both decades can account for the American theatre's "inadvertent revolution," to borrow Beth Bailey's term for a sea change in social behavior enabled not only by the innovations of self-proclaimed rebels, but by widespread, systematic shifts allowing a broad based accommodation of the new rhetoric by many Americans.[11] The American Little Theatre movement was a modernist project, but it is important to understand that American moderns, as Christine Stansell spells out, less often gravitated toward the stylistic and narrative innovations with which high modernism is often associated than they embraced a "renovated realism . . . as a solvent of bourgeois society."[12] Even if abstract, rhythmic, stark productions garner(ed) more attention in print, the pull and fascination of realism and the recognizable made Little Theatre usable for "bohemians" and reformers in the 1910s as well as for educators, civic boosters, and the spiritually hungry in the radio-linked, therapeutically inclined, consumerist 1920s. In short, the two phases of the movement share more than is usually acknowledged.

Taxonomies

Many theatre histories locate the "innovative" Little Theatre movement
in the years between 1912 and 1918, with a devolution into "community"
theatre occurring in the 1920s.[13] The need for "Little" to mean "art" theatre and to be different from the presumably lesser "community" theatre
is not only a latter-day interpretation. In 1926, Lee F. Heacock's "Community *or* Little Theatre—Which?"—based on observations in Buffalo,
New York—insisted that "the two are absolutely incompatible," as Little
Theatre "aims to raise the appreciations of its audiences . . . to a higher
intellectual level" while "the function of the Community Theatre is to give
opportunity of expression to those in the community who wish to try
their talents."[14] Yet from the outset, Little Theatres combined the two
aims, often producing dramaturgically negligible plays in the name of
self-expression. The Provincetown Players, for example, may be best remembered for the work of Eugene O'Neill and Susan Glaspell, but the
vast majority of plays written by members are forgotten and forgettable.
Jane Heap, coeditor of *The Little Review,* which first offered *Ulysses* to
American readers, found little in the Provincetown fare to raise her appreciation or challenge the intellect. She complained in 1919 that the
Provincetowners "presented plenty of plays about romantic triangles and
an abundance of works offering 'a problem from [the playwright's] own
little psychological laboratory. . . . But plays there were none.'"[15] Also in
1919, an anonymous editorial writer for the *Nation* saw the fluidity and
multipurpose value of Little Theatre work from midstream, looking
ahead and observing simply that "the Little Theatre movement is now
in its second and perhaps its most difficult stage," while astutely seeing
the purpose of several kinds of simultaneously existing groups. "The
various little theatres encourage American drama, the laboratory theatre begets it."[16]

Unquestionably, there were literary and organizational changes that
occurred within the movement following World War I. The repertoire
of the mid-1910s drew heavily on British and Irish plays, with works by
Lord Dunsany, George Bernard Shaw, and John Millington Synge among
the most popular. Early Little Theatres around the country also grabbed
Zona Gale's "Neighbors," Susan Glaspell's "Trifles," and Alice Brown's
"Joint Owners in Spain," all original one-act plays about ordinary American women.[17] In 1924, *The Drama Year Book* catalogued several hundred
Little Theatres and listed repertory for about 10 percent of them.[18] Many
whose repertoire is listed continued to present the favorites from the

1910s, which suggests that the impulses and interests of the original movement were not abandoned. Some groups, preferring recent Broadway hits, for the 1924 season chose the domestic/romantic comedy *Dulcy,* the costume romance *Captain Applejack,* and A. A. Milne's drama *The Truth About Blayds.*

But if Broadway fare and strategies infiltrated Little Theatre operations, it is equally important to note that Little Theatre sensibility had a major effect on Broadway. As Ronald H. Wainscott traces in *The Emergence of the Modern American Theatre 1914–1929,* the Broadway on which his study primarily focuses is a Broadway with key players who honed their skills as writers and designers in Little Theatres. A short list includes Susan Glaspell, Paul Green, Robert Edmond Jones, O'Neill, Elmer Rice, the Theatre Guild, and Lula Vollmer. While Sheldon Cheney and Hiram Kelly Moderwell had extolled "art theatre" in the 1910s, by 1925 there was a market for Oliver Hinsdell's book *Making the Little Theatre Pay.* By "pay," Hinsdell meant stay solvent and in operation, not necessarily turn a profit. Cheney and Moderwell lobbied for an as-yet unfamiliar and antirealist scenographic aesthetic—shorthanded as "the new stagecraft" and valorizing abstraction over pictorialism, although useful enough to back realist texts—for American art theatre. Hinsdell, writing in the 1920s, could assume ten years of description, experimentation, "how-to" articles, and well-circulated photographs and sketches, including those from Broadway productions, manifesting Little Theatre influence. In a brief mention of *Theatre Arts,* the seminal journal that Cheney founded, Wainscott points to the magazine's effects on Broadway and off: "Inspired by the publication, theatrical mavericks and dissenting professionals joined amateurs of the little-theater movement in transforming stagecraft, directing, and dramaturgy."[19] Cheney himself cautioned that community theatre "is at best only a relative term . . . [which], moreover, does not necessarily mean a theater which is designed to serve a majority of the people of its city, or even any considerable percentage of the population."[20]

In arguing for a continuum rather than a golden age of enlightenment followed by a capitulation to popular taste, I am interested in something that the various and evolving Little Theatres did take as a common cause—something beyond particular literary genres or design aesthetics. I am calling this ongoing concern "audience construction." By audience construction, I mean the creation of attitudes and behaviors concerning theatregoing in the minds and bodies of actual or potential spectators as well as other Americans. The purpose of audience construction was, beginning in the Little Theatre movement, and remains in the United States, to create and maintain a permanent audience class and a public belief in the importance of theatre in civic and personal life. Audience construction may be imposed from the outside in the form of actual instruction by an usher, a columnist, a teacher who is about to take a group of students to their first play, or program notes requesting or forbidding certain behavior. Or it may be generated by playgoers who create their own theatre in order to inhabit it as spectators and to fill it with others who are like-minded. Audience construction may also involve theorizing about audiences for a particular play or a new kind of theatre. The audience being constructed ideally would include a citizenry that, even if not all its members attend the theatre, could change their attitudes toward the theatre, thus facilitating governmental support, theatre in schools, and perhaps the participation of family members. In W. B. Worthen's analysis, "the modern theater's history of innovation is directly concerned with producing a certain kind of experience for the audience, and so with producing the audience itself."[21]

This production of audience was essential during the 1910s and 1920s if theatre was to survive in the face of the entertainment challenge offered by movies and radio, as well as by restaurants, amusement parks, and even driving and riding in automobiles. Little Theatre theorists recognized this. In 1917, Thomas Dickinson (1877–1961), a professor of English at the University of Wisconsin and founder in 1911 of the Wisconsin Dramatic Society, wrote that "the organization of the audience represents a great advance toward a *solution of the problems* of the theatre" (emphasis mine).[22] The "federated audience" he touted would comprise playgoers who could be counted on to subscribe, often in groups, to serious theatre endeavors.[23] Underscoring that the project was national and not only rooted in New York, or even only in the largest cultural centers, Sheldon Cheney asserted that "*potential* audiences for the best drama do exist in the average American city" (emphasis in original).[24] In 1923, critic Walter Prichard Eaton (1878–1957) asserted that "perhaps the most important dramatic work in America is . . . the creation, through rural America, of an audience for the spoken drama."[25] For Eaton, hope lay in the schools. Dickinson, as late as 1952, had not changed his mind. In a letter to a graduate student researching his early work, Dickinson wrote that "while not primarily a theatre man I knew the theatre well enough in all its angles to be aware that its chief bottleneck was the audience."[26] Mary Heaton Vorse, owner of the wharf where the Provincetowners gave their first productions for each other in 1915, summed up in her response what the Little Theatre movement wanted: "a creative audience."[27]

Audience construction did not and could not, of course, take place outside the production of particular plays, designs, scripts, workshops, classes, publications, and even buildings. The style and content of these changed as the social milieu changed. But shifts in textual and production modes represent not a failure of earlier models or even necessarily a rupture between past and present; rather they denote an evolution resulting from and in an ongoing negotiation with a never static cultural field. As the ensuing pages show, Little Theatre practitioners and theorists sometimes had an adversarial stance towards actual or potential audiences they saw as unenlightened in relation to the work they were trying to do—a stance that continues to be shared by many artistic directors in regional theatres three-quarters of a century later.[28] Some of those who asked what the theatre could do for them, including many of the early participants, went quietly into the night after the war.[29] Among those who asked what they could do for the theatre were the others who came to embrace summer workshops, university training programs, Little Theatre tournaments, and shared resources into the 1920s and beyond.

A strategy used by all of the Little Theatres examined in this study is some version of what Shannon Jackson calls "reformance." This neologism combining "reform" and "performance" suggests a constitutive doing in which change occurs through active participation.[30] For Jackson, reformance is a process of mutual influence. The initiators of the activities respond to and are affected by the work of recruits; the recruits shape their behavior to the prescribed task while subtly putting their own stamp on it. At the most obvious level, Little Theatre practitioners engaged in reformance activities with recruits who did actual work on scripts, productions, and institutional maintenance. But this work was not necessarily distinct from audience construction and recruitment. In their 1938 study of noncommercial theatre in the United States, Jean Carter and Jess Ogden found considerable overlap between participants and audience in the noncommercial theatre. One Little Theatre in their study reported that 25 percent of their subscription list participated in their productions.[31] Audiences who did not take part in productions were also encouraged to see themselves as participants in creating a more meaningful and purposeful American theatre by virtue of their attendance, response, and eschewing of lesser forms of entertainment, thereby embodying Vorse's idea of the creative audience. George Pierce Baker

(1866–1935), the Harvard professor credited with making playwriting an accepted part of the American university curriculum, put the audience at the center of shaping new drama by making their written responses to original plays the price of admission to attending these plays. Not only shared viewing and writing projects, but shared reading of journals and plays for Little Theatre supporters "recursively reflected and constituted the feeling" of being an active and important community.[32] Both Baker's project and the construction of a Little Theatre audience through shared journal reading are discussed at length in chapter 3.

Little Theatre workers were, in effect, creating what Benedict Anderson calls an "imagined community" of theatre audiences nationwide. Anderson's thesis is that modern communities are united by shared ideas about themselves that are fictive but reified by the behavior and self-images of people who identify with one another even though they may never have met or even seen each other. Modern nations, Anderson suggests, forge sociological solidity by shared ideas of simultaneously existing, separate, yet comparable sociological plurals. A nation's prisons, in his example, are alike in their "prisonness."[33] Although each is a discrete entity, all are recognizable as exemplifying the same ideals and values. American Little Theatres, while locally inflected, were much alike in their "theatreness," because of a combination of what they resisted, who traveled among their ranks, and how they circulated ideas about production. Texts and people in positions of leadership were the means of sharing ideas and building conceptual consensus; local participation and consumption were the means of individualizing and particularizing projects and experiences. As the following chapters show, imaginings of the ideal audience were often soaked in nostalgia, a nostalgia constructed, as Joseph Roach asserts nostalgia always is, "with designs on the culture of the future." Such nostalgia takes the form of a yearning for and belief in the "role of the audience, mythologized as an organic cultural whole and reified as a mass-cultural simulacrum of the body politic."[34] That the audience the leaders imagined and the community particular Little Theatre audiences imagined themselves to be were not always isomorphic is part of the performed dialectic by which the modern audience engaged in the process of composing itself.

The flow of practitioners from university programs to work in what would now be called regional theatre and the national circulation of scripts in magazines and journals devoted to serious theatre are now ordinary. Such sharing of personnel, texts, and theories was crucial to the development and success of the Little Theatre movement. To give just one example, Frederick Koch studied with George Pierce Baker, who pioneered the playwriting/production workshop model at Harvard, before Koch moved to North Dakota to work in and on rural Little Theatre with Alfred Arvold, founder of the Little Country Theatre. In 1918, Koch went to the University of North Carolina, where his Carolina Playmakers and his courses in playwriting (including attendant productions, à la Baker in the latter's 47 Workshop) with an emphasis on the folk play (a legacy of his rural work) fostered the work of Paul Green. Green's "The No 'Count Boy" was picked up by the Dallas Little Theatre when one of the DLT's influential members read Green's script in *Theatre Arts* in 1924. The Dallas production, discussed in chapter 6, became an award winner in 1925 at a New York City–based Little Theatre tournament, not long before Green's *In Abraham's Bosom* was produced on Broadway and won a Pulitzer Prize.

Other legacies of the Little Theatre movement include the nonprofit model, the sometime ambition for visibility in New York, and the expectation of government support for theatre. The 1930s Federal Theatre Project (FTP), the 1960s creation of the National Endowment for the Arts, and the various state councils on the arts are ideas for which the way was paved by Little Theatre theorists. Indeed, Hallie Flanagan, head of the FTP, had studied with George Pierce Baker and taught experimental theatre at Vassar College before being tapped for her post in Washington. Elmer Rice (then Reizenstein and not yet the author of *The Adding Machine*) was an early member of the Morningside Players, a Manhattan Little Theatre group, in the 1910s before serving a short term as an administrator in the New York City branch of the FTP.

In arguing for the Little Theatre movement's role in creating a cultural space and need for educational and government support of theatre, I am not making any global claims with regard to aesthetic excellence or egalitarian inclusion. As the ensuing pages show, much of what was touted as serious, uplifting, educational, and universal in Little Theatre rhetoric and productions was often racist, sexist, self-absorbed, and exclusionary. I am, rather, arguing that Little Theatre rhetoric about the worthwhile nature of thoughtfully produced theatre came to infiltrate the thinking of educators, many audiences, cultural theorists, and funding sources nationwide. This rhetoric still serves American practitioners and educators who continue to fight battles about inclusivity, legibility, activism, social worth, and aesthetic innovation.

If the term "Little Theatre" poses taxonomic challenges, so, too do the terms "American Theatre," "legitimate theatre," "mainstream theatre" or even the separate words "American" and "theatre" in the context of this study. In his now infamous beginning to the 1951 *History of the American Theatre,* Glenn Hughes denied that "Aztec rituals, transplanted Spanish mysteries, Eskimo festivals, and various other exotic manifestations of the dramatic instinct . . . the antelope dance . . . or the potlatch" belonged in his study. American theatre, for Hughes, was that which "began with the settlements of Europeans on our shores."[35] The advent in the 1980s of performance studies as a discipline widened the scope of the definition of "theatre," although even in the 1920s, *Theatre Arts* had published articles about rituals and performances of Pueblo Indians, puppet theatre, Chinese theatre, modern dance, and the difficulty of interpreting movement qua movement, suggesting an awareness on the part of some Little Theatre leaders of a larger performance world. Nonetheless, when Little Theatre practitioners and reformers talked about American theatre, they nearly always meant "legitimate" theatre. Within the context of the Progressive Era, Mark Hodin argues that "*legitimate* theatre [emphasis in original] . . . proposed and promoted . . . that, in *relation* to other competing forms of commercial amusement, the particular value of conventionally staged drama was that it provided the best occasion and opportunity available for acquiring cultural prestige, 'literary' value . . . ."[36] An early study by the Twentieth Century Club of some of these "other competing forms" in Boston found that in the 1909–10 season, just 13.1 percent of all theatrical entertainment comprised "legitimate" performances. Vaudeville and moving picture shows made up 85.4 percent.[37] Of the "legitimate portion," Little Theatre would largely ignore minstrelsy, melodrama, musical comedy, and dancing, leaving drama, comedy, farce, and, to a lesser extent, Shakespearean drama, in its purview, these all totaling slightly less than half of the "legitimate" area in the study and less than musical comedy and melodrama alone. Richard Butsch's term "drama theater" is a useful name for the small corner of the "legit" staked out by Little Theatre workers.[38]

Within this already-narrowed area, however, as Hodin also notes, the concept of "legitimate" made "no distinction between good and bad plays."[39] Its value as cultural capital lay in its literary basis qua basis. Because a "legitimate" theatre experience could be had in the context of a bad script (not that anyone overtly lobbied for such a thing), the Little Theatre movement was able to recruit audiences via reformance activities even as it might encourage the writing or supporting of derivative, quickly dated, or self-indulgent plays. Susan Harris Smith, in her comprehensive study of the sidelining or outright ignoring of American drama as a field of literary study, cites aspects of the Little Theatre movement as contributors to the problem she outlines. By elevating text as the scaffold of theatre performance over text as literature, both George Pierce Baker in his playwriting workshop and Progressive Era pedagogy that stressed self-expression via dramatic literature over exegesis were able to encourage a love of theatre without focusing on plays outside their performance possibilities.[40] This contradiction continues to plague school and community theatre productions where participant focus on collaboration can be at odds with administrative, directorial, or even audience concerns for texts that fulfill literary requirements ranging from being recognizably canonical to being overtly offbeat.

The emphasis on the experiential and the importance of persuasion and efficacy over experimentation or unusual aesthetics can in part be traced to a pedagogical affiliation between theatre and speech—a legacy evident in the number of college departments whose names and missions combine the two. In 1920, E. C. Mabie (1892–1956), shortly to found a theatre department at the University of Iowa, cited dramatic art as "a splendid means of democratic, educative, public recreation," embedding his remark in an essay on the value of speech training in "the discharge of the duties of the citizen."[41] Mabie based his argument about the linkage of speaking and citizenship on the experience of soldiers in World War I, and he had in mind young adults. Teachers of young children also embraced dramatic activities, especially in areas where lower-class or immigrant students seemed to cultural elites to require reform in speech habits. "Dramatics was . . . particularly useful when teachers made 'a great point of the use of the voice of pronunciation and diction; and what could not possibly be taught in one play a year, can be inculcated in one play a year for ten years.'"[42]

Little Theatre reformers and practitioners did in fact have much to say about dramatic literature as literature. Yet ultimately they were more concerned with the value of attending, creating, and discussing "legitimate" theatre than with the necessity of putting a particular kind of writing at the center of that experience. J. Ellen Gainor suggests a possible reason for this in her study of Susan Glaspell. Glaspell, like may other Little Theatre playwrights, was a journalist and published in a variety of genres. Therefore, the choice to use drama to explore a social or personal concern was made with a "keen understanding of what narratives are well served by theatrical representation."[43] The choice by a close-knit group to present plays for, and often by, their own community meant that particular ideas about what would engage an audience without alienating it would prevail. Since most Little Theatre practitioners were in positions of some social influence (e.g., because they were writers, teachers, or monied), their work got public attention and eventually affected the thinking of many commercial theatre workers and audiences.

To say that Little Theatre constructed an audience for mainstream American theatre invites the question of what is meant by mainstream. While mainstream theatre often implies "legitimate" (predicated on dramatic text) theatre, mainstream also suggests a particular point of view both about and generally embedded in the text. Ideas and images that are often called mainstream and accepted as universally American both in cultural histories and "in the ambient culture generally," are the ideas of the professional middle class. The professional middle class comprise "all those people whose economic and social status is based on education, rather than on the ownership of capital or property," although this hardly means that this class eschewed money.[44] Their ideas and values circulate not only in "literate" writing, but more commonly in mass-produced images, where they pass as norms. In the Progressive Era, they would have appeared widely in magazines, newspapers, window displays, advertising, plays, and textbooks, promulgating standards in everything from clothing, hygiene, family, and courtship styles to public behavior, diet, and preferred vocabulary. Because Little Theatre naturalized professional middle-class interests, tastes, and anxieties as universal, even some kinds of theatre that technically qualified as "legitimate" in being text-based were ignored. Among the latter were circle repertory and tent theatre, both of which were popular in the rural Midwest among audiences who also enjoyed vaudeville and medicine shows. Most workers' theatre was also ignored, except when it comprised contemporary European drama. These forms were either of little interest or were invisible to the urban, suburban, or college-educated class that fostered much Little Theatre.[45] Accordingly, what Little Theatre workers challenged as an American theatre in need of reform represented a particular piece of a much larger theatrical and performance pie—the piece that was consumed by their class and cohort.

One of the forms the challenge took was in literally embracing littleness. Most Little Theatres set up shop in small venues that were geographically close to the groups they served rather than being in traditional entertainment districts. Typical choices were renovated storefronts or churches, studios or school auditoriums, grange halls, settlement houses, and, occasionally, private homes or overhauled saloons. Audience members were likely to know each other. The coterie ambience flew in the face of the impersonal glitter of a commercial theatre outing and ideally reinforced a communitarian ideal. One of the challenges Little Theatre posed—and faced—was in the encounters it staged in audiences comprising both members or sympathizers and guests or outsiders. Sinclair Lewis offers a brief sketch of such an encounter in *Main Street* (discussed in chapter 4) when the idealistic Carol Kennicott and her meat-and-potatoes husband attend a Little Theatre evening of one-acts by Schnitzler, Yeats, Shaw, and Dunsany at a drama school in Minneapolis circa 1911. Both Kennicotts are outsiders in being from a small town and not knowing anyone affiliated with the school. Carol is an insider in that she sympathizes with the idea of self-expression through contemporary European drama. Will Kennicott has no interest in the plays, but he goes because his wife wants to and because he can brag that he's seen theatre in the big city. In the end, neither understands much about the literature or the mise-en-scène, but both are captivated by one actress's work.[46]

The self-selected Little Theatre audience, regardless of class, geographical, or even internal differences, was very uniform in one sense: it was almost always racially segregated. Yet Little Theatre work to reform audiences and production of mainstream theatre was, with regard to representation of Americans of color, often more sympathetic and nuanced than in much commercial theatre. It nonetheless did not present a world through the eyes of its subjects. Rather, it offered them in depictions created by and for white audiences, perpetuating what Maurice Berger calls "white lies." White lying may avoid overt negative remarks but can never escape an internalized hierarchizing in which persons of color are understood in some way as lesser.[47] Such classifying, with the assumption that white, Anglo-Protestants were at the top, "received structural reinforcement from other American social ladders—particularly those of civic politics and the industrial division of labor—[giving] such categories and hierarchies . . . the spontaneous and taken-for-granted character of common sense."[48] Thomas Dickinson, for instance, argued in 1915 for the importance of representing "the race borderland between the Indian and the white man" in American drama.[49] Yet his view of the Amerindian was that "he was lost in a miasma of thought he could not fathom, of a civilization he was unprepared for."[50] Dickinson's Wisconsin Players presented "Glory of the Morning," a one-act written by a white university professor and featuring a romanticized view of a nature-based Amerindian life.[51] "Negro plays" (discussed in chapter 6) similarly featured poor, rural blacks in "timeless" settings and were pointedly tragic or comic but rarely modern or urban. These plays offered generally sympathetic and sometimes ethnographically very informed portrayals, but they did so in ways that did not challenge whites' ideas of universalism and that avoided the point of view or insider particularities of those represented. Little Theatre work often demonstrated interest in and sympathy for lack of visibility per se; it did not, however, challenge entrenched hegemonic assumptions about white social superiority.

The presumed audience—both that to be constructed among the young, the inexperienced, or the new immigrant, as well as that to be reconstructed among "debased" but presumably rescuable theatregoers— was never large. Recall that the Twentieth Century Club report indicates how much in the way of resources (number of theatres and number of performances) were devoted to "legitimate" theatre: 13.1 percent, of which perhaps half was of interest to Little Theatre reformers. Maurice Browne (1884–1961), the charismatic and visionary founder of the Chicago Little Theatre, stipulated clearly what was wanted for his "temple of a living art": "about one per cent of the population going to the theatre about once a month as a matter of course and preferring to enjoy itself while there." Recall, too, Sheldon Cheney's idea of community theatre not being designed to serve a majority of the people of its city, or even any considerable percentage of the population. Browne's 1 percent comprised "average" Americans, "men and women, without overmuch money or brains, but with a great deal of that splendid, pitiful, underrated quality which is common to all—ordinary humanity; ... your cousins ... my aunts ... Mrs. Lake Avenue's cook's young man ... store-clerks and college professors and club-women and policemen and members of the Drama League of America and elevator boys ... all who are compact ... of laughter and tears and the divine childish gift of 'let's pretend.'"[52] The requirement for admission, in other words, was one of sensibility. Practitioners and recruiters often conflated "ordinary humanity" with the interests and viewpoints of their own class, but the ideal and rhetoric did make room for strategic challenges to the mainstream point of view regarding commercial theatre and for interclass inclusiveness. Much of this study is occupied with the tensions between the ideal and the realization.

Timeframes

While I have been arguing for a continuum of Little Theatre audience construction over the 1910s and 1920s, it is important to situate those decades of theatre activity within the larger culture and also to stake out a claim for the specific 1912–1925 timeframe that this book covers. The Progressive Era saw reform in many areas. Labor practices, public health policies, Victorian mores, Romantic and neoclassical ideas in art and literature, trust monopolies, and public education were all scrutinized, criticized, and overhauled to greater or lesser extents. The United States participated in World War I; the country also approved Prohibition. Between 1890 and the early 1920s, some twenty-three million immigrants arrived, largely from southern and eastern Europe and Russia.[53] Both the new citizens and new world of ubiquitous consumer goods, propped up by inexpensive, popular publications, later by cinema and radio, and by advertising, yielded concurrent and dialectical effects: on the one hand, anxiety about change, especially on the part of elites and hereditary Americans who felt their comfortable status and familiar ways being challenged; on the other hand, a certain thrill in the face of new technology, new ideas, and the titillation and/or exoticism offered to white elites by emigrants from abroad or migrating African Americans within national borders.[54] In the wake of the war, the nation cooled its public tolerance for self-proclaimed anarchists, international involvement, and for immigration; women got the vote but did not, in the main, use it as a bloc to challenge the political status quo. The ensuing 1920s hardly "roared" equivalently for all Americans, but the middle classes enjoyed more consumer goods than ever, and political concerns (or a turning away from them) earned them the label "isolationist."[55] A rise in the number of professional organizations, systematized understandings of the workplace, special interest publications, and widely circulated beliefs that the fast pace of modern life required certain kinds of therapeutic and/or professional advisory interventions were recognizable features of the 1920s.[56]

Still the 1912–1925 timeframe may not be an immediately obvious one for examining the Little Theatre audience construction project. The starting point is clearer as a theatre beachhead than the latter, which may seem, as a terminus, to leave off *in medias res*. The year 1912 is a visible and vibrant one of assertive rebellion. The Lawrence, Massachusetts, textile mill workers' strike led by the International Workers of the World brought international attention to the plight of the thousands of workers who "in the greatest woolen center in the country could not even afford the overcoats they produced."[57] Three of four presidential candidates were Progressives, although they belonged officially to different parties, and the incumbent, Taft, was put in the position of conservative, receiving less than half the votes of Wilson and Roosevelt.[58] Chicago-based *Poetry* magazine was started that year, soon to be followed by Margaret Anderson's *Little Review* in the same city. Preparations took place in New York for the Armory Show of January 1913, which exposed Americans to "every variety of contemporary non-representational, non-moralizing, untraditional experiment: the postimpressionists, the Fauves, the expressionists, the primitive, the cubists, and the abstract sculptors."[59] The start of the Little Theatre movement was an important part of this mosaic. There had been noncommercial theatre groups formed earlier. What distinguished the two companies that started production in 1912—the Boston Toy Theatre and The Chicago Little Theatre—as well as the first show spearheaded by Irene and Alice Lewisohn with the people who were to become the supporters, audience, and participants in the Neighborhood Playhouse, was a commitment to the new stagecraft in the first two cases, and an interest in the cultural input of immigrants and in formal experimentation in the latter case. All three used buildings that were off the commercial beaten track: respectively, a renovated carriage house, a building that housed offices and artists' studios, and a settlement house. The ethos of community and fulfillment underpinning these new theatre projects is underscored by the fact that 1912 also marked the first appearance of the term "interpersonal relations."[60]

The 1925 endpoint is less dramatic but is, I believe, a clear benchmark. Clarence Perry's *The Work of the Little Theatres* (1933) argued for four more formative years, settling on 1929, which was, among other things, the year that the National Thespians (now called the National Thespian Society), a dramatic honor society for high schools, was founded. An argument could be made for 1927, the year in which the Neighborhood Playhouse succumbed to an inability to come to terms with changes in the professional theatre to which the founders, in many ways, aspired. (The Neighborhood Playhouse is discussed in chapter 2.) The tastes of many theatregoers in all parts of the country must have undergone a shift as the "talkies" entered the entertainment arena in 1926 and took hold in 1927 with the production of *The Jazz Singer*. Also in 1927, George Pierce Baker, by most accounts the most influential member of the university community in the Little Theatre movement, sent three thousand invitations to representatives of nearly every branch of (legitimate, mainstream) theatre to attend a national conference about the development of the American theatre.[61] It is significant that professional, amateur, and university theatre representatives agreed, after the hard, effective work of the Little Theatres, to confer with each other about their endeavors and did not cavil about different agendas or audiences.[62] In fact the new order was in place by 1925, which Bernard Beckerman says "conveniently marks the year when theatre study began to achieve departmental legitimacy."[63] Baker's national conference was preceded by a 1925 Conference on the Drama in American Universities and Little Theatres, which was sponsored by the Carnegie Institute of Technology in Pittsburgh, the first university in the United States to offer a degree in theatre. The preliminary announcement cited "universal agreement" that the regenerative forces in the American theatre were centered in the universities, community, and Little Theatres. Invited speakers included educators, scholars, and representatives of the commercial theatre, among the latter, Broadway director Brock Pemberton; Otis Skinner, a Broadway star known for classical roles and by then an eminence grise (he had starred in Clyde Fitch's 1894 *His Grace de Grammont* and the 1911 *Kismet*); and Otto H. Kahn, a wealthy investor known for his support for theatre both on and off Broadway who had been the leading financial force behind the 1909–1911 New Theatre, a failed attempt at a large, serious repertory theatre in New York outside the geographical bounds of the Broadway district.[64] Sheldon Cheney issued a revised edition of his seminal 1917 book *The Art Theatre* in 1925. In his new introduction, Cheney noted that ten years earlier, when he had been preparing the first edition, American experimental theatre had seemed "tentative"; in 1925, it was setting standards for Broadway.[65] Of great symbolic importance was the fact that *Theatre Arts Monthly* resituated Little Theatre that year. The journal began as a quarterly issued by the Detroit Arts and Crafts Theatre in 1916 with a focus on Little Theatre work, ideas, and theories, and exemplars in other countries; in 1924, it renamed itself "A Magazine of World Theatre." In 1925, it began to issue a Little Theatre Yearbook. So pervasive was the Little Theatre outlook in criticism, sophisticated scenography and lighting, award-winning playwriting, and educational theatre endeavors that actual Little Theatres could now be treated as a subcategory of the mindset they created.

Ideologies

The above timeframe still does not immediately answer the question of why has it been usual to view the Little Theatre movement either as end-

ing around 1920 or as beginning around that year to devolve into something watered down, less fine, or less significant. I want to suggest that
one way to think more productively about the ongoing work of the
movement might involve an examination of some ideologically loaded
words that are often used to discuss Little Theatre. Two of these are "bohemian" and "modernism," sometimes accompanied by "avant-garde"
and "bourgeois." All four are useful, but frequently they are the victims
of undercoding, a practice defined by Keir Elam as "the formation of
rough and approximate norms in order to characterise a phenomenon
which is not fully understood or which is only vaguely differentiated for
us."[66] In the usual (undercoded) schema, the Little Theatre movement
of the 1910s was the work of bohemians who were antibourgeois and
whose best artistry was modernist in its embracing "innovatory narrative schemes . . . fragmentation, irony, self-referentiality, lack of closure,"
"arcane allusion, juxtaposition, [and] indeterminacy."[67] Recent scholarship has investigated and problematized these words and categories with
regard to literature. Less attention has been given to parsing the terms
for a consideration of theatre beyond its playtexts as literature or its scenography as decoration, which is what I want to attempt here.

The bohemians of pre–World War I Greenwich Village, primarily those
who formed the Provincetown Players and the Washington Square Players, are the usual suspects in the traditional argument. They were atypical of "America" in their quest for a fulfillment they found thwarted in
ordinary middle-class routines, often in the midwestern cities they left
behind;[68] they were also a very unusual cohort of bohemians in that their
members included the creative team of the Paterson Strike Pageant, several writers for the *Masses,* some facilitators of the Armory Show, the sin-
gular Mabel Dodge, the visionary and soon-to-be-famous Robert Edmond
Jones (1887–1954), and the much lionized Eugene O'Neill.[69] A fuller picture of the American bohemian includes the likes of Carol Kennicott,
whose transgressions on the fictional *Main Street* extended largely to a
superficial, although heartfelt, interest in theatre, art, architecture, and
conversation; impatience with provincialism; hosting a party decked out
in Chinese pajamas; and befriending a young newcomer to town who, although Lewis never says so outright, is probably gay.[70] What is the connection between the two versions—Greenwich Village's and *Main Street's*—
of resistance and rebellion, both of which included amateur theatre?

In his 1964 study of the original nineteenth-century Parisian bohemians, *Bohemian Versus Bourgeois,* Cesar Grana staked out clearly delineated

practices and values. Both camps prized individualism, but for the bohemian, this was "centered on the person as an intellectual and imaginative reality," while the bourgeois had "economic and political targets." The bohemian was "the servant and, if necessary, the victim" of romantic values that elevated beauty, creative work, and the free individual above predictably coded behaviors.[71] Yet Raymond Williams insists that avant-garde (which in this context he deliberately conflates with modernist) artistic movements bearing cultural and political agendas are the product of "*bourgeois* dissidents" (emphasis in original), noting that "a main element of modernism was that it was an authentic avant-garde, in personal desires and relationships, of the successful and evolving bourgeoisie itself. The desperate challenges and deep shocks of the first phase were to become the statistics and even the conventions of a later phase of the same order."[72] Williams's description and chronology are worth more unpacking with regard to the New York bohemians and their Little Theatre legacy, since I believe that it is their rootedness in their bourgeois status that made much of their work usable—often very quickly—for others in the "successful and evolving bourgeoisie" of both the 1910s and the 1920s, as well as later. Floyd Dell, a Provincetowner and writer for the *Masses* noted that the "*real* Villagers . . . paid their bills and bathed regularly" and were "schoolteachers, college professors, social workers, doctors, lawyers, engineers and other professional people. As for the artists and writers—such as John Sloan and Art Young, Mary Heaton Vorse, Inez Haynes Gillmore, Susan Glaspell, Theodore Dreiser—they already had positions of importance in the realm of arts and letters. . . . They had most of the familiar middle-class virtues . . . ."[73] Susan Glaspell (1876–1948), a cofounder and arguably the playwriting doyenne of the Provincetowners, wrote, specifically with regard to her cohort being called "radical, wild . . . Bohemians," that "it seems to me we were a particularly simple people, . . . needing each other as protection against complexities, yet living as we did because of an instinct for the old, old things, to have a garden, and neighbors, to keep up the fire and let the cat in at night."[74] Some recent critics of these bohemians see them lacking in intellectual or political coherence, pursuing the incompatible goals of Marxism and Freudianism simultaneously, and ultimately, as "children of fantasy," both confusing idea with desire and bending their reading, their political involvement, and their theatremaking to their need for personal fulfillment above all else.[75] Christine Stansell generously refines this understanding of multiple agendas as "sociable radicalism . . . depend[ing] on habits of conflation, culture collapsed into politics, ideas collapsed into performance," thereby recognizing bohemia's "symbiotic relation to bourgeois culture rather than . . . opposition to it."[76]

Even as dissidents signaled their distance from bourgeois uses and understandings of art and culture, they carved out their own ways "to parley that dissent into careers."[77] The Little Theatre bohemians might best be seen as proto-Bobos, the latter the neologism coined by David Brooks for "bourgeois bohemians" of the 1990s and early twenty-first century.[78] Bobos have exercised their influence in areas of culture more than politics, something that is surely akin to the Greenwich Village bohemians' contribution to social reform being largely the promotion of artistic sensitivity.[79] Brooks advocates seeing such a population not as failed radicals (which they mainly were in terms of, for example, socialist politics), but rather as successful social forces in the "lifestyle" areas of everything from food to sports to religious practice to arts consumption to child rearing, making these more varied, colorful, and richly wrought for non-Bobos.[80]

Glaspell's self-created community yearning for "old, old things" as protection against complexity is redolent of Joseph Roach's "nostalgia constructed . . . with designs on the culture of the future." Such nostalgia yielded what Williams calls "defensive cultural groupings" of modernists paradoxically invested in old technologies such as writing, painting, sculpture, drama, and "little" magazines, while eschewing, for example, the truly modern cinema and photography.[81] Stansell makes much of the Village and Chicago moderns' lack of interest, both as children and as adults, in forms of entertainment other than reading, writing, and talking, despite the availability of melodrama, minstrelsy, dancing, cinema, and even concerts. Theirs was "a politics constructed from books, magazines, and the talk that surrounded them."[82] Popular culture was often the whipping boy of Little Theatre idealists, who fretted about debased use of leisure time, especially at the movies. But it is worth considering the extent to which popular entertainments were refused not because they were too well understood, but because they were annoyingly irrelevant or threateningly illegible to bohemians.[83]

Marjorie Perloff suggests two schools of modernism, T. S. Eliot's familiar "make it new" and also the "make it old." The latter, rooted in Anglo-Saxon romanticism, "takes the lyric paradigm for granted" and may include "a slight influx of French Symbolisms to add piquancy." The other seeks a rupture with the immediate past.[84] Little Theatre bohemians combined the two strategies, particularly in the early days of mixed bills of diverse one-acts, thereby appealing to possible audiences and recruits in both camps. Folk plays and others compared to the work of Synge and influenced by the Irish Players tours of the early and middle 1910s followed the "lyric paradigm." Plays featuring abstract scenography or topical subjects forced a rupture with pictorialism and romanticism. That Little Theatres across the country embraced the plays of Dunsany (who favored allegory and exoticism), Zona Gale's "Neighbors" (which portrays the homespun support of a group of small town midwestern women for one of their own when she is disappointed in her plans to adopt a child), and Glaspell and George Cram Cook's (1873–1924) "Suppressed Desires" (certainly a comedy and arguably a farce, which traded on an awareness of Freudianism and the capacity to laugh at its more extreme possibilities), suggests an ability to work along both axes. Daniel Joseph Singal calls modernism a "full-fledged historical culture ... that ... supplies nothing less than the basic contours of our current modes of thought."[85] He notes (and seeks to correct) the common tendency to equate modernism only with the life of its early artistic avantgarde at the turn of the twentieth century while ignoring the later, possibly less glamorous phases in which previously radical ideas infiltrate the larger culture, creating a "bourgeoisie seeking bohemian delights"—the latter, Leslie Fishbein's assessment of the 1920s America that absorbed the earlier stage of modernism.[86] This absorption represents not the end of the movement, but its next step. In theatre, one of the "absorbed" ideas was that participation and creation belonged at the center of proper modern appreciation. Another common thread in modernism generally and, for my purposes, in Little Theatre, was a quest for authenticity. That the vehicles and rhetoric in the quest shifted along with changes in the cultural, political, and mass market worlds should not be a surprise. One of the ongoing paradoxes of the Little Theatre movement is the varieties of kinds of work that were touted as modern or experimental and the apologias for some work that actually did push the envelope but that was promoted in ways that would entice audiences by assuring them that the productions were not highbrow or "longhair."

A crucial vehicle in transmitting and validating Little Theatre was the embedding of its values and practices in university programs and secondary schools. While the history of theatre (in) education is often treated separately from other theatre history, in this era the two projects overlap, a phenomenon that meshes with Thomas Strychacz's assertion that one of modernism's most important projects was installing the reading and legitimizing strategies for its emerging discourses in the realm of professional university training. Courses in theatre practicum (as opposed to literature) entered college curricula in the first quarter of the century, and the newly instituted theatre major arrived during the 1910s and 1920s.[87] The founders of many of these programs also worked with, and in many instances founded, Little Theatres (several are discussed in chapters 2, 3, 5, and 6). Strychacz points out that such training in university programs not only yielded practitioners for the profession; it resituated that profession in the minds of the public. "[A]cknowledgement by educated and uneducated alike that a particular discourse demands special skills, and can therefore be performed or understood only by those who are specialized, lies at the foundation of professional power and cultural power in the twentieth century."[88]

Professional theatre was something that its workers previously learned on the job or in an apprenticeship system and that American audiences largely encountered in theatres as fun or escapist. The modernist alliance of university with theatre training did at least two things. First, by controlling graduate studies, the alliance made it possible for universities as gatekeepers to "institutionalize a mechanism whereby forthcoming teachers would perpetuate—indeed require for their legitimacy—a similar professionalized outlook."[89] It also made theatre "respectable," and a locus of cultural capital for those who attend it. The specialist language that universities sought to professionalize and keep esoteric was in circulation even among non-university Little Theatre theorists, a number of whom were later to find income-producing possibilities in affiliations with schools. Maurice Browne scorned the devotee lacking in insider knowledge, writing "I wonder how many of the millionaires who endowed the New Theatre knew what a dimmer was, and I wonder what Mrs. Hybrow N. Thusiast, the director of the Pure Provincial Players, would do if she were suddenly told that her second border was unmasked," going on to note that such skills are not merely technique, but the means of "establishing a living convention on a dead one . . . which shall be the temple of a living art."[90]

The Little Theatre movement yielded not only opportunities for training in production, but, in the aggregate, a comprehensive manual for how the audience should perform its role. The movement sought to construct an educated audience that could fully appreciate the difficulty of bringing a piece of theatre—a handmade artifact with hundreds of working parts—to fruition. Such an audience appreciates a production not unproblematically because the artifact is labeled "worthwhile," but because the audience has been taught the fine points of how complicated, labor-intensive, and full of meaning-laden elements the artifact is. Along with this technical, functionalist education comes the less overt message that to know these things is the mark of a superior, minority population, one whose sensibilities are simultaneously protection against a stultifying or overwhelming present and the hope for a future predicated on caring values (arguably Glaspell's recipe). This audience is asked to identify itself and to engage in the ongoing project of self-construction through Little Theatre work. Such an understanding of the value of engagement and participation in developing a fulfilled and versatile self meshed not only with John Dewey's Progressive Era idea of education as an ongoing formation of character through the construction of experience; it also serves Walter Benn Michaels's observation that "American modernism . . . is both the privileging of identity and its transformation into a project."[91]

It is crucial to recognize that Little Theatre's identitarian project lay, as I have been arguing, not primarily in the realm of literature, even though most Little Theatre productions were plays with scripts and even though scripts remain easy to reproduce, circulate, and codify, and even though most of the earliest innovators were themselves inveterate readers. The project required that audiences experience revised signals in the realm of the aural and visual as well as the textual. In each of these areas, Little Theatres broke with preexisting commercial practice. The Wisconsin Dramatic Society as early as 1911 eliminated the ubiquitous orchestra as well as spotlights routinely accompanying the entrance of major characters. The Chicago Little Theatre's *Trojan Women* (1912–1915) had one setting throughout, rather than the usual pictorialist creation of a physical setting for each change of locale mentioned in the text; the company's *Christmas Mystery Play* was given completely in silhouette. The Little Playhouse of St. Louis instituted program notes, then familiar enough to symphony orchestra programs but not to theatres. Audiences at the Neighborhood Players' productions in Newark, New Jersey, were asked to hold all applause until the end of the play, in contrast to the usual practice of breaking in to recognize star turns, entrances, scenery changes, and other high points.[92] Unlike the modernist novel or poem or art exhibit, which could be read at a rate determined by each individual audience member, the Little Theatre production, like any live theatre performance, stipulated that the multitracked artifact was to unfold in real time at a rate controlled by the artists. Part of the performative nature of the work was that it asked audiences, among other things, to go to a venue that was often not in a traditional theatre district, to interact socially, and to accept amateurs as actors with something valuable to communicate. All of these challenges were efforts at constructing a new audience.

Consider, for example, the Provincetown Players' two 1916 productions of Louise Bryant's "The Game." Bryant, a novelist, did not go on to have a career in the theatre. Her one-act is an allegory in which Life and Death play dice to see who will win Youth, a male poet, and The Girl, a beautiful dancer. The text fits Marjorie Perloff's "make it old" model, with its "lyric paradigm" and "slight influx of . . . Symbolisms for piquancy." It is heavy-handed and traditional with regard to gender, as the young man traffics in words while the young woman is valued for her beauty and bodily expression; the play is also narcissistic with regard to what kind of life is of value as Life wants "geniuses," who happen to be artists, and she eschews soldiers, until the last line of the play, where she adds on a tag line: "They are the flower of youth—there are dreamers among them."[93] But the production fit the "make it new" paradigm in its mise-en-scène and gesture vocabulary. The art nouveau backdrop, barefooted performers with the women in loose garments, and angular hand and arm movements meshed with the sort of orientalist and freedom-of-movement styles in circulation in the realm of dance, particularly in the work of Isadora Duncan, Ruth St. Denis, Maud Allen, and Vaslav Nijinsky with the Ballets Russes (see fig. 1.1).[94] So central were these elements to the piece that the initial notes in the published text state the play

> is an attempt to synthesize decoration, costume, speech and action into one mood. Starting from the idea that the play is symbolic of rather than representative of life, the Zorachs have designed the decorations to suggest rather than to portray; the speech and action of the players being used as the plastic element in the whole unified convention. As the gestures and decorations of this play are as important as the written speech it is essential that theatres wishing to produce The Game [sic] should send for photographs and directions.[95]

The play was presented in Provincetown, Massachusetts, in a refurbished fish house and later in the year in Greenwich Village at the

Fig. 1.1. "The Game," by Louise Bryant, presented by the Provincetown Players in 1916. *Left to right:* John Reed, William Zorach, Martha Ryther-Fuller, and Kathleen Cannell. Design by Marguerite and William Zorach. Photo courtesy of The Harvard Theatre Collection, The Houghton Library.

Provincetowners' new theatre in a renovated rowhouse. Death and Youth were played, respectively, by John Reed, the Soviet sympathizer and a founder of the Communist Party in the United States who was to die in the Russian Revolution, and William Zorach, the painter and sculptor who designed the set and costumes for the play with his wife Marguerite. The semiotics of the text, decor, gestures, identities of the amateur actors (known to many of the audience members), and of an offbeat site as serious bearers of theatrical meaning, challenged the audience's received ideas about theatre. Moreover, the play shared the bill in each of its performances with Eugene O'Neill's "Bound East for Cardiff," a slice-of-life play depicting a dying sailor and his mates at sea on a hardscrabble voyage. The ability to shift moods and digest diverse packages of meaning was also a Little Theatre demand on its audience, diverging from late Victorian "legitimate" theatre practice of presenting a single, full-length play alone, sometimes with a short one-act as a curtain-raiser. (This practice, in turn, replaced the earlier one of interspersing acts of a play with variety entertainments, preceding the play with other music or scenes, and ending the evening with an afterpiece.)

An early Provincetown example may, in retrospect, seem too predictably "typical," both geographically and temporally. Another mid-1910s, and non–New York, attempt to make it both old and new was the 1916 "Mirage," a one-act play set in a Hopi village in Arizona and first presented at the University of Pittsburgh. Later, the 1922 *Salut au Monde!,* a Neighborhood Playhouse production featuring poetry by Walt Whitman, an original score, extensive choreography, a non-pictorial setting, and a visual world derived from many Asian and premodern European sources, combined abstraction with orientalism in a fascinating old/new dialectic, the meaning of which can still be debated.

"Mirage" charts little new territory dramaturgically. It features a thirty-something East Coast WASP ethnologist, Grayson Stone, who is dwelling among the Hopi and suffering from amnesia. His plucky Brahmin wife, Christine, and their psychiatrist friend track him down, only to find him engaged to Polaina, the nineteen-year-old niece of the tribe's chief. Polaina (which means "Butterfly," a name derived from her hairdo, but also reminiscent of Puccini's abandoned heroine) may be pregnant by Stone. The psychiatrist restores Stone's memory in a deft half-page, and Stone, realizing he is already married and far from home, prepares to leave the village. Polaina, unable to persuade him to stay with her (he offers money as thanks for her care; she says her claim is greater than Christine's because the latter has no children), shares poisoned water with him. His memory again disappears, and, wracked with thirst, he exits with Polaina to pursue a mirage in the desert. The text is larded with descriptions of Hopi dress, hairdos, jewelry, pottery, and architecture. The playwright, George M. P. Baird, a University of Pittsburgh professor, stipulates that the chants in the song are only available in *The Indians' Book,* by Natalie Curtis Burlin, and includes them in his dialogue. Traditions are both carried out and explicated, as when two women sort ears of corn noting that it is "evil medicine" if red and white be mingled. Aurally and visually the play takes the Hopi world as foreground, not background, although the dramaturgy is causality-driven and realist. It is the white wife who appears hysterical and out of place in her ecru pongee motorcoat, while Polaina emerges as cagey and strong-willed (albeit compliantly vengeful and suicidal on the Victorian "other woman" as well as the art nouveau femme fatale models). The exotic setting and ritualized behavior in the context of a university gymnasium setting would have challenged conventional ideas of theatregoing in Pittsburgh in 1916, as would the combination of one-acts on the evening's whole bill. The other two offerings were the antiwar "The Terrible Meek," by Charles Rann Kennedy, and "The Marriage," a lyric piece by Lady Augusta Gregory based on the

Gaelic of Douglas Hyde. "The Terrible Meek" features a peasant woman who is revealed at the end to be Mary at Golgotha; "The Marriage" has a blind poet bringing prosperity to the home of a newly married couple.

Salut au Monde! was presented in 1922, but work on it began in 1919 with a desire for a feeling of oneness in the United States in the wake of World War I.[96] The piece used a Walt Whitman character to salute humankind's progress and the various races and religions of the world. These were depicted through song, chant, and dance. The orchestra and singing chorus were positioned throughout the theatre, thereby challenging even usual ideas of sound directionality in theatrical performance. Part 1 featured humankind evolving from the dawn of time to a generalized premodern existence as farmers. Part 2 offered the Jewish prayer Kol Nidre by a New York cantor, a Hindu chant in Sanskrit by a native of Bengal, a hymn to Apollo, a Mohammedan ritual performed by a native Persian, and Gregorian chants. Part 3 returned to Whitman, who catalogued the peoples of the earth while these paraded behind the open circle-within-a-curtain that comprised the setting (see fig. 1.2). Whitman, outside the circle, was the mediator between the present-day, American audience and the (arguably too premodern) peoples of the rest of the world. The production also featured elaborate lighting against a cyclorama, the latter a relatively new convention in progressive theatre and more common in Germany than in the United States at the time.

Salut au Monde! could have been the poster child for Horace Kallen's 1915 *Nation* essays "Democracy *versus* the Melting Pot," which challenged Americans to embrace actual inclusive democracy rather than the idea that there is only one way to be a real American. Kallen, pulling no punches, jumped in by saying that Anglo-Saxon "pride of race," an idea that would have been anathema to the founders of American democracy, was now being invoked in democracy's defense. The melting pot, in which all were acceptable so long as their own "pride of race" would "melt," was, for Kallen, antidemocratic, and he urged acceptance of multiple ethnicities coexisting in harmony. He went so far as to state that "the hyphen attaches, in things of the spirit, also to the 'pure' British-American."[97] *Salut au Monde!*, with its celebration of the premodern and lyrical (make it old), took up the challenge of cultural pluralism (make it new), but it was up to individual spectators' reading strategies whether the final vision of various cultures being welcomed to America was one in which Whitman, positioned outside the frame, stood for the "timeless" values of WASP America, or whether the new arrivals were acceptable on their

Fig. 1.2. *Salut au Monde!* at the Neighborhood Playhouse, 1922. Photographer: Mary Dale Clark. Courtesy of the Billy Rose Theatre Collection, The New York Public Library for the Performing Arts, Astor, Lenox and Tilden Foundations.

own terms. Were the immigrants to melt and blend in or to contribute while maintaining their own values and traditions?[98] The location of the Neighborhood Playhouse on Manhattan's Lower East Side underscored the question. For uptown spectators, it was an out-of-the-way locale whose denizens might be seen as in need of melting or equally possibly as entertainingly exotic. For the locals, a few of whom participated in this production, the theatre might have felt WASP and highbrow (it was becoming increasingly professionalized by the 1920s), but it still eschewed Broadway ideals and drew heavily on ethnic sources. Whatever response *Salut au Monde!* generated along a spectrum of ideological possibilities, it was theatrically innovative.

The majority of people who embraced Little Theatre work as a Progressive/modernist project were members of interpretive communities already predisposed to see art, literature, and the ideas of aesthetically concerned social elites as being of value. Serious experiments in theatre and/or theatre undertaken by people in positions of intellectual prestige drew supporters in accordance with what Pierre Bourdieu calls "the logic of the homologies," in which objects or activities from different "systems of interest" are embraced because they "are situated in roughly equivalent positions in their respective spaces."[99] Participating in or attending such theatre fit with "elective affinities" that created a sense of distinction.[100]

Shared predispositions and educational experiences did not, however, obviate the need for negotiating or accommodating the multiple attitudes and consumer patterns of various constituencies within the larger community containing potential audiences or even within the actual assembled audiences themselves. One obvious example is that of multiple generations within an audience, as projects with young people drew friends and siblings but also parents and grandparents to the theatre. Even among the educated, urban spectators attracted by the quintessentially "bohemian" Provincetowners, however, there were fault lines in the small audience. Robert Károly Sarlós points out that the first New York season might never have happened if John Reed had not sold two hundred subscriptions to members of the New York Stage Society, an uptown Manhattan organization that supported purposeful, serious theatre, often in the form of European imports.[101] While the Provincetowners were supposedly more comfortable among their "friends and fellow torchbearers" than among the "more formidable" uptowners, the latter outnumbered the former eight to one, making some kind of blending of interests probable.[102] The Stage Society's president was Emilie Hapgood, wife of Norman Hapgood, whose younger brother Hutchins Hapgood was an active Provincetowner. In this family, the uptown/downtown distinction began in part over theatre itself, as Norman reviewed for New York's *Commercial Advertiser* and helped his brother get a leg up as a critic by letting Hutchins "cover all the plays he didn't particularly care about," including many in the German, Yiddish, or Italian downtown theatres.[103] The downtowners were "scared off" by too much symbolism and poetry, evidenced by the mystified response of audiences even as they claimed they "want to do our own thing in our own way."[104] The Provincetown group eventually split over the question of whether or not to aspire to moves to Broadway and validation by reviewers and commercial theatre audiences. An observer of the Washington Square Players as early as its second season breathed relief that the shows "please both High-brow and Hofbrau."[105] In short, even the earliest, most bohemian modernist Little Theatres were affected by the desire to be popular and accessible while being specialized and serious. Later groups might choose recent Broadway hits to produce yet still seek to facilitate personal growth and foster an appreciation for the hand-made via these very productions.

Al Pacino's interviewee, the man whose spiritual home is serious, now culturally validated theatre, and with whom this chapter began, represents one facet of the Little Theatre legacy in the 1990s. Another appears in the 1997 film *Waiting for Guffman*. Here, the eponymous figure, like the Godot he is supposed to call to mind, never appears. He is a New York theatre agent whose impending visit motivates the fictional, small-town Missouri amateurs who are the focus of the film to regard the historical pageant they write and perform as the possible route to a Broadway production and new lives. The show is directed by a flamboyant, intense, and very stagestruck one-time Broadway chorus boy, and it affords the performers a sense of self-importance as they gear up for an occasion that their fellow citizens very much enjoy. So, too, does the man they take for Guffman, who turns out to be in town on the occasion of the birth of a great niece and who ends up in the agent's seat because, arriving late, he can find no other. For the director/ex–chorus boy and one young woman with talent and troubles, the production leads to moving away from the town. For the others, it is a moment of glory for themselves and the community. We are meant to laugh at their delusions (this is "community" not "Little" theatre), but not to discredit their locating worthiness in the creation of a piece of amateur theatre. We recognize both the value(s) and the self-delusion because we have the legacy and social experience as audiences to do so.

Both *Richard* and *Guffman*—and the results implied by their accompanying gerunds "looking" and "waiting"—depend on accepting the ideas that theatre can redeem leisure, that audiences often misunderstand or fail to serve the dreams of artists, and that theatre on any model other than the Broadway musical needs to work hard to build audiences locally. These credos were forged during the Little Theatre movement when twentieth- (and now twenty-first-) century American theatre audiences took the first steps in composing ourselves.

Imagining the Little Theatre Audience

Precedents and Prejudices

> Europe has centuries of culture behind her and her Little Theatres have found their audiences ready and waiting. In the United States the Little Theatre in many cases had to create itself and its audience at the same time. In each of the European countries Little Theatres have centered the intellectual life of such larger cities as Moscow, London, Berlin and Paris. In the United States, cities and suburbs, seashore villages, prairie towns and mountain farm-lands have their little theatres.
>
> —Constance D'Arcy Mackay, *The Little Theatre in the United States*

In her 1917 book about the first American Little Theatres, Constance D'Arcy Mackay observed that constructing a new American audience was an imperative adjunct to creating a new theatre. The differences she noted between American and European Little Theatre point to several recurring tropes in the American undertaking. American theatre reformers knew their country was spread out, diverse, and had its own traditions; in this context, they embraced the local in the name of the national. But they also measured their cultural activities against a European yardstick. This measuring was full of contradictions and ironies. For example, the Moscow Art Theatre was considered an exemplary art theatre, while immigrants from Russia were often seen as social problems. German plays and theatre buildings were admired until the American entry into

World War I, when they dropped out of most American discussions of art theatre. Fluency in European languages was a fairly ordinary skill for many Progressive drama aficionados; European immigrants who spoke the same languages were targeted by educators or social workers for social improvement through theatre.

In some cases, these incongruities were largely instances of class difference: the "art" theatre is good in the eyes of the privileged arts reformer while the peasant does not pass cultural muster. But Little Theatre leaders also found much to admire in the cultural habits of poor immigrants. Sometimes activists romanticized practices they only dimly understood, but sometimes—especially regarding theatregoing—they genuinely respected the fervor and involvement displayed by audiences of recent arrivals from Europe. In a tangle of ongoing negotiations, American practices were used to instruct European immigrants even as European experimental theatre was held up as a model of pioneering work. At the same time, Europhilia for its own sake was criticized by those Progressives who found its knee-jerk adulation a form of stultifying resistance to change. And, as much as centering the intellectual life of any city, Little Theatre was often used to center social life within neighborhoods or communities. In places where recently arrived Europeans actually lived, intellectual and community life could be linked through theatre, with inevitable criticism from within and without that one was being sacrificed to the other.

This chapter investigates key cultural precedents and prejudices underpinning the work of Little Theatre reformers and traces the multiple ways these played out. Some precedents had to do with theatre and theatregoing per se; these were drawn from recent and historical European practice and in a few key instances included ideas borrowed from classical Athens, whether accurately understood or based on received opinion. Other precedents included hereditary American beliefs about education, social service, use of leisure time, and commerce. Progressives were improving everything from conditions in the workplace to traditional school curriculum and from federal trade laws to local fire codes. Theatre reform, in this context, was one more means of challenging monopoly and validating individual experience. Yet this very pairing—challenging monopoly and validating the individual—is Janus-faced rather than simply two-pronged. Reformers were both reactive and proactive, nostalgic and forward-looking. They self-interestedly defended their own values and tried to convert others to their own way of thinking; they also worked disinterestedly to eliminate practices that constrained others' comfort and mobility, whether or not they interacted personally with those others or even liked them. Both axes of activism served as means of maintaining personal security in the face of change, even as both aimed to bring about change.

Since much of this chapter has to do with cultural othering, it is important to situate those whose ideas were privileged and circulated in print. The activists who pioneered the Little Theatre movement differed in a few key ways from those who created the symphony orchestras and art museums of the Gilded Age.[1] Foremost, rather than being members of high society who controlled great wealth, they were part of what Richard Ohmann calls the PMC—professional-managerial class—that emerged in the last twenty years of the nineteenth century.[2] The PMC comprised about 12 percent of the population in 1910, they gravitated towards cities, and they worked for rather than inherited most of their money. They were the market for many kinds of leisure activities, such as vacationing, eating in restaurants, and attending legitimate theatre. They sent their children to college so that the latter, too, could engage in "privileged work," such as writing, law, teaching, medicine, upper-level administration, or publishing. With an emergent set of fairly coherent values and attitudes, the PMC shared a class consciousness.[3] The oldest of the Little Theatre workers, those born in the 1860s, such as George Pierce Baker and Hutchins Hapgood, would have come of age along with the PMC itself. Those born in the 1870s, including Thomas Dickinson, Zona Gale, Frederick Koch, George Cram Cook, and Susan Glaspell, for instance, would have participated in it with some mentors or at least role models ahead of them. The younger members of the early movement, those born in the mid-to-late 1880s, and including Eugene O'Neill, designer Robert Edmond Jones, Sheldon Cheney, and Constance D'Arcy Mackay, never knew a world without mass-circulation magazines, mass-produced and -marketed foods and clothing, and professions that were self-conscious fraternities increasingly concerned with standards and entry requirements. Young recruits to the Little Theatres of the 1920s might already be second generation PMC, arriving not only with assumptions about the organization of markets and professions, but, in some instances, with college training in theatre under the aegis of an earlier Little Theatre pioneer.

Work to build a creative audience for a creative theatre involved imagining possibilities and then entering into "reformance" projects that combined reform and performance in ways that mutually reconstituted the understandings of both the reformers and their students, colleagues, charges, and followers. This work was characterized by endless negotiating of such opposite concepts as past and future, self and other, valuable and worthless, artistic and commercial, and American and European, many of which were blended and blurred in the mixture of generations, cultures, and ideas that Little Theatre facilitated.

Anti-audience Precedents

Between 1890 and the early 1920s, critics and theatre practitioners announced their concerns in such pointedly titled articles as "Disintegration of the Theatre,"[4] "Is the Theatre Worth While?"[5] "What the Stage Should Be," "What's the Matter with the Road?" "The Menace of the Movies,"[6] "A Plea for the Theatrical Manager," "Why Theatrical Managers Reject Plays,"[7] "The Extirpation of Culture,"[8] "What's Wrong with the American Stage?"[9] "The Audiences of Yesterday," "The Real Revolt in Our Theatre,"[10] "Theatricitis,"[11] and "Elevating the Audience."[12] And all drew on longstanding precedent. Blaming the audience for the ills of the theatre is nearly as old as Western theatre itself, beginning with Aristotle's assertion that tragedy's reputation as inferior to epic was the result of accommodating an audience who required too much spectacle in order to understand what was going on.[13] In the late nineteenth century, Nietzsche railed against the effects of audiences on artistic authenticity: the more an artist's work finds an audience, he believed, the more that work is surely debased, no matter how much it might have begun as a unique vision.[14] Constantin Stanislavski, whose ideas were new at the time of the Little Theatre movement, posited that "natural" acting involved performers working out characterizations in relation to each other and not the audience. "Theatrical" acting—aimed across the footlights and with a focus on audience response—was construed as inartistic and false.[15] In an American context, Washington Irving had roundly criticized audience behavior in 1802, complaining of spectators' eating during performances and bullying performers, and comparing the noise issuing from the gallery as "the yells of every kind of animal."[16] An essayist writing for the *Knickerbocker* in 1836 excoriated audiences for their trivial choices of entertainment, accusing them of having "vitiated their healthy appetite by extravagant spectacle, melo-dramatic absurdities, and other grossly physical exhibitions," thereby rendering themselves "no longer able [to] enjoy the strong intellectual food" of more worthwhile fare.[17]

The early American critiques were launched during an era when much theatrical entertainment was presented in a variety format and included singing, dancing, and possibly individual acts from more than one play interlarding the presentation of a main piece. Prior to the advent of electric or even gas lighting, when the audience was frequently as well lit and visible as the players, it was ordinary for spectators to call out to performers or to talk with each other. By the end of the nineteenth century, in a phenomenon that Lawrence Levine calls the "sacralization of culture," American elites had enshrined "high art" in buildings and performance schedules that removed it from the mixed bills, long evenings, and multiclass venues that had characterized presentations of opera, orchestral music, and theatre earlier in the century.[18] Elites sought to use the arts not only to secure their own sense of well-being, but also to overhaul the thinking and taste of the general public. Sacralization emerged from a split view of the arts as "a force with which to proselytize among the people or . . . an oasis of refuge from and a barrier against them." In either category, though, cultural leaders were concerned with "disciplining and training" audiences.[19] Both the split agenda (a force with which to proselytize/an oasis of refuge) and the "disciplining and training" would be prominent themes of Little Theatre reform.

Pleas for theatre reform targeting the PMC, already possessed of the income and predisposition to attend the theatre and to be concerned about cultural capital, appeared in magazines aimed at this class. The earliest of these critiques drew on two kinds of precedents: that the values of high culture would yield "good" audiences and that theatre professionals were in the best position to determine what was good theatre. The advent of the Little Theatre critiques would reverse these assumptions: high culture as commonly recognized would be seen as derivative and moribund and theatre professionals as unable to see or do what enlightened amateurs could.

At the start of the reformist continuum, consider M. Esteve's answer, offered in 1890, to "what the stage should be":

> Why cannot the more intellectual number of citizens demand the representation of better plays than are now in vogue, and, by united votes, carry the theatre managers, so as to bring about a renaissance epoch in the histrionic word[?] . . . I repeat my wish to see the true actors and managers decide upon the play to be performed, and not to notice that a mass of people, whose education has not been of the broadest, and whose appreciation of the classics is merely embryonic, should be catered to.[20]

Esteve's insistence on "intellectual numbers of citizens" rather than those without a "broad" education or an "appreciation of the classics" smacks of Matthew Arnold's now-clichéd "best that has been thought and said." Culture, for those Americans who thought about it, at least until the 1910s, meant "a particular part of the heritage from the European past, including polite manners, respect for traditional learning, appreciation of the arts, and above all an informed and devoted love of standard literature."[21] But flattering the audience was, for Esteve, a ploy to support the interests of those who really knew best—the "true actors and managers," who presumably shared and, in his schema, are put forth as beacons of this background and set of values. In 1890, such a constituency would have been minuscule, as actors had no systematic way of training in the United States, were not drawn primarily from the ranks of the university-educated, and were, by and large, interested in sustaining and not overhauling the business that fed them.[22] Nonetheless, in his circuitous way, Esteve assumes that existing professionals are the ones to make the change.

In 1893, A. M. Palmer, a seasoned commercial producer, blamed the theatregoing public and its demand for "absolute amusement" for his having to choose certain kinds of plays and reject others. He was dismayed that the "hard to please" public that "knows what it wants" was drawn to new American plays featuring "men and women who talk through their noses, the *habitants* of the realistic New England kitchens . . . the precocious children who talk baseball slang . . . and the thousand and one *outre* and (to the refined mind) disagreeable characters and things with which the American play is generally crowded." He called for plays with "correctly-talking and correctly behaving characters." The appearance of his article in the *Forum,* one of several expensive magazines aimed at eastern elites, assumed a readership that would see itself as "hard to please" but also possessed of good taste and able to support his agenda.[23] That they were also the very audience attending the popular new American plays was the problem but was not analyzed. Palmer's didacticism reemerged as near-sarcasm in 1904, when Lionel Strachey diagnosed "the virulent disease theatricitis americanus" as the affliction of the obtuse "theatromaniac . . . the most unprejudiced of individuals where 'amusement' is concerned. To him 'Götterdamerung' and the Siamese Twins are equivalent in their respective capacities to make the hour fleet."[24] Local color, photographic realism, and a willingness to embrace popular entertainments along with high art were all criticized as violations of good taste, which was implied but not defined.

A literal invocation of the slippery concept of "taste" was Edward A. Dithmar's strategy in 1897, when he blamed the unsophisticated parvenus of the 1890s for the low level of dramatic criticism in the New York theatre dailies. Unlike the theatregoers of the 1870s who had "inherited a taste" for theatregoing, the later products of "social revolution after the Civil War" had unfortunately reached maturity "long before the acquisition of sufficient money and leisure made them actually aware of the stage as a source of entertainment." Dithmar made no mention of any particular plays or theatres. The problem was simply the audience, who had acquired disposable income without "breeding." Dithmar was either suggesting that his audience was sophisticated as readers of the *Forum*— how else could they ingest and grasp the article?—but boors as theatregoers, or he was suggesting that his readers were superior to other theatregoers, even though they attended and enjoyed the same plays. The latter was exactly the argument made to genteel readers by Lorin Deland, who, in 1908, assured his *Atlantic* readership that, among "Good Taste," "Bad Taste," and "No Taste" audiences, they were the first. They were distinguished not by actual choice of dramatic fare, but by sitting in the first ten rows of the orchestra. Deland, too, wanted better plays, but his recommendation was "segregating the classes on the line of mental and aesthetic appreciation."[25] Somehow if the audience could totally sort itself into discrete communities, not merely within an existing arena, but rather by removing itself to a setting containing only the socially likeminded, the theatre itself would improve. Little Theatre idealists would work with precisely the idea of self-selection and separate venues; their acid test, however, was to be ideology rather than social status.

Progressive Precedents

In the 1910s, critiques of audiences drew on the then relatively recent precedents of what would now be called "segmenting the market" and appealing to the educated interests of cultured sophisticates, as had Dithmar, Deland, and Strachey. But notions of what comprised culture and good taste began to be questioned with regard to the arts in general and, for my purposes, theatre in particular. Annie Nathan Meyer complained in the *Atlantic* in 1913 that theatre was "lagging behind the other arts" so far as its audiences' abilities to grasp and demand modernism were concerned. "It is astonishing," she wrote, "to hear people of fair intelligence—at least in other matters—assuring us that these players from Dublin do not act at all." Meyer assumed her readers knew full well who the Irish Players of the Abbey Theatre were. Indeed, the Irish Players' 1911–1912 American tour inspired Little Theatre founders in Boston,

Philadelphia, New York, and Chicago.[26] But, while Meyer's readers as culture mavens might have been aware of the latest experiments in European theatre and might even have sought out the Irish company during its U.S. tour, once in front of the actual artifact, they were too inexperienced and too untrained to know precisely what they were looking at. Credentials that distinguished the reader in other areas vanished when that reader was part of a theatre audience. As a result, Meyer noted, "the stage in many ways has held curiously aloof from the spirit of its age."[27] Like A. M. Palmer twenty-one years earlier, Meyer was upset by the popular taste for what passed as realism in the theatre. But while Palmer found attempts at realism too crude, Meyer found them out of sync with modern times. Hadn't photography wrought a change in what painters now called "real?" Why, she asked, was theatre still in the thrall of phony grandiloquence at worst, photographic reproduction at best? Meyer wanted an updating of reading strategies among those likely to attend theatre.[28]

Meyer's criticism of theatre audiences was embedded in a larger Progressive critique of arts and culture. This complaint was articulated by Randolph Bourne in the *Atlantic Monthly* as a plea for the educated to get with the program of modernity and Americanism. In 1914, Bourne gently but firmly pointed out the hollow snobbery of an American "bourgeoisie ... [for whom] Europe became so much the fashion that it is now almost a test of respectability to have traveled at least once abroad."[29] Actual Europeans were more interested in "discriminating the good of to-day than in accepting the classics," and Bourne admonished Americans who went slack in the face of evaluating their own culture: "culture is not an acquired familiarity with things outside, but an inner and constantly operating taste, a fresh and responsive power of discrimination and the insistent judging of everything that comes to our minds and senses. It is clear that such a sensitive taste cannot be acquired by torturing our appreciations into conformity with the judgments of others, no matter how 'authoritative' those judgments may be. Such a method means a hypnotization of judgment, not a true development of soul."[30]

Two years later, Bourne took up the same topic in more aggressive terms in the pages of the left-wing *New Republic.* Calling the acquisition of reverence for the classics in art an "unpleasantly undemocratic" ideal, Bourne also pointedly critiqued the passivity engendered in audiences by such an Arnoldian arts education. "If your training has been to learn and appreciate the best that has been thought and done in the world, it has not been to discriminate between the significant and the irrelevant that the experience of every day is flinging up in your face."[31] He scorned "The Cult of the Best," as promising the mere "mechanics of art education." In line with John Dewey's desire for education to comprise critical engagement and active experience, Bourne's call for the conscious development of a "sincere and general public taste" was wholly the opposite of Esteve's recoiling at a "mass of people, whose education has not been of the broadest." Bourne, in fact, saw the "cult of the best" (Esteve's "broad" education) as dangerously and stultifyingly narrow, except for the wealthy few who were to the manner born, since for them it did comprise a sort of real world. For the rest of the citizenry, attempts to inhabit that world comprised mimicry or sham at best and actual retreat from reality and selfhood at worst.

While the earliest Little Theatres did embrace European plays, for the most part what they favored among these were contemporary works and not canonized classics. In that sense, they were approaching part of Bourne's ideal, although, to be sure, the favored plays—those by Hermann Sudermann, Shaw, Chekhov, and John Galsworthy, for example—had already enjoyed runs and reviews in Europe, making them preapproved as respectably, and perhaps, therefore, oxymoronically, avant-garde. The companies that specialized in writing and producing original American plays, such as the Provincetown Players, the Little Country Theatre of Fargo, North Dakota, and the Carolina Playmakers (Chapel Hill, North Carolina), risked the production of more chaff than wheat, but they did commit themselves to grappling with the "significant . . . that the experience of every day is flinging up" both for their playwrights and their audiences.

One European high art precedent that underlay the work of at least two important Little Theatres was a love of classical Greek theatre and ancient Athenian culture.[32] In his study "Hellenism and the Independent Theatre Movement in America," Eric Wiley points out that both Maurice Browne of the Chicago Little Theatre and George Cram Cook of the Provincetown Players were ardent Grecophiles, had studied classics as undergraduates, and self-consciously pointed to Greek precedents in founding their companies. Studying Greek and Latin was, in the late nineteenth century, an ordinary route to college admission. Both Browne and Cook also cited the influence of the Irish Players on their thinking. Hellenic aesthetic values were a clearly articulated part of the Irish Players' agenda, including a belief that their work should embody "ethical idealism" and local mythological subjects. Both Yeats and Synge, whose work anchored the Irish Players', used "poetic diction and the tragic form . . . echoes of

Greek theatre."[33] Kenneth Macgowan (1888–1963) concluded his generally forward-looking study, *The Theatre of Tomorrow,* by modeling desirable "apocalyptic" civic theatre on the religious passion of the Greeks.[34]

Browne and Cook had differing interests in classical Athenian theatre and, in any case, each of them based his understanding on a retrospective reading colored by contemporary values.[35] Browne was a self-proclaimed aesthete who had, as an undergraduate at Cambridge, worshipped Oscar Wilde. Poetic drama was a priority in his company, where his goal was to bring to life his "conception of art as a religious service to beauty."[36] Browne used work on *The Trojan Women* during 1912 not only to mount a production of that play in 1913, but also to train his players and audience in an appreciation of "rhythmic drama," which he believed he would find using a "road-map . . . concealed somewhere in the Greek chorus: a choreographic map based on the beat of the verse; a map of perfectly synchronized mood, movement and speech; a 'dance' with words."[37] His Hellenism undergirded his creation of aesthetic objects and his preference for plays that used verse, elevated diction, and abstract settings, whether they were Greek or not. Cook, on the other hand, sought a communal way of working based on his understanding of societal organization and democracy in ancient Athens. His goals were less aesthetic per se than they were social and cultural, and he continued to maintain a "democratic, quasi-socialist, political orientation."[38] He sought a "group consciousness" that was focused on the creative possibilities of the Provincetown participants, whose pooled energies were to enhance each other, yielding a "serious theatre capable of redeeming society." Cook wanted all participants to learn and do all of the tasks it took to mount a play rather than to specialize in just one area. He also favored "inspiration and intoxication, not training and craftsmanship."[39]

Both recipes—Browne's for abstraction, poetry, and aestheticism and Cook's for spontaneity, naiveté, and self-expression in the context of communal support—made specific demands on participants and other specific demands on audiences. Both artistic directors were autocratic, Cook despite his stated ideals and Browne perhaps because of them.[40] (Browne literally wrote that dramatic aspirants must be willing to submit to the will of "an artistic oligarchy," a function he reserved for himself, often surrounding himself with young, pretty, admiring women and rehearsing long hours for many weeks.)[41] Both men also sought audiences who would pay for their Little Theatre experiments, preferably also agreeing with the creators' ideals, but in any case subsidizing them, sharing intimate theatre spaces with them, and recognizing their value in reflecting certain social interests.

Amateur Precedents/Mercantile Precedence

Shared beliefs and values between audiences and players was not necessary in commercial theatre, where it was unlikely that most audiences knew or interacted with the performers or writers of the Broadway or touring shows that prevailed in the United States from about 1870 until around 1912. These productions traded on a certain luxurious escapism rather than on intimacy, an escapism that, in large cities, often also included lavish meals in showy restaurants following the performance.[42] There was, however, at least one precedent for the Little Theatre model in the mid-nineteenth-century phenomenon of parlor theatricals. Popular in the 1850s and 1860s, parlor theatricals were offered by middle-class people in their homes for like-minded friends and family. The entertainments featured charades, tableaux vivants, and the enactment of playlets, all mounted on elaborately tricked-out stages in parlors where typically the front room was the audience area and the back room the stage, with a curtain dividing the two. (This was roughly the layout of the Provincetown Players' first New York venue, a remodeled brownstone, where the former front parlor served as the audience area, the dining room as stage, and the former butler's pantry as a tiny backstage and storage space.) Guidebooks to parlor theatricals were readily available for the amateur of the 1850s as manuals and journals would be to the Little Theatre amateur of the 1920s. Karen Halttunen links these performances to self-definition and notes that "the audience was carefully restricted. . . . No vulgar intruders who might undermine the performance through their lack of tact would be permitted to witness a parlor theatrical."[43] While it is unlikely that any of the Little Theatre founders—especially those born after the 1870s—would have participated regularly (if at all) in parlor theatricals, it is not at all unlikely that some of their parents or parents' friends might have done so and shared anecdotes. Young participants in parlor theatricals would have been early forgers of the PMC or the parents of the first generation of PMC Americans, from whom the Little Theatres' founders and audiences emerged. Accordingly, there was a precedent among the social class that spawned the Little Theatre movement for intimate amateur theatre that did not question the values and sense of self-worth shared by participants and audience, who were expected to come from the same ideological neighborhood.

The parlor theatrical, of course, did not depend on paid admission, nor was it intended to yield anything like a long run, ongoing production company, permanent venue, or reviews. Little Theatre pioneers of the 1910s and 1920s, despite protestations of adherence to an amateur ideal, followed a basically mercantile—albeit small-scale and frequently subsidized—model. Consider one example of an alternative template for morally purposeful, self-expressive amateur theatre—one also predicated on an interest in Hellenism—that was more widely available to a like-minded audience than were parlor theatricals, but that did not leave itself open to the financial pitfalls that were to color and often defeat many Little Theatres. In 1890, the Saturday Morning Club of Boston mounted a production of *Antigone*. The club was founded by Maud Howe, daughter of Julia Ward Howe, and was made up of socially prominent young Boston women interested in "general enlightenment and cultivation," according to the *Boston Advertiser*'s unnamed reviewer for the production.[44] The purpose of the group's all-female production was to suggest that modern women needed to reinhabit Antigone's stance in order to combat Creon's present-day law. The choice of a Greek play was based on the belief that the "Greek idea of fate was the cause of the sense of impasse that characterized all history up to the 1890s. Under the philosophical mandate sanctioned by the Greeks, suffering was viewed as a permanent condition. In contrast, the young women of 1890 testified that their generation believed that 'the old ideas of the gods had become too small' and that justice was the new spirit."[45] The play was presented four times in Bumstead Hall, following a year of preparation that included dramatic coaching. The production was a hybrid of public and private theatrical undertakings, referred to in the *Boston Transcript* as a "semi-public presentation."[46] Tickets were sold (with proceeds going to charity), and newspaper reviewers were invited, but the audience was all women and the performers were amateurs whose goal was neither a springboard to professional careers in theatre nor the creation of an ongoing producing company.

When the Little Theatre movement emerged in the 1910s, it was a curiously unspoken yet almost axiomatic tenet that, despite the amateur status claimed and championed by most of the groups, mercantile ideas of ongoing production prevailed. Nearly all Little Theatre leaders saw it as important to seek sponsorship, to charge for tickets, to publicize in newspapers, and to set up shop in buildings that would be available to them on a continuing basis. In other words, projects that might have been paid for by participants and offered to supporters on a limited basis in venues available for a short time for the purpose of self-expression or alternative artistic options did not accommodate all that the groups wanted. Conceivably, this was because Little Theatre founders were the unquestioning heirs to what Alan Trachtenberg calls the "incorporation of America." Well-organized companies and a view of the nation in terms of markets for goods replaced, between 1865 and 1895, an earlier, more localized way of organizing commerce that was often family-owned and dealt basically with customers known personally to the business people. For those born during these years, the sea change would have comprised a normal way of doing things and of understanding the public. Robert Wiebe sees Americans' "search for order" yielding by the mid-1910s "a bureaucratic orientation [that] defined a basic part of the nation's discourse. The values of continuity and regularity, functionality and rationality, administration and management set the form of problems and outlined their alternative solutions."[47] Progressive movements supported by members of the new upper middle class were all about expanding outward, as reformers "formulated their interests in terms of continuous policies that necessitated regularity and predictability from unseen thousands."[48]

The result of trying to combine regularity and predictability with a handmade and an amateur ideal meant that the Little Theatre contract with both audience and participants was often problematic regarding the wedding of artistic aspirations and ordinary commercial practice. In September 1916, for instance, just as the company was preparing to open in New York, an article about the Provincetown Players appeared in the *Boston Post* suggesting that "they do it all for fun."[49] Nonetheless, some time during the previous summer, founder George Cram Cook had sent a letter to people who had seen the season's early offerings on Cape Cod asking them to pay for admission to the remainder of the summer's plays. Shortly thereafter, the Provincetowners began a subscription drive for "associate members" to fund a continued project in New York that was ultimately to include renovating not one but two buildings. Officially, the Provincetown was a private club in which associate or club membership entitled people to buy tickets, while no one else could legally walk in off the street and do so. Moreover, members were supposed to demonstrate that they were "interested and engaged in the production of plays or other work of the Provincetown Players Theatre."[50] When sales were needed, however, members could be recruited en masse, as was the case with the bulk ticket sales to the members of Emilie Hapgood's New York Stage Society. Certainly the Stage Society members were "interested in the production of plays"; they also provided the financial support necessary to guarantee rent and production for an anticipated season and were not expected to participate in production.

Institutionalization was a given almost from the outset. While the private membership strategy enabled the group to circumvent New York City ordinances, in no way did the Provincetown Players resemble the amateur theatricals of the mid-1800s nor the occasional, themed use of theatre exemplified by the Saturday Morning Club.[51] For example, although the "view of amateurism as a stepping stone to professionalism" was defeated by the early Provincetowners in their rejection of the name "Try-Out Theatre," the group soon recruited a director who, along with the business manager, was paid; they began providing free passes to newspaper critics from the mainstream New York press in the middle of their third season; and, in the wake of Eugene O'Neill's success with the move of *The Emperor Jones* to Broadway in 1920, Cook opened—with disastrous results—his play *The Spring* on Broadway in 1921.[52] The tension between wanting professional careers and supporting a more amateur ideal was a famous cause of the group's demise; increasing professionalism and failures to achieve it surely also colored audience experiences and expectations as well as the perspective of newspaper critics.

In analyzing the Boston Toy Theatre, Constance D'Arcy Mackay noted: "The Toy Theatre in Boston failed because it was what its name implied. Its workers did not take it seriously."[53] Perhaps. But perhaps the group started out with a tacit professional model at odds with their stated amateur ideal. Founder Jane Winsor (Mrs. Lyman) Gale (1868–1952) renovated a stable in Louisburg Square, which was then, as it is now, an upper-class enclave. From the beginning, the theatre had a multipage program booklet with extensive advertising, a tearoom with specially made cups sporting the theatre's monogram, the support of Harvard's president, and, briefly, the participation of patrician-bred poet Amy Lowell as well as that of an heir to the Jordan Marsh department store fortune. Newspaper publicity was sought and was forthcoming. Yet the articulated ideals were modest, with Gale herself praising the handmade and simple in the analogy with literal playthings: "Toys that people make themselves, toys made of string, and wood, and anything that comes to hand mean more to the children and are far more valuable, both in educating and amusing their owners, than the finest ready-made toys the shops can afford."[54] Here Gale was drawing on a rhetoric familiar to proponents of the Arts and Crafts movement, which had begun in England with the socialist ideal of reuniting crafts workers and laborers and their increasingly assembly-line-wrought products. The movement devolved, in one strand, in the United States to an upper-class taste for handmade, expensive, artisanal objects (consumerism with taste) and in another strand—the one the Toy espoused—to a belief in participatory hobbies and do-it-yourself projects as a way to combat ennui, with emphasis on "enjoyment" and "growth."[55] The Toy Theatre's raison d'etre was "to produce simply and with artistic seriousness plays of a more limited appeal than are usually risked by professional managers and plays suited only to a small and intimate auditorium."[56] "Artistic seriousness" here resulted in an expensive undertaking that did not seem imaginable to its leaders outside a commercial model. In fact, when the original Toy closed after two seasons, Gale started a new and much larger venture, also called the Toy Theatre, and also destined to fail, but clearly understood by journalists and the ticketbuying public as "among the regular playhouses of the city."[57]

One Little Theatre that aimed from its outset to achieve professional status was Beulah Jay's Little Theatre of Philadelphia. Within two years of opening, the undertaking had become semiprofessional, using amateur actors but offering royalties to some playwrights, maintaining a building, and seeking publicity in the mainstream press. Jay produced and directed offerings herself and operated with the belief that she could run a semiprofessional theatre based primarily on her background as a student of acting and opera. Her short-lived venture foundered during World War I, and the small theatre building she had renovated at her husband's expense was taken over by the wholly amateur Plays and Players of Philadelphia.

The pitfalls of naively imagining that professionalism is a pick-and-choose arrangement with no particular rules or obligations are nowhere so well shown up as in a letter Jay received from George Bernard Shaw in 1917. Shaw excoriated her for presenting his *Misalliance* without having obtained legal rights to do so. Since he had sold the rights to the first production of the play in all major American cities to William Faversham, Jay had, Shaw stated, caused him to defraud Faversham. "The difficulty in dealing with you is that you have not had sufficient business training to understand the legal importance of the things you do," wrote Shaw tartly. While Jay claimed to have sent him royalty checks, he pointed out that neither these nor four other letters she said she had sent had ever reached him.[58] "How is it possible to do business with a woman who does things of this kind and imagines that they are only romantic adventures?" Shaw went on to point out that he had no interest in her description of her theatre as "simple and dignified in design," nor in the datum of its holding 330 people. "The number of people a theatre holds is of no consequence compared to the quantity of money it holds. What are the prices of the seats; and how many are there of each denomination?" He further scorned her speaking of a law and an interpretation, presumably regarding permission to operate her theatre as simply "splendid," without spelling out either the wording of the law or the nature of the interpretation. In a particularly pointed moment of irritation, he wrote, "It is not a question of going to prison. As you have never been there (though you really ought to be), you probably think that a few months of it would be amply repaid by having your fancy about somebody else's play. . . . Don't do it again, Beulah; you will not find Jewish theatrical syndicates as easy to play with as I am."[59]

Shaw's virulent attack on Jay and on the commercial power of, among others, the Shubert brothers on Broadway and across the nation, brings together two key underpinnings of the Little Theatre movement. One, discussed above, is that reformers both refused but in many ways shared the same desire for widespread recognition and interest in attracting monied spectators drawn to "the best" that motivated commercial producers. Their desire to reform commercial theatre by example spilled quickly into wanting to displace actual commercial ventures. Even when not literally focused on attracting the well-off—which many were—Little Theatre practitioners understood audiences in commercial terms compatible with the idea of Wiebe's "continuous policies . . . [toward] unseen thousands."

The second key feature of Little Theatre reform betrayed in Shaw's letter is a tacit understanding that stereotyping groups outside the Anglophone mainstream—here Jews as avaricious, ruthless in business, clever, "other"—was an ordinary way of seeing. Most, although not all, Little Theatre reformers were Protestant and born in the United States. Maurice Browne and the Washington Square Players' Lawrence Langner were born in England, and Irene and Alice Lewisohn were nonpracticing Jews. Even among these, audiences, participants, and role models who were foreign born seemed simultaneously appealing and disturbing. Theatre reformers wrestled with ideas about ethnicity, race, and Anglophilia that shaped and challenged thinking about Americanism and American theatre audiences. Reformers unquestionably trafficked in prejudice, but, like so much else in the Little Theatre movement, this prejudice was multifaceted and sometimes inconsistent. It included prejudices for, against, and in the interest of re-visioning several European heritages and kinds of cultural praxes.

Prejudices

The term "cultural pluralism" was coined by scholar and social philosopher Horace Meyer Kallen to denote a belief in both the unique nature and the collective value of multiple ethnic identities evident in American life. Kallen, by his own account, began developing the concept around 1905 and put the term into circulation in academic conversation during the 1910s and into print in 1924.[60] These years coincided not only with the Little Theatre movement and its immediate antecedents, but also with roughly the last half of an era of European immigration that challenged the social perceptions and economic concerns of many native-born Americans. John Higham points out that the proportion of foreign-born to the total population actually remained the same from 1860 to 1920.[61] What changed, beginning in the 1880s, besides the size of the overall population, were the countries from which immigrants came, the numbers in which they arrived, and the economic arrangements under which many Americans lived. Earlier immigrants had been largely Irish, German, or Scandinavian and had been more or less tolerated as, respectively, English speakers, or Teutonic or Nordic exemplars of industriousness and fair-skinned familiarity. Many of these, especially the Scandinavians, became farmers in relatively sparsely settled parts of the country. After 1880, European emigrants were far more likely to be Jewish, Slavic, Italian, or Greek, to be rural in origin, and to cluster in large cities. Their darker skins, unfamiliar social behaviors, peasant backgrounds, crowded slum dwellings, and, in the case of Jews, their non-Christianity, by virtue of being outside native ken, challenged the assumptions of many hereditary Americans. Blue-collar workers in the factories and mines that had become sources of livelihood for many, including many of the earlier immigrants, within only a few decades were threatened by the presence of large numbers of uneducated, newly arrived laborers willing to work for little money or to compete for scarce jobs; industrialists alternately urged or objected to immigration based on their fluctuating labor needs and on labor unrest.

Little Theatre reformers, as members of the PMC, were, by and large, beset by neither the first-hand anxieties and resentments of nativist labor who feared loss of work nor by the profit motive of the powerful industrialists who saw laborers less as individual humans than as depersonalized parts of a production machine. The Little Theatre practitioners and supporters were, moreover, among those most interested in configuring difference in terms other than the strictly ethnic or racial. David Kadlec's study *Mosaic Modernism* investigates a writerly ability to think about difference as something that "turned on a distinction between motion and stasis rather than on a distinction between 'us' and 'them.'"[62] It was exactly such a notion of difference that enabled many Little Theatre leaders to work with immigrants based on an idea of cultural pluralism that, as John Dewey approvingly observed, "was not the fixed standard of 'Anglosaxondom' but rather the ongoing measure by which Americans 'assimilate[d] themselves *to one another*'" (emphasis in original).[63]

Efforts at assimilation—either mutual or expected on the part of immigrants only—were, however, fraught with unresolved tensions. Both the melting pot and the multicultural ideals were predicated on difference as a problem. In the former, all ethnic differences were to be "melted" away in pursuit of a monocultural (WASP) ideal; in the latter, difference might be either celebrated or scorned, but it was noted, and lines were drawn.[64] As we shall see below, theatre practitioners and reformers were interested in the performable customs and ceremonies that immigrants might bring to the creation of theatre events as well as in the theatregoing habits they brought from Europe. Also, despite Higham's claim that the aesthetic and cultural "contributions that charmed sympathetic progressives had no bearing on American institutions or ideals," it was a willingness to work with such contributions that facilitated social change at the level where it was, and some would argue still is, most immediately perceived: the local.[65] As native and immigrant Americans worked together on performances, both the artists and their audiences were challenged to "assimilate themselves to one another." Nonetheless, Anglosaxondom and nativism often trumped other contributions and practices even within group attempts at mutually shaped theatre. Moreover, as the interests and needs of the immigrant groups evolved, it was sometimes the Little Theatre workers who resisted adjustment, preferring to focus on models of creativity that gratified PMC rebels and their sympathizers rather than neighborhood denizens.

Little Theatre reformers did not exist outside the gestalt of their times, even if they challenged or tried to reconfigure aspects of it. Theorists and officials in many walks of American life contributed to an idea that the foreign-born were dangerously inferior, even if they deserved sympathy. Clergyman John Denison in 1895 labeled recent European arrivals examples of "specious humanity" and a socialist threat to liberty-loving Anglo-Saxons. Edward A. Ross developed the idea that Asiatic immigration could lead to the annihilation of the American people if the "higher" race did not reproduce at an adequate rate to keep pace with the "lower" one. That fear was picked up by others and bandied about as "race suicide," a term Theodore Roosevelt used in arguments against birth control for native-born whites. Between 1905 and 1909, over thirty-five articles dealing with this topic appeared in general-interest magazines. Eugenicist Charles B. Davenport lent biological authority to his argument that many immigrants came from immutably "degenerate breeding stock," not subject to change through environment or education. Around 1913, novelist Jack London wrote two books "which showed 'the dark-pigmented things, the half-castes, the mongrel-bloods' of southern and eastern Europe swamping the blond, master race in America." Patrician Madison Grant, the wealthy scion of family that had enjoyed social prominence in New York since colonial times, published *The Passing of the Great Race* in 1916. Among other things, he argued that any intermingling of races always resulted in a "reverting" to the more ancient, "lower" type. Grant's book enjoyed its greatest vogue between 1921 and 1923, when new editions appealed to nativists who, in the economic depression and emergent isolationism following World War I, pursued immigration quotas. Calvin Coolidge published an article in 1921 asserting that "Nordics deteriorate when mixed with other races."[66]

The slippage (my own) between the terms *race* and *ethnicity* reflects a historical shift that began in the 1920s. Differences later called ethnic (e.g., Slavic vs. Teutonic vs. Italian vs. Greek vs. Celtic vs. Ashkenazic, etc.) were, during the Progressive Era, firmly understood as racial. Based on then-current science as well as in popular thinking, these categories were taken as biologically hard-wired and immutable.[67] The period of greatest anxiety about white "others" was concurrent with the forging of Little Theatre and its audiences. Therefore, understanding negotiations with those later to be called white ethnics—and to be recruited as theatre sympathizers along with other hereditary Americans for the rest of the century—is crucial, as is a close look at how theatre reformers understood and used difference. In examining Little Theatre ideas about white "others," I neither mean to ignore nor elide work with, about, or by black Americans. African Americans, who comprised the majority of blacks living in the United States, occupied a different position from white others in the minds of most theatre reformers. Among other things, Little Theatre practitioners in the Northeast and Midwest encountered few African Americans before the early 1910s, which is when migration from the South began to occur in significant numbers.[68] As native-born, English-speaking Protestants, African Americans presented another register of othering for Little Theatre practitioners and audiences from immigrants. At the crudest level, African Americans' biggest "difference" was skin color, which could not be "melted" through cultural practice. But when PMC theatre reformers began to pay attention to African Americans in great numbers, the latter by and large functioned as a doppelganger within more than as an alien force from without. By the 1920s, African Americans had started their own Little Theatres, and some were, by the end of the decade, contributing plays to a national Little Theatre competition held on Broadway. This was the opposite of what happened with theatre for and by immigrant groups, which largely disappeared with the graying of the first generation.[69] Accordingly, negotiations with black Americans within a theatre devised for spiritual, intellectual, social, communal, and artistic betterment are examined in the final chapter.

The Anglosaxondom that so often served as a touchstone of both normalcy and excellence had particular valence in the world of theatre and theatre reform in no small part because its prime literary exemplar was Shakespeare. Appreciation of and participation in productions of Shakespeare's plays were posited as keys to overcoming the taint of foreignness as well as to developing character. This prejudice circulated among hereditary Americans and was also often eagerly adopted by immigrants wanting to better their situation in the United States. In 1882, A. A. Lipscomb published an article in *Harper's* urging the study of Shakespeare as a means of arousing "the intellectual consciousness" and providing education beyond "formulae . . . repetition, and . . . exactness," something seemingly akin to the Progressive recipe later favored by Randolph Bourne. Shakespeare facilitated "the art of *applied* mental philosophy" if only the student would "store up his materials and give them time to adapt themselves by hidden interaction to one another, so that they may shape themselves *intuitively* to their own ideal." Shakespeare was "the master-teacher outside of the Holy Scriptures."[70] Lipscomb, writing before the huge waves of southern European immigration, could not have anticipated an urban America teeming with non–English speakers; moreover, the readers of *Harper's* were the WASP elite who could afford the magazine. Accordingly, the "intuitions" that Shakespeare was to nourish were envisioned in the Anglo-American mold.

In 1901, *Harper's* published an article that explained what, precisely, made Anglo-Saxons a superior "race." Neither the magazine nor its presumed readers were any longer the only game in town, as twenty years of southern European immigration, increased industrialization, and the advent of the less-expensive popular magazine had created a climate in which such an explanation might seem necessary (or at least comforting) to an increasingly anxious elite. The author, Professor Brander Matthews (1852–1929) of Columbia University, was the first American to be appointed Professor of Dramatic Literature, and, therefore, wielded influence in the emerging recognition of drama as a legitimate area of study. Here, though, Matthews contributed as much to a divisive racial theory as he did to a progressive theatre program. He asserted that "the peoples that speak English are, and always have been, self-willed and adventurous . . . and they have always exulted in the untiring energy and the daring imagination which are the vital elements of poetry."[71] Celtic influence added delicacy and sentiment to the original Teutonic characteristics, all of which coalesced in Elizabethan literature and character, to which, Matthews added, turn-of-the-century Americans were the true heirs, as Britons had become characterized by "insularity and inarticulateness."[72]

American theatre reformers of the Progressive Era, even as they found much to identify with in work like Matthews's, also found much to admire in immigrant audiences and the theatre the latter supported, especially when theatre events depicted and aroused passion and political commitment. This split identity resulted in an anxious concern for a we/they division that colored assessments made by WASP or WASP-identified critics. A careful reader may note a difference between critiques of individual productions and critiques of audiences for those productions. Particular shows could be assessed or ignored; even the longest run eventually comes to an end. But the audience—Joseph Roach's "simulacrum of the body politic"—could not be too foreign and still be entirely safe.

In 1898, John Corbin published a long essay in *Harper's* in which he reported on ethnic white theatres and audiences in lower Manhattan. Corbin would go on to distinguish himself both as a drama critic for the *New York Times* (he did three stints as chief critic between 1902 and 1924) and also as an anti-Semitic racialist. His 1910 play, *Husband,* promotes racial separation, as the idealistic Jewish "New Woman" in the play is constituted as a threat to the marriage and reproduction of the WASP family. In the 1930s, Corbin was to lament Jewish influence on the New York theatre in an article for *Scribner's*.[73] His 1898 title, "How the Other Half Laughs," paid direct homage to photographer Jacob Riis's *How the Other Half Lives*. Both projects expressed empathy while also reinforcing boundaries. But while Riis's readers probably never inhabited situations akin to those of the photographs' subjects—living and dying in poverty and urban squalor—Corbin's readers presumably could and did see themselves as actual or potential theatregoers with a socially significant purpose. Corbin visited Italian, Yiddish, and German theatres; he reminded his readers that his essay was an exercise in tourism for "us" to exoticize "them" through repeated references to "our plays in English," "our uptown manners," and "our moral code."[74] This stance, far from being exclusive to elites, echoed textbooks and popular culture of the time, both of which differentiated between the native and the foreign-born, both also reasserting the cultural authority of the WASP bourgeoisie.[75]

Corbin praised Yiddish theatre audiences for the financial sacrifices they made to attend the theatre, "a patronage of art infinitely beyond that of the families uptown who parade their liberality in supporting the Metropolitan Opera House."[76] He admired the "rapt enthusiasm" of a Jewish audience for the philosophical play *Uriel Acosta*, in which the eponymous protagonist struggles with his opposing loyalties to intellectual freedom and rabbinical power. "I know of no American theatre audience where so nobly intellectual a theme would meet so keen an appreciation," he wrote in praise of an "artistic people."[77] Here, the immigrant theatregoers are salutary exemplars precisely to the extent that they do *not* resemble the privileged (nonartistic) and indifferent native-born. Likewise, Italian audiences were praiseworthy because they "hung on every bar" of music, offering audible praise that was not mere indiscriminate cheering, but rather full of "infinite shadings of expression."[78]

The admiring observations, however, oscillate with anxious and defensive ones. Corbin's Italians have "instinctive strength and delicacy of affections," but these "may be more nearly allied to the animal than a sympathetic observer suspects."[79] His Jews comprise a "downtrodden people . . . leaping into individuality . . . through the new liberty they have found" but are also taken in by glamour because of "the very Oriental luxuriance of their temperament" and are suspect because of a "racial instinct" for opportunism.[80] A behind-the-scenes tour with a WASP stagehand who speaks Yiddish ends with Corbin's expression of relief that his guide has maintained his "racial pride in the face of the immigrating people. It is almost compensation for our lack of the sympathies and the assimilative powers that make up an artistic people."[81]

Assimilation was a goal but also, ironically, an arts problem. Even as Corbin's article appeared, the Italian theatre he had hoped to visit again had closed. He predicted the demise of Yiddish theatre, too, in no small part because the comforts of American life would lure the young into abandoning their parents' ways, including their theatres.[82] These very comforts underpin the jibe with which Corbin challenges his readers in his conclusion, wondering whether, "in the course of years our souls should cease to fulfill their largest hopes in out-of-door sports and porcelain baths," and, therefore, whether it is reasonable to think that only something "beautiful" will be able to satisfy our longings?[83]

As a contribution to the rhetoric of audience reform, Corbin's article is valuable not only for the stereotypes, positive and negative, that it reveals, but also because of two ideological strains that are present in the form of blind spots. First, Corbin misrecognizes immigrant theatres as compelling and authentic to their audiences because "in the truest sense of the word they are national arts." More accurately they are the arts of displaced subcultures. Indeed these theatres were dealing with "the life and interest" of their audiences, but they were doing so in ways having less to do with nationhood and its attendant sense of centrality than with adjustment, negotiation, acculturation, nostalgia, and often a generational divide between parents who remembered Europe and their children who didn't. To yearn for the devotion to the theatre that such audiences exhibited was to yearn for something that a self-satisfied uptown audience who benefited from and defined hegemonic values had no equivalent reason to achieve. The immigrant project, which Corbin recognized, was to overcome the limitations and injuries of the very outsider status that enabled a commitment to ethnic ("other half") theatre. Second, what Corbin did not see, but Little Theatre reformers believed, was that discontent itself, more than racial or even shared social characteristics, would be the seed from which purposeful theatre and theatregoing could grow. In other words, being educated WASPS together would not spontaneously produce an improved theatre in the face of some finger-wagging or against the lure of the metaphorical porcelain bath. Embracing David Kadlec's "motion"—here the motion bred of dissatisfaction and emptiness—in place of "stasis" was the preferred recipe; and the desire for motion was the glue bonding a "we" with immigrants in the context of theatremaking. Little Theatre projects with immigrant colleagues and audiences were endeavors that sought to Americanize immigrants discontent with their displacement and one that some re- formers hoped would lend passion and commitment to their own (dis- content with commercialism) nativist cohort's theatregoing.

Play-mates

Jane Addams's (1860–1935) Hull-House, one of the most successful late- nineteenth- and early-twentieth-century settlements on many fronts, used dramatic and other arts activities as a means of social betterment and per- sonal growth for immigrants, beginning in the 1890s. Hull-House is rec- ognized as perhaps the earliest prominent locus of using theatremaking to these ends; Irene and Alice Lewisohn's Neighborhood Playhouse started related work at the Henry Street Settlement on Manhattan's Lower East Side beginning in 1912. The Lewisohns began teaching and directing at Henry Street in the first decade of the century, mounted their first play proper in 1912, and opened the Playhouse building in 1915, usually con- sidered the first official year of the Neighborhood operation. Addams and the Lewisohns had radically divergent attitudes, however, towards theatre and performance-making. Addams saw commercial theatre as tawdry, debasing, and "soiled" yet found theatremaking valuable as "an agent of recreation and education . . . [and] as a vehicle of self-expression."[84] The Lewisohn sisters were trained in acting and dance, and Alice performed as a very young woman on Broadway; the sisters sought their own as well as their immigrant cohorts' betterment and outlet in creativity. Addams also saw good literature as crucial to good theatre while the Lewisohns pur- sued what would now be called interdisciplinary work, with an empha- sis on dance, rhythm, music, design, and collective composition.

Despite the differing interests, both settlements' theatre endeavors suffered from the same split attitudes regarding audiences. On the one hand, each sought to serve immigrants in their neighborhoods; on the other, both were lured by the Little Theatre values promulgated and re- spected by reformers who were experimenting with theatre to satisfy their own ideas of aesthetic and social excellence. Many analyses of theatre- making at these two prominent settlements favor and sympathize with the frustrations of the artist/directors who struggled against what they saw as unsophisticated immigrant tastes and/or philistine commercial tastes. Yet such analyses presume that the "best" audience is the one that recognizes and favors theatre in which the analysts' and theatre directors' own concerns and repositories of cultural capital were present and legible—a prejudice that is sympathetic to self-expression and experimentation only for certain kinds of social selves and aesthetic trajectories. At both settlement houses, the aesthetic theatre goals and the social service work eventually diverged, in part because of arts directors' interest in appealing to audiences that were more like themselves than like their clients and students. Yet the immigrants who embraced Americanization emerged able to join that audience if they chose. Since the process of working together to create theatre was just that—a process—change occurred to some extent in both camps.

Theatre activities at Hull-House began with dramatic readings (1890), followed by a class in Shakespeare (1890) and one in Greek tragedy (1892). In 1893, Hull-House youth presented their first production. Thereafter, plays were sponsored by individual clubs, many of these organized around ethnic identity. The appeal of theatre to economically impoverished young people prior to the advent of the movies was not lost on even the disapproving Addams, who noted sympathetically that the "phrases of stage heroes" and the words of melodrama were the ones in which boys and girls expressed their dreams and ambitions, an expressing she favored, but whose terms she wanted to revise.[85] In 1896, an adult professional was put in charge of supervising various youth club–sponsored dramatic activities. One club's *As You Like It* was presented in 1897 and then had encore performances in the wealthy suburbs of Kenilworth and Winnetka.[86] Immigrant work with Shakespeare was a way to show native elites that the newcomers were educable and assimilable—not surprising in light of Lipscomb and Matthews's ideas—and therefore a good advertisement for the project before an audiences of potential funders or even powerful enemies needing persuading.[87]

Later that year, the Hull-House Dramatic Association was announced. This group, which came to be known as the Hull-House Players, differed from its forerunners in that membership was restricted and based on talent and skills. In 1900, Laura Dainty Pelham, a former actress, became the group's adviser; she led the Players until her death in 1924. The group earned wide recognition and publicity, but internecine battles around the time of the beginning of the Little Theatre movement reveal tensions between social and aesthetic concerns and the assumption that the two cannot merge without one of them suffering. Pelham's success rested, in part, on focusing almost from the beginning of her tenure on the interests and values of audiences that included not only the working classes, but also people from wealthy areas of Chicago.[88] J. Dennis Rich's account of

Pelham's shift to an interest in social realism, taken from a 1916 article by Pelham herself, reveals the tensions between what is legible and meaningful to theatre professionals—even those engaged in educational and social reform—and the effects of this on the potential audience community.

> The decision to give a new direction to theatrical activity at the settlement coincided with a change in the Halsted Street neighborhood. Pelham had secured a following for her actors by producing plays which were popular in the community. She observed that her audience consisted, in the main, of Irish and English-speaking French. But these "neighbors were being crowded out by Italians, who did not care for performances in English, and we were compelled to look elsewhere for our audiences." This change freed the director from the pressure of having to attract the immediate neighborhood to the theatre. The immigrant community continued to be served by the Hull-House clubs and by productions, sponsored by the immigrants themselves, in languages other than English. Pelham abandoned the effort to attract local audiences and, as a result, she was more easily able to undertake the production of a different kind of drama. Jane Addams's desire for socially significant theatre could now be satisfied. A new following was gained by "presenting plays which the commercial theatre is apt to overlook but which a certain group in every community really desires to see."[89]

Addams's ideas about social significance included seeing the "function of the stage as a reconstructing and reorganizing agent of accepted moral truths," a notion she says came to her "with overwhelming force as I listened to the Passion Play at Oberammergau one beautiful summer's day in 1900."[90] The anti-Semitism of the Passion play, both in the text and the production's traditional casting, was either illegible or irrelevant to Addams, just as the ongoing needs of the non-English-speaking immigrant community moving into the Halsted Street were written off by Pelham, leaving them, as Rich reports, to sponsor their own theatre activities.[91]

Meanwhile, the Hull-House players attracted the attention of influential visitors such as Joseph Jefferson and Maurice Browne, spokesmen and guides for Rich's "certain group," understood by Pelham as "our audience." Pelham introduced new Irish work in 1912 following the Irish Players' American tour. The two companies saw each other's work, and the Hull-House players raised money so they could visit Ireland in 1913. When they returned from the trip, they sought more autonomy in running the company, casting, and choosing plays; they expressed dissatisfaction with Pelham's "outdated style of direction," articulating a desire for a more integrated, up-to-date style of production in the interest of satisfying "the public, our public" and their demands. While Addams sided with Pelham and supported the latter's continued artistic control of the official Hull-House Players, the dissatisfied actors left the group, one eventually acting for Browne's Chicago Little Theatre.[92] Here, ironically, the professional actress who has learned to work with neighborhood actors is rejected by those same locals as they seek membership in the vanguard of their leader's abandoned profession. An outsider may have trouble seeing the difference between Pelham's "our audience" and the Players' "our public." To local groups who sought their reflection in the eyes of specifically like-minded supporters, such differences felt crucial. They also suggest that statements framed in terms of "the public" or "the audience" may have less to do with the population at large or even with potential ticketbuyers than with a handful of particular funders or members of other theatre groups.

The tensions and ironies in the above account are parsed with nuance by Shannon Jackson, especially regarding the immigrant community "left behind." She notes, among other things, that the members of the Hull-House Players who traveled to Ireland and then rebelled against Pelham were themselves largely Irish-American, so that, while the "language of artistic success and theatrical fame effectively denationalized their 'Irishness,'"[93] they were already themselves among the most "American" of the immigrant groups in the area, being English speakers, light-skinned, and Christian, and, therefore, easily adoptable by theatre and arts aficionados or social reformers interested in melting-pot ideals. But Jackson situates the work of the Hull-House Players as merely one of a nexus of projects exemplifying "the participatory fieldwork of theater making."[94] Refusing the social/aesthetic split common to historians who want to validate the high art Little Theatre ideals of the Hull-House Players and elide or ignore the other performance work created in the name of amateurism or self-expression, Jackson focuses on the efforts of theatre director and teacher Edith de Nancrede, whose dance classes and directing at Hull-House were all about disciplining bodies so that grace, comportment, and style (as understood by elite or PMC Americans with northern European forebears) would become second nature to young, working-class, or immigrant participants. As such, reforms in speech, bodily carriage, choice of dress or home decoration—all acquired in significant part through theatremaking under the guidance of educated settlement workers—enabled student performers to better themselves economically as they became able to pass in their performances of self in everyday life with an audience of already-privileged Americans.[95] The "embodied cultural capital" learned in theatre and dance classes and productions, whether or not the latter drew a high art audience, was also part of the Little Theatre movement in the settlement house.[96] Whether or not participants continued as arts performers, they learned the skills and values of audiences for serious theatre.

Theatre criticism, journalism, and historiography helped and continue to help construct theatre audiences based on prejudices about amateurism, professionalism, and immigrants. Dennis Rich accepted and reinscribed the idea that "socially significant" American theatre satisfies the art ideals of a certain kind of audience, the non–English speakers be damned. Perhaps it is no surprise that some of the Players that Pelham trained chafed at her leadership in the name of "the public, our public." For the rebels, the segment of the public that mattered was not only English speaking, but interested in Abbey Theatre and soon-to-be Chicago Little Theatre values. Contemporary criticism supported that view. Sheldon Cheney drove a clear wedge between what constituted proper stimulation for "the best" American audiences and what was good for immigrants in his short-hand assessment of the productions offered at settlement-affiliated theatres. In Chicago, Hull-House's project was "a little too closely linked with the redemption of slums to maintain a high artistic standard. We want art theatres in which the best life of the city, and particularly the art life, revolves around the dramatic center."[97] In New York, "theatregoers on the lookout for the best will be drawn down to Grand Street['s Neighborhood Playhouse] two or three times a year. The rest of the time they will stay away with the knowledge that the playhouse is fulfilling its other destiny of giving the East Side a variety of things and a means of self-expression."[98] Cheney, the founder of *Theatre Arts* magazine and by 1917 the author of two books about the Little Theatre movement, was not an isolated, unimportant, or atypical respondent. Whether knowingly or not, he was, in his settlement theatre remarks, embracing the idea of theatregoer as customer and was, moreover, showing concern only for a certain kind of customer. The mercantile and the elitist, never absent even from the earliest Little Theatre endeavors, are here fully validated, even as "self-expression," a key tenet for such exemplars as the Provincetown Players, is written off because it is an expression of the wrong selves.

The active "selves" at the Neighborhood Playhouse did, indeed, include many immigrants, largely eastern European Jews. The Playhouse on Grand Street was affiliated with the Henry Street Settlement; youngsters in the settlement's catchment took classes in acting and dance, joined choruses, and appeared in original pageants and plays at the Playhouse. Old Testament stories and Jewish customs, prayers, and holidays were tapped as sources for several large-scale productions involving dozens of participants.[99] But the dominant and dominating selves were the Playhouse's founders, artistic directors, and benefactors, Alice (1883–1972) and Irene (1892–1944) Lewisohn. The Playhouse was devised and largely funded by the two sisters, heiresses with a serious interest in theatre, dance, and social service who also directed and choreographed most of the major productions as well as performing in several of them and training a cadre of teachers. They began their tenure at Henry Street as volunteer teachers working for and with Lillian Wald, the settlement's founder and a proponent of Americanization. The Lewisohns' father and uncle started the largest copper sales company in the world, and, when Irene and Alice's brother joined the business, it merged with the Rockefeller family company and United Metals. The independently wealthy sisters traveled to India, Egypt, Jerusalem, Burma, Japan, and Germany in pursuit of performance traditions that would stimulate and challenge both their audiences and themselves. Over the course of the thirteen years of the Playhouse's existence (1915–1927), however, the audience they both imagined and attracted was decreasingly made up of neighborhood immigrants and increasingly comprised uptown arts aficionados. More obviously than many other Little Theatre practitioners—perhaps because more aesthetically sophisticated and financially powerful—the Lewisohns exemplify T. J. Jackson Lears's observation that many Progressive Era reformers were led by their own psychic dilemmas in an emerging modern society to "create the doctrines of modern culture for largely personal reasons."[100] When immigrant and neighborhood needs meshed with personal reasons, the former were included in theatremaking; when local audience needs changed, the artists chose not to adapt, preferring the modernist doctrines they had "fixed" to an actual modern process of ongoing reconstruction.

The Lewisohns did not predicate their work on the idea that Anglo-Saxon texts, especially Shakespeare, defined universalism. Nonetheless, universalism was their goal, and they systematically erased, elided, or misread customs or practices from various traditions in the pursuit of a "oneness" that Alice later clarified in terms of Jungianism. In her memoir of the Playhouse, she describes both her first trip to the Henry Street Settlement and her arrival in Palestine in similar terms. In each case, she—the inexperienced visitor—finds herself surrounded by crowds of exotic natives, and in each case, she is quickly removed from the crowds to dine with wealthy hosts. Her foreign hosts are of most interest to her when they are least individualized or modern. For example, Passover is nearly spoiled for her at the home of the Bokhara Rabbi in Palestine because the family has "exchanged their colorful traditional dress for the stiff, quasi-modern substitutes." The most moving feature of the dinner is what she imagines to be the Rabbi's disappearance into the past, as he seems to lose awareness of his immediate surroundings and turn into a "symbol." In other words, actual people and their evolving traditions in their real world were disappointments, at least as arts fodder; "symbols" were what Lewisohn wanted them to be. She speaks of the seder informatively as a "ritual meal still repeated in Jewish homes the world over" and elsewhere of Chanukah as the "midwinter festival,"[101] universalizing a tradition that she seems to wish to pretend is neither unique in historical origins nor specific to her own heritage.[102]

The Lewisohns' parents were Orthodox Jews, but, like many other German Jewish philanthropists, the sisters were assimilated. German Jewish social work and philanthropy targeting the newer Jewish immigrants was colored by xenophobia and a predilection for Americanization as much as it was motivated by sympathy and identification.[103] The Lewisohns' productions evolved from using Jewish participants and material of direct interest to the neighborhood to using professional actors and designers and branching out to draw on other traditions. For instance, the first Henry Street production, undertaken in 1912 (before the Playhouse building, funded by the Lewisohns, was erected) was *The Shepherd* by Olive Tilford Dargan, chosen because its subject, the conflict between revolutionary methods and Tolstoian non-resistance in Russia, had resonance for many of the neighborhood's recent arrivals from czarist Russia. The first production in the new Playhouse—a building whose plan was researched and wholly funded by the Lewisohns— in 1915 was an original piece, *Jephthah's Daughter,* using the Old Testament as a source, and incorporating both modern dance, an original score, and a pacifist message. The Playhouse offered, like other Little Theatres, plays by Dunsany, Yeats, Shaw, Galsworthy, Chekhov, Glaspell, O'Neill and Mrs. Havelock Ellis. In addition, the sisters' interest in foreign performance traditions, at least as they understood them, led to *Tamura,* a Noh play offered in the 1917–18 season; *The Royal Fandango,* a Spanish ballet in the 1920–21 season; *An Arab Fantasia* (subtitled "an impression of Arab life") in the 1923–24 season; *A Burmese Pwe* (an impression of Burma) and *Kuan Yin, The Goddess of Mercy* (a Chinese fantasy), both in the 1925–26 season and both directed by Irene; and, perhaps most famously, *The Little Clay Cart,* a Hindu drama based on a play written by King Shudraka some time between the fifth and the tenth centuries, the first offering of the 1923–25 season and revived in the middle of the final (1926–27) season.

Melanie Blood's study of the Neighborhood Playhouse repeatedly points to class differences between the founders and their settlement constituents and to a growing distance between the two, with fewer neighborhood participants and smaller numbers of spectators drawn from the local area as the years passed. Blood asserts that the shift to using a professional company beginning in 1920 marks a clear preference for artistic over social goals.[104] Uptown validation, reviews, and audiences became important to the Playhouse producers. The local immigrant audience was left either to assimilate, to choose movies that were more affordable than the (increasingly expensive) Playhouse shows, or to be written out of the Lewisohns' quest, although individual dedicated participants from the community were still used in larger cast lyric productions with vocal or dance ensemble work. The immigrant audience was no longer useful to the Lewisohns' art. In this sense, unlike Edith de Nancrede, the sisters backburnered reformance and mutual understanding in favor of aesthetic quest and one-way audience construction.

Understandably, the immigrants around Grand Street had a different relationship both to their own "exoticism" and to their customs and history than did the Lewisohns. The neighborhood newcomers were not self-identified structuralists who could afford to seek "that inner world of reality" or "those depths that link the individual to the mystery of nature" in the face of pressures to learn a new language and set of social habits. Alice touted the value of a "trained" audience in receiving experimental forms with appreciation, but the actual audiences she most admired were those she saw on her foreign travels, particularly in Burma and India, while Americans exemplified a "corrupted remnant of the relationship" between performer and audience. At the same time, she repeatedly described people she observed in her travels in plant and animal terms, feminizing both sexes and always preferring the "ancient" and the "lyric" to the immediate or the contested. Her own identity seemed firmly uptown and WASP, as, for example, in her description of rehearsals for *The Silver Box*, where, for weeks, dinners and tea parties at the sisters' Fifty-seventh Street home were made "the occasion for [others in the cast] acquiring familiarity with Anglo-Saxon customs at the board" while Alice herself worked at her role as an Irish char, learning to peel potatoes and to "concentrate my emotion in my back. . . . Bushels of potatoes were sacrificed to my study of the role."[105]

In the end, the Lewisohns seemed to be seeking an audience created in their own image, "trained" to appreciate the emergent interpretive and modern dance, researched orientalism, and new stagecraft that appealed to the sisters. Alice cited the "exigencies of an audience" as one of the things that had made it impossible to continue to pursue "the cultural values of production" in the latter days of their Playhouse. "Cultural value," as sociologist Paul DiMaggio points out, does not inhere in the intrinsic attributes of aesthetic goods, but rather in meanings that arise for individual consumers because of the identities of these goods' other consumers, and for what the goods say "about their consumers to themselves and to others, as inputs into the production of social relations and identities."[106] The "interplay" between audience and player that Alice touted in her memoir ceased when the desires of the actual audience failed to mesh with those of the artist/producers, with the locals drifting away because of lack of interest and expensive tickets and the uptowners because of the location of the theatre and some of its continued ethnic offerings. Here, the Lewisohns played both the roles of Laura Dainty Pelham and the rebellious members of the Hull-House Players. As producers, they refused to compromise or accommodate the neighbors whose interests did not quite match theirs; as rebels who wanted an audience that fit their construct ("the public, our public") they closed their downtown doors and continued their work on a limited basis in a series of orchestral dance dramas presented at the Manhattan Opera House, at Cleveland's Severance Hall, at the Library of Congress, and in Irene's cofounding a costume collection that was the basis of the Metropolitan Museum of Art's Costume Institute.

Urban settlements were not the only Little Theatre sites that worked with immigrants in a dialectic of inclusion and othering that built an audience for locally created theatre while Americanizing its constituents. In 1912, Alfred Arvold (1882–1957) founded the Little Country Theatre in Fargo, North Dakota, on the campus of the state agricultural college.

In an early pamphlet about the project, he construed three quarters of the population of the state as not American, citing those who were "either foreign-born or of foreign descent" as needing "social betterment." His foreigners comprised one hundred thousand Norwegians, sixty thousand Russians, forty-five thousand Germans, and "large settlements" of Canadians, Swedes, Danes, Austrians, Irishmen, Englishmen, Hungarians, Scots, Icelanders, Frenchmen, Welshmen, Bohemians, Dutchmen, Bulgarians, Greeks, Turks, and Italians. Arvold's crusade was not primarily against foreignness per se; country life itself was stultifying and bad for the human spirit. He saw "drama and all that goes with the drama, as a sociological force" to fight "moral degeneracy" born of rural stagnation. This was not Arvold's private invention; rural boredom was a concern addressed by the U.S. Department of Agriculture, which "sent out hundreds of letters to country women, asking them what would make life more attractive." Arvold's answer to overcoming "stupid monotony" and "social stagnancy" was to lift people out of the morass by helping them "find themselves" and "find their true expression in the community."[107]

In just such an effort, Arvold facilitated and praised a production called *A Farm Scene in Iceland Thirty Years Ago,* in which twenty young men and women of Icelandic descent depicted the "national life of their fathers and mothers." His hope that bringing together some of the forms "of social recreation of their previous national life" would "contribute much toward making our American life happier and better" sounds liberal and future-oriented, especially as he notes the specific goal of getting people "acquainted with each other" with drama as the medium of exchange. Arvold enthusiastically described a scene in which "an old grandfather [is] seated in an armchair near the fireplace reading a story in the Icelandic language . . . [with] several young ladies dressed in Icelandic costumes, busily engaged in spinning yarn and knitting, a favorite pastime of an Icelandic home."[108] The selves that his young participants are expressing are safely located in the past; the performers did not portray their own experiences. Arvold's tourist gaze, not unlike the Lewisohns', romanticizes and aestheticizes activities that seem quaint to him—spinning and knitting—failing to see these as economic practicalities, ordinary aspects of self-preservation, and possible sources of the very boredom he believed to be dangerous and stultifying. Emphasizing the past as the true locus of ethnic identity bypasses the possibility of characterizing ethnicity in terms of contemporary political or cultural concerns; it simultaneously positions ethnicity itself as something to be left behind.

Nonetheless, Arvold's white ethnic participants were not denied their past, their own history, nor an opportunity to perform rather than bury their heritage. Such permission did not extend to nonwhites in North Dakota, suggesting, again, the limits of racial inclusiveness in Little Theatre social reform. Arvold praised the 1920 Larimore, North Dakota, pageant, *The Story of Grand Forks,* in which a representation of the area's history featured the retreat of the Amerindians to make way for the "real Americans."[109] The latter were portrayed by the teacher who wrote the piece as those who "stand for order, law, and right, for all that's good and true." The Natives, meanwhile, realize "our hunting here is done, / The white man comes and we must go, / On towards the setting sun."[110] The "foreigners" of Arvold's earliest endeavors now meld into Americans, united in their whiteness and work ethic against the demoralized, failed, red-skinned Natives.

One way in which Arvold's project differed from settlement house work involving hands-on work with immigrants was that it set up a "package library system" to provide scripts and production materials to anyone in the state requesting help or advice in mounting a play. Arvold neither supervised nor needed to approve all the amateur theatre he encouraged. Examples of plays and pageants he cites now seem rife with teleology touting American life as the best history has ever known, doggerel, and sentimental storytelling. But Arvold's commitment to rural denizens' creating and attending their own theatre in the interest of working together for recreation and sociality extended to his visiting and training workers for rural theatre in other states. Moreover, because of his university affiliation, institutionalization and continuity could be identified outside of the founder's personality. In other words, regardless of his own views of ethnicity, his system was built to accommodate others' work as well as his own, and to allow individual audiences to formulate their productions to suit their own needs.

An exception to the myth of immigrant recuperability through good theatre as a route to Americanization was Germans. John Corbin briefly praised the Irving Place Theatre in his 1898 article. Corbin's contemporary Norman Hapgood went further in praising the Irving Place, calling it "our only high class theatre," and, like Corbin, chastising American audiences for their "impatience," while warning that "those who dine at eight or even seven have much artistic degeneration to answer for."[111] In 1915, Emanuel Reicher, a German director with experience in the Berlin Deutsches Theater and the Volkstheater, established the Modern Stage

Company in New York. Despite his knowledge of publicly supported theatre and experience in finding financial backing and the support earlier in his career of Henrik Ibsen, Reicher was chastised by Little Theatre founder Thomas Dickinson for offering "alien fare" and for "aliena[ting himself] from the American audience" by joining with the People's Theatre and The Wage Earners' Theatre.[112] Reicher's nationality and class sympathies were grounds for severe criticism in 1917, despite his repertoire of Hauptmann and Ibsen, among other European playwrights. "The" American audience was construed by Dickinson as uninterested in, or perhaps unaware of, class struggle, preferring myths of classlessness.

Other Little Theatres that worked with immigrants in both cities and rural areas accepted working-class participants, but these participants were seen either as a source of exoticism or as a cohort in need of help—especially help with the personal and language skills that would enable them to work to become (or to behave like the) middle class. An immigrant intellectual in a leadership position was a different matter, especially given the particular fear of Germanness at the height of American awareness of World War I. Cheney's fledgling *Theatre Arts,* for example, moved from Detroit to New York, following an August 1917 article praising German theatre architecture that caused the parent Detroit Arts and Crafts Society to withdraw support for the journal. Cheney's December editorial stated that "an art magazine was not the place for discussion of war or peace questions except as they affect art . . . ."[113] Here, the politics of Little Theatre activism were reactive rather than proactive and appear nationalistic and perhaps even jingoistic. Yet such politics can also be read as survival tactics for a marginal but determined community of arts innovators struggling for credibility.

Part of achieving credibility in light of the precedents and prejudices addressed in this chapter was for Little Theatre to gain recognition as simply being valuable to the populace at large, whether or not great numbers attended or participated. In other words, a shared goal was for theatre to have status as cultural capital. Paul DiMaggio differentiates between cultural capital and what he calls cultural resources—a distinction that is clear in the Lewisohns' dilemma. Cultural capital is proficiency in discourse about nationally validated cultural goods, while cultural resources "refer to any form of symbolic mastery that is useful in a specific relational context."[114] As enterprising Little Theatre reformers succeeded in circulating their values, which were often local values, these became national standards for theatre cultural capital, although, as we have seen, cultural resources that failed "uptown" (such as those of the Henry Street locals, Emanuel Reicher, or even Arvold) were left to wither or go their own way. Value accrued to the products easiest to circulate in print, including certain kinds of scripts, designs, and aesthetic theories. These trumped other, less quantifiable manifestations of self-expression or teamwork, such as staging, choreography, parody, or casting. The combination of mercantilism, careerism, and an increasing interest in professional standards meant New York City quickly came to be the community that ambitious Little Theatre artists wanted to impress or emulate, even when their work was generated far away from Manhattan. Moves to Broadway, to professional theatre careers, or even Cheney's concern about the importance of being in the right neighborhood, quickly colored earlier idealism and also came, for many, to be understood as part of it.

The Neighborhood Playhouse was not the only experimental theatre project that moved away from a local, white ethnic focus. As immigrants assimilated and as quotas reduced the number of new arrivals, urban work with foreign-born "play-mates" lessened.[115] Also, arts training per se in settlement houses became contested by the National Federation of Settlements in the 1920s as an instance of "overspecialization."[116] Ann Larrabee's view of settlement theatre is that it was most powerful in "instructing and positioning its subjects in the dominant culture's symbolic exchange, the hegemonic interests of the powerful."[117] Whether this interpretation suggests silencing the individual voices of immigrants in the interest of creating high art legible to the influential, or whether it is read as offering Americanization via theatre or reformance activities affecting everyday behavior, the analysis focuses on homogenization.

Artists and audiences who accepted Little Theatre ideals did not always acknowledge or recognize the precedents nor state outright the prejudices discussed in this chapter, nor did they consciously conflate self-expression and conformity in their writings.[118] They did not "trash" hereditary American audiences so much as try to inspire them with a more purposeful understanding of theatregoing through information and participation. They rarely demeaned immigrants intentionally, even though their orientalist fantasies or work to reconstruct speech and comportment look colonialist from a present-day perspective. Their work did rest on the assumptions outlined in this chapter. The largest task was to carve out a recognized place for theatre within a national landscape that embraced movies as a primary form of popular performed entertainment, consumerism as a means of self-actualization, and compulsory education as the currency of both accommodation and advancement. The succeeding chapters chart some of the ways that Little Theatre workers fought for a place at the cultural table for their own views by constructing theatre audiences through available channels and in terms of other national discourses.

3

Producing the Audience

The time in which the theatre throve in the ignorance of its patrons was followed by the time when its only hope lay in the knowledge of its patrons.
—Thomas H. Dickinson, *The Insurgent Theatre*

It is only when the audience has demanded the artistic commodity, when it is pledged to pay the bills, when it feels itself on trial for the success or failure of its work, that it begins that responsible participation which makes art live.
—Hiram Kelly Moderwell, *The Theatre of To-Day*

Little Theatre theorists believed that the "whens" shared by the two quotes above had arrived. This chapter investigates influential innovators' projections for the knowledgeable audience and two undertakings that were powerful means of audience construction. *Theatre Arts Monthly,* the foremost and longest-lived publication of the Little Theatre movement, built via national circulation a point of view about what to look for and value in theatre through its articles, illustrations, reviews, scripts, and invitation to use its material in local productions. George Pierce Baker's 47 Workshop at Harvard handpicked a local audience and insisted, as a condition of membership, on active critical participation in developing new plays via detailed written responses to performances. The R_x these undertakings were trying to fill was sometimes vague, shortsightedly specific, or wont to stint on detailed procedures. Two strains, however, recur in the recommendations: the audience must function as an informed participant in the creation of serious theatre, and the audience must be organized so as to guarantee payment for that theatre.

Prescriptions

"Movements," if they amount to anything, have their roots in the audience as much as in the artists and producers.

—Kenneth Macgowan, *The Theatre of Tomorrow*

The myriad magazine articles discussed in the previous chapter were specifically aimed at general readers ("general" as understood by the mostly upper-middle-class publications) who were among the educated and theatregoing class, whether as individuals they were theatregoers or not. Longer texts about theatre reform invited special interest readers. Such books are valuable sources of ideas about audiences because these ideas are embedded in treatises that also address what the theatre as a whole should be. In other words, these books offered broad-spectrum prescriptions for righting drama, design, and audience as an interrelated project. Many theatre reform books included recommended reading lists as appendices.[1] A glance at even a few of these lists makes it possible for the present-day reader to appreciate how many and how quickly books about theatre and dramatic theory appeared, many of them how-to manuals or play anthologies, and how quickly many of them disappeared.[2]

A handful of theatre reform books, however, appeared regularly as recommended reading not only through the 1920s but into the 1990s; this ensemble provides a useful map of the evolution of audience theory during the Little Theatre movement. While the key tropes—intelligent participation and banding together to guarantee funding—occurred in some form in all of these texts, the books can be read as a continuum, suggesting the subtle adjustments that practitioners and leaders made to maintain currency with potential and actual audiences. The earliest book, written by Hiram Kelly Moderwell, a young enthusiast who later integrated art criticism into his theatre journalism, focuses on the superiority of innovative European scenic artists and the need for audiences to make the spiritual grade. The middle three, written by theatre workers Sheldon Cheney, Thomas H. Dickinson, and Kenneth Macgowan, who either taught theatre in universities or wrote several theatre books or both, balance aesthetic and social ideals with organizational responsibility in a specifically American context. The last one, written by a director who began his career in Little Theatre and went on to Hollywood to coach actors for Paramount Studios, foregrounds business sense as the primary problem to overcome in delivering meaningful theatre to a presumably already-willing segment of a community. Not only did these writers know each others' work, but in various groupings they knew each other personally and well. They did not so much refute as refine each others' beliefs in an ongoing effort to construct American audiences. As they adjusted their language, focus, and recommendations, they recognized the changing social climate in which Little Theatre and its audiences were developing.

Hiram Kelly Moderwell's (1888–1945) 1914 *The Theatre of To-Day* begins with a lofty ideal, extolling theatre as the only art that "can concentrate all the arts in the service of all men." It is clear throughout the book that Moderwell's referent for humankind encompasses Europe and the United States only, but his ability to champion both abstract design and socialist audience organization bespeaks willingness to foreground cross-class inclusion in his portrait of iconoclastic artistic modernity. Moderwell concluded his career during World War II working to promote an understanding of the United States' role in world peace. He attended Harvard, where he roomed with Kenneth Macgowan and where he also knew Robert Edmond Jones. His book was written just a few years after he graduated, and it radiates the fervor of a new convert recently returned from a research year abroad. Moderwell's later interest in writing about other arts as well as theatre (under the name Motherwell) is foreshadowed in *The Theatre of To-Day*'s extended and articulate examination of dramatic meaning not just in scripts, but in the innovative scenic and lighting design work of Gordon Craig, Adolphe Appia, and Max Reinhardt. Moderwell's theatre design credo, arguably recognizable as the most salient legacy of the Little Theatre movement, was "selection instead of imitation, and suggestion instead of representation."[3] How was the audience to support this new ideal?

Moderwell's answer was both simple and complicated. The audience must make its demands known, and the theatre must respond. Theatre is only theatre if it exists in "organic relation" to its audience. The audience, however, must also pay in full for what it wants and "owns the institution which serves it." The model institution was Berlin's Neue Freie Volksbühne (New Free Folk Stage), founded in 1892, which, by 1912, served a membership of fifty thousand. This audience, for Moderwell's proselytizing purposes, was defined as displaying the admirable pursuit of "exalted artistic enjoyment, . . . moral improvement, and . . . powerful intellectual stimulus in the dominant questions of the day" in the form of thirteen visits a year to the theatre, and of being from "the laboring classes."[4] If mere laborers—albeit Germans, and therefore, in 1914, still acceptable as exemplary European art lovers—could support purposeful theatre, what excuse did educated Americans have for not doing so?

Moderwell outlined in detail the financial workings of the member-owned folk theatre, with an almost obsessive concern for the bottom line in phrases such as "not a charity," "interest is paid," and "desired commodity . . . reducible to cold cash." American readers were thereby assured that idealism and socialism didn't obviate the need for double entry bookkeeping; but they were simultaneously to realize that audience ownership was for audiences who understood and cared about such things as plays with a "revolutionary spirit," "autocratic" artistic administration, and a willingness to let minorities have influence. Moderwell ignored the fact that the sort of drama he advocated was simply more familiar to large numbers of Europeans than to Americans because it was native theatrical fare already available in some local theatres. For German workers, the key issues were price and access; Americans needed much more inculcation. Moderwell's touchstones were local organization and anticommercialism; his desire was for an audience who, as participants in a grand artistic scheme, would recognize and pay for "one of the greatest influences in the new international culture."[5] As he wrote, exposure to the truth (as he saw it) and an exhortation to do better were the blunt-edged carrot and stick. If Moderwell himself was not concerned with the hands-on procedures for familiarizing American audiences with the sort of theatre he wanted them to demand, other projects would address that aspect of the problem.

Three years later, in 1917, Thomas H. Dickinson's (1877–1961) *The Insurgent Theatre* tempered youthful idealism with pragmatic examples and generally chattier writing. *The Insurgent Theatre* is one of the few Little Theatre books to be reissued more than fifty years after its first appearance. It specifically focuses on organization and management, in contrast to the literary and production concerns of Dickinson's earlier book, *The Case of American Drama.* Dickinson was older than the other theorists in this group. A native Virginian who earned an undergraduate degree at Columbia University, he served on the home front as a chaplain in the Spanish-American War, worked as a newspaper reporter in Columbus, Ohio, and had a play, *The Unbroken Road,* presented in 1909 by commercial producer/actor Harrison Grey Fiske. Dickinson earned a PhD at the University of Wisconsin, where he joined the Madison faculty and, in 1911, started the extracurricular Wisconsin Dramatic Society.

Dickinson's overriding theme was the "federated" audience, by which he basically meant a subscription audience, and which he offered as the only reliable way to serve a community continuously with regard to providing an ongoing theatre presence. His definitions and prescriptions shuttled between the earlier elitism of Moderwell and the sort of "pep" that would characterize much social prescription in the 1920s. Dickinson clucks fondly over the "faith in the absolute art principle" that had guided the many young producers who had simply acted out of ignorance and inexperience and that would no longer do. But he also carps about the ordinary Joe, warning that "[i]f there is anything in the world [theatre] needs[,] it is to be freed from the control of the man of the street." The dialectic between elitism and popular taste would plague and color virtually all attempts to build theatre audiences. Dickinson balanced the extremes by staking out a specific segment of the public who should offer the mental and financial support that define an audience's role. He criticizes the "Puritan" who influences the theatre by virtue of being part of a large cohort but who basically disapproves even while attending. The "theatre-goer" is dismissed for failing to discriminate between vaudeville, movies, and legit. "Connoisseurs"—also known as highbrows—are equally problematic because they offer more overrefined criticism than they do actual support. Dickinson's target group are "theatre-lovers," because they have "taste" but favor enjoying the theatre over judging it. His Little Theatre is "a place of entertainment for intelligent people,"[6] a package offering, in an ego-flattering come-on, the reassurance of fun without drudgery.

"Intelligence" is a word that appeared often in descriptions of desirable audiences, but in an era that preceded IQ tests, SATs, and the concept of multiple intelligences, it meant something social as well as mental. In her autobiography, playwright Alice Gerstenberg (1885–1972) locates in "intelligent" activity the basis of a fulfilling life, one free of stress and replete with purposefulness.[7] Such activity includes sports, time spent outdoors, conversation, intergenerational outings, reading, and doing things for and with members of one's community. While music, art, and theatre figured routinely in Gerstenberg's privileged world and would have been part of conversation and intergenerational outings, these are not particular or favored touchstones for deploying intelligence. Rather, for her, the word denotes something more holistic and in this sense is useful in understanding what some Little Theatre theorists seem to have intended in their own usage of the word.

Dickinson's pragmatism may have evolved in part as a result of his working at a land grant university in a city that did not have a major commercial theatre district that might tempt amateurs to move a show in the hope of a potentially money-making run. He allows that insurgent theatres may aspire to professionalism if this means "order and crafts-manship," but not if it means the "false order and artifice" of the past. Audiences deserve dependability, and he calls on theatre organizers to earn their subscribers by building this reliability into their business and scheduling practices. He respectfully discusses Maurice Browne's concep-tual scenographic work but confesses that he neither understands Browne's "rhythmic" project nor fully knows whether to call the visual work properly dramatic or not.[8] Dickinson's "intelligent" audience need not embrace "universal" principals on the (European) New Stagecraft models of Craig, Appia, or Reinhardt—models privileging simplicity, suggestion, and unification over pictorialism or simulation—because this audience is understood to be a local federation entitled to some local principles. Even Dickinson's understanding of theatre in higher educa-tion took into account differing ways of creating artists and understand-ing.[9] He offers a generic recipe that local leaders could adjust to their own tastes: intelligent theatre-lovers are good; too much Europeanism and abstraction is understandably off-putting although worthy of respect; subscription guarantees a sense of ownership.

Sheldon Cheney (1886–1980) took his passion for purposeful theatre well beyond his 1917 *The Art Theater,* which was revised and reissued in 1925. He had already published *The New Movement in the Theater,* a survey of mostly European tendencies, in 1914 and was founding the journal *Theatre Arts* as he completed *The Art Theater.*[10] Cheney's strat-egy throughout *The Art Theater* is to alternate between European and American examples as he urges greater American participation, organi-zation, support, and understanding. Berlin appears again as a site of good audience organization (with the Neue Freie Volksbühne audience so admired by Moderwell now at one hundred thousand), but so do Ypsilanti and Santa Barbara. Cheney had worked for five years as a drama critic after graduating from the University of California at Berkeley and before becoming part of the Theatre Committee of the Society of Arts and Crafts in Detroit, where *Theatre Arts* started. He would go on to write a total of thirteen books, among them the 1929 *The Theatre: Three Thousand Years of Drama, Acting, and Stagecraft,* which was reputed to be the first comprehensive English language history of the theatre.[11]

Cheney did not shy away from idealism as topic and desideratum, but his experience with American productions and audiences resulted in a book that continually tempers ideals with practicality. Cheney's biggest ideal—one he wanted all audiences to appreciate and demand—was unification in production. In the balancing act that typifies *The Art Theater*'s outreach, he discourses on synthesis, inner rhythm, harmony, and individual genius but also points out that his "synthetic ideal . . . has room not only for the imaginative, the symbolic, and the expressionistic, but for the realistic and the romantic."[12] Cheney reassures readers of his awareness that audiences resist the self-proclaimedly "difficult," and that most are not interested in experiments on the workshop models of either Harvard (described by Dickinson as hewing to a "German standard of research") or Carnegie (with it focus on "technology of the arts").[13] Rather, Cheney recommends a "workshop annex" to art theatres—something like the second stage or blackbox or reading series that regional theatres would adopt much later in the century—to perpetuate experimentation, while also promising presumably down-to-earth audiences something more established in the main theatre. His prescription is a generalized but useful mean: "keep ahead of business standards, but never go so far into untried fields or toward the art of particularized appeal, that the audiences of the moment will be antagonized."[14] "Of the moment" suggests that with audiences as with art, attention must be paid to process as well as product, allowing for growth. Presumably, if readers-as-leaders built it (on Cheney's model), audiences would come, pay, and stay.

Cheney's language throughout the book as well as his chapter on audiences and his epilogue reveal an emerging challenge for art, experimental, Little, community, and regional theatres for decades to come, namely how to offset an urban sensibility, shared by many theatre innovators, with the gestalt of the smaller town, and how to resist the idea that New York offered the surest examples of "the best." Indeed, references to the "best," the "finest," and "high standards" pepper the entire text, sometimes with a frustrating lack of referent and sometimes with clear reference to European abstractionists (Dunsany or Maeterlinck) or authors of serious problem plays (Shaw, Ibsen, John Howard Lawson). In the chapter on audiences, Cheney eschews a discussion of New York in favor of small or "average" town audiences, although his concluding praise for communities that strive for "the best in drama" delights in the belief that audiences from these places will gravitate to high art productions when they visit New York, which he seems to assume they will.[15] He deals firmly with national goals and with examples from many cities. His model audience—unquestionably part of an imagined community that would recognize its members even on a first visit to a new city—admires unified productions, federates to buy subscriptions, stays out of the way of artistic directors (all holdovers from Moderwell and Dickinson), and does all of these in the interest of building a national consciousness. "Each progressive center," he wrote, "no matter how small or how amateurish, reflects its good work on the activities of all the others." Cheney's "new dramatic map of America" is predicated on an informed theatrical sensibility, one that can be achieved through trained appreciation and educational work, two ideas that were to move to the forefront of audience construction for the rest of the century. "National Endowment," now a familiar if contested concept, was a pipe dream ghosting Cheney's ideal scheme.[16]

Kenneth Macgowan's (1888–1963) *The Theatre of Tomorrow* (1921) looks, at first glance, very much like a rerun of *The Theatre of To-Day*, to which it acknowledges its titular debt. Macgowan wrote his book at the height of what Thomas Bloom calls Macgowan's romance with "the aesthetic paradigm," and the text continues the familiar admiration for the work of Craig, Appia, Reinhardt, and Meyerhold. Macgowan, who supported and wrote extensively about his Harvard friend Robert Edmond Jones's design work, would, less than two years later, team up with Jones and Eugene O'Neill to run the Provincetown Players' spinoff, the Experimental Theatre.[17] Despite its name, the Experimental Theatre emerged because of O'Neill's interest in commercial possibilities and in working with professionals. Macgowan's book, its idealistic tone notwithstanding, sits on the cusp of esoteric experimentation off the beaten track and revitalization of a larger commercial theatre world through Little Theatre practices. In this position, Macgowan recognizes that the audience of tomorrow—surely an idea the book summons although not a term he literally uses—is supposed to disdain the commercial "same old" but is also expected to assess serious theatre in light of an awareness and appreciation of movies and other popular entertainments.

Macgowan expected readers to recognize the expressionism of both the playwright Georg Kaiser and of the film *The Cabinet of Dr. Caligari.*

More importantly, he acknowledged that neither theatre nor cinema held a purchase on pictorialism or on "imagination"—each could deploy either. The screen, however, pointed the way to the dramaturgy of the future, with its multiple, rapidly changing scenes; condensed dialogue; periods of silence; and refusal to be held hostage to the particular artifice of the three- or four-act form. In fact, movies demonstrated how right Shakespeare had been and how wrong his logic-driven Victorian restructurers had been. The value of cinematic dramaturgy for Macgowan was its ability to "come closer than the stage to our unconscious mind, because it has operated through sight . . . and . . . has, therefore, often avoided a great deal of the false rationalizing of the conscious mind."[18] Macgowan invoked Freud and Jung just as his potential audience might have: casually and in the terms of the ambient culture rather than the specialist. His interest in rapid cuts, visual coding, and flashbacks had to do with his understanding of how the mind works. He attributed to all potential audiences the inherent ability to grasp the difference between realism and Realism, casting his vote for theatre audiences who would prefer the former in its multiple possible manifestations.[19]

In this vein, Macgowan went farther than any other major Little Theatre worker or theorist to incorporate some of the spatial and performance practices of vaudeville and Broadway as being of value for theatre reform. He discussed Al Jolson and Fanny Brice and how their playing styles provoked audiences to think outside the dictates of photorealism or the box set. In Brice's interpretation of "Second Hand Rose," for example, "all the time there is the most curious and fascinating undercurrent of intimacy between the actress as actress and the audience as audience. We see both the player and the played. The player introduces her own work to us, she almost criticises [sic] it, she certainly criticises Rose. In the slang of Broadway, she 'wises up' her audience to this odd little Jewish girl." The passage now seems almost proto-Brechtian in its invocation of awareness, commentary, instruction, and direct audience address as useful components of performance. In eschewing "peep-show realism," Macgowan invoked Jolson's "demoniac" energy on the runway of the Winter Garden theatre, a kind of vaudevillian *hanamichi* that forges intimacy through a spatial rather than a textual close-up. Following up on this in a chapter on architectural figurations, Macgowan urged lessons from the circus with regard to actor-audience and intra-audience intimacy. A thrust or arena configuration allows a player to be closer to a greater number of spectators than does a proscenium house, unless the latter is quite small. Moreover, the performer who can galvanize the larger crowd in the arena setup creates both intimacy with individual audience members and a shared intensity within the house—exactly the things Little Theatre originally wanted in its small venues. Readers who were practitioners were prodded to think about drawing on challenging performer-audience relationships poachable from popular entertainments. Readers as audience members got the message to keep their critical antennae up in all performance contexts and not to fall prey to mistaking genre alone for substance. Such audiences would fulfill Macgowan's prescription for a tonic no practitioner— or spectator, for that matter—could resist: audiences of "life-giving vigor."[20]

Oliver Hinsdell's (1889–1967) 1925 *Making the Little Theater Pay* differs from the books above almost to the point of seeming like another species. Subtitled *A Practical Handbook,* it favors charts, budgets, tips on purchasing materials and selling tickets, rehearsal schedules, recruiting events, and lessons in how to departmentalize and delegate. What gave the book credibility in its time was the status of the Dallas Little Theatre, of which Hinsdell was artistic director during its period of greatest growth and prestige. In 1925, three years into his eight-year tenure, the DLT was building its second theatre, had just won the New York–based, David Belasco–sponsored Little Theatre Tournament, and was organizing regional Little Theatre events for participants drawn from several states in the south and southwest. Hinsdell's focus in the book was not the ideology of aesthetics, although he was perfectly well aware of the favored plays and design trends of the previous dozen years. A graduate of Northwestern University, where he was invited back after his 1918 graduation to found what was then called the Department of Play Production within the School of Speech, Hinsdell had worked as an actor in stock for seven years (briefly with Philip Ben Greet) and had spent two years as director of Le Petit Théâtre du Vieux Carré in New Orleans before going to Dallas. He left Dallas in 1931 to work for MGM as an acting coach, switching to Paramount in 1936, and visiting Dallas to recruit talent in 1937.

Hinsdell's understanding of audience construction began with assuming Cheney's "keeping ahead of business standards without antagonizing" the target segment of the community. Unlike Dickinson, though, whose theatre-lover (the ideal audience member) was distinct from the theatre-goer (who was not discriminating enough because the latter also enjoyed movies and vaudeville), Hinsdell seemed to understand that he was competing for recreational time that potential audiences might choose to spend elsewhere. While he never mentions movies (nor sports, social dancing, or restaurants, for that matter), he everywhere recognizes that potential audiences cannot be expected to materialize simply because theatre is worthwhile; rather they must be wooed, attended to, and reminded of all the ways in which Little Theatre supports and extends their other values and tastes. Hinsdell's model Little Theatre gets obligatory lip service as the locus of "spiritual freedom and a better understanding of the things that govern our universe," a source of "self-expression," and a "clearing house for ideas." The audience he pursues, though, is clearly one seeking distinction through its choices about consumerism, including the consumption of ideas. Hinsdell understands that serious theatre-going fits into the lifestyle of those who are homeowners, department store shoppers, Kiwanis members, women's club members, bank customers, habitués of Dallas's downtown business district, and frequenters of book shops. Accordingly, he outlines publicity campaigns in places already serving these constituencies. Hinsdell even tackles Dickinson's "Puritan," by urging Little Theatre workers to show those who see theatre as objectionable on religious or ethical grounds that "Little Theater stands for the highest ethics of the drama" and is "constructive, educational, civic."[21] He goes so far as to warn against scheduling rehearsals on Sundays. He posits, in other words, that Little Theatre must fit within rather than refuse bourgeois society. Earlier theorists, of course, were always targeting a bourgeoisie, but the positioning of the activity was often oppositional and the acknowledgement of the symbiosis generally covert.

Unlike his predecessors, Hinsdell offered concrete suggestions for staging audience encounters outside the performance of plays and beyond public relations events at stores and luncheons. His book urges free readings of new plays, at which attending to audience response can be useful to reader and director alike. He also urges Little Theatre practitioners to listen to the audience as they leave the theatre. Hinsdell's recommendations in the "campaign for new members" overlap with his audience recruitment recommendations, acknowledging that Little Theatre audiences and participants are drawn from the same pool. So sure is he of the general social and aesthetic predisposition of this pool that he relegates his discussion of scenography to the end of his book, a reversal of all the other texts discussed above. Unification, simplicity, and alternatives to pictorialism are now a given. Hinsdell's focus, when he latterly gets around to discussing design, is not on how to get the audience to recognize and accept these; it is on how to achieve them on a limited budget.

Hinsdell, like other Little Theatre theorists, prescribed a democratic audience policy. His well-chosen season "makes a point of offering something . . . that will appeal to every element in the community—from 'tired business man' to intellectual—without compromising or lowering the dramatic standard of the theater."[22] Little Theatre is educational and should attract and cooperate with schools and colleges. Plays should appeal through their "human qualities," thereby resonating for all members of the group and with potential recruits for both sides of the footlights. Hinsdell's book lays out the rhetoric that would serve various regional theatres—including Little, community, and LORT (League of Resident Theatres)—in the United States for the rest of the century. The book also perpetuates the gaps and blind spots in Little Theatre ideas of inclusion and democracy. The exhortation to erect a building downtown and to provide parking, as well as the suggestion of luncheons and teas for members, indicate that African Americans, working-class people, and people outside the business loop were still de facto, if not de jure, irrelevants.

Resistance from minorities or the working class was not perceived by middle- and upper-middle-class white theatre promoters as a problem in 1925; the enemy was indifference of the privileged. For most Americans, theatre was of less interest and had less immediate appeal as "intelligent" diversion than movies, books, or even other forms of popular entertainment. Gilbert Seldes called the high arts of the 1920s the "bogus arts," accusing their promoters of appealing to people's snobbery.[23] Perhaps. But Little Theatre appeals involved gratification through participation and through self-actualization—hallmarks of 1920s educational theory, advertising practice, and both popular and professional psychology—even if this was the self-actualization achieved through becoming in-the-know as an audience member. Like most social change, Little Theatre audience construction took time; it worked when it was able to alter thinking through repeated exposure to new ideas in inviting forms and, as with any piece of theatre, when its participants had ample time to study their scripts and rehearse. Two venues for audience construction allowed for exactly such repeated exposure; they achieved and maintained national significance over a period of many years. The first, a publication, served as a kind of script or reference manual; the second was an actual audience construction laboratory with a version of auditions and performances required of spectators.

Theatre Arts and the Evolving Audience

Few dramas are as interesting as the attitude of the audience toward them.
—Walter Prichard Eaton, "Audiences—A Spring Grouch"

[O]ne more step is taken toward creating a nation-wide audience for the developing art theater.
—Sheldon Cheney, *The Art Theater*

"A Record and a Prophecy" was the slogan by which editors of *Theatre Arts* wanted the publication to be remembered after it passed into the hands of new owners in 1948.[24] "Part and parcel of the growing up of the modern American theatre" was critic and author Barrett Clark's description of this pioneer publication.[25] The magazine was founded in 1916 at the Detroit Arts and Crafts Society by Sheldon Cheney, who was its first editor, publisher, and owner. Cheney was joined by coeditors Kenneth Macgowan, S. Marion Tucker, and Edith J. R. Isaacs in 1919 after moving *Theatre Arts* to New York in 1917. Isaacs (1878–1956) became editor in 1924, with Ashley Dukes as English editor and Stark Young—simultaneously serving as drama critic for *The New Republic*—as associate editor; Isaacs, who also became one of the magazine's financial mainstays and who worked without a salary, made the publication a monthly and remained at the helm until the 1948 transfer.[26] She championed what she and the magazine called "the tributary theatre," which might now be called regional and educational theatre. New York was the center of American theatre production, but *Theatre Arts* was not going to conflate the city and the nation. The magazine, called by one modern critic "the principal organ" of the Little Theatre movement, continued in a revised form until 1964 and remains one of the most widely available contemporary sources on Little Theatre.[27]

Theatre Arts aimed from the outset to establish a national audience for serious theatre. It addressed and constructed its readers as a wholly new kind of theatre audience, assuming they were educated but never allowing them to treat their social positions or university credentials alone as adequate grounds for coming to terms with innovative theatre. The magazine's stance was that important theatre was not merely stylish or topical, but ideally groundbreaking, and at the very least aesthetically purposeful and socially valuable. To consume *Theatre Arts* was to map the new into one's thinking about theatre, which, for the magazine, also embraced a tentative version of what was much later to be called performance studies. From the beginning, *Theatre Arts* included articles on American Indian performance traditions, modern dance, African American culture, nonlinear texts, and outdoor venues, as well as the more predictable concerns with actor training, the New Stagecraft, and later, scripts of new plays.[28] *Theatre Arts* was, in short, "concerned ... with the American theatre as a whole."[29]

Theatre-dedicated magazines were not a new phenomenon in the United States. By one count, close to seven hundred theatre-focused publications came and mostly went between 1798 and 1967.[30] Some of the better-known and long-lived emerging in the decades preceding *Theatre Arts* included *New York Dramatic Mirror* (1879–1920) and *New York Clipper* (1853–1924). Their names suggest their primary concern: Gotham's commercial stage. Both were founded well before the turn-of-the-century shift in style and advertising that facilitated magazines' special role in helping Americans understand and construct themselves as citizens and consumers. A "magazine revolution" occurred around 1900, getting started about ten years earlier and reaching its apogee in the 1920s.[31] Topical magazines offering "inside dope" on any subject achieved a centrality in American life during the Progressive Era that was never duplicated before or since.[32] *Theatre Arts*'s most high-profile compatriot in helping an upper bourgeoisie negotiate the world of theatre was *Theatre* (1901–1931), a glossy monthly founded with what Susan Harris Smith calls a "distinctly popularizing mission" and the central concern of which was Broadway and stars.[33] Nor were these two the only niche publications to stake a theatre claim within the magazine heyday; shorter-lived magazines than *Theatre Arts* included the *Play* (1905–6), the *Dramatist* (1909–1923), the *Drama* (1911–1931), the *American Playwright* (1912), *Critic* (1919–1920), *American Theatre* (1920–21), and the *Drama Yearbook* (1924). On the latter list, only the *Drama* was much like *Theatre Arts*. *Drama* ceased publication in 1931, a victim of complicated social and financial circumstances. As the house organ of the Drama League of America, it was associated in fact and in the public mind with women's clubs and their theatre activities with churches, schools, civic groups, and children.[34] Both magazines appealed to amateur practitioners, but the *Theatre Arts* editors operated with a clear awareness that readers included other New York critics and theatre artists as well.

Like all magazines, *Theatre Arts* addressed and constructed its audience at a material level as well as through editorial content. A consumer encountering the magazine would know, even without much reading, certain things about what it was and was not. The magazine was small (6 ¼ x 9 ¼" at the outset, then 7 ¾ x 9 ¾" by 1924; it did not go to an 8 ½ x 11" format until 1930) and had, initially, a plain brown cover of noncoated heavy paper bearing a simple line sketch of a solo performer. It aimed, from the start, at a "tradition of elegance . . . [and] book-like permanence."[35] The first issue's cover had a female dancer in a long, flowing, Greek tunic; for the remainder of its first year, *Theatre Arts* settled on a line rendering of an ivory statuette from the second century AD representing a masked performer in high headdress, draped robe, and thick-soled boots. Volumes 2 and 3 featured on the cover an image of Razullo, one of the commedia dell'arte characters, as depicted in a 1621 engraving by Callot, although the figure, depicted jauntily playing his long-necked lute, was not identified anywhere in the magazine. These images were about two inches tall and anchored but did not dominate the cover. From 1920 to 1923, there was a different woodcut or line drawing on each cover, depicting such things as a shadow puppet, the facade of the Deutsches Theater, or the seagull logo of the Moscow Art Theatre. In 1924, what became the signature cover appeared. It featured a frame suggesting a completely rectilinear modernist proscenium with steps, surrounding the magazine's title and highlights of the contents of each issue, on a background of green and then, for ten years, bright yellow. This would remain the standard cover (except for a reversion to varying background colors) through the 1930s. The cover could not have been more different from the much flashier *Theatre*'s, the latter in full-color on much thinner, coated stock, always depicting either a glamorous performer— usually a woman—or a moment from a current Broadway production.

Theatre Arts ran very few advertisements.[36] In this way again, it was wholly unlike *Theatre,* which served as a primer on fashionable life via its many pages of advertisements for expensive stockings, cruise ships, luxury resorts, automobiles, personal hygiene goods, liquor, phonographs, and cigarettes, thereby situating its readers as lovers of the high life—whether they experienced it in actuality or vicariously—and consumers for whom theatre was one among several sources of entertainment. The few ads *Theatre Arts* did run at first were for books about the theatre and for the literary magazines *Poetry,* the *Quarterly Notebook,* and the *Dial.* The connection was a means of creating what Charles U. Larson calls "nuances of meaning" by "the brushing of information against other information."[37] *Theatre Arts* added a directory advertising theatrical goods and services such as schools, manuscript typists, costume rentals, and vocal coaches. Except for pianos, one interior decorator, and a small number of jewelers whose ads were always understated and restricted to the inside front and back covers plus one succeeding side of one page of the magazine, *Theatre Arts* did not advertise consumer goods or non-theatre-related services. The editors spelled out this policy of selectivity in a 1925 editorial that affirmed a commitment "to limit our advertising to the arts and the industries allied to the arts," with a 1926 issue going further and calling the advertising "an editorial expression."[38]

Yet it would be a mistake to stereotype *Theatre Arts* as an esoteric, cult "little magazine." As Mark S. Morrisson argues, many modernist little magazines, despite their adversarial stances towards Babbitry, did not represent a retreat from mass culture. Rather, their editors believed passionately that art had a public function and, in opposing commercialism, they devised a canny way to fight their rhetorical enemy with its own means. That is, magazines like *Theatre Arts* were created by modernists "to *promote,* to *market* their own efforts to ... shape public culture" (emphasis in original).[39] They relied on and benefited from the relatively low cost of producing a magazine, which was possible because of technological advances and the market for paper and printing; such magazines adopted the unique position of eschewing mass appeal at the intellectual level while embracing some version of it rhetorically. *Theatre Arts*'s goal, in this schema, was to retool the thinking of its readers in the interest of improving all American theatre. Cheney stated plainly that "what we stand for" was "a new point of view," and a "clean cleavage between a purely commercial theatre ... and a new professional art theatre.... [W]e hope to see rise a chain of *local repertory art theatres,* serving every art-loving community from Maine to California" (emphasis in original).[40] The idea was that if enough people insisted on such things as unification in production, the value of interdisciplinarity and research, and the importance of experimentation, the reception waters would lift the boats of commercialism.[41] *Theatre Arts* was high-minded, but it was never stuffy, and it balanced an appeal to both youth and authority. The first issue dedicated the journal to "a new generation of artist-workers" and to "the theatregoer who is awake artistically and intellectually." Workers and audiences alike were to take up the "good fight to fight" and "to conserve and develop [the] creative impulse in the American theatre."[42] The audience, then, as well as the artist, had an active and creative role to play.

Theatre Arts instructed its readers to refuse provincialism of three sorts: geographic, aesthetic, and cultural. The very first issue contained short news blurbs as well as articles about Little Theatre activities in Cincinnati, Boston, Los Angeles, Chicago, and Detroit. From the beginning, too, there was a section of small-print news from Little (later "Little and Experimental") Theatres, which carried brief announcements—possibly sent in by subscribers—about the activities and productions of companies from San Francisco to Indianapolis to St. Louis to Montclair, New Jersey.[43] No one region owned either excellence or experimentalism. The idea was to help readers recognize that both were possible nationally. Broadway was never ignored. Cheney did a roundup of "New York's Best Season," in the first year, praising not only the experimental companies whose work he saw, but admiring commercial productions of *The Yellow Jacket*, a long, episodic fable tricked out in oriental trappings that he called "a delight to the eye and a spiritual experience"; *Good Gracious Annabelle*, a tame comedy he admired for its directing; and Shaw's *Getting Married*.[44] Meanwhile, Zona Gale assured readers that "the new drama" of the Wisconsin Players, "far from being 'high-brow,' . . . is inherently democratic."[45] Real theatre-lovers needed to look beyond locale to content, something *Theatre Arts* would help them parse. The Great White Way could deliver worthwhile theatre; experimental groups were not inherently esoteric.

The magazine's ingredients never changed, although the way the categories were positioned did; in 1924, *Theatre Arts* used the subheadings "A Magazine of World Theatre" and "The International Magazine of the Theatre." These were later dropped, but news from other countries, especially England, became a staple, as did regular roundup style reviews of the Broadway season. Little Theatres per se got less space, but one issue a year until 1947 was devoted exclusively to the Tributary Theatre. While Little Theatres themselves were no longer the central focus, Little Theatre values remained definitive.

Cheney's own passion for the nontextual elements of theatre set a tone that remained in place even when the magazine began publishing plays in 1919. From the first volume, the "synthetic ideal" was presented as "the most important thing in the theatre."[46] A 1921 article spelled out that "unity of production" meant "an organic fusion of movement, light, sound, and stage decoration. These four factors . . . together make up the theatre."[47] Sketches and photographs of the work of innovative designers appeared in every issue, as did pictures of the interiors of exemplary theatres. Articles about design and designers ran the gamut from the theoretical, to the reportorial, to the "how to." For example, designs by

Robert Edmond Jones, Raymond Jonson, Lee Simonson, and Norman-Bel Geddes appeared along with photographs of scenery from the Moscow Art Theatre and Max Reinhardt's New Theatre throughout the 1920 issues. The 1923 issues, expanded in length, included designs by Mordecai Gorelik; photographs of and articles about puppets in Slovakia, Italy, and the United States; drawings of Pueblo corn dances; photographs of "plastic make-up"; sketches of circus theatres; and Lee Simonson's design for *R.U.R.*, the play that put the word "robot" into the American lexicon and criticized totalitarianism as well as capitalism and their attendant dehumanization long before *1984* or *Brave New World*. Visual lessons from theatre history that year included two images of Italy's Teatro Olimpico, the first indoor theatre to adopt classical principles and perspective scenery in its stage design; a photograph of the Teatro Farnese, home of the earliest extant proscenium frame in Europe; and photographs of two Greek theatres. A number of the images accompanied articles, but many were also scattered through the magazine's pages, offering quick bursts of visual input minus any long, contextualizing argument. The magazine itself was the context, and those who even browsed through its pages could not help but absorb a visual world that was varied, that configured space for multiple kinds of audience-performer encounters, and that eschewed pictorialism. For instance, two costume sketches by designer Anna Wille for Richard Boleslavsky's *Twelfth Night* at the American Laboratory Theatre were captioned with the brief note that Wille "has been primarily interested in the recapture of . . . rollicking Elizabethan gusto and gaiety, and makes use of uncompromising contrasts in line and color. There is no attempt to reconstruct with photographic accuracy the actual costumes of Tudor England, but rather to translate its vitality into modern times."[48] Fabian's disguise costume is a full-length cape with bold, abstract designs calling to mind both orientalism and cubism. There was no accompanying article.

Who were the targeted readers for this synoptic, flexible package of theatre journalism? Nafe Edmund Katter's study of *Theatre Arts* defines the readership as "specialists"—theatre artists, teachers, and students.[49] Still, this cuts wide swaths regarding age, level of professionalism, and geography. At the end of the first year of publication, Cheney provided demographics about subscriptions, obviously hoping to get more, but also suggesting that progressive ideas about theatre could emerge anywhere where smart people cared. Philadelphia was lambasted for having only one subscriber. Detroit and New York had the most, but right behind them was Berkeley, with thirty.[50] Chicago, with just eight subscribers, was told that its lack of interest was "both disgraceful and intolerable."[51] Oregon had more subscribers than all the southern states combined; California outdid New England; "little places like Northampton and Montclair" put Indianapolis and Milwaukee to shame. Introducing *Theatre Arts* to someone interested in theatre was called a "distinct service"— something a committed audience member could do for the cause. Cheney was probably addressing fewer than two hundred subscribers and perhaps at most a few hundred more people who bought or perused the magazine at the bookstores that carried it in New York, Chicago, Boston, Los Angeles, San Francisco, Washington, D.C., and London (with the shops' addresses helpfully listed in early issues.) Circulation would peak in 1957 at seventy-seven thousand.[52]

What was supposed to happen to an American theatre audience member who read *Theatre Arts*? And what characterized this person? An audience talk-back article of 1918 announced that "any sort of person can have adventures at the theatre." The writer, Claire Dana Mumford, positioned herself squarely as a viewer, and not a practitioner, and announced that she was about to "drop a bomb from Philistia" declaring that the "new . . . Movement was moving in every direction at once—save towards us—the Audience—and towards the professional theatre." Professionalism, for her, was not about venue or budget but about "the quality of being a complete fit in a vocation," while the amateur was "second class in [an] avocation." So-called artists were blasted as ineffectual and self-serving if they failed in "unceasing reference to an audience." Mumford informed her fellow audience-member readers of the ecstasy they might expect to experience when being unceasingly referred to by an artist completely fit to his vocation. The essay turns into a paean to Rollo Peters's scenic artistry for an otherwise forgettable play called *Josephine,* spelling out the effect of such artistry on an audience. In his good New Stagecraft, Peters created a "sense of the whole," achieving "apposite beauty communicable to the audience by a creative faculty, owning nothing at all to reproduction." At *Josephine* (the eponymous character was Napoleon's empress), the attuned Mumford was "wrought upon by needles, when the triangular shaft of light cut the high Dark of Notre Dame."[53]

Mumford, of course, was not just "any sort of person" at the theatre, offended by esoteric ideals until a consummate artist's work elicited from her a spontaneous, positive response. She was a writer and painter who in 1907 had founded the all-female Query Club, a luncheon club whose members gathered to hear lectures on art or social and political issues and many of whose members were affiliated with the Greenwich Village–based, feminist Heterodoxy Club. The flattering notion posited in her article— that the willing self can be galvanized into recognition of the best all on her own if only the artist knows what he is doing—was not anything *Theatre Arts* was leaving to chance. Mumford would not have had the vocabulary with which to define the real thing without some prior knowledge of design, and her article mentions Gordon Craig, Joseph Urban, and Leon Bakst, as well as symbolist playwrights Dunsany and Maeterlinck. She never says where she acquired this prior knowledge. As a New Yorker, she herself had access to many productions, but what Mumford referred to in her essay was available to anyone who regularly read *Theatre Arts*. By planting information and experiences in editorial and pictorial form, the magazine assured that these could then be cued in future encounters.[54] An article by Rollo Peters himself tartly confirmed that reception could not be trusted to "the latencies of . . . an audience—intensely modern, inexperienced in picturesque imaging." Peters knew one could not instantaneously "divide the suburbanite from Suburbia."[55] Audiences would undergo conversion through exposure that could then be experienced as spontaneous recognition in the presence of genuine theatrical art. The individual reader joined the imagined community constructed among *Theatre Arts* readers, with implanted aesthetic sensibility that would flower at the right kind of prompting. Arguably the idea was precisely to divide the suburbanite from Suburbia in one of the more overt instances of wording that reveals audience construction goals along Manhattan or European lines.

Theatre Arts was an early proponent of what might now loosely be called multiculturalism and multidisciplinarity. There is no question that the target audience/readership for this version of inclusiveness was solidly WASP and urban or suburban, rhetorically if not always in fact. As Patrice Pavis would note decades after the Little Theatre movement, exotic materials are like "grains of sand in an intercultural hourglass: the mass of the source culture, metaphorically situated in the upper chamber, must pass through the narrow neck controlled by the target culture of the bottom chamber with, in this neck, a whole series of filters that keep only a few elements of the source culture selected according to very precise norms."[56] *Theatre Arts* was such a filter-laden neck, but it tried to be a capacious neck by including examples from and about disciplines and cultures then normally excluded from discussions of mainstream theatre. For instance, modern dance innovator Ruth St. Denis was a contributing editor for the two years the magazine had these. Her 1916 essay explained that dance required the integration of many arts to be more than "steps to music."[57] In 1917, Isadora Duncan argued that the "new school" of dance was nothing less than "a museum of the living beauty of the period," in contrast to ballet, which was "sterile" and "unnatural."[58] Both essays presented dance as a form of theatre in its own right, neither a handmaiden to musicals nor an alien species. Andre Levinson's 1925 essay praised ballet's flexibility as an evolving expressive code, but of more interest to the progressive performance historian is Levinson's critique of an inability to "consider . . . motion itself as such. We cling to things at rest as though they were landmarks in a turbulent chaos." The artilleryman was, for Levinson, better equipped to consider the principle of a dancer's leap as trajectory than "some loose-thinking poet, however magnificent his style." The dancer's vocabulary "is useful only to himself"; Levinson urged his audience to develop a critical vocabulary for movement, arguably one of the key challenges to performance analysis that would live up to a synthetic ideal embracing more than text and tableaus.[59] In 1925, D. H. Lawrence contributed two pieces describing southwestern American Indian dances in New Mexico and Arizona.[60] Again, dance was a full theatre form of its own; it also might emerge in an America not concerned exclusively with European or beaux-arts precedents.

Ethnic inclusiveness that tried to expose habits of insensitive othering had begun in *Theatre Arts*'s pages with Zona Gale's report on the 1917 *Three Plays for a Negro Theatre*, Broadway's first presentation of African American actors in serious, nonmusical roles.[61] The three plays were by poet/playwright Ridgely Torrence and dealt respectively with the American dream, miscegenation, and early Christianity, all with black protagonists. Gale offered the prescient observation that the integrity of the project confronted white Americans with representations that did not follow hereditary American models of stereotyping minorities, foreigners, or regionalists. "Here is a race, infinitely potential, moving before one in individuals highly differentiated, and as terribly intent . . . on their own living as any Anglo-Saxon is intent on his own. The Colored Players strike at a provincialism which has been in one's way, it appears, not only socially, but artistically."[62] The same year, a short excerpt from a book on Indian theatre and gesture appeared under the title "Oriental and Western Acting," positing that Indian acting was an interpretation of life, while modern European acting was an imitation.[63] Playwright Mary Austin wrote in 1917 about Amerind (her word) poetry and performance as something that required aural sophistication and that offered textual meaning without linearity or Aristotleanism. In 1920, there were articles about Jewish Art Theatre in New York and about contemporary Chinese theatre. Jewish art theatre was still the product of racial "others," but Rebecca Drucker's emphasis on "folk experience" linked Jewish work more to American local color than to Europeanism, which had been the earlier way of assessing the values of Jewish immigrant theatre. Folk life was something hereditary Americans could identify as native; Europeanism had generally been presented as something to adopt. A 1923 article reported on Chinese theatre in Boston and also provided an introduction to Asian performance, with additional examples of gestural technique from Java and India and a focus on formalism.[64] The article explains that Asian drama "does not depict the emotion felt in the given situation, but puts forward the situation itself," using emotions not for their own sake but "like terms of an equation."[65]

Exposure alone was not enough, however, in the years of Little Theatre. The construction of an enlightened, progressive audience for American theatre required proactive as well as reactive behavior on both sides of the producing-reception divide. A handful of articles dealing directly with audiences indicate that audiences were supposed to develop a conscience that would guide their ticketbuying choices, while serious artists were supposed to attend to such audiences' tastes. Walter Prichard Eaton (1878–1957) contributed much to the discussion of how to prod mainstream audiences. Eaton was a Harvard graduate who started publishing theatre criticism at the turn of the century. He was a long-time champion of the non–New York theatregoer who recognized intelligence and purposefulness on the stage and who also enjoyed realism, although Eaton was careful to define this as a realism that was "representative, not necessarily imitative," and he refused the "idea that realism in art means only pointing a camera at a pig-sty."[66] Eaton had, as early as 1908, taken to task his fellow critic Clayton Hamilton for Hamilton's snobbish "The Psychology of Theatre Audiences," which had asserted that individuals regressed to childlike animalism when part of a crowd, although Hamilton plainly held himself exempt. Eaton allowed Hamilton his point in cheap theatres in the seamier parts of Manhattan but pointedly asserted that millions of Americans went to the theatre "without checking . . . personal intelligence and refinement at the coat room."[67] Eaton's intelligent audience is characterized by openness to new ideas more than patrician credentials.

In 1919, Eaton published in *Theatre Arts* an article aimed at that same intelligent and refined American audience. This time, though, he criticized them for their "radical divorce between life and art," a disconnect nowhere so manifest as on Broadway during the war. Hungry Russian audiences had "dodged machine gun bullets and shrapnel to enjoy Gorky's *Night Refuge* superbly acted at the Moscow Art Theatre" while "well fed, we dodged, at the same time nothing more deadly than a taxicab, to view the silliest and most blatantly chauvinistic of melodramas . . . or the trivialities of musical comedy."[68] Americans have the wrong attitude toward theatre, argued Eaton, but the fault was largely that of laissez-faire capitalism, which had resulted in a country where only in two cities, New York and Chicago, could Americans see theatre other than that aimed at the lowest common denominator. (Eaton's ignoring Little Theatre is curious, but it went unremarked by the editors.) New Yorkers had a special responsibility to make intelligent choices; they also had to realize that this was a responsibility that came with privilege, since "New York, unfortunately, is not America."[69] Eaton's essay was a reprint of a talk he had given to the New York Drama League a month earlier. His argument was for a national network of theatres that would enable many people in the country to see new plays at roughly the same time, without having to travel to New York or wait for a tour. He also chastised dramatists for not addressing America. Rather, they addressed Broadway. Eaton believed artists could do better if only audiences would work harder. Even as he distinguished between blasé but earnest New Yorkers and intelligent but inexperienced Americans, *Theatre Arts*'s inclusion of the essay for a national readership united the two. The second-person address originally aimed at a Manhattan club now arrived in the hands of the very deprived Americans Eaton valued. The savior was the "sincere artist," but audiences needed to come to the artist's rescue. Those audiences presumably read *Theatre Arts* and they were nationally distributed.

In a rare use of the word that most reform rhetoric eschewed in favor of "intelligent" or "democratic," Eaton declared that American theatre "depends for its patronage almost entirely on the adult *bourgeois* class" (emphasis mine).[70] The class from which most theatre reformers emerged, the class on which they depended, and the class to which most wanted to belong—albeit with "bohemian delights"—did, in fact, prove itself capable of federating nationally on behalf of serious theatre in the hands of the Theatre Guild. It would be 1930 before the New York–based, nationally touring guild could boast seventy thousand subscribers to rival the Neue Freie Volksbühne of the mid-1910s, but in 1921, the Guild's producer, Theresa Helburn, told *Theatre Arts* readers how to federate an intelligent population of theatregoers craving what they understood as the best. For once, it was the artists who needed to do some adjusting, albeit in the service of quality. Helburn's experience in the Guild's experimental and developmental trenches gave her arguments credibility for the *Theatre Arts* readership.

The Theatre Guild was the postwar reincarnation of the Washington Square Players, one of the best-known early Little Theatres.[71] The WSP had begun in 1915, emerging from the same Greenwich Village community as the Provincetown Players, but with a slightly different focus. Its mission was to produce plays of "artistic merit," with some preference given to American plays, and with attention to European works turned down by commercial managers.[72] It never developed a core membership of playwrights, nor did it have a single charismatic leader. It had an elected committee of department heads, it sought subscribers from the outset, and it offered its productions in commercial venues outside of Greenwich Village. After excellent reviews for its first season, the WSP rented a Shubert Theatre for its succeeding three, going broke in the face of high rents and ranks depleted by wartime conscription. When the group reformed in 1918, the goals were to be "fully professional" and to produce "great plays." The group also adopted the subscription principle and aimed to be self-supporting. Their subscriber base grew steadily from 150 in 1919 to 600 in 1920, 1,300 in 1921, and 14,000 by 1925.

Helburn's article for *Theatre Arts* was called "Art and Business," and it announced at the outset that pure art was an impossibility in the theatre because theatre was—to borrow and turn on its ear Cheney's favorite word—"synthetic." Cheney's synthesis was one in which a single artist's vision would curb and direct the previously independent workings of actors, designers, and technicians. For Helburn, synthesis meant an organized compromise with front of house. She called her audience "special," while clarifying that these were "the public that buys Edith Wharton and Bernard Shaw."[73] Both Wharton and Shaw were known quantities in 1921; neither proffered a rhythmic ideal or the need for translation. Indeed, the Guild learned a lesson with its very first production, *The Bonds of Interest,* a fantasy by modern Spanish playwright Jacinto Benavente. Critics preferred the commedia set to the acting or directing; the house was filled with men in uniform admitted free; and the Guild ended its four-week run with nineteen dollars to its name. They were saved by a production of St. John Ervine's *John Ferguson,* a play with a naturalistic setting and melodrama's familiar poor family, mortgage foreclosing, and daughter's threatened virginity. Although kitchen sink realism was never to be their métier, the Guild was forced to think about how to appeal to a critical mass of Dickinson's "theatre-lovers."

The key to turning this "special" segment of the public into subscribers, according to Helburn, was to assure them that the board selecting the plays was "an audience in miniature." The Guild board included a banker, a lawyer, an artist, an actress, a producer, and a playwright, all, in Helburn's words "keenly interested in the theatre, [but] not all *of* it."[74] It is hard to see how the last three are not "of it," but the mix was meant to make readers feel that they were represented both as artistic and as executive selves. (The list also suggests who is excluded from the audience, either actual or potential.) Within a decade, the Guild was challenged from its own ranks by young members who found its work stultifyingly "uplifting" and artsy while failing to arouse passion or deal with issues of the day. The upstarts would found the Group Theatre; the parent organization, meanwhile, did fulfill the Little Theatre and *Theatre Arts* goal of availing many parts of America of new, nonfrivolous plays. A short list of their offerings includes Shaw's *St. Joan, Heartbreak House,* and *Back to Methuselah;* O'Neill's *Strange Interlude* and *Marco Millions;* Strindberg's *Dance of Death;* Elmer Rice's *The Adding Machine;* and DuBose and Dorothy Heyward's *Porgy. Theatre Arts* readers who sympathized with Helburn's middle-of-the-(high)-road schema were reassured about their important role in American theatre.

In 1923, Eaton published a *Theatre Arts* article simply called "Audiences." Again he spoke about the needs of "the sound core of middle class America" outside of New York, where multiple kinds of theatre didn't exist. This time his answer was organizing amateur efforts in the schools to satisfy audiences craving good plays. What is remarkable about the essay is Eaton's belief that productions in public schools will create an audience for spoken drama even as he notes Americans' mistrust of any kinds of amateur endeavors. He prescribes well-trained teacher/advisers, better equipment, and incentive, but he never accounts for how better amateurism—not as a training ground for professionals but as a source of local recreation—is supposed to eliminate a preference for the professional in the first place. He dismisses movie fans as "morons," attendees of traveling bedroom farces as "yahoos," and Little Theatres as out of sympathy with the community. Imagining that there is no reason to embrace popular entertainments other than ignorance or boredom, he recommends amateur theatre as a means to reach the "same vast audience which has created our public schools, our vast State universities, our parks and libraries, our highways and towns." In an eerie middlebrow echo of Moderwell's 1914 revolutionary battle cry, Eaton concludes that "once this audience demands a theatre, they will have it."[75]

The pitfalls of Eaton's logic—snobbery, out-of-hand dismissal of the main entertainment forms of the day, belief that school participation would produce adult commitment—would not prevent his basic ideas from being adopted. To insure that a bourgeois public would regard theatre as important, many theatre supporters in the 1920s embraced the idea of school as a training ground for theatre appreciation. A 1920 *Theatre Arts* editorial noted the proliferation of plays being performed for and by children around the country, suggesting approvingly that "if we want our American trees inclined toward the love and appreciation of the drama, we must begin to bend our American twigs that way."[76] Also in 1920, Samuel J. Hume (1885–1962) organized the Drama Teachers Association of California. Hume was not only the close friend of *Theatre Arts*'s founder and first artistic director of the Arts and Crafts Theatre of Detroit, but it was arguably he who had introduced America to innovative European stagecraft with the New Stagecraft exhibitions he organized in Cambridge and New York in 1914. Hume had a strong affinity for Hiram Moderwell's ideas, and Moderwell spoke at the exhibit's opening carrying the first, unbound copy of *The Theatre of To-Day*.[77] In six years, Hume had shifted his target audience for building theatre awareness beyond social elites in the east to classroom teachers in the west.

By 1924, *Theatre Arts* was helping to circulate the sort of thinking that would become an accepted feature of mainstream pedagogy in the near future and that signaled both recognition of and restrictions on the values of the Little Theatre movement. Helen Louise Cohen's "Education in the Theatre Arts" stressed the importance of seeing and doing theatre for New York City's high school students. In a throwback to earlier ideas about creating good Americans from flawed foreigners by means of salutary Anglo-Saxon theatre endeavors, Cohen cited the "inestimable assistance" to students of theatre in realizing "worthy citizenship, worthy use of leisure and ethical character."[78] Now it was hereditary Americans who could grow into being valuable citizens via serious theatre endeavors. It would be seventy-plus years before Alice Goldfarb Marquis would point out that schools "expose" (quotation marks hers) children to all sorts of disciplines that they never choose to pursue as adults, and that neither theatremaking nor discount tickets turns more than a small minority of upper-income and upper-education-level adults into theatre supporters.[79]

In the 1920s, the value of these ideas was still being hammered out and filtered into the national consciousness. School figured prominently in this later phase of Little Theatre. In 1925 *Theatre Arts* articulated a clear stance with regard to theatre, higher education, and democracy: college was no longer the province of gentlemen alone; even if it were, why should gentlemen not have the right to study theatre as a complicated craft? "Is the theatre too good, or not good enough? . . . And would that study not be worth while to the theatre even if it offered as its only result a more understanding audience?"[80]

Little Theatre per se was no longer the focus of *Theatre Arts* by the mid-1920s; rather, examples of work, wherever it originated, that exemplified longstanding Little Theatre ideals and goals filled the magazine's pages. What had been the province of small groups and innovative professors a decade earlier was now affecting Broadway, high school, and community theatre.[81] Despite its awareness of students and teachers as valuable audiences, though, *Theatre Arts* never established an editorial stance that assumed these were its primary target, as did, for instance, *Players,* which was started in 1924 as the official publication of the National Collegiate Players. *Players*'s readers were presumably university-educated young adults, but *Players* nowadays seems a sanitized, pedantic, and a step-behind-the-beat version of *Theatre Arts.* As late as 1929, for example, in an admittedly extreme example, an editorial in *Players* argued for an endowed theatre because theatre can show that "the wages of sin are death . . . [and the] rewards of virtue are life."[82] *Theatre Arts* never addressed its readership this way no matter how many of them were educators or students; rather, all were treated to a mode of address that suited New York sophisticates. Nonetheless, the editors came to understand the necessity of appealing to educators qua educators. In 1934, the magazine advertised a "teacher's chart," available with each issue to instructors using *Theatre Arts* in class. The charts suggested assignments, listed references, and summarized "features adapted to class work." Discount subscriptions were also made available to groups of students and teachers. Elsewhere on the audience construction spectrum, *Theatre Arts* acknowledged those who wanted to combine serious theatregoing with travel. In 1929, the magazine started a column called "The Audience on the Road," a calendar of productions and performances at summer theatres and festivals.

No single branch of the Little Theatre movement—educational, community, experimental—single-handedly catapulted serious theatre to a position of importance on the national agenda. *Theatre Arts* supported multiple strands of the effort to build an audience for the idea of nationally distributed and locally generated American theatre that, for nearly two decades prior to Hallie Flanagan's coining the slogan for the Federal Theatre Project, was theorized as free, adult, and uncensored.

Workshop for Watching

Twenty years ago to have said that the art of the theatre should receive recognition as a fine art and count as points toward a college degree would have seemed like suggesting the wildest nonsense. Yet today it is accepted as an interesting rather than a revolutionary fact.

—Constance D'Arcy Mackay, *The Little Theatre in the United States*

In 1925, *Theatre Arts* published an item it called "The Baker Map."[83] The drawing depicted the forty-eight states, noting places where more than one hundred former Harvard and Radcliffe students of Professor George Pierce Baker were living and working in the theatre. Various symbols were used to denote critic, actor, designer, playwright, producer, manager, Little Theatre worker, and college teacher—their "job titles"—yet none of Baker's students had earned degrees in any of these areas. Baker taught dramatic literature and playwriting in the English department and created a small, member-funded program where students could do production work. Whatever the professional destinations of his students, however, Baker strove in his classes for an emphatic "yes" to *Theatre Arts*'s question whether the "study not be worth while to the theatre even if it offered as its only result a more understanding audience?" Beginning in 1899, Baker had lectured on campus and off about theatre's importance as a "force in modern life," and of the necessity for audiences to learn "to seek in the theatre not a sedative or excitant, but an art to be respected and admired."[84] A *New York Times* editorial declared that his thirty-five year career at Harvard had "raised the prestige of the theatre enormously. In addition to the many students it sent directly into the theatre, it has, in one way or another, graduated a host of educated theatregoers."[85] A British royal commission report of the relation of drama to adult education said that the success of the Little Theatre movement in America was mainly attributable to Baker.[86] Such success depends on audiences and artists making meaningful use of each other; Baker showed students how to create this symbiosis. He eventually left Harvard to accept Yale's offer to start a professional theatre training program, but he never stopped publicly advocating the need for theatre appreciation classes to eliminate "audiences which in spite of a growing understanding of the theatre are still preponderantly made up of people who blindly follow their emotional responses along the lines of least resistance. This means liking what is tritely theatrical . . . ."[87]

Baker's direct work with audiences emerged as part of his 47 Workshop, an extracurricular project that mounted original plays with the stated purpose of helping playwrights develop their work by seeing it produced in front of an audience.[88] The Workshop was developed in conjunction with Baker' playwriting class, English 47. The class, in turn, was something he was allowed to create based on his experiences teaching dramatic literature almost from the start of his tenure at Harvard in 1890. His expertise in the evolution of English and European drama led to an interest in contemporary drama and this, in turn, to an interest in guiding students to write as well as to analyze plays. Baker was a leader in introducing modern theatre studies to the university curriculum. The idea of academic specialization in drama was so new that when Baker was made Professor of Dramatic Literature in 1910, he received a letter of congratulations from Brander Matthews of Columbia welcoming him "to the seat in the chair which I, alone in all the world, have occupied now for ten years and more."[89] Participants in Baker's classes and the 47 Workshop form a veritable who's who of American theatre for the first third of the century. The list includes playwrights Eugene O'Neill, Percy MacKaye, William Vaughn Moody, Edward Knoblock, Edward Sheldon, Philip Barry, and Sidney Howard; designers Lee Simonson, Stanley McCandless, Livingston Platt, and Donald Oenslager; Little Theatre directors Agnes Morgan, Sam Hume, and Irving Pichel; producers Theresa Helburn and Winthrop Ames; drama professors Frederick Koch, Alexander Dean, and William Lyon Phelps; critic/authors Walter Prichard Eaton, John Mason Brown, Robert Benchley, and Norman Hapgood (Hutchins Hapgood was Baker's graduate assistant in forensics); Federal Theatre Project Director Hallie Flanagan; erstwhile theatre dabblers John Reed and Thomas Wolfe; and veteran Broadway director and legend George Abbott.

The Workshop was founded in 1912 and lasted until 1924. Its audience was carefully selected to help fledgling playwrights get an idea of what commercial theatre audiences in major cities across the country would supposedly be likely to accept and appreciate in the way of serious or adventuresome playwriting. The "Shop" audience numbered around four hundred per season. Radcliffe's Agassiz Theatre, the performance venue, had two hundred seats with acceptable sightlines and each play was given twice. The audience, like Theresa Helburn's board of directors, was meant to represent bourgeois playgoers nationally; the social restrictiveness of the control group was either invisible or irrelevant to the Workshop directors. As much as Baker was working to produce successful playwrights, he was also working to produce an audience with ideas about itself, about theatre, theatregoing, dramatic literature, and dramaturgy.

The process of audience construction began with the 47 Workshop membership policy. Membership in the audience was, like membership in the Workshop in any other capacity, by application. No money was collected for tickets, but members were urged to make contributions. Workshop production programs contained information on membership:

> Past and present members of English 47 and 47A at both Radcliffe and Harvard naturally make the nucleus of the audience, but other persons interested in the art of the theatre are welcome. The committee on Membership is always ready to consider new names for the audience, but membership is rigidly restricted to persons believed to be interested in such experimentation as the 47 Workshop offers and ready in some way to co-operate. The name of each candidate proposed and seconded by a regular member of the audience should be sent to the chairman of the membership Committee. A statement of qualifications should also be submitted.[90]

Tickets were not to be transferred without permission, absenteeism was noted, and members who missed two successive productions without returning their tickets were warned and then dropped if no satisfactory explanation was made. Most important, audience members were required to "sign a card promising cooperation by written criticism handed in at the appointed times."[91] Audience members, like other Workshop participants, were addressed as students. Once approved for Workshop participation, many audience members responded to the setup by behaving like students, gauging their acceptability in terms of the professor's tastes and values. One member actually wrote that "after reading over the program of the last play I feel like a college boy when the professor forgets to assign a lesson for I note there is no request for a criticism. Is it a new policy? Were our remarks so poor they were less than of no value?"[92]

The construction of the theatre audience as students is evident in the many letters of application that bypassed the committee and came directly to Baker or his assistant. The spectrum of qualifications often included attending or teaching at Harvard and Radcliffe, or a degree from another Ivy League school or a university with a reputable theatre program, as these emerged.[93] Experience in professional theatre was sometimes mentioned, but usually only in conjunction with academic credentials. Women were occasionally recommended as good potential members because they were "charming" or "pretty." General terms such as "discriminating," "cultivated," and "artistic" were frequent. One applicant's letter was her resume, including her grade in a course with the Washington Square Players. Another letter referred to an applicant as "quite inordinately well-read" and concluded with a promise to send the Workshop "its little present . . . half of what I make next week."[94] Baker's admissions policies, like those of many elite private colleges of the era, favored candidates with social or family connections, previous experience in recognized institutions, attractive appearance (especially for women), and the ability to make financial contributions. This is a familiar enough Ivy League pattern and, in the case of private institutions interested in self-perpetuation, is understandable even as its exclusivity now looks like silly snobbery.[95] But if part of the project of reforming the theatre was to "elevate" a broad-based audience, the narrow representation of the body politic in the laboratory experiment is problematic. Baker's use of his local, elitist audience as a stand-in for nationwide communities invited a collapsing of the difference between cultural capital (proficiency in discourse about nationally validated cultural goods) and cultural resources ("any form of symbolic mastery that is useful in a specific relational context"[96]), encouraging in the minds of Baker's playwrights the idea that Middletown could be understood in terms of Cambridge, while also suggesting to Middletown that Cambridge's values were the right ones and not themselves defined by a particular local context. The overdetermined control group resituates the project as one of self-perpetuation, albeit one in which the limited group's own ideas might be challenged internally.

The cultural capital that Baker sought in the Workshop audience reflected his own life of Yankee privilege. Born and raised in Providence, Rhode Island, he was the only child of a Harvard-educated doctor, and he attended the city's leading private school. He spent most of his adult life living on a section of Brattle Street nicknamed Tory Row. When he did encounter American populations outside his Brahmin ken, his written responses ranged from the nervous to the dismissive. Minutes of 47

Workshop Committee meetings from 1918 reveal anxiety about offering performances to men in uniform; the adopted suggestions include
making the soldiers come without guests and issuing tickets to "men
selected by the authorities."[97] An essay filed with the *Providence Journal*
in 1888 reflects Baker's response to Hispanic New Mexicans as he experienced them while visiting a Harvard classmate's family ranch. He calls
them "lazy," "impressionable, superstitious," and "more like animals than
men" and cites their "shiftlessness, lack of moral stability," "taciturnity,"
"moroseness," and "tendency to pilfer," in which they resemble "the
Negro." He adds that the women can rarely be called pretty, and that
they dress badly, "combin[ing] colors in a way to distract an artist and
load[ing] themselves with cheap jewelry." These women, whose faces in
old age looked to Baker "as hideous as a death-mask" are, in his essay,
possessed earlier in life of a "languid, half-stupid gaze."[98]

Baker's prejudices are of interest not because they were unusual for
members of his class, but because of how they problematize his ideas
about individuality and the unique voice in the theatre. His book *Dramatic Technique* was published in 1918 and comprises material from
classroom and public lectures. In the book, he urges playwrights not to
"truckle" to their audiences, pointing out that the most successful, indi-
vidualistic playwright is one who, "determining to make his interests and
his sense of values the public's, labored until he had accomplished the
task. Forthwith a delighted public begged for more and what was declared
impossible became the vogue."[99] The book eschews generalizing labels
such as "ingenue" or "tragic heroine" or "comic relief," except in the case
of the character of a "wizened Jewish picture dealer," whom Baker refers
to as "the Jew."[100] The rubric is especially interesting in light of the fact
that a probable impetus for the 47 Workshop came from Lillian Shuman
Dreyfus, the (Jewish-descended) president of the Radcliffe 47 Club. In
1912, she went to Baker with a rough plan and some money for an experimental theatre. Within weeks, Baker had mapped out the main features of what was to become the 47 Workshop.[101] Presumably Dreyfus
could pass as "American" rather than "Jewish" due to her own cultural
capital, behavior, and attitudes. Nonetheless, Baker's goal of encouraging "individual" voices (a repeated desideratum in *Dramatic Technique*)
needs to be carefully considered in light of his ideas about both America
and theatre audiences.

Unlike some other Little Theatre workers, Baker did not eschew commercial recognition for his playwrights. The 47 Workshop was the crucible

for plays that went on to Boston's successful, mainstream Castle Square Theatre and to Broadway. Baker encouraged his students to seek New York productions of their scripts. He acknowledged the importance of working with an actual body of theatregoers in mind, noting that a playwright who would be convincing must "not run completely counter to what an audience thinks it knows about life."[102] The public was the final arbiter of stageworthiness, and Baker warned that "until a dramatist has considered his material in relation to the public, his play is by no means ready for production."[103] Yet the assemblage Baker sought as a stand-in for "the public" avoided diversity and reflected neither the Boston, nor the New York or Chicago of the period (to mention only the biggest locales with commercial theatres).[104] Lists of 47 Workshop audiences reveal a preponderance of Yankee names and high-rent addresses. The 1918–19 audience list has 209 names. By informal count, it includes two Italian, thirteen Jewish, four Hispanic, and eleven Irish names—a total of thirty, or about fourteen percent. Intermarriage and wives whose birth names disappear when they are listed as Mrs. John Doe make it important to allow for a margin of error. Still, the homogeneity is noticeable.

The point is not that Baker failed to meet some sort of political correctness criterion, an anachronistic idea in any case. Rather, by claiming a concern for both the individual writer's voice and also for wanting to create excellence for a public of commercial theatregoers which, however white, was not exclusively the product of Harvard or universities, or theatre training, or even of wealth during the 1910s and 1920s, Baker established a practice of studying and using audiences that was to go largely unchallenged by university theatre departments for decades to come. That is, university audiences were unproblematically studied as stand-ins for "the public" by scholars and practitioners who considered everything from simply what kinds of plays people preferred to which lines within plays in performance caused increased somatic levels of excitement.[105] As universities were to become the training grounds for both theatre artists and administrators, the practice of remaining within the university community was easy enough to embrace, especially since audiences, too, were being trained in the same institutions. Nonetheless, the failure to see beyond the immediate group within the university when questioning public taste is noticeably shortsighted. Audience surveys and studies throughout the century would reveal that theatregoers are educated and financially comfortable. Such surveys provide data about those who choose to go to the theatre; they do little about investigating why others stay away. One simple observation is that much American theatre reflects, both on stage and in the house, the concerns and ambience that make a white bourgeoisie comfortable while ignoring the interests and preferences of other groups. Again, the point is not to do retrospective finger pointing or to say Baker should have done otherwise; it is to note that by doing what he did as a pioneer, he created a model that had blind spots and would largely go unexamined for many decades.

The 47 Workshop audience was, however, an excellent collection of willing subjects for at least two reasons. First, since they were comfortable in each other's presence, they could construe the entire theatregoing event as salutary, minus any of the possible distractions of a heterogeneous assemblage, unfamiliar venue, or otherwise unknown social quantity.[106] In the absence of any such challenge or frisson, the Workshop audience could focus on the assignment of assessing the onstage event in an environment they could take as normal. Second, this audience comprised forthcoming, generally articulate writers. The bulk of the audience responses have few spelling or punctuation mistakes, show some mastery of dramaturgical ideas, and suggest that care went into either typing them or presenting them on good stationery. Responses were signed, but the signatures were removed (although estate letterheads were not) when the letters were given to the playwrights. The remainder of this chapter is based on seventy-eight responses for Lydia Garrison's play, *The Trap*, presented in 1923, for which the playwright apparently never claimed the critiques.[107] They demonstrate the ongoing construction of the 47 Workshop audience from student to theatre critic and also to social critic.

The Trap was construed by its author and the audience respondents as realism, although today we might call it melodramatic regionalism. It features a middle-aged couple with three children and a blind, doddering grandfather. The family is trying to scratch out an existence on a sterile New England farm. The "nagging" wife drives her husband away. Ten years later he returns. Disappointed at the wife's continued carping and at her forcing his favorite daughter into a loveless marriage, the husband rises up against his "hopeless" lot by stabbing his wife with a carving knife. Local color and generational and gender affiliations are conveyed through the wife's piecing quilts, the grandfather's reciting biblical homilies, the husband's remaining unemployed, and the young son's playing baseball.

The audience responses varied as to content and sympathies. Statements such as "I consider *The Trap,* [*sic*] the best play I have ever seen produced at the Workshop," vied with others such as "Alltogether a most disappointing play," while one respondent sat on the fence with "It was interesting even though it was boring." Several spectators concurred about Garrison's "astonishing and deep understanding of all her characters," as did others in the opinion that "she sees only surfaces and . . . has failed to pierce beyond . . . into the motives." One wrote, "I do not quite see the significance of the name," and another, "*The Trap* is well-named! I mean as regards the poor husband . . . ."

If feelings and opinions were all over the map, however, no one questioned the principles of cartography. The structure of the responses is remarkably similar, as are the vocabulary, the things to which writers responded, and an idea that the play represented a slice of real life, something that the writers, despite their quotidian distance from the community represented in the play, felt competent to assess. The greatest amount of critical space is given nearly always to theme or characterization. Discussions of structure and acting occupy the next greatest amount of space. Observations about the mise-en-scène are the shortest and nearly always appear last. Despite the fact that the responses are intended to serve the playwright, the most frequent comment is "well-acted," which appears by informal count in thirty-one responses. This is followed by "well-drawn characters," which appears in nineteen, and which often conflates the work of the actors with the work of the playwright.

Many respondents used the rhetorical tactic of defining the audience, or an audience, or the public, or the spectator, as extensions of themselves: "Three acts are too much to expect an audience to sit through unless there is a promise of hope and light somewhere." "The unrelieved depression of 'The Trap' was too heavy for any audience to stand." "The spectator is prompted to say to himself, 'Isn't that Aunt Susan to the bone!' or 'There's Uncle John!'" "The spectator cannot endure more." "There was no doubt of the entire absorption of the audience nor of the power of the sordid story." But this coherent sense of themselves as a theatre audience, evident in their collapse of the individual and the group, did not prevent Workshop respondents from differentiating between their assemblage and what they envisioned as a less refined, less tolerant public for whom they saw themselves running interference: "It is a play for only a limited audience and not suited to be the recreation of the average." "Miss Garrison's 'The Trap' . . . portrays such characteristics that our public has least need of."

Judgments about realism reveal a conflation of actuality and dramatic convention. The audience respondents, armed with Baker's vocabulary and empowered by the experience of frequent theatregoing, confuse their familiarity with commercial plays with authority on sociology. "I wondered what the outcome would be. What else could it be? I fancy many an unsolved crime owes its inception to similar causes." "I felt a sudden piercing shriek that broke with a gurgle would make the murder more convincing." "I cannot seem to feel that a man who could actually kill would have seemed just like that." "She writes of people and their actions as they really are." "Most of the Alex [the husband] types I have seen—the shiftless, well-meaning, ineffective persons—have had a certain loveableness that endeared them at least to the people who didn't have to live with them." "As a bit out of real life it is remarkable." In a standoff between the concerns of psychological motivation and those of stage-worthiness, three audience members queried the plausibility of incompatibility and nagging as causes for murder while three others wondered if strangling might not be more palatable. Pierre Bourdieu defines this tendency in middlebrow art, with its "recording of the social picturesque, whose populist objectivism distances the lower classes by constituting them as an object of contemplation" as "the self-legitimating imagination of the 'happy few.'"[108]

Baker's audience project with the 47 Workshop no longer seems radical now that "audience development" is a job description. He worked to fill his seats with members of a preexisting interpretive community whose enlightened self-interest made them useful to his efforts to educate a wide(r)spread playgoing public. He experimented with acclimating his volunteers to new drama and the possibility of bending conventions. He offered his writers a limited audience, not necessarily one that reflected the larger theatregoing public, but one that represented what he would like that theatregoing public to be. He chose an elite to stand in for a broad public who, in turn, were to be the recipients of the elite's choices. His was the now-familiar balancing act between the commercially safe and the crusading desire to push the envelope—Cheney's keeping ahead of business standards but never so far as to antagonize audiences of the moment. If Baker did little to encourage the attendance of an actual heterogeneous audience, he was, at the very least, concerned with challenging the one that existed in his purview.

Baker's model remains both useful and troubling. The 47 Workshop took seriously the idea that original theatre needs a committed audience and that the actual members of this audience can work actively as co-makers of meaning in the theatrical event. Culling this audience from the same group (not just the same geographic locale) as the artists guaranteed a certain sympathy, but it did little to address the multiclass public to which Baker and other Little Theatre reformers and educators so often referred. At worst, Baker perpetuated a notion that the public who should influence playwrights should be white, upper-middle class, and urban in outlook. At best, he offered a model of two-way influence that his followers could reshape to suit other locales and other publics. The following chapters examine some of those reshapings, replete with triumphs and surprises as well as with fears and blind spots.

"Fall Girls of Modernism"

Women and/as Audiences

It is the women who make or break a play. *See any manager.*
—Edwin Carty Ranck, "What Is a Good Play?"

[T]he theatre is to-day the one great public institution in which "votes for women" is the rule, and men are overwhelmingly outvoted.
—Clayton Hamilton, "Organizing an Audience"

The Little Theatre movement began at a moment when middle- and upper-middle-class women attended "drama theatre" with enthusiasm and without shame. Clayton Hamilton asserted in 1911 that any attempt to reform American theatre would have to be aimed at the women of the nation.[1] Around the same time, New York's Frohman office surveyed audiences at its various productions and concluded that women comprised 70 percent of the attendees.[2] In 1913, *Drama* reported that 80 percent of American theatregoers were women.[3] Yet such observations were rarely issued with outright approval. Rather, they came as part of a nexus of warnings and critiques. American women's enthusiasm and ubiquitous presence in theatre audiences generated a backlash against them as a counterpoint to their new roles as theatre advocates and theatre reformers.

This chapter investigates that backlash as a parallel to women's work—

side by side with men—to develop American theatre. Even the largest-scale and longest-lived women's undertaking for theatre reform, the nationally distributed Drama League of America, was the target of skepticism from outside and within because it was woman-identified. Much of the public disparagement took the form of journalistic constructions of women as flawed theatre supporters. What marks the remonstrance is not any consistency within its arguments, since women were censured in print for being too Victorian, prissy, or domestic and were equally chided for not hewing to decorous, old-fashioned ideals; in a compromise 1920s stance, they were berated for failing to package Victorian values in flapper clothing. Characterizations concocted for the delectation of readers are, assuredly, not to be read as ethnographic renderings of the real lives of women participating in theatre reform. Still, the ongoing disparagement of women theatregoers from the earliest years of their embracing commercial reform right through the key years of the Little Theatre movement says something about the anxiety provoked by the actual referents for the lampoons and derision.

Just as *Theatre Arts* sought to educate an ideal American theatre audience through its editorial and advertising policies, other publications focused on circulating an image of women as troubled theatre artists and troubling audiences. Many of these complaints—which showed up in genres as diverse as cartoons, reviews, short stories, and essays—collapsed the difference between women interested in Little Theatre and those with more commercial tastes. Where the critiques are consistent is in their insistence on gender as a category of failure. As generational and geographic differences became clearer within the Little Theatre movement, these came to inflect the nature and content of the condemnations. Regardless of date or geography, though, women remained the moving targets of disciplinary comments ranging from gentle ribbing to hostile ridicule and leveled at them for behavior spanning a spectrum from indifference to zeal. One of the sobering ironies of the era is that however much and hard women worked to support and improve theatre, they were ignored, laughed at, scorned, or asked to step aside in many of the same publications that shared their general goals. Moreover, it was not only men who made the attacks. The perpetrators of the broadsides were sometimes women themselves as they learned the ropes of modernity.

Emergent Status

Middle-class women had not always been a sufficiently important part of the American theatre audience to warrant such notice. Colonial and

Jacksonian audiences in cities were largely male, with exceptions made for particular plays or particular days of the week, when middle- or upper-middle-class women attended with male family members or escorts. Working-class women who attended alone in the antebellum years were sometimes mistaken for prostitutes.[4] Commercial producers began actively seeking middle-class women as patrons in the middle of the nineteenth century by foregrounding "respectability" both in their offerings of plays and, perhaps more importantly, in their advertising, decorating, and scheduling practices.[5] The matinee was management's way of targeting women *as women* to buy tickets, with theatres in New York offering a site of escape and pleasure located near the emerging department stores and ice cream parlors of which women were the habitués. Shopping and theatregoing were positioned as means of satisfying desire and fantasy.[6] Saturday matinees meshed with children's afternoon out of school, and they were welcome with their mothers.

The earliest attempts at safe, "moral" plays suitable for the whole family were offered in "lecture rooms"—beautifully appointed theatres given an educational name—attached to museums owned by Moses Kimball and P. T. Barnum in the 1840s. Other commercial producers followed suit, eliminating liquor and redecorating with plush seats and chandeliers that signaled elegance and refinement. The post–Civil War emergence of an evening devoted to a single play in place of the longstanding practice of a mixed evening served both to shorten and to homogenize the entertainment, enabling spectators to know just what to expect and to get home earlier. The trajectory of the second half of the nineteenth century was toward quieter audiences who no longer smoked or drank at the "legitimate" theatre. The very term "legitimate" came into use at the end of the century to distinguish drama theatre from other stage entertainments.[7] The audience's ability to interact with both the stage performance and each other—formerly a standard feature of American theatregoing—was quelled not only by separating variety entertainment offerings from legitimate theatre, but also by the darkening of the audience area, something made possible by improvements in gas lighting and then by the advent of electricity. Men who found all of this stultifying or boring and wanted something racier, less domesticated, or more interactive could opt for minstrel shows or, later, the leg show. By the 1890s, "legitimate theater was a woman's entertainment."[8]

The attraction of theatre for middle- and upper-middle-class women was the result of more than producers' promotional guesswork or convenient access. A network of social changes and values had yielded an urban-influenced American culture in which women were the guardians of virtue, home life, morality, religion, and an interest in the arts, while men were breadwinners and protectors. If the schism seems an ordinary feature of the popular imagination regarding "traditional" American life, it is worth remembering that Colonial women in a more agrarian context had often worked side by side with their men or had run their own small businesses, for example as brewers or printers. Increased industrialization in the nineteenth century meant, in broad terms, that men, in the east at least, earned the money while married women spent it, albeit largely on the home and on family members. A steady increase in mass-produced goods over the course of the century made possible for women in the cities and suburbs the kind of stay-at-home consumerism that Thorstein Veblen would describe in *The Theory of the Leisure Class.*[9] In the "cult of true womanhood," women embodied piety and domesticity within a proscribed "sphere." This sphere included, besides devotion to parenting and wifely submission, the appreciation, consumption, and perpetuation of certain kinds of literature, art, music, and nonintellectual religious ritual and church activity. Accomplishments and interest in the arts, especially playing the piano, singing, drawing, and painting on china or velvet, were acceptable for women, primarily because these activities could be construed by both sexes as contributing to the comfort and supposed inspirational function of the home. Women were the guardians of this soft realm of culture, while they were largely excluded from business, law, industry, most of medicine, politics, and the rigorously intellectual aspects of theology or philosophy.[10] Not all women, of course, participated in this straitened privilege. Middle-class "oases" for some families depended on female servants whose own homes could not function as analogous retreats.[11] It was "true women" and their descendants, however, who comprised the backbone of the theatre audiences that were both cultivated for profit and criticized for their feminized values. Accordingly, the feminization of American audience values was forged in the image of a particular idea of "woman"—an idea that excluded many actual women. Those who supported cultural and spiritual activities in the nineteenth and the early twentieth centuries took these activities seriously and therefore are important to their growth. Nonetheless, these women's positioning poses two problems in considering them as theatre supporters: first, their exclusion from the loci of male privilege kept them out of the public and financial arenas where ideas were backed and institutionalized; second, their blindness to their own class privilege made them read and promote as "universal" norms that were unfamiliar, unavailable, or uninteresting to others.

Feminized values and exclusion from the professions did not, however, preclude activism or self-improvement, both of which were provinces of the women's clubs that emerged in the nineteenth century. Temperance, religion, public health, and educational betterment were areas where nineteenth-century women crusaded outside the home. But even bids for suffrage often fit the mold of "domestic feminism," a term that broadly describes women's work for social reform through "applying their moral qualities to the world at large."[12] Little Theatre reform derided many beliefs that underpinned domestic feminism and Victorian womanhood; it also depended on the support of women with leisure, many of whom came from a tradition of using some of that leisure in club activities. Women in the Little Theatre movement resisted many aspects of Victorianism but often lived with newer versions of a feminine sphere. As Christine Stansell notes of the infamous bohemian free speech movement in the Greenwich Village of the 1910s, women could not necessarily speak really freely, since old habits don't die merely in the face of the assertion of newness. Gender rules still applied.[13] Cheryl Black observes in her study *The Women of Provincetown* that even the most feminist and urban of the well-known Little Theatres exhibited gender bias in everything from casting (the forty-three-year-old Ida Rauh was deemed too old to play a character who ages between acts and is fifty for half the play) to job assignments, where women always made the costumes, decreasingly served as directors, and almost never designed sets. In the 1920s, as Little Theatre ideologues secured a space for theatre in university as well as high school education, women participated in the push-pull of new job opportunities that had been nonexistent a generation earlier, when there had been no drama specialists, but that were nonetheless understood as feminine and lower-paying than men's theatre-related work, such as chairing university departments, or working as stagehands, to cite only two examples. Theatre activities were liberating for middle-class American women for many decades. Yet the overall context in which this liberation occurred— one of limited, albeit growing, education and employment opportunities— meant that it was often compensatory, decorative, or transitory, evaporating in the face of marriage, spousal disapproval, or family pressure.

I have been arguing that Little Theatre was one of many modernist projects in the arts and that support for it was predicated on earlier tastes and habits, even as these were criticized and overhauled. Nonetheless, among the arts, theatre was a particularly "loaded" domain for women. For actresses, it had been among the few relatively equal opportunity sources of employment in the nineteenth century. At the same time, actresses, unless they were stars, had generally been regarded by the bourgeoisie as disreputable. Moreover, the very independence that actresses enjoyed was negatively deployed to reinforce accepted images of women, recuperating passivity, sexual taint, and conventional desirability, something evident in some of the fiction and articles discussed in the next section of this chapter.[14] The Little Theatre movement would yield professional and university programs for studying acting, thereby making it somewhat easier for young women to enter the field without necessarily scandalizing friends and family. Yet the roles actresses played underscored older values. Consider, for example, Rachel Crothers's assertion that she regarded herself as very avant-garde "when among other innovations she made her heroines over thirty years old."[15]

On the other side of the footlights, women in the theatre audience were also on display—there to be looked at as much as to do the looking.[16] The same might be said of a woman at a concert, of course, or of even a woman strolling through a museum, but theatre invited emotional responses to the socially recognizable ideas depicted in plays; also, these emotional reactions were experienced in the company of others and, in response to dramaturgical construction, more or less on cue. Bruce McConachie observes that in theatre for bourgeois audiences, more than in any other nineteenth-century arts endeavor, "the role of high culture was tied to the bottom line."[17] His reference is to financial gain, but this was linked to a sort of social bottom line. Plays succeeded and made money if they validated the desires and beliefs of their audiences. Women in theatre audiences displayed their womanliness—arguably their ticket to support or a place in society—by responding to predictable onstage situations in predictable ways; these were the opportunities theatre offered and encouraged. If legitimate theatre was woman's entertainment, the price of women's tickets was still primarily underwritten by men who, whether they themselves enjoyed theatre (and clearly many did), were willing enough to have their wives, daughters, sisters, mothers, and sweethearts attend, so long as what they attended was understood by all concerned as not threatening.[18]

Little Theatre threw down a gauntlet to many features of commercial theatre. It was a realm where sentimentality and passivity were challenged and women were active participants as writers, producers, promoters, and educators in unprecedented numbers. But in an ongoing series of paradoxes, women were simultaneously encouraged and excluded, cultivated and scorned, relied upon and ignored. Were women in Little Theatre what Ann Douglas calls "fall girls of modernism—given false tasks to perform?"[19]

Ambient Images

It is hard to find a print medium that did not include derogatory images of women as theatre audiences in the Progressive Era and for several years beyond. Newspapers, magazines, cartoons, unpublished essays, memos, short stories, and novels reflected the idea that women qua women were the silliest, most tiresome, and least intelligent form of theatre audience. In the aggregate, these texts suggest that women degraded the industry, kept male playwrights from being able to do their best, drained actors' energy, annoyed husbands, sought self-fulfillment in laughable ways, failed to understand theatre even when they did embrace it, and ate too many fattening things in the bargain. Women were foolish because they were vain and sentimental. They were dangerous because their interest in theatre kept them from being motherly enough or, conversely, since they were not masculine enough their interest and influence in theatre meant that men who attended somehow had their own masculinity diminished as a result of sharing feminized fare.

Criticisms that included men were much less pointedly personal and never attacked their masculinity. Usually these were either assaults on audiences in general or jibes at the "tired businessman" and his preference for lightweight theatre. Certainly some gendered audience critiques addressed men and woman as separate but equal problems. For example, in the early 1890s, the Keith and Albee vaudeville circuit began efforts to stop men from lighting up cigars during performances and to require women to remove their large hats.[20] Men who thumped their canes or rattled their programs in the theatre were criticized along with women who rustled candy wrappers.[21] Such scolding, though, sought merely behavior modification, not aesthetic overhaul; it was never as pointed or searing as critiques aimed at women alone.

In the years just before and at the start of the Little Theatre movement, women were portrayed in print as "the chief offenders in the matter of bad breeding in the theatre."[22] One can see in these assaults a critical stance with one foot in Victorian values, even as the younger among the critics struggle to embrace modernism. Critic Ludwig Lewisohn in 1909 blamed "drama's saccharine and uninteresting lack of 'virility' squarely on 'the American girl' and matron." Another critic the same year attacked the "'illiterate candyeating women' who infantilized the American stage."[23] Clayton Hamilton's extended 1907 assessment of audience psychology damned women with a particular vengeance. Dramatists, he said, must appeal to crowds instead of individuals, and crowds—in an analysis swallowed nearly undigested from Gustave LeBon's nineteenth-century polemic *The Crowd*—are "emotional," "uncivilized," "uncultivated," "easily credulous," and "carelessly unthinking." In the theatre, the "crowd is composed largely of women . . . [and] is lacking in the judicial faculty and cannot look upon a play from a detached and disinterested point of view." The female hand that fed also choked the playwright: "It is to an unthinking and over-feminine mob that the dramatist must first of all appeal . . . . [S]ince women are by nature inattentive, the femininity of the modern theatre audience forces the dramatist to employ the elementary technical tricks of repetition and parallelism, in order to keep his play clear though much of it be unattended to." The practical effects of this inferior drama, according to Hamilton, were that "very few men go to the theatre unattached; and these few are not important enough, from the theoretic standpoint, to alter the psychologic aspect of the audience."[24] Hamilton did not suggest that men self-segregate and devise their own civilized, thinking, disinterested theatre. Men did, in fact, attend performances in genres from which women were largely absent in the audience, but these were sexually titillating shows, for which, of course, there was no middle-class female analogue and which hardly addressed Hamilton's complaint. One way to parse Hamilton's analysis would go something like this: women have co-opted legitimate theatre, ruining it for men. Men still have other entertainment options (unlike women), but they deserve a range of alternatives (unlike women). Therefore, women should be more like men at men's rational best, so as to guarantee men a cultivated, civilized option at one end of a continuum of (male) choices while insuring that women, with no such continuum, would conform to (presumed) male ideals at their loftiest (and least popular among men themselves) in the sole option women are to be allowed. It was not necessary to wait for Freud's essays on femininity to recognize that "appropriate" womanhood necessitated a tortuous set of accommodations.

Women critics also chastised women theatregoers. In 1911, Ann Peacock acknowledged the importance of the female theatregoer's opinion to producers, "however valueless it may be, critically considered." Women, after all, only went to the theatre to see favorite stars, "gorgeous gowns," or stories of personal interest. In choosing a play, moreover, they always preferred the opinion of a female friend to that of a professional (nearly always male) critic. Feminist historians and critics of the last three decades have pointed to the ways in which the consumption by women of stories that are of immediate and emotional interest—particularly when the stories represent recognizable situations in relation to men—can be empowering, even when the women in the audience are solidly entrenched in economic and domestic realms circumscribed by a powerful patriarchy.[25] Also, the act of gathering with friends to attend or discuss plays was itself a step out of the home and into the public realm. But women who wrote criticism in the early decades of the century were, as often as not, accepting views erected on ideas of behavior and taste that refused the overtly feminine as they knew it.[26] Consider Ella Costillo Bennett's 1914 judgment of the "matinee girl"—basically a teenage fan who went regularly, often with girlfriends, to the same shows her parents might attend at night. She was "a nuisance that the management of the theatre should abate, just as he would any other kind of a nuisance— biped or quadruped." The girl's crimes included conspicuous chattering, giggling, and non-stop fixing of her hair. A "governess or attendant would not be out of place with the young misses," whose "lack of good breeding . . . ruins the grand finale of every matinee."[27] Dorothy E. Nichols facetiously envisioned an ideal theatre of the future in which audience members would be seated according to a sort of theatre IQ test. The lowest rank would be accorded to the woman who wanted to "*modrenize*" [*sic*] the ending of *Romeo and Juliet*.[28] Even women writers who attacked others of their cohort found accusations of enjoying theatre and food powerful means of assault. Rose Caylor, who worked as a journalist and as an actress before marrying playwright Ben Hecht, went after Hecht's first wife, Marie, a sometime theatre critic, in "An Essay Concerning the More Maniacal Sex." Caylor skewered the culture-loving matron for smothering and torturing her husband, describing this victimizer—really Marie Hecht—as "woman, the theatre-goer, patron of concerts, acquisitive buyer, who caresses herself with silks until her dotage, who is obsessed with vanity and advancement, who often eats like a lumberjack . . . ."[29]

Another string of jibes was built on the premise that while women may love to go to theatre, they are unorganized and uninformed about that very activity. "When Milady Shops for Seats" (1922) lambasted the female ticketbuyer who emptied her purse on the box office counter in search of her cash, yammered to the ticket seller about sightlines, took up his time wondering what the play was about, fretted that the Thursday matinee was inconvenient for her, dished about her closest girlfriend, inquired whether the ticket price included tax, and finally, after her purchase, struggled to gather the possessions she had scattered.[30] A 1925 humor piece recounts the laugh had by a ticket speculator at the expense of a women's club whose members had written to request twelve aisle seats for a Friday matinee. In his reply, he regrets to inform the ladies that the play they want to see closed several weeks ago and that, as each row has only one aisle seat, they would not in any case have been able to sit together. Moreover, there is no such thing as a Friday matinee. The women have also failed to enclose payment for the tickets. Their organization, an audience improvement enterprise called "The Friday Afternoon Discussion Club for the Promotion of Better Contemporary Drama," is thereby rendered one huge bastion of laughable incompetence with regard to the group's very raison d'etre.[31] Even women who do manage to purchase tickets don't understand what they are seeing. In "Mrs. Blabb Goes to the Matinee," an out-of-town matron sits down to breakfast with her daughters in a New York hotel and attempts to answer their questions about the plays she has seen. Her conversation is a mishmash of malapropisms and mispronunciations in which she cannot get past descriptions of ticket speculators, actors' appearances, gossip about other theatre personalities, and neighbors from home. The exasperated daughters finally beg for an account of the story of one of the plays. "'Story!' echoes Mrs. Blabb, 'Heffens! I don't know; I never have time to bother about the story when I'm enjoying the play.'"[32]

Who was reading these jibes and critiques? Many appeared in *Theatre*, the glossy monthly that covered Broadway, opera, and stars' lives, offered newsy reportage about Little Theatres and movies, and ran advertising for luxury and personal grooming goods. Since commercial theatre, gossip, fashion, and consumerism were supposedly the pronounced provinces of bourgeois women, a logical guess is that the readership was largely female, although nothing in the editorial content ever stated this outright. Also, while most readers of *Theatre* had an interest in commercial New York theatre, the inclusion of Little Theatre news and activities suggests some editorial interest in crossover. *Theatre* offered its audience insider information in the form of articles and fiction about women who actually worked in the theatre, including Little Theatre. These women were not lambasted in the way female audiences members were; rather, they were routinely presented as exemplars of true womanhood who managed to work in theatre but never forgot the high ideals of femininity. For the reader-as-audience-member, this might be seen as encouraging, since it offered reassurance that "good" women could and did work in the theatre, making it respectable to watch—and perhaps imitate in an amateur context—their undertakings. On the other hand, such reassurance could also function as a warning not to go too far.

A 1916 profile of actress Blanche Bates was called "Motherhood and Art." Bates, the mother of two, was interviewed at her country home, and the (female) writer created a domestic tone by describing in detail a bucolic setting, duly noting that Bates would not sit down for their conversation before attending to her toddler's nap. "I am a suffragist, a feminist, an individualist, and an ardent subscriber to every 'ism' and 'ology' that has to do with the advancement of my sex, but I hold as my firmest, my highest, my most irrefutable belief, that the highest good that can come to a woman is motherhood."[33] A similar story about Emily Wakeman Hartley, who built and ran a theatre in Stamford, Connecticut, informed readers that she did her fund-raising "in odd times she could spare from her mothering and home duties."[34] Another piece entitled "Acting Helps a Woman to Live" described how the profession prepared the actress to endure trials in her marriage through imitating in real life the self-effacing, tolerant, noble characters she has played onstage.[35] Two teenage girls who started a theatre dedicated to presenting the work of Shaw, Ibsen, and Wilde were infantilized in a short feature as "cute," "saucy," or "fluffy-haired." Their financing came in the form of a Christmas gift from their father; their own economizing would occur in the areas of "sodas, ice creams, boxes of candy, [and] filmy, fluffy creations so enticing as they hang in Fifth Avenue shop windows."[36] Alice Gerstenberg, interviewed for a New York daily in 1915, was described as a "little, blond-haired, blue-eyed schoolgirl . . . perched on the arm of a chair with a letter from her daddy." Gerstenberg had just published her second novel and was known in New York for her stage adaptation of *Alice in Wonderland* and her Little Theatre one-act, "Overtones." Since she was not married, this portrait rendered her acceptably ingenuish. She was thirty at the time.[37] An article about Elizabeth Schober, the unmarried manager of the Temple Theatre, assured readers that this former shoe factory manager ran her theatre "with a certain sympathetic femininity which even commerce cannot eradicate from the character of a level-headed woman."[38] In every instance, regardless of the women's actual personalities, ages, or accomplishments, journalism fit them into one of a few standardized models guaranteed to shore up femininity and to situate business or artistic accomplishments in the realm of recognizable, familiar, gendered behavior. Short fiction buttressed the idea that domestic femininity was the paramount female virtue and that a woman was best off in the audience and not on the stage. In the 1919 story "A Woman of No Imagination," an actress who is separated from her husband wins a role in a Broadway show by convincing the producer's sister that being a wife is superior to a career as an actress. The actress succumbs to her own performance, turns down the role, and returns to the husband she had previously left.[39]

Between 1924 and 1926, *Theatre* ran a series of cartoons lampooning theatre audiences. The audiences depicted included both sexes and ran the gamut of highbrow, middlebrow, and lowbrow preferences. Of these, only the genuinely highbrow were rendered as gender-equal, with their laughability resulting from their hyper- (or pseudo-) intellectualism. The protagonists in "the lobby at the highbrow theatre"—one male and one female—are both tall, small-chested, posing with hips thrust forward in a debutante slouch, looking bored and superior, and seemingly in agreement that the play is "rather inadequate, [and] not metaphysical enough in it's [*sic*] rotation" (see fig. 4.1). The person in the background could be either male or female.[40] Similarly, devotees of off-beat or Theatre Guild plays were ribbed because of their pretenses as eccentrics and culture mavens. Men and women in this group again consume and love the same kind of theatre. Here the critiques are again of the separate but equal sort and take on gendered self-presentation in the self-consciously bohemian cohort. This survey of "All Sorts and Conditions in New York Audiences," depicts downtown audiences as a cross between tourists and tourist attractions: "Down below the Forties, where the roaring is done mainly by Italian babies and untamed tea-lions, Greenwich Village audiences congregate in the name of ART, wearing much or little hair as the sex may determine and garments as loose as their domestic affiliations" (see fig. 4.2). Devotees of Theatre Guild offerings offered an occasion for non–New York readers (since Theatre Guild plays both toured and played in New York) as well as Manhattanites to recognize the uptown and heartland analogues to the Village crowd: "Theatre Guild audiences refute completely the argument that the intelligentsia is composed of the great 'unwashed,' for here may be seen, worshipping at the shrine of sophisticated drama, young men with Brooks tuxedos, Van Dyke beards, and five-foot bookshelf intellects, accompanied by young women who know how to manipulate with equal grace a volume of Nietzsche and a Spanish shawl" (see fig. 4.3).[41]

RATHER INADEQUATE, NOT METAPHYSICAL ENOUGH IN IT'S ROTATION."

IN THE LOBBY AT THE HIGHBROW- THEATER.

Fig. 4.1. "The Box-Office Angle: What the Public Wants Revealed by Hans Stengel, Who Went to the Play to Review the Audience," *Theatre,* February 1924.

Men and women who were supposed to be "average," that is, not ethnic, intellectual, or radical, were also ridiculed in the cartoons in gender-specific ways for shoddy audiencing. All-male audiences were out to ogle chorus girls, and men from ministers to hot dog vendors had the same thing on their minds (see figs. 4.4 and 4.5).[42] In the female camp, young wives who meet after a morning's shopping in the city indiscriminately choose any theatre "in which they can sit down and tell each other how 'dead' they are." "Thrill-proof flappers" yawn that matinees are "dumb," even as they pause to primp in the theatre lobby (see fig. 4.6).[43] Men chose theatres as peepshows; women marked time there in order to gossip and complain.

Down below the Forties, where the roaring is done mainly by Italian babies and untamed tea-lions, Greenwich Village audiences congregate in the name of ART, wearing much or little hair as the sex may determine and garments as loose as their domestic affiliations

Fig. 4.2. "All Sorts and Conditions in New York Audiences," by Ethel Plummer, *Theatre*, September 1925.

Theatre Guild audiences refute completely the argument that the intelligentsia is composed of the great "unwashed," for here may be seen, worshipping at the shrine of sophisticated drama, young men with Brooks tuxedos, Van Dyke beards and five-foot bookshelf intellects, accompanied by young women who know how to manipulate with equal grace a volume of Nietzsche and a Spanish shawl

Fig. 4.3. All Sorts and Conditions in New York Audiences," by Ethel Plummer, *Theatre*, September 1925.

The little blonde, second from the left, is a knockout with the boys from Buffalo.

Fig. 4.4. "The Boxers: The Exclusive in Their Mad Pursuit of Pleasure," by Helen Hokinson, *Theatre,* January 1924.

There is no club-house equal to the New Amsterdam, for here assemble ministers, hat-box manufacturers, talcum-powder sales-men, deans of universities, frankfurter vendors, all believing with Ziegfeld that, be it ever so unadorned, beauty is beauty still

Fig. 4.5. "All Sorts and Conditions in New York Audiences," by Ethel Plummer, *Theatre,* September 1925.

The flappers, thrill-proof, remarking, "Don'tcha hate matinées?" "Yeah, ain't they dumb!"

Fig. 4.6. "Matinee Girls of 1924," by Helen Hokinson, *Theatre*, June 1924.

But women were criticized as incompetent in a way that men never were. In a group of five cartoons depicting ushers, it was female patrons who were portrayed as ignorant and helpless, while men merely went through routine interactions.[44] A blasé female usher informs a nondescript male patron with his back to the viewer that his seats are three flights up to the left. In contrast, an irritated-looking male usher tells a lumpy, disgruntled-looking, and clearly very ignorant woman patron, "No, Madame, the balcony is not downstairs" (see fig. 4.7). Men who sat in the balcony needed traffic directions; women who sat in the balcony needed to be brought into Western civilization. An usher with a flashlight has to lead by the hand a female theatregoer whose face is upturned as if she were heading ceilingward. The patron announces, "I can't see a thing," even though the usher's light is fully on and pointing right to a seat inches from her hand. It is unclear in the drawing whether the woman theatregoer's eyes are even open (see fig. 4.8). In another cartoon, middle-class women were clearly marked as a drain on male fun. Dour spectators include "the poor wretch who had to miss a meeting of the Rotary Club to go with the wife to the Moscow Art Theater; and the Mrs. constantly sobbing: Ain't it wonderful?"[45] The biggest difference between the laughable men and the laughable women in *Theatre* magazine's audience depictions was that women were risible simply for their genuine enjoyment of plays and musicals. Middle-class, middle-aged women were fools by themselves and killjoys for men. These resolute hausfraus were also, in the age of dieting and boyish flappers, depicted as fleshy, and, therefore, coded as unstylish and unappealing.[46]

Various strands of antifeminist audience criticism come together in a 1923 cartoon accompanying an article entitled "Main Street Comes to Broadway" (see fig. 4.9).[47] The sketch depicts a young woman who might otherwise be "attractive," except for her unflapperlike attire, including a dowdy jacket, high collar, straw hat, pince-nez, and her round-shouldered posture. The confused box office agent does not quite know what to make of the single coin she proffers; basically only movies and vaudeville the-

Fig. 4.7. "Other Aisle, Please," by Helen Hokinson, *Theatre,* September 1924.

"I cant see a thing"

Fig. 4.8. "Other Aisle, Please," by Helen Hokinson, *Theatre*, September 1924.

atres sold tickets for less than a dollar in Manhattan's theatre district in the 1920s. The caption reads "Prominent Rotarians and Drama Leaguers of Main Street visit the Show Mart of Gotham with no sense of inferior standards. Their battle cry beginning—'Now, Back Home'—rings ominously in managerial ears." The cartoon's punch depends not only on the ideas of out-of-towners as rubes and women as hapless theatregoers; it draws on a presumed recognition of Sinclair Lewis's novel *Main Street* and of the Drama League of America. The Drama League, treated in more depth in the final section of this chapter, was a national women's organization dedicated to improving theatre and educating audiences. *Main Street* satirized small-town life, using theatre as a way to trace the desires of the frustrated heroine, Carol Kennicott. The cartoonist's sketch matches Lewis's description of Carol, looking in her mirror at age thirty, only to recognize fading youth and creeping provincialism: "Neat rimless glasses. Black hair clumsily tucked under a mauve straw hat which would have suited a spinster. Cheeks clear, bloodless. Thin nose. Gentle mouth and chin. A modest voile blouse with an edging of lace at the neck. A virginal sweetness and timorousness—no flare of gaiety, no suggestion of cities, music, quick laughter."⁴⁸

Theatre on Main Street

That the cartoonist might have known *Main Street* is not remarkable. The novel sold three hundred thousand copies when it was published in 1920,

Fig. 4.9. "Prominent Rotarians and Drama Leaguers of Main Street visit the Show Mart of Gotham with no sense of inferior standards. Their battle cry beginning—'Now, Back Home—' rings ominously in managerial ears." Drawing by Wynn, *Theatre*, June 1923.

another hundred thousand before cheaper editions appeared, and by 1929, having sold eight hundred thousand copies, it was called "the most sensational event in twentieth century American publishing history."[49] *Vanity Fair* nominated Sinclair Lewis to the Hall of Fame for adding the phrase "Main Street" to the spoken language. The Pulitzer Prize committee chose *Main Street* for its annual novel award (although Columbia University went against their selection and awarded the prize to Edith Wharton's *Age of Innocence*).[50] As recently as 2002, a critic ranked the publication of *Main Street* with that of *Uncle Tom's Cabin* as "one of the few literary events in American history that proved to be a political and social event as well."[51] Women readers then and later identified with Carol Kennicott's position as an unhappy woman in a sexist community, recognizing the plight of Lewis's "woman with a working brain and no work."[52]

The fictional Carol matches in age, temperament, and experience many of the actual women involved in the Little Theatre movement as participants and as audiences. The daughter of a professional father who has relocated from New England to the Midwest, Carol graduates from college and works briefly between 1909 and 1912, at which point she marries a small-town doctor, gives up gainful employment, and experiences herself as superior to her new environs and neighbors in Gopher Prairie. Lewis plots much of her self-actualization in terms of the appeals and limitations of theatre for comfortably middle- and upper-middle-class white women of the late Progressive Era, and he balances sympathy with critique. Carol is brought up on books and charades at home. In college she pursues an education described by one critic as "entertaining and shallow."[53] This education includes a graduate seminar in drama; a sociology class taught by a Bostonian who has lived among poets, socialists, and Jews; and an inculcated (but unfulfilled) desire to read Bernard Shaw. Outside of class, she joins a half dozen arts societies and paints scenery for the dramatic club. Part of Dr. Will Kennicott's wooing includes his bid to her to "make the town . . . artistic. . . . Make us change" (22).

The town, of course, wants only to change in painless, commercial, boosterish ways and resents Carol's playing princess, Joan of Arc, and Lady Bountiful—three labels Lewis uses for her. Nonetheless, she does manage to start a Dramatic Association in 1914, and Lewis makes clear how vague her knowledge of theatre is in contrast to the drama of her own desires:

> She knew from some lost magazine article that in Dublin were innovators called The Irish Players. She knew confusedly that a man named

Gordon Craig had painted scenery—or had he written plays? She felt that in the turbulence of the drama she was discovering a history more important than the commonplace chronicles which dealt with senators and their pompous puerilities. She had a sensation of familiarity; a dream of sitting in a Brussels café and going afterward to a tiny gay theater under a cathedral wall. (204)

Carol projects her fantasies of escape, glamour, and recognition onto the site of "theatre," by which she means a particular version of the umbrella category that allows her to mark herself as special and separate from her neighbors. In fact, people in Gopher Prairie enjoy performing "stunts" (rather like vaudeville acts) at parties, and her husband proves adept as an end-man in an amateur minstrel show, so the desire to witness or participate in performances per se is not the issue. The citizenry cheers a traveling tent show production of *Sunbonnet Nell: A Dramatic Comedy of the Ozarks* and flocks to a Chatauqua that is rife with the same sorts of vaudeville and elocutionist turns they themselves do for fun. Carol's sympathetic cohorts in her Little Theatre endeavors are all female, effeminate, or outsiders and include the prissy Raymie Wutherspoon (whom her husband calls a "gentleman hen"), two female schoolteachers (one of whom is driven out of town by the unctuously religious busybody whose drunken son assaults the young teacher and then blames her for the encounter), the artistic farm boy turned tailor, Eric Valborg (whom the townies refer to as "Elizabeth"), and the socially and professionally impotent lawyer Guy Pollock. Pollock defines for Carol the "village virus" that immobilizes educated thinkers, rendering them simultaneously unable either to leave the town or to keep up with the broader culture's intellectual current. He offers his services to Carol in theatrical and feminized terms, saying he will be the sympathetic friend akin to "the confidant of the old French plays, the tiring-maid with the mirror and the loyal ears" (157). Those who embrace Carol's idea of theatre are smart and sensitive but ostracized and fairly powerless within the community. They are also seen in heightened gender terms.

Resistance to Little Theatre emerges in *Main Street* as a form of antifeminism, acted upon even within the Dramatic Association, as Carol's choice of *Androcles and the Lion* (albeit in some ways itself rather antifeminist) is voted down in favor of *The Girl from Kankakee*. The latter recuperatively "narrates the success of a farm-lassie in clearing her brother of a charge of forgery" before she goes to work for a millionaire, is social counselor to his wife, and marries the boss's son (214). Carol's research for her production involves a trip to Minneapolis to see an evening of one-act plays being offered at a school of oratory and dramatic arts. Her husband would prefer a "regular play . . . real Broadway stuff, with the New York casts," such as *Lottie of Two-Gun Rancho* or *Cops and Crooks*. Here Lewis offers a hint of the kinds of negotiations women needed to make both in choosing plays for production and even for a single evening of sitting in the audience, providing insight into some reasons why not all Little Theatre projects were as innovative or daring as latter-day observers might wish they had been.[54] Kennicott agrees to the evening of Dunsany, Yeats, Shaw, and Schnitzler because the title "How He Lied to Her Husband" sounds as though it might be "racy" (205). His later response to the Shaw play is that it was "darn fresh." The difference between "racy" and "fresh" is the difference between permissible titillation (masculine and commercial) and transgressive plays with ideas that challenge hegemony (feminine and amateur). Negotiating this continuum would be a challenge for the many Little Theatres that were tainted (according to high arts purists) with the label "community" in the 1920s and beyond.

Carol as spectator is thrilled but, despite her education, is utterly lacking in any critical tools to assess what she has seen. She is "amused" by the Shaw play but restless at the Dunsany. She is most moved by the girl who plays Maire Bruin in Yeats's "Land of Heart's Desire," seeing herself in the actress, as "transported from this sleepy small-town husband and all the rows of polite parents to the stilly loft of a thatched cottage where in a green dimness, beside a window caressed by linden branches, she bent over a chronicle of twilight women and the ancient gods" (210). The land of Carol's heart's desire is a mishmash of Brussels, New England, Paris, and Never-Never Land. As she leaves the theatre, she is energized by her need to "make the dramatic association understand her aspiration" (211), never thinking that the other participants may have motives outside of validating her ego. Her understanding of Little Theatre comprises a thrilling to her own inchoate emotions. Her production, staged in 1915, is a disaster, with hammy performances, actors arriving late for rehearsal, and too much makeup. Carol, who has bought three books about directing and design, realizes she has no talent for directing and is, moreover, perceived as bossy by the cast. She gives up on theatre. After a two-year hiatus, she tries to resuscitate the dramatic association with the help of two newcomers. They fail and, in short order, each newcomer is driven from town.

Lewis wanted his book to represent America, and not just Minnesota or even just the Midwest.[55] He carefully mapped Carol's terrain, adding to the New England forebears, the Chicago year of library school, and the Minnesota marriage, a honeymoon in the Rockies and the southwest, a second honeymoon driving through the south, and a stint in Washington, D.C., where Carol does war-relief work and achieves an independent sense of self before returning to home and husband. The one place that is conspicuously absent from his arts lover's experience of America is New York City, arguably the one place where her "heart's desire" might seem ordinary and fairly easily satisfied among the like-minded. The omission was surely deliberate and a reminder to astute readers then and now that trying to understand American Little Theatre primarily through the "big three" that most theatre histories use as examples of the whole movement—the Provincetown Players, the Neighborhood Playhouse, and the Washington Square Players—misses the issues and challenges that defined endeavors nearly everywhere else.

Two other brief mentions of theatre round out Carol's story and suggest how Little Theatre and women's involvement developed over the 1910s. In 1919, during her Washington stay, Carol attends a film in which she recognizes Eric Valborg, the effeminate and genuinely talented young tailor who was her protégé but a misfit in Gopher Prairie. The film depicts the life of artists, and Valborg portrays a composer, appearing in a beret and velvet jacket. Carol is "wretched" and speculates that she could have "made so much of him" (416). In the face of Eric's affectations, the film's false fronts, and its cheap props, her husband's dull letters now seem real and compelling. Lewis chooses a transitional moment in both Little Theatre and in American culture for Carol's mini-epiphany. A change in mood and a sharp turn away from Progressivism occurred almost immediately after the Armistice. Sympathy for anarchism virtually evaporated, lynchings increased, and, in short order, Wilson was out and Prohibition was in. The war "purged the pent-up guilts, shattered the ethos of responsibility that had permeated the rhetoric of more than a decade [and] convinced the people that they had paid the price for such comforts of modern life as they could claim . . . ."[56] The international battle had been won, in a manner of speaking; energy for social battles at home was shifted to domestic, consumer, and business concerns. Carol returns to Gopher Prairie with a new sense of adulthood and responsibility, which plays itself out in the hopeful form of standing up to her husband and insisting on good treatment and good education for their children (including the desire that her daughter become a radical and do-gooder). She has no more room for theatre. Conceivably, Lewis was tweaking the excesses of Little Theatre as much as he was writing it off. The self-serving, snobby, models in which Carol had believed offered no map for accommodation or revision.

Just before her return to Gopher Prairie, Carol encounters four debutantes in a tearoom. They are her youthful analogues, and she is suddenly made to feel decidedly un-chic, as the eighteen-year-olds clatter in "smoking cigarettes with the correct ennui and talking of 'bedroom farces' and their desire to 'run up to New York and see something racy'" (414). As Carol once did, these young women define themselves partially in terms of theatre. But as proto–jazz babies, coming of age not during muckraking Progressivism and open immigration but as Harding and quotas are about to replace Wilsonian idealism, these girls do not talk about feelings. Rather, they appropriate Kennicott's vocabulary to describe their own taste: "racy." Ann Douglas's "feminist misogyny," a shorthand for how young women in the twenties forged their ideas of independence by trying to "kill off" the effects of the Victorian matriarch, lurks about the girls, whose ennui was won, in part, by the battles fought by their feminist elders—Carol's generation.[57] It is unclear whether Carol has failed the theatre or the theatre has failed her. In either case, a connection has been severed and culturally rewired in a less inchoate but also less spiritual and idealistic way. Carol's no-nonsense concern is her children's future. Nonetheless, theatre would continue to be a piece of the puzzle comprising the ambitious and modern bourgeois woman's understanding of how to be independent, sophisticated, and emotionally fulfilled.

In 1924, Sinclair Lewis wrote an article for the *Nation* called "Main Street's Been Paved." In it, the author reports on a fictional visit to Gopher Prairie, where he himself talks to a few of the citizens—personalities well-known to American readers—about the upcoming presidential election. Lewis and the *Nation* supported the aging populist La Follette. Kennicott, who anticipates Lewis's portraying him in the article as a yahoo, is pro-Coolidge. Carol, who is "growing dumpy and static, and [has] about her an air of having lost her bloom," waffles. She admires La Follette and observes that Davis, the Democratic candidate, must be genteel, since he has been ambassador to the Court of St. James. With so many bank failures, however, she thinks it risky to experiment this year and will vote for Coolidge. As an afterthought, she brightens and asks Lewis if he has seen *The Miracle* or *St. Joan* in New York and if they were really as "lovely and artistic as people said." The last words Lewis wrote for Carol were about the theatre. Her reading still keeps her tangentially aware of and tantalized by theatre, but adult responsibilities and social context have taken their toll, producing more immediate battles to fight, as well as a partial retreat into Victorian values (gentility and the Court of St. James). One reading of this revisiting is that Lewis is criticizing former Progressives for abandoning their best ideals. Such a reading, though, may fail to take into account gender as a category. A young mother with no visible means of financial support outside her husband's income and who has experienced the derision and excoriation of her neighbors for her ideas and high spirits might understandably waffle on any number of ideals as she negotiates her own and her children's future.

Not only the fictional Carol Kennicott, but actual married women interested in theatre had a balancing act to perform. Many juggled the Victorianism into which they were born with the Progressivism, postwar consumerism, and heady isolationism in which they spent a good part of their adulthood. Nearly all had access to some money—some much more than others—but few among the married could get to it directly without spousal approval. Many were educated but also had racial and ethnic prejudices, rendering certain possible theatre projects too nervous-making.[58] Lewis hinted at all of these conundrums and was, indeed, prescient about the directions many middle-class women's lives would take in the 1920s. But women did not abandon Little Theatre in the postwar years. For twenty years that included the prelude to as well as the aftermath of World War I, middle-class and well-to-do American clubwomen, fuelled by idealism about improving audiences and by an interest in self-expression, ran one of the largest theatre development entities in American theatre history. The Drama League of America, whose rise paralleled that of Carol Kennicott and the Little Theatre movement itself, lasted until the early years of the Depression. The obvious reason for its demise was the economic climate; but with many well-off members, there were other issues. A more nuanced assessment takes gender into account.

A (Drama) League of Their Own

The Drama League of America (1910–1931) was the only project within the nexus of theatre reform activities of the 1910s and 1920s that focused from the outset on audiences. In keeping with common wisdom about theatre audiences, it targeted women as recipients of its information and as participant-members. It shifted its focus from support of "worthwhile" commercial theatre to an outright alliance with Little Theatre undertakings and goals as Little Theatre emerged. Perhaps no other undertaking of the Little Theatre movement offers as rich and as troubling a site for thinking about the role of gender and social construction in creating and supporting theatre in the second two decades of the twentieth century. The Drama League created and ran a dizzying array of projects and offered myriad member services, yet it suffered from perpetual financial difficulties and abandoned nearly as many programs as it ran. Its leaders imagined a national market and target clientele for their offerings that too often construed the larger public (or a national membership) as expanded versions of their immediate communities, failing to recognize how individual chapters had varying values and interests.

The league was founded in 1910 in Chicago as an outgrowth of the drama interests of a network of women's clubs; the league's longtime leader, Marjorie Ayres (Mrs. A. Starr) Best (1874–1942), described its founders as "a group of eager, disinterested women."[59] Single women and professionals were in the minority in virtually all the clubs that began to emerge shortly after the Civil War, and, while there were black clubs, integration was virtually unheard of. The typical clubwoman sought a role outside the home, but she imagined that public role in terms of her primary position as mother and housekeeper. Domestic feminism branched into what was called municipal or civic housekeeping as immigration, mass production, increasing numbers of children enrolled in public schools, and an industrialized workforce created social phenomena to which clubwomen might turn their energies, even if superficially, for "betterment" of the polis or just the neighborhood.

The idea for the Drama League of America originated with a special interest women's club, the Drama Club of Evanston (Illinois), which had started at the home of Alice Riley (1867–1955) as a reading group in 1901. Riley herself wrote and published children's plays, and the focus of the "Riley Circle" became drama in 1902. By 1910, her group had the enthusiasm and interest to call together sixty delegates from women's clubs representing a membership of ten thousand to a founding meeting in Chicago. The response to her invitation indicates how ready women's clubs in many locales were to embrace theatre reform. The initial goal was to improve the quality of commercial theatre, basically by supporting the good and "discouraging the bad by non-support."[60] This was achieved through published bulletins that described and recommended productions considered worthwhile (a favorite Drama League word). Marjorie Best was elected president of the new DLA. Membership cost individuals a dollar a year. Affiliate members were people belonging to a club or social group affiliated with the Drama League, a relationship established by the satellite organization paying five dollars annually. By 1912, there were ten thousand individual and one hundred thousand affiliated members; individual membership peaked in 1917 at just under 23,100, with eleven cities boasting centers with over five hundred members. Centers—at one point 114 of them—were located all over the United States with a few in Canada and included groups in Duluth, Kalamazoo, Atlanta, Cincinnati, Buffalo, Ottawa, Los Angeles, and Boston, whose membership of twenty-five hundred in 1910 made it the largest at start-up.[61]

The Drama League of America is, on the simplest level, an example of domestic feminism writ large, as members unabashedly trafficked in the rhetoric of "uplift," eschewed bedroom farces and Sunday performances, provided theatre for underprivileged children, and finally joined forces with the Church and Drama Association. The DLA's demise raises troubling questions. The relatively small amount of money that could have kept the organization going might easily have been provided by one or a few wealthy members—if one considers their assets in the abstract, minus personal inclinations or spousal control of purse strings. Yet this did not happen. (World War I hurt membership proportionally more than the stock market crash did.)[62] At the same time, the collapse of the national organization did not mean that individual constituent Drama League branches ceased to function, suggesting that local rather than national interest was what appealed to active members. Nearly all of the DLA's presidents, convention speakers, authors of study guides, and writers for its journal were men, while virtually all of the organizers, conference participants, and local representatives were women. Official rhetoric posited this male leadership as positive, but one recent historian of the league believes that it was male dominance that finally made women lose interest.[63] Perhaps the very idea of a "league of their own" began to feel to younger members like a covert version of separate but equal. By the time the DLA gave up the ghost, members had had enough. Or perhaps not enough.

For the entire existence of the DLA, gender figured in how the organization saw itself, presented itself, and was seen by outsiders. Best, a key player throughout the life of the league, was one of only two women to serve as president, both within the first five years of the organization's existence. They were followed by eleven men. The longtime editor of *Drama,* the league's journal, was a man, Theodore Ballou Hinckley; editors of individual sections of the publication and contributing editors were also all men. No matter how the league configured its activities, men were the majority of department chairs, speakers, and authors. When the league was formed in 1910, it set up eight departments, including Drama Study, Library, Junior, Plays for Amateur Acting, and the Lecture Bureau. The departments created publications and services available for local use by members, educators, or group leaders around the country. Only the Junior, Teachers, and Plays for Amateur Acting departments (focusing on women, children, and schools) were headed by women. George Pierce Baker chaired Drama Study (relieved by Columbia's Brander Matthews while Baker was on a study leave). In 1916, when the league shifted its focus from audience enlightenment concerning commercial theatre to the promotion of amateur theatre, it retooled its committees. Wellknown men were again appointed as heads, although women did much of the less glamorous labor. For instance, the Stagecraft department was formed in 1919 under Irving Pichel (who would go on to run the student sponsored Little Theatre at the University of California's Berkeley campus and then to become a character actor and director in Hollywood), but women ran the mail order department and compiled play lists for amateurs "accompanied by copious notes on costumes and make-up for the plays."[64] Gilmor Brown (best-known as artistic director of the Pasadena Playhouse) was appointed chairman of the Little and Community Theatre department in 1922. The Little Theatre State Circuit Committee was chaired by E. C. Mabie of the University of Iowa. Dr. Clarence Stratton of the St. Louis public school system chaired the DLA's High School department. Women were chairs of the Junior department (Cora Mel Patton) and the Religious Drama department (Clara Fitch), again situating them as experts in areas dealing with children and the nontheological ("soft") aspects of religion. The majority of the study guides prepared by the DLA and available to members were written by men. Most speakers at most of the league's annual conventions were men, as were the vast majority of the members of the board of directors.

It is impossible to determine whether or to what extent the choice to have men in the forefront was proactive or reactive. Marjorie Best seemed to want to do everything possible to overcome any perception that the DLA was second-rate or provincial in outlook because of being associated with women. In 1914, she proclaimed that "in its short term the [Drama League] movement has outlived the 'ignominy' of being a woman's movement . . . and now has men as presidents in nearly half of the established centers; there are more men than women on its National Board of Directors, men representing all parts of the country and all types of interests."[65] "Ignominy" was not a figment of her imagination. One New York paper ridiculed "the brand-new organization, which sweetly and blithely has undertaken to improve the intellectual tone of the American stage," making fun of both Best's name and Evanston, "the Parnassus of all the bad amateur poets in America." The article was forthrightly titled "Good Ladies Drama League the New Menace to American Stage." It concluded with a warning—quoting Walter Prichard Eaton—about the dangers of "the establishment of a censorship in the hands of any committee composed of women unfamiliar with the theatre and its possibilities."[66] (Eaton was to be elected president of the league immediately before it closed shop in 1931, suggesting that he had served as a guide to "the theatre and its possibilities," at least as he construed these.) A Chicago columnist warned of the "danger of intellectual pose," alerting readers to "beware of trickiness and intellectual snobbery."[67] Women, the backbone of the American theatre audience, and specifically those who chose to study and analyze drama were nonetheless seen by male critics and journalists as poseurs unfamiliar with the theatre. Even after fourteen years of work, the league's judgment was supposedly resented by managers and New York critics, as Heywood Broun reported that a Drama League endorsement for a play "hurts business instead of helping it. If the news gets out that the Drama League likes a play, the general public is rather apt to get the impression that here is something tedious and pretentious, to be avoided at all costs."[68] Broun did not elaborate on who comprised the "general" public, something that can itself be a journalistic construction in which a writer projects his or her values (or parochialism) onto citizens at large.

In looking for reasons other than a Manichean "male is good/female is bad" for a New York critic's idea that DLA values were not "general" values, it is worth noting that there is something slightly smarmy about much of the league's language and some of its ideas. What washed with older, midwestern members was distasteful to the New York chapter and possibly out of step for younger members, especially in the 1920s. Marjorie Best articulated the league's awareness of "the danger inherent in the powerful influence of the drama over the public, if that influence is not ennobling, uplifting."[69] "Uplift" was coupled with "the best that is done today, or the best that has been done in days past, in the shape of drama," situating 1911 activism in terms of Victorian Arnoldianism.[70] In 1912, the Junior department was reportedly "to inculcate in the young wholesome dramatic standards which shall tend toward the perfection of a fine and high national drama."[71] Ten years later, the tone had not changed. *Drama,* the league's journal, praised the efforts of three thousand members of the Federation of Women's Clubs of Youngstown, Ohio, who took up arms against Sunday performances. "Sunday is a sacred day," the women asserted, "ergo let us at least on Sunday be clean and cleansed of the 'pyjama' and 'chemise' dust which A. H. Woods presents in *Up in Mabel's Room." Drama* went on to ask how one could "blame those federated protestants, when the *revusical* comedy stresses the special value of a production in the words 'Spectacular! Pretty girls!'"[72] Marjorie Best could still claim in 1925 that part of the ongoing mission was "to crowd out vicious plays."[73] Even efforts to be more democratic smacked of piety and civic housekeeping. The 1919 eschewal of "art for art's sake" in order to pursue possibilities for self-expression in all classes was motivated by a desire to "secure certain social relations . . . . The League's chief concern is that many persons shall find delightful recreation in drama . . . people will be provided with a moral safety-valve which will assist them in maintaining a proper poise during these and troubled times."[74] Delightful recreation and a moral safety valve are a hard sell as equivalents on many adult value scales.

But the DLA did accomplish a great deal. It provided skills, training, information, and reference materials to hundreds of women who helped create and support the five thousand American Little Theatres claimed by *Variety* to exist in the mid-1920s.[75] Its original project of "bulletins" to recommend worthwhile plays had a wide reach: the 1912 bulletin had a total circulation of 95,444 copies. From 1910 to 1916, the DLA issued bulletins on 250 productions; by 1923, when the National Bulletin was discontinued, six hundred plays had been bulletined. If the early work was trained on commercial productions, it nonetheless dovetailed with many of the concerns that would underlie Little Theatre work, enabling an easy move to an alliance with Little Theatre workers and sympathizers as DLA focus shifted in the mid-1910s. The DLA's various publications served many amateurs. For example, eighteen thousand copies of a "List of Plays for Children to Act" were published in 1914; the list was successful enough to be followed by 23,500 copies of a "List of Plays for

High Schools to Act" in 1916. The Publications department selected plays for issue by Doubleday, Page and Company. The twenty Doubleday drama volumes appearing between 1913 and 1916 were among the first in what was to become a trend among many publishers to produce editions of plays.[76] More than seventy-five thousand league-created study guides were sent out on forty-four different phases of drama by 1925.[77] The DLA convention, held annually except in 1919, 1929, and 1930, was an occasion for members to hear nationally known theatre experts, visit arts sites in the sponsoring city, see Little Theatre productions, and, of course, socialize and trade ideas. In 1920, the league started a ten-day Summer Institute that offered members hands-on classes during the day and the opportunity to see productions in the evening. By 1925, the institute was a three-week offering, with classes in everything from make-up, dance, and puppetry to stagecraft and Little Theatre management. Local Drama League groups also had national impact. The Chicago Drama League's summer project of 1917 offered free classes to urban children and continued throughout the 1920s, with the inclusion of performances, as the Children's Civic Theatre at the Municipal Pier. Other league branches in other cities created similar summer programs, forging alliances with playgrounds and recreation departments. The New York branch started the Drama Book Shop—still a Times Square fixture and national resource—in 1923.[78] The DLA promoted National Drama Week beginning in 1922, when two hundred organizations in twenty cities participated. The event was carried on until 1931; its goal was to "make the people of the country understand that drama is influencing and molding their standards and ideals and that it behooves them to determine what the influence shall be."[79] The idea that dramatic presentation structures the national imagination, helping "shape and promote certain understandings of who 'we' are, of what an American looks like and believes in," is one that is still being addressed by theatre advocates as a reason to take theatre and theatre studies seriously.[80]

For every ongoing undertaking, though, there seemed to be a DLA project that was announced and abandoned, a procedure that could not have been good for credibility, either with the general public or with affiliate members. Two postwar playwriting contests were publicized in 1918, one for the best patriotic play suitable for amateur production, and the other, endorsed by Herbert Hoover, for a food conservation play. No winners were announced, and neither contest was offered a second time. A program to tour plays to remote communities, especially in Iowa, started in 1922 with E. C. Mabie as chair. A central booking office was planned for each participating state, but the project was abandoned in 1924 for lack of funds. A Better Plays Bureau, which was to negotiate reduced royalties on "high-grade" plays for groups with limited funds, was abandoned for lack of interest in 1926 after being in existence less than a year. A 1925–26 project involved weekly broadcasts of radio dramas on WLS in Chicago as the Drama League Hour. The league, WLS, and sponsor Sears Roebuck ran a nationwide Radio Play Contest that received six hundred entries. The winning play was broadcast in 1926. The contest was never repeated and the broadcasts themselves became irregular and then ceased.[81] In 1930, the league scrapped a plan to institute a Printed-Play-a-Month department, but not before the plan had been announced prior to executive approval and fifty applications received to join the club.[82] Major fund-raising efforts were undertaken in 1922, 1925, and 1927. All failed, and each had had a different target. Contributions from philanthropists did not materialize in 1922; grant applications to the Carnegie Foundation and the Laura Spelman Rockefeller Foundation were turned down in 1925; the 1927 attempt to establish a trust fund with $75,000 yielded no contributions and cost the League $4,500 in fund-raising agency fees, not to mention the $14,000 debt on which it defaulted. It ended the calendar year with more than $24,000 in outstanding bills and less than $113 in the treasury.[83]

The erratic path of the DLA's rise, success, scramble to adjust its identity to perceived social and membership needs, financial ineptitude, and limping demise is nowhere so evident as in saga of its publication, *Drama*.[84] Since a hundred affiliate members of the DLA were colleges and universities and since, as a benefit of membership, they received the publication, *Drama* was guaranteed safe harbor in the world of paper trails and research. Because *Drama*'s primary readership always comprised DLA members—predominantly women—gender is a necessary component in an assessment of the publication's cultural and intellectual role in addressing and constructing audiences.

Drama began as a quarterly in 1911 with a dual agenda: it was intended as a forum for any reader interested in new developments and issues in contemporary American theatre and drama, and it was to keep DLA members informed about league business. From the outset, however, there were few nonmember readers; DLA dues funded the publication, and members received it free as a benefit of belonging. For its first eighteen months, the *Drama—A Quarterly Review of Dramatic Literature* (the original title) was published by Chicago's Dramatic Publishing Company; in 1912, the league took over publication itself and in 1913 appointed Theodore Ballou Hinckley as editor, a position he held until his death in 1930. In 1916, the league added a new publication called *Drama League Monthly,* which was created to deliver news from local centers, reports from the various DLA departments, occasional editorials from the league president, and information about the annual conventions. As noted earlier, individual membership in the League peaked in 1917 around twenty-three thousand. Paid membership dropped precipitously to under six thousand in 1919. *Drama*'s history thereafter reads, in some ways, like a series of attempts to recoup former prestige without serious investigation into why membership was dropping and programs were being scrapped.

The quarterly and the monthly coexisted until 1919, when the two were combined as the *Drama Magazine* under Hinckley. The eight years of the quarterly's existence featured articles by many of the same writers whose work appeared in *Theatre Arts* and who were influencing the Little Theatre movement as practitioners, professors, and freelance critics. Among these were Alfred Arvold, George Pierce Baker, Maurice Browne, Barrett Clark, Jacques Copeau, Archibald Henderson, Edith Isaacs, Frederick Koch, Brander Matthews, and Stark Young. Translations of modern European plays were a staple, and a number of articles were lengthy think pieces. This profile changed with the 1919 merger, which promised a drama magazine "within the reach of all" that would not be a Drama League "organ" and whose style would be "more brief, crisp and popular than that pervading the somewhat academic quarterly."[85] Later, in 1925, the New York league's publication the *Little Theatre Monthly* was absorbed by *Drama Magazine,* appearing as its own section and focused on amateur activities.

Each shift was intended to woo readers and thereby take in enough money to stay in the black, but the fixes were temporary at best. Only three times did the league finish a year without owing money for the magazine. Under the one-term presidency of John M. Stahl (1919–1920), a Chicago businessman, membership was increased, annual dues were raised, and the salary of the *Monthly* editor/business manager was eliminated in the merger with the *Quarterly.* The history of the magazine from 1920 to 1931 is one of forming corporations, selling and giving away stock, falling woefully short on income, using various advertising executives and schemes, instituting new departments, relying on personal loans, and tending towards safety rather than challenge in editorial policy.

The 1924–25 volume showed a profit as the result of a self-conscious attempt to be more popular and to devote minimal space to experimental or "advanced" work. Nonetheless, DLA membership dropped. Attempts to sell the magazine to another publisher failed. The addition of the *Little Theatre Monthly* was concurrent with the New York chapter reaffiliating after severing its ties with the national organization shortly before. This boost in membership came close to eliminating the deficit, but it was short-lived. The New York chapter—1,289 members strong—again withdrew in 1927 because its members were not interested in the league's amateur focus and inability to affect commercial theatre.[86]

By the spring of 1929, only seventeen constituent member centers were still active in the national organization. Affiliation with the Church and Drama Association, announced by the board in 1929, dealt a blow to the DLA, as six large centers dropped their national charters in response to this. The affiliation was annulled a year later, but it proved impossible to regroup successfully. *Drama*'s final chapter has all the melodrama and all the banality of a soap opera. Hinckley begged Mrs. Best to relinquish her stock in the separate corporation that owned the failing magazine so the publication could be turned over to the Church and Drama League—an alliance he had supported but to which she had objected. She refused; *Drama* remained in the hands of the corporation and was never part of the short-lived Church and Drama League. Albert Thompson, a sometime journalist and publicist, was approached concerning the possibility of his replacing Hinckley as editor. Thompson, backed by his wife's money, purchased the magazine in June 1930, against Hinckley's wishes, judgment, and advice. Hinckley remained as coeditor and died at the end of the year. None of Thompson's plans worked out, and the magazine ceased publication the following year.

Why is gender important to this story? What did it say to and what does it say about women as audiences and DLA women as educators of audiences beyond their own membership? Why is this not merely the chronicle of an arts organization with ambitions beyond its resources and a lack of access to professional business advice? In some ways, of course, it is the latter, as much as it is, at the very end, the story of a project hurt by the financial hardships and attendant realignment of personal priorities brought on by the stock market crash. Yet a single individual who wished to finance the magazine might have done so, and well-to-do Drama League members were theoretically in a position to underwrite the publication. In fact, it was Drama League member Edith Isaacs who financed *Theatre Arts.* Isaacs, a member of the New York chapter, was one of two women who underwrote *Theatre Arts* from her arrival as an editor in 1919 until the magazine's transfer in the 1940s. She worked without pay for her entire tenure as editor-in-chief; she also made significant loans and grants to the magazine. Beginning in 1923, through Isaacs' negotiations, the magazine also received large subsidies from Dorothy Whitney Straight Elmhirst, first in the form of a $10,000 grant and later not only via direct grants but also in the form of shared resources when the magazine was incorporated into a four-publication consortium organized by Elmhirst.[87] No such person emerged for *Drama*.

To ask, though, why an individual woman did or did not support singly one magazine or another still begs the question of what was problematic about gendering a national audience construction project, not to mention the question of who fit the bill of "Woman" as imagined target for that project. Arguably it was precisely the gendered status of the project that made it iffy for anyone attuned to the idea of, say, Broun's "general public." Also, women's opportunities within theatre—a direct result of Little Theatre undertakings—shifted over the course of the 1920s, as did the focus of many women's clubs, so that even the interest of women who remained comfortable with being female-affiliated might have waned regarding the DLA in particular.

A useful starting point for thinking about these questions is Harold Ehrensperger's 1927 article "Women and the Little Theatre," which was published in the *Little Theatre Monthly* section of *Drama*. Ehrensperger was neither an occasional freelancer nor an outsider unfamiliar with the league or with theatre. A Harvard graduate who studied with George Pierce Baker, Ehrensperger had directed the Indianapolis Little Theatre and was an instructor of English at Northwestern University when he was tapped in 1923 by the president of the DLA to serve as its first full-time, paid national executive secretary. He was already editor of the "Drama League Activities" section of *Drama* and had been associate Chairman of the league's Playgoing Committee. In 1927, he became the paid editor of the *Little Theatre Monthly.* Ehrensperger's piece was a plea to women to "come to the rescue" of the "sick" Little Theatre as unsalaried, "outside" help.

There was nothing ambiguous about how the hierarchy of the theatre world was gendered for Ehrensperger and, one has to assume, for the audience he imagined responding positively to his call for aid. Citing a nameless woman who struggled to get recognition and support for her

city's Little Theatre, and having succeeded, made way for a male professional to become director, Ehrensperger touted her praiseworthiness
because "she has retired to an advisory position . . . . She represents the
role that women have played. The fine courage and robust faith that they
have shown is undoubtedly responsible for the success of the exemplary
theatres of this country. This 'suffering servant' capacity is no mean
task."[88] "Suffering servant" was, for Ehrensperger, a worthy goal for
women, even as he noted that new university programs in theatre welcomed women as students intending to work in theatre after graduation.
These women graduates expected to work for salaries and gratification,
not to suffer as unpaid servants.[89]

The DLA recognized that schools were providing theatre activities and
courses for children and that dedicated women could get training at
universities. Therefore, in 1925, they dropped the Summer Institutes,
acknowledging that these were no longer needed. DLA policies otherwise, however, did not seem to recognize significant ways in which many
American women's priorities and alliances changed after World War I.
The General Federation of Women's Clubs, with which Drama League
centers had been affiliated and which had attracted all sorts of clubs in
the heyday of municipal housekeeping, lost ground in the 1920s. The
federation's stance was, and remained, the "propagating woman's sphere
and its possibilities for altering the world, rather than working to blend
those spheres."[90] Women interested in a woman's sphere for the sake of
social change through political means might, after World War I, join the
new Women's Joint Congressional Committee, Association of University
Women, or League of Women Voters, the latter of which was openly opposed by federation groups in many states.[91] Women's professional organizations attracted those interested in gender issues and advancement
in their particular fields—fields that had barely included women when
the federation was formed in 1890. But many younger women had little
interest in political, public, or professional movements and understood
social and gender freedoms through consumerism and personal fulfillment, the latter often having to do with lifestyle in a companionate marriage. Older-style women's affiliations, whether forged to win the vote,
to achieve self-assurance through practice speaking in front of an all-
female audience, to fix social ills through civic housekeeping, or simply
for camaraderie, gave way to a revised ways of understanding independence that yielded a preference for mixing with men at work or at school,
albeit often to attract one so as to be able to vacate those very mixed are-

nas. Here was Ann Douglas's "feminist misogyny." As one writer notes, feminism in the 1920s came to mean "merely sexual liberation within the confines of domesticity."[92] The ambivalent response to this shift was expressed by Ruth Pickering, who wrote in the *Nation*, "I have traded my sense of exhilarating defiance (shall we call it feminism?) for an assurance of free and unimpeded self-expression (or shall we call that feminism?). In other words, I have grown up."[93]

Could the notion of "growing up" be applied to women as theatre audiences? Joseph Mersand would do just that in 1937, plenty late for the seeds planted by the Little Theatre movement to have come to fruition and undergird his observations. Mersand, director of the Institute of Adult Education at Boys High School in Brooklyn, wrote a paper entitled "The Woman in the Audience Grows Up: A Study of the Contribution of Female Audiences to American Drama," in which he praised female theatregoers for having moved beyond "dripping sentimentality and pish-tushery" to supporting plays on such subjects such as labor disputes, yellow fever, miscegenation, child labor, "sordidness," and "the shams of war." In a remarkable mix of paternalism, Victorianism, and Progressivism, all linked to being in-the-know about Broadway plays, Mersand saw women as "the guardians of the culture of the race" in their capacities as mothers, teachers, and "socially-minded individuals." They were valuable to the theatre because of their support of authors, producers, and directors (primarily male), about whose work they learned both by attending theatre and taking courses in drama. They presumably had the time and leisure to this because they were not gainfully employed; moreover, any woman not engaging in such activities would "undoubtedly have wasted her time gossiping or playing the latest time killing game." Women proved their mettle by embracing Clare Booth Luce's play *The Women,* which Mersand admired because it "presents the female at her worst and New Yorkers love it."[94] Mersand's stance was that women were admirable to the extent that they accommodated male-centered ideas about art that ignored (or ridiculed) many women's immediate interests and activities, especially those interests that reflected a proscribed sphere of propriety and putative appropriateness. And, again, paradoxically, actual men needed to be dragged to such serious drama since, left on their own, after having worked hard all day, they would prefer lighter theatrical fare. Women's value as "intelligent audiences" propped up male theatrical work, in part by forcing it on those other males who would have preferred something else. This value, ironically, depended on women's not actually entering the male sphere (e.g., as part of the work force), because this would eat into the time they could devote to supporting male-dominated theatre work.

The meeting place of toughness, male hegemony, and eschewing a sphere in which women might assert independence by refusing, rather than embracing, a heady mix of consumer chic and "sordidness" was, arguably, the rocky ground on which women theatregoers found themselves in the 1920s. Like the young debutantes who upset Carol Kennicott's equilibrium with their blasé smoking and plans to run up to New York and see something "racy," women audiences were encouraged by critics to accept "feminist misogyny" as a form of sophistication. Like the flappers in the *Theatre* cartoon who drop into a theatre because the are "dead on their feet" but see matinees as "dumb," women could assert independence and mark themselves as in-the-know by going on their own to, rather than by opposing, places that marketed derogatory or infantilizing images of their sex.

In many Little Theatres the plays that were the mainstays of the 1920s repertory reinforced the idea that women were silly or simply not suitable as the subject of serious drama. Frank Shay compiled *One Thousand and One Plays for the Little Theatre* in 1923. A glance at any page of this book reveals a substantial majority of male characters in most of the plays. Eugene O'Neill is particularly problematic. Few would argue with the ideas that his dramaturgy is bold, his characters strong, and his dramatic situations compelling. In this collection, his thirteen one-acts listed with cast requirements portray more than twice as many men as women, and in the "sea plays" women make mostly cameo appearances as prostitutes. The single play in which the female predominates is the one-woman "Before Breakfast," in which domestic life drives a husband to suicide. Women who might have been looking, as audiences, for a play addressing their concerns, or as amateur actresses for one in which to showcase their work, might understandably not choose O'Neill, even as they might see reasons for his critical acclaim. Plays in Shay's anthology that do feature more women than men often have titles like *Miss Myrtle Says "Yes," Womankind, Dancing Dolls,* and *Why Girls Stay Home.*

Women could pursue independence by participating in the production of plays in their communities; such plays often criticized them for being too sexual, not sufficiently interested in supporting their husbands, too materialistic, or a host of other "too's." Such plays were Broadway mainstays, resulting in the phenomenon of Little Theatres pursuing a version of mimetic sophistication by presenting recent commercial hits that depended for their arch knowingness on putting upper-middle-class women in their place. These offered the ironic comfort of selling tickets ("making the Little Theatre pay") by means of belittling its workers. Two of the most popular Little Theatre choices between 1925 and 1929 were George S. Kaufman's *Dulcy* and George Kelly's *The Torchbearers.* In *Dulcy,* a wealthy, busybody wife arranges a disastrous weekend party at her Westchester home in order to help her husband clinch a business deal and, on the side, to do some matchmaking for the potential boss's daughter. Everything that can go wrong in the world of butlers, grand pianos, golf, and millionaires does. In *The Torchbearers,* a Little Theatre group run by wealthy society matrons in an exclusive suburb mounts a ridiculous production, rife with fluffed lines, missed entrances, abysmal acting, and egos galore. The women in the play are "pampered, pompous, talentless, and brainless."[95] Only the level-headedness of the leading lady's skeptical husband diverts her from what she imagines will be her future life as a star. Such plays are, ironically, seen as having "good" (read "large and showy") roles for women. Even plays by women that represented strong characters seeking to alter the dominant discourse about women began, as early as 1915, to emphasize the primacy of women's domestic role and to see widespread feminist change as somewhere on the spectrum from impossible to deceptive.[96]

The collapse of the Drama League of America hardly meant a collapse of women's enthusiasm for going to the theatre, participating in Little Theatres, or drumming up audiences for the latter. Women, in fact, remained the core constituency of Little Theatre throughout the 1920s and whenever it resurfaced or looked for renewed support in the 1930s.[97] The first steps of the regional theatre movement in the late 1940s were spearheaded by women, notably Nina Vance in Houston, Margo Jones in Dallas, and Zelda Fichandler in Washington, D.C. But addressing women audiences as women rather than as "general" audiences went against many ideas of both sophistication and business-as-usual for middle- and upper-middle-class white women in the 1920s, and "general" audiences were assumed to share a critical stance that was dismissive of women qua women, as we have seen. Ruth Schwartz Cowan locates the start of the feminine mystique not in the 1940s or 1950s but squarely in the 1920s, when housework and consumerism came to be seen as expressions of women's fulfillment, successfully keeping women who could afford to be there at home, and encouraging the belief that unmarried women were suspect and female camaraderie old-fashioned.[98] Women who worked, joined professional associations, or remained enmeshed in politics were a decided minority and did not capture the imaginations of those women who may not have participated in activists' actual campaigns but could, in theory, have admired or supported them. Activist and working women, moreover, did not always thrive as a special minority. They continued to experience lower pay, isolation, exclusion from positions of control, and employment in gendered industries. In the realm of theatre, this meant that women as audience members, seeking acceptance, respect, and male company, often expressed themselves as women by embracing plays that shored up the social and economic status quo and that moved away from either the activism of True Womanhood or the feminist rebellions of the 1910s.

Consider the dilemma within the ranks of Drama Leaguers. The doyenne of the Drama League, Marjorie Ayres Best, was representative of, not unusual for, those few who did stick with the Drama League of America. In a Victorian or even early Progressive context, her brand of uplift, focus on children and study guides, church-friendly work (even before the official joining of forces, religious drama had been a focus of the DLA), and willingness to have members toil without pay or even official leadership positions, was appealing to many women who, like her, were born in the 1870s. By the 1920s, this profile was not so appealing, especially among younger women.[99] A 1928 datum offers insight via fashion into women's impatience with the burden of older mores and responsibilities. In 1913, three years after the start of the Drama League, the amount of fabric required for a woman's everyday outfit of clothing was 19 ¼ yards; in 1928, three years before the League's demise, it had declined to seven yards.[100] For a woman of Best's generation, the "light" look was certainly new, and possibly it felt transgressive on some level; for women born in the twentieth century it was ordinary.

Yet age is not the only way to figure group identification, as some people embrace (or even forge) new ideas more readily than others. Edith Isaacs, a peer of Best's generationally but not ideologically, was one powerful New York Drama League member who was determined to keep the New York chapter out of the national organization.[101] It is not hard to see how Isaacs, an urban Jewish woman with in-depth experience as a theatregoer and as a business professional, would have little patience for the suburban- and small city–inflected DLA brand of working with women as theatregoers and uplifters. Yet Isaacs's progressive championing in *Theatre Arts* of nuanced, nonbombastic acting, of new playwrights, of international traditions in theatre, and of the New Stagecraft, also favored a "tough" modernist aesthetic with antifeminist strains. For example, she adamantly refused to publish plays by Tennessee Williams early in his career, describing them as "'pussy' and therefore not theatre-worthy."[102] Isaacs also disliked the work of George S. Kaufman, scorning its "journalistic" style; her critique did not extend to what a later critic saw in the Kaufman and Hart collaborations: "a body of work that aches with misogyny."[103] Audiences—even some very sophisticated ones—with women in the majority, seemed for the most part indifferent to this ache, if they experienced it at all. Here, theatre played out the same feminist split that the larger culture did with regard to political and labor activism of the 1910s and 1920s: civic housekeeping struck some as too Victorian, while a tough egalitarianism paid too little attention to the materialist realities of the lives of most married, nonprofessional, nonmonied women.[104]

Seventy years after the collapse of the Drama League of America, the New York State Council on the Arts Theatre Program appointed a special task force to study the status of women in the American theatre. Their 2002 report showed that women's representation among playwrights, directors, and producers remains skewed and located largely in the amateur and the local and in theatre for young audiences, with the lion's share of Broadway and major regional theatre credits and long careers going to men. For instance, during the 2001–2 season at regional theatres, the researchers found that just 16 percent of directors and 17 percent of playwrights produced were women. But in one sense, "votes for women" is going strong: women comprised 61 percent of Broadway ticket buyers in the 1999–2000 season. Women buy tickets; they do not prefer, insist on seeing, or even necessarily note the lack of, work by women. Completing the syllogism is not difficult, but lest its readers miss the point, the NYSCA report spells it out: women audiences regard plays by women, regardless of subject or thesis, as "women's plays" and less "universal" than plays by men, regardless of subject or thesis. As one participant succinctly put it, the common wisdom is that "men are universal; women are specific."[105]

How, nearly four generations after the heyday of the American Little Theatre movement, can experimentalism, university degrees in theatre, government support for theatre, and an ongoing avant-garde tradition be a regular part of the theatre landscape, while women's participation and ways of seeing remain marginalized, ignored, or discouraged in the name of "universalism" and "professionalism?" How were the genuine achievements of the Little Theatre movement with regard to audience knowledgeability, support, and expectations still deficient with regard to women's place in theatre on both sides of the footlights? A significant part of the answer lies in the institutionalization practices of universities, secondary schools, critics, and historians, all, ironically, seeking progressivism as they understood it. The specifics of some of their undertakings are the subject of the next chapter.

Textbook Cases

Learning to Be and See Little Theatre Women

[A]udiences . . . are more interested in themselves than in anything else in the world. The selves in which they are interested are the selves that have been revealed by schools and by tradition.

—Walter Lippman, *Public Opinion*

It has been one of the ongoing arguments of this book that Little Theatre practitioners sought recognition and incomes for the same work with which they positioned themselves as rebels and critics. Not only were Little Theatre workers striving to provide "an alternative image of society to an audience that desires one";[1] as much as anything else, they worked to guarantee the existence and perpetuation of precisely such an audience. In other words, they were creating a need as much as they were satisfying one, and to do this better than haphazardly required some kind of system and ongoing visibility. The project of institutionalization gained ground in the 1920s as the number of amateur theatres grew and as theatre earned a permanent place in American schools. Seating at the public school and university table assured not only continuity but also the imprimatur of credibility; it also forced a certain amount of conservatism and safety.

149

The installation of bona fide theatre studies in the schools and universities offered a push/pull invitation to women. Just as (bohemian) free speech was not entirely free for women and Little Theatre was not a free ride to equal representation, positions for women as students and teachers of theatre in the 1920s meant being simultaneously encouraged and excluded, cultivated and scorned, relied upon and left behind. Young women claimed places as students in brand new university departments of theatre and filled slots as teachers with a specialty in high school dramatics as fine arts degrees and high school drama emerged concurrent with the "lost generation"'s women being poised to find themselves. "Lost generation" was Gertrude Stein and Ernest Hemingway's phrase for writers and others of an artistic bent born around 1900 and suffering the malaise of displacement and rootlessness resulting from coming of age during the Great War and starting their professional lives in a decade of retrenchment from political passion. The label was parsed by Malcolm Cowley with telling (if unintended) signs of how gender determined second class status even in the midst of literary and artistic lives characterized by intellectualism and dissent. Cowley noted that those who felt "lost" shared comfortable, middle-class backgrounds and a naiveté about the battles their immediate bohemian predecessors had fought on social, artistic, and political fronts. They entered adulthood in "the new era of installment buying and universal salesmanship" while "in their hearts they looked toward the past."[2] The "system of ideas" characterizing his urban writers' 1920s includes, among other things, self-expression, liberty, living for the moment, psychological adjustment, and female equality—a list that, on the surface, meshes with many Little Theatre ideals. Tellingly for both the lost generation and its noncommercial theatre, female equality is explained as comprising the "same pay, the same working conditions, the same opportunity for drinking, smoking, taking or dismissing lovers."[3] Few items on even this short list were equally accessible to both sexes, even among educated thinkers. As we shall see, though, self-expression proved a malleable enough term that it could fit with a gendered, two-tiered system of both artistry and place in the workforce.

Nowhere is it clearer how gender assumptions were being scripted onto Little Theatre enthusiasts and audiences in the name of innovation and self-expression than in educational theatre, where the ground floor was being laid in the 1920s. The implications of this gendering are two-fold. Historians of the 1910s and 1920s can, in hindsight, see and chart the emerging job titles, programs, and rhetoric that hardwired gender divisions into progressive theatre education. Such gender division meant, for example, that women as high school drama teachers not only received less pay than men but could lose their jobs for smoking, drinking, or—taking lovers aside—for marrying. That phenomenon is the subject of the next part of this chapter; the career trajectory of Dina Rees Evans, arguably the first women superstar among theatre educators, provides a preliminary map of this bumpy terrain. But students of the more recent past and of the present are often blind to the ways in which theatre history itself can do disservice to women of the Little Theatre movement through our own rhetoric, periodization, and romance with the discourse and achievements of professionalism, both scholarly and artistic. The latter part of the chapter takes up the life of Alice Gerstenberg, a one-time darling of the Little Theatre movement who is now nearly forgotten. The variety of Gerstenberg's work and the vicissitudes of her professional reputation offer a site for considering how institutionalization that is intended to create a free space for resistant discourse can double back on itself to curtail or contain the complexities of the very "difference" it purports to privilege. In that containment, not only practitioners but also audiences can be misled or shortchanged.

Little (Theatre) Women in the Classroom

The single greatest opportunity for women to be involved in noncommercial theatre in an ongoing way emerged in the 1920s as high schools instituted drama programs and universities started to offer systematic training in production leading to degrees. Young women could take advantage of the opportunity to become teachers—a respectable endeavor for those from the social class that comprised most college students—while also immersing themselves in the study and practice of drama and theatre. As a teacher, a young woman could direct, design, and even write plays while earning a steady paycheck. Her paycheck, though, would be smaller than that of her male counterparts, and she would have received her theatre training in an environment that would only thinly disguise its own "knowledge" that there were "too many" women interested in theatre and no need for them within the various adult-focused professions understood to yield a living wage in New York or at Little Theatres with paid staffs.

Kenneth Macgowan outlined the situation for women participants in most American theatre in his synoptic study *Footlights Across America*. The study surveyed all aspects of amateur theatre in the United States.

Macgowan did his research at the end of the 1920s, and virtually all of the institutions on which he reported were the products of Little Theatre activism in the late 1910s or early 1920s. Macgowan was well-suited to the undertaking to the extent that he had had his finger on the pulse of the movement since its earliest years.[4] Despite his insider status, Macgowan saw Little Theatre women as a "problem"—his assessment of the predominance of women in university drama programs of the day.[5] Elsewhere in the movement, according to Macgowan, the presence of women was either cause for annoyance, an outright embarrassment, or inappropriate. For example, in semiprofessional companies that offered some pay, Macgowan advised that it was more important to hire men than women, since it was "easy to supplement the women with amateur actresses." While this could be seen as an opportunity for amateur women to work with professional men, it could equally be read as a way of discouraging emerging professional actresses by telling them they were expendable in a way that men were not. Macgowan cavalierly noted that women who taught pantomime were laughable and that writing plays was a "man-size task." He observed without comment that there was a "decided prejudice" against women directing in Little Theatres even while noting that most members or patrons of Little Theatres were women.[6] In fairness to Macgowan, who does not discourse on these observations at any length, it would be wrong to pretend that none of those with an antifemale prejudice were themselves women who, for one reason or another, also perceived directing and playwriting as "man-size" tasks. In mentioning gender as if it were an independent category, however, Macgowan ignores the professional or class status that may have fostered such prejudices. In other words, when presented with the opportunity to work with a paid/outside/professional/successful (male) or an unpaid/local/amateur/inexperienced (female) director (or playwright), Little Theatre participants may have preferred the former because of the credentials and cachet attendant on the resume and the financial transaction.[7] Professional status became entwined with gender, but invisibility and incompetence were ascribed to gender alone, as if women were constitutionally incapable of professionalism (an essentialist argument) rather than being systematically excluded from its ranks (a materialist one). Macgowan perpetuated in print the idea that separate spheres were, if not natural, then certainly acceptable, and possibly inevitable, even as, ironically, he reported on the very systems that fostered and extended ghettoization.

   Separate spheres in the realm of formal schooling meant that gender differences were being packaged along with textbooks, productions, lectures, and labs as part of becoming "educated."[8] In his report on the thirty-five universities whose theatre departments he knew well, Macgowan found that female students constituted three quarters of the majors.[9] Among all students majoring in drama, 75 to 80 percent planned to become teachers.[10] Since 85 percent of high school teachers in America were female by 1920,[11] that preponderance of theatre majors who intended to teach was likely almost all women. Macgowan claimed they had little choice. With the prejudice against them as directors in Little Theatres, the already-gendered idea he presented of playwriting, and the absence of any mention of the design field, he observed—likely with reference to acting—that "Broadway is ready enough to receive them, but there the field is overcrowded."[12] A particular cohort of Little Theatre women came of age with largely unquestioned attitudes regarding gender as part of their educational and professional worlds, even as they were forging new identities within an emerging area of schooling and theatre.

   The appeals of both teaching and acting had precedents; their intersection was characterized by irony and a certain amount of friction. Women had been schoolteachers in American public schools since Colonial days. At first they taught the youngest children and were hired primarily in New England.[13] They became an increasing percentage of the teaching population for all ages and in all regions beginning around the middle of the nineteenth century for two reasons. First, parents and administrators were happy to have women—supposed beacons of morality and spirituality—in the classroom, where they were construed in part as surrogate mothers. This was a consideration as schools were beginning to be regarded as agents of cultural standardization. This new idea replaced the earlier, more instrumental functions schools had served as loci of acquiring minimal literacy and ciphering at one end of a short spectrum or preparation for university work—with much Latin and Greek—at the other. Schooling increasingly came to be about a vast middle realm of fitting into the social and economic order.[14] Second, women teachers commanded significantly lower salaries than men who, even with the prospect of higher salaries in the classroom, had more enticing commercial and industrial opportunities beckoning.[15] Women's lesser mobility sometimes made them much more loyal to a local school system. The Little Theatre movement dovetailed with a surge in high school teaching opportunities, as high schools were being constructed in the United States at the rate of one a day between 1890 and 1920.[16] The combination of opportunity and respectability made teaching attractive at a time when few fields were open to women at all and when a number of areas that did employ women (dressmaking, domestic service, mill-work, and factory work) were not of interest to daughters of the profes-sional-managerial class.[17]

Acting had been a professional drawing card for some American women at least since the last third of the nineteenth century. In 1870, more women professionals were employed as actresses than as anything else except teachers.[18] It was among the few professions where women's limited access to formal higher education made little difference, as most performers trained on the job. The appeal of performing as a means of self-actualization, glamour, or a last-ditch route to a paycheck runs throughout Progressive Era fiction and some drama, offering a sugges-tion of the kinds of actual frustrations and anxieties the acting might (or could be imagined to) alleviate. Middle-class Carol Kennicott's yearnings in *Main Street* (1920) for exoticism, recognition, and escape via some-thing called "theatre" were not an isolated invention of Sinclair Lewis's. Theodore Dreiser's working-class heroine in *Sister Carrie* (1900) seeks work as a show dancer when all else seems bleak. She finds her Ameri-can Dream and leaves the factory—and dependence on male support— behind when she wins accolades as an actress. Interestingly, although much of Dreiser's book focuses on financial independence and luxury, commercial musical theatre and comedy fail to satisfy Carrie once she has met the intellectual Bob Ames. He awakens in her a "call of the ideal," and she, as if foreshadowing the Little Theatre impulse, begins to con-template serious drama as an antidote to perpetual feelings of unsatis-fied desire.[19] A dozen years later, the emptiness Carrie felt was in full force for the socialite heroine Alice Gerstenberg's *Unquenched Fire*. Here, the restless and intelligent daughter of a millionaire becomes an actress when the debutante world seems to promise nothing more than an endless round of shallow social events, marriage to the highest bidder, and an obligatory damper on creativity. Theatre offers artistic fulfillment, but at the expense of family life and marriage. Consider, for instance, George Kelly's well-off suburban wives and widows fancy themselves avatars of culture among yahoos in *The Torchbearers* (1922). Of all the ways Kelly's emotionally and professionally thwarted women might seek recognition, acting is singled out by the playwright, who mocks his female characters' desires but who also touched a nerve among audiences and Little Theatre companies, who embraced the play with enthusiasm. The heroine of Henry James's *Tragic Muse* (1890)—the only one of this sampling of Progressive Era heroines to achieve greatness as a serious actress (and the only non-American heroine)—is labeled by many of the characters in the book, herself included, as pursuing an endeavor that is grotesquely about exhibitionism and display. She is also portrayed as an outsider in that she is fatherless, her mother supports her pursuit of a career, and she is Jewish. Nonetheless, she achieves the admiration of many of the novel's more conventional, elitist characters through her artistry and commercial success.[20]

Bourgeois theatre is, even in a world of separate spheres and separate gender expectations, a sanctioned site of exhibitionism, emotional display, commanding attention, and speaking with authority. If the majority of its playtexts "put women in their place," actual onstage presence defies the dramaturgy. This schema allows for both flouting and asserting authority via theatre.[21] Actresses, of course, were far less welcome in most bourgeois homes and families than they were as objects to observe onstage—a phenomenon that provides tension in the novels mentioned above. For the young woman seeking respectability and her own income but also craving creative outlet and a means of rebelling in a limited way against a restrictive social order, earning a university degree in order to become a teacher at first glance looks like a way to have her cake and eat it, too.

Women who used university study as an entrée to paid work as theatre professionals were a particular segment of a group that was itself a distinct minority. Only 3.8 percent of all American women between the ages of eighteen and twenty-one were enrolled in college in 1910, rising to 7.6 percent in 1920 and 10.5 percent by 1930.[22] Women who attended college were far less likely to marry than were other women; from the 1870s to the 1920s, between 40 and 60 percent of women college graduates did not marry, compared with 10 percent of all American women overall who did not.[23] Within the small population of women who attended college during the first three decades of the last century, theatre students were special for another reason. They participated in more coeducational classes and activities than were typical for female students.[24] Still, their situation was far from egalitarian within their departments. Women theatre students shared with their sisters in nearly all areas of study a general lack of women professors as role models in powerful positions. Throughout Macgowan's study, it is clear that theatre department chairs were men; women were most likely to be voice or elocution teachers, costume designers, or specialists in drama for children.[25] Vassar's theatre program, led by Gertrude Buck and then Hallie Flanagan in the 1920s, was an exception; not even all women's colleges favored women faculty. Women's colleges were in many instances oblivious to the "problem" of the "predominance of women" leading to "drafting faculty actors or working the better men to death"[26] and simply cross-gender cast male roles. This solution to meeting the needs of the many women students interested in performing was not part of the coeducational agenda. The fact that cross-dressing was a regular, albeit limited, part of the commercial theatre of the day did not sway this thinking.[27] Women-focused solutions to women's dilemmas in finding acting opportunities were not generally taken up outside of all-female communities.

The realm of high school drama—where unmarried female teachers with theatre training were especially employable—burgeoned between 1900 and 1925 for one major reason: it meshed with and, according to its ardent supporters, was a key means of meeting the overall goals of American secondary education. These were "health, command of fundamental processes, worthy home-membership, vocation, citizenship, worthy use of leisure, and ethical character."[28] Drama was supposed to promote teamwork, cooperation, self-discovery, good speech, understanding of self and others, and appreciation of theatre as good recreation.[29] Helen Louise Cohen's *Theatre Arts* article "Education in the Theatre Arts" cited the "inestimable assistance" to students of theatre in realizing "worthy citizenship, worthy use of leisure and ethical character."[30] The schools wanted citizenship skills that theatre could accommodate; Little Theatre workers found ways to persuade insiders and outsiders that theatre—in the hands of trained professional theatre educators—could serve America's needs. Just as women teachers in the nineteenth century had been valued as beacons of spirituality and morality whose main task was to produce citizens with a work ethic, those of the early twentieth century were supposed to impart the building blocks of citizenship within an industrialized world characterized by systematized schemas for nearly everything from the production of goods to ideas of personal hygiene. Teachers were part of the overall system that now took for granted work within Alan Trachtenberg's "incorporated" America and emphasized the need to fit in, be popular, consume in accordance with one's peers, and seek professional advice in an increasingly complex world of ideas and knowledge.[31]

The high schools that hired young women as drama teachers were also beginning to emphasize the "practical" for students. Home economics and business courses such as shorthand, bookkeeping, and what later came to be called "shop" all entered the curriculum in the first quarter of the century. All were designed along gendered lines. Girls were expected to treat homemaking as a "vocation"; only boys took shop. The commercial courses favored typing for girls and encouraged boys to prepare for work as managers and administrators.[32] As theatre teachers prepared their students for worthy citizenship via the cooperative artistry of playmaking, domestic science students made costumes, boys studying carpentry built sets, and boys in print shop provided programs. The "values and objectives" of high school dramatics were in place by 1925 and would change little over the next several decades.[33]

These values and objectives are exemplified in the work of Dina Rees Evans (1891–1989), a teacher and scholar who did much to codify and circulate them for theatre educators. Evans started her career as a high school teacher in Bozeman, Montana, and a quarter of a century later, after earning both MA and PhD with thesis and dissertation on theatre education topics, received the top high school award of the American Educational Theatre Association (A.E.T.A.). Although her advanced scholarship was unusual, Evans was in other ways typical of the drama teachers of her day. She was a member of the professional middle class (a minister's daughter) and attended a large state university (the University of South Dakota) in preparation for a teaching career. She read *Theatre Arts* and cited the magazine as a key influence during her early years in Bozeman in making her "revolt" against the painted scenery "held sacred through the years against any violation of change." Her graduate work was also undertaken at a large midwestern university (Iowa), and her master's thesis examined a typically "feminine" sphere of work: high school dramatics. In the 1920s, graduate schools had begun to encourage research in this area, and by 1930, at least eight theses had addressed some aspect of this subject.[34] Six were by women, repeating almost exactly the percentage of theatre students who were women as well as the percentage who planned to go into teaching. Evans's 1929 work "A Preliminary Study of Play Production in Secondary Schools" was singled out for enthusiastic attention by Kenneth Macgowan in his book. After completing the thesis, Evans took a job as a high school dramatics and English teacher in Cleveland Heights. Her 1932 doctoral dissertation, again at Iowa, was a study of "the effect of participation in dramatic art on social behavior and emotional attitudes" in seventy-five of her students. After completing the PhD, she began to develop a technique of "rapid analysis to enable her to discover the speech and personality needs of students and then to outline courses for their speech and per-sonality development."[35]

This spectrum from "revolt" to social engineering reflects the evolution of theatre's position in schools and universities from its arrival in the 1910s to the solidification of its status in the 1920s. The poles also reflect the ongoing conundrum for women teachers of theatre, some of whose students likely did desire "an alternative image of society," while others were probably placed in classes because of administratively or parentally determined "speech and personality needs." Moreover, not only was the student population divided into at least these two possible categories, but the teacher needed to negotiate another set of divided loyalties: to administrators as well as to students. School superintendents were characteristically male, native-born, rural-born, middle-aged, married Anglo-Saxons; the student body over which they presided mirrored a nation that, in 1910, comprised 40 percent first- or second-generation immigrants. By the 1920s, this population was overwhelmingly urban in outlook.[36] The female teacher's task was to guide students in negotiating the social needs of the present and future while embodying feminine ideals that sometimes seemed like throwbacks to the past. She was expected to be a social exemplar and was held to standards neither required of her male colleagues—who were not expected to give up their jobs if they married—nor of her professional counterparts in other fields. The number of women college graduates who married increased in the 1910s and 1920s,[37] creating a paradox for teachers: as they understood their options increasingly in terms of companionate marriage and sexual self-expression—the 1920s model of self-determining womanhood—they were virtually committing professional suicide. In other professions, the choice to marry might produce difficulties in the areas of juggling responsibilities, but it did not demand instant retirement. Teachers were caught between the rock of low pay and possible suspicion of asexuality or homosexuality if they did not marry and the hard place of no income and no professional status if they did.

Teachers were subject to public scrutiny and were urged in teacher education textbooks to control and deny themselves, since community approval was of paramount importance.[38] If the teacher's area was theatre, the potential for tension between "revolt" (her own in terms of the larger society) and social engineering (a key part of what she was expected to perform) becomes clear. One teacher education text explicitly advocated a split self, noting that "the schoolma'am must constantly be two persons of opposite tendencies. She must be the one who sees and re-presses undesirable traits and unsuitable behavior; at the same time she must also be the one who stimulates the thinking and draws forth the expression from her pupils . . . ."[39] Another noted explicitly that "an excellent teacher would not be interested in entertainment of which the community disapproved" and would be loathe to criticize "limitations on freedom."[40] Teacher education texts almost uniformly assumed that their target audience was women. Accordingly, it is impossible to dissociate entrenched beliefs about gender from "general" ideals about educational standards. Moreover, the connection between conformity and success (the latter understood to a large extent in terms of consumerism) meant that teachers who were supposed to be trafficking in ideas, creativity, expression, self-actualization, and the ability to critique social wrongs—a virtual laundry list of the goals of both Little Theatre and Progressive education—were expected to package those very things as a kind of safe product.

Dina Rees Evans's research in the mid-1920s for her master's thesis charts both the growth and the gendering of theatre studies in American high schools. The study was based on responses she received to 2,088 questionnaires she sent to American high schools ranging in size from fewer than one hundred students to seven thousand. Evans received replies from 927 schools and tabulated information about their play choices and course offerings. Just under a third of the 927 schools were teaching play production for credit.[41] She recontacted those schools and then focused on her findings from the first fifty replies she received to the second query. Finally, she visited a high school in Omaha, Nebraska, and reported in detail on her observations there. Her findings show how much the profile and practices of theatre in high school were in place by the mid-1920s. Thirty of the forty-five theatre courses reported to be regular, credit-towards-graduation courses were in existence by 1925.[42] The most popular choices among 154 full-length plays produced by high schools in the 1927–28 school year were popular Broadway shows of the early 1920s. The high schools, like the adult Little Theatres, were emphasizing production and teamwork over original writing or the development of new techniques. They straddled a line between self-fulfillment/expression (production and teamwork) and popularity/outreach (the Broadway hits). If this looks like a watering down of early Little Theatre ideals, it is worth remembering how early groups' interest in recognition, reviews, institutional support, and continuity were often stymied by a lack of attention to how to cull an audience and keep its faith, loyalty, and dollars. Four of the high school top ten plays matched four of the community theatre top ten reported in the "Billboard" section of *Drama* from October 1925 to May 1929. Those written before 1925 were *Captain Applejack* (1921) by Walter Hackett, *The Goose Hangs High* (1924) by Lewis Beach, and *The Youngest* (1924) by Philip Barry. All are sentimental and domestically oriented, although *Captain Applejack* involves swashbuckling scenes set in romantic milieus from the past as a springboard back to the present. The only Shakespeare play on the list of works produced by at least ten high schools in the country was *The Taming of the Shrew.* Students involved in high school drama learned, if only at the level of text and casting, that women's place was as sweetheart, wife, mother, and submitter to male control.

Playtexts were not alone in reinforcing gender codes in the process of learning by doing theatre. Evans's report on her visit to Technical High School details the ways in which gender lessons were part of virtually every encounter with school theatre, beginning with faculty assignments. The visit was handled by the head of the public speaking department, Mary Irene Wallace, who was in charge of all dramatic work. Evans also met the head of the English department and two drama teachers, both women, as well as the principal and teacher in charge of stagecraft, both men. Wallace's training had taken place at the Chicago Conservatory of Dramatic Art under Beverly Colfax, "instructor of social etiquette in New York City," at the Cecil Sharp School of Stratford-on-Avon, and with Irving Pichel, a colleague of Sam Hume at Berkeley who was active in the Drama Teachers' Association of California and had worked with educational projects of the Drama League of America. This department head's credentials and status reinscribed the value of deportment, Anglophilia, and urban hegemony in theatre studies—nineteenth-century values yoked to twentieth-century reform.

Evans discusses play production methods noting, not surprisingly, that the domestic science department constructed the costumes for productions while the "Stage Craft Class" provided the boys who built the sets. Stagecraft had its own class as a specialty; costume construction was, presumably, something that could be executed by any willing girl who could sew. The boys were chosen by the teacher, worked outside of class time, served as running crew for the show, and emerged from the class and the extracurricular work "so well trained that they can go on to any professional stage in the city and are frequently called on when additional help is needed in the down town theatres. They leave school with a trade." The stagecraft teacher also taught radio. Professional work, twentieth-century technology, innovation, and the popular media were associated with the male teacher and his handpicked students. The girls and their teachers embodied domesticity, taste, social etiquette, skills dissociated from ideas of marketability, and "appreciation of the finer things in life," the latter listed as a goal of the public speaking department in its grade twelve elective drama course.[43]

The close embrace among theatre, English, and speech provided a balance of credibility and rigor (English), social and professional better-ment (speech), and a mixture of fun and self-expression (theatre) with theatre insuring its worthiness by its attachment to the rhetoric of the other disciplines. Evans situated her own work within this context in part by referring to earlier studies of high school dramatics. Her study is by far more geographically and numerically comprehensive than some of the others she cites, but it offers few ideological surprises. For instance, the 1915 report issued by the National Council of Teachers of English (N.C.T.E.) refers repeatedly to "supervision," "control," and, most fre-quently, "taste." It complains that "when . . . students want dramatic en-tertainment they throw the standards of the English class to the winds." The piece wonders, how can the teacher "hope to cultivate good taste and create a demand for clean, artistic entertainment?" Control—so impor-tant to the teacher education textbook writers—showed up clearly in the Technical High School Drama class syllabus, where the teacher issued a "Caution: Do not try to read any drama until reading is assigned." The N.C.T.E. report for 1917 said that the "teacher can do for the pupils what the drama league [sic] is trying to do for the public generally." A 1924 study by Margaret Robb, "Aims and Methods of Dramatic Work in Sec-ondary Schools," noted that there should be two key objectives of such work: first, the "strengthening of certain mental functions, namely: se-lective thinking, imagination, memorization, emotional control of the body, and aesthetic appreciation for the theatre," and second, the "satisfac-tion of certain social needs, namely: education for constructive use of lei-sure, a good social spirit, and the rendering of useful services to the the-atre, a social institution." Evans cited the work of high school teachers whose drama curriculums were noteworthy. Indeed, by present-day stan-dards, some of these are rigorous enough to be suitable for college work. Occasional academic rigor aside, though, most stressed social construc-tion and citizenship in some manner. Frequently mentioned objectives were "to train individuals to meet the demands of a good environment. To help students to think health and enthusiasm. To develop the self-conscious and subdue the exuberant." Positive results were noted, in the words of teacher Mary Z. Hebden of Louisville, when "shy people 'come out' [and] forward ones . . . draw in to suit the purposes of drama; balance is the result."[44] When theatre qua theatre is mentioned, it is always in the service of either personal adjustment or, secondarily, preparing for professional work, the latter usually in technical areas, as was seen with the boys in the stagecraft class.

Women theatre educators embodied the conundrum that ran through the activism of the entire Progressive Era. A belief in the value of social change and a general desire to improve the lives of many Americans characterized the work of both conservative and liberal reformers for several decades.[45] In this context, introducing theatre to the public school curriculum was forward looking and inclusive since it embraced as goals individual expression, self-development, and problem solving across class and ethnic lines rather than rote memorization and traditional subject matter. But it was conservative and even repressive to the extent that it was marshaled to serve the objectives of producing conformist citizens via performed identities taken on during classroom exercises and productions. The female teacher with a college degree in theatre was, therefore, in some ways as much a victim of public taste as was any woman working in commercial theatre. Yet the teacher had spent some time in an environment where, to quote Alain Locke on university theatre of the late 1910s and early 1920s, "laboratory and experimental conditions have obtained."[46] Moreover, a central area of her work—teaching "expression"—was itself subject to misunderstanding and to opposing interpretations.

"Expression," which appears frequently in all theatre literature of the era, is usually left undefined and can have several referents. It was often the term used to denote what we might now simply call acting, as schools of expression trained people to do everything from interpreting roles in plays to doing public readings or simply excelling as public speakers. (Every issue of the *Emerson College Magazine* bore over the title, a quote from founder C. E. Emerson: "Expression Necessary to Evolution.") Yet the idea that expression (of ideas, feelings, self) is a key function of theatre was relatively recent. It emerged in the nineteenth century along with Romanticism and replaced earlier beliefs that theatre either existed to affect or influence audiences or to serve as a vehicle for the autonomous work of art that was the playtext.[47] Expression etymologically denotes a squeezing out of something residing deep within. This loose definition suggests reasons why expression might be construed as something amorphous and undisciplined and also as something authentic. John Dewey would argue against the former by stating that true expression was anything but an instantaneous emission and that artistry requires not only the mastery of a medium but a careful process of blending self and emotion with objectivity and idea.[48] Too much control yields a "cold" product, too little merely an outburst. With regard to acting, Dewey himself straddles the line between the individual and the collective need, noting that a part in a play is just that: "part" of a whole. Moreover, that "whole" both unifies a collective life and can remake that life. For the theatre teacher, expression, like free speech, suggests openness yet is subject to self-monitoring by the woman who cannot afford to be cast out of her job. Too, "self-expression" was a goal of many kinds of extracurriculars, not only dramatics, leaving the theatre teacher needing to locate the particular values of theatre participation in the acquisition of "cultured manners," improved oral English, and the ability to do well in the better-respected area of debate.[49]

Dina Rees Evans would be at the center of educational theatre and its advocacy for her entire career. In 1936, she was elected to the executive council of the brand new American Educational Theatre Association, forerunner to today's Association for Theatre in Higher Education and started by her university adviser, E. C. Mabie. She became vice president in 1939 and president in 1940 and won the organization's top award in 1959. Her writing during the early years of American educational theatre presents a clear picture of the gendering of an industry, whether that gendering was objectionable or even legible to most activists and participants. There are many reasons to accept that a working, middle-class woman—even one with an interest in experimental theatre—might acquiesce (or at least turn a blind eye) to restraints and prejudices affecting both her life and work in the interest of taking two steps forward for every one step back that kept her from getting fired. Educators, whatever they recognized or sacrificed privately, set public examples via their activities and proscribed spheres for their students—the audiences of the future.

The same restraints and prejudices also affected explicitly feminist theatre artists even when they could afford to subsidize their own art. Here, gender's effects on the reception of Little Theatre women's work and activism were not only the predictable resistance to the women's achievements and stated beliefs in their own lifetimes; theatre history has worked retrospectively to minimize, belittle, or ignore Little Theatre work that saw through the double standard.[50] Alice Gerstenberg, a Chicago heiress who was active in the theatre until she was sixty and continued writing plays into her eighties, might have met Dina Rees Evans at the 1959 A.E.T.A. conference both attended. But while Evans's work with youngsters and social change was lauded in the world of educational theatre, Gerstenberg's endeavors became hard to categorize, in part, perhaps, because she did not safely stay put in one job title. Theatre history's failure to account for Gerstenberg's decades of Little Theatre work is a failure to see how Little Theatre values continued to have a genuine effect on Americans years after the heyday of the movement. Audiences in Gerstenberg's long lifetime and after were taught to overlook the ironic double agenda of "innovative nostalgia," missing—in the quest for "good" literature or "cutting edge" styles—a chance to consider Little Theatre goals of community and self-expression via theatre as they might play out over a feminist lifetime.[51] The Little Theatre movement produced an audience interested in itself as revealed by (progressive) schools and by (reformed) tradition. Gerstenberg had a stake in both, as do present-day feminist scholars with a stake in the disappearance of many Little Theatre women.

Alice Gerstenberg's "Transitional" Life

Then Jane, the artist, and Jane, the woman, came face to face in the mirror, and both were smiling.

—Alice Gerstenberg, Unquenched Fire

"Overtones" (1913), a one-act play by Alice Gerstenberg (1885–1972; see fig. 5.1) is among the most anthologized plays of its era. It and Susan Glaspell's "Trifles" are the favorite examples of innovative women's writing from the Little Theatre movement. The inclusion of "Overtones" in the 1916 collection *Washington Square Plays* made it visible and easy to find as part of the history of the Washington Square Players, who presented the piece during their second season. A 1927 Greeks-to-the-present anthology of plays intended for college study included both "Overtones" and "Trifles" as exemplary modern one-acts; these were, moreover, the only two plays by women in the collection.[52] After a four-decade hiatus, interest in women dramatists of the Progressive Era resurfaced; beginning in the 1970s, Gerstenberg and Glaspell again enjoyed pride of place both in themed studies and in college surveys.[53] In the new millennium, these two writers remain central to the collection *American*

Plays of the New Woman, with Gerstenberg again represented by "Overtones."[54] "I am stamped by it as with a label," she wrote in 1950.[55]

Gerstenberg is largely forgotten outside of "Overtones." Her career challenges the familiar inherited taxonomies of Little Theatre, especially with regard to the opportunities the movement held out to and withheld from women. Her work and what could be called her lifestyle ceased to fit standard progressive, modernist, or revisionist paradigms for theatre and literature. Yet both her plays and her investment in community embodied the concerns for fellowship, self-expression, and anticommercialism that Little Theatre fought for. Moreover, her feminism—present

Fig. 5.1. Alice Gerstenberg, ca. 1915. Courtesy of Alice Gerstenberg Papers, The Newberry Library, Chicago.

in virtually all her plays—is too easily lost in critiques of her work that see only the upper-class milieus or the satirized women's behavior. Her characters' actions are often silly or extreme, but Gerstenberg is lampooning the social roles that constrain actual women as much as she is portraying individual women. She wrote more than four dozen plays[56] and two novels. Gerstenberg acted in Maurice Browne's Chicago Little Theatre for its first season (1912–1913). She started the Junior League Children's Theatre in Chicago in 1921 and in 1922 founded the Playwrights Theatre, which operated until 1945. She lent her support to a third amateur company that was named for her and founded in 1955. She was one of only two women (the other was Edith Isaacs) invited to speak at the 1936 National Drama Council and National Theatre Conference meeting, jointly sponsored by the University of Iowa's Department of Speech and Dramatic Art and the Extension Division of the State University of Iowa. She was an invited speaker at three A.E.T.A. conferences. Gerstenberg recognized that people interested in other arts were good prospects to tap as theatre supporters. She also recognized that understanding and respect for theatre lagged behind the other arts', necessitating both educating by critics and some nudging and encouragement by people who, like herself, were in a position to make theatregoing fun and comfortable for some who might otherwise stay away. She also remained involved in theatre long enough to determine that the emotional and social problems of old age could be interesting dramatic subjects.

Nonetheless, because one of Gerstenberg's earliest plays has been singled out for its formalist innovation, and because most of her later work as a writer was not of interest in New York, she has been pigeonholed—even by those who have studied her career—as a writer who made an initial splash and then failed to develop. In terms of canonicity, this is hardly inaccurate. But as an analysis of an active and visible life lived by Little Theatre principles on many fronts, it falls short. Moreover, it invites a rethinking of how the very terms used to situate the Little Theatre movement favor professional status, an idea of community based on off-Broadway rather than local ideas, and a disregard for the genuine ways in which women saw and wanted other possibilities in Little Theatre endeavors than "growing up" to write or support hard, tough plays about "serious" issues, the latter a virtual litany of Modernist and theatrical concerns vis-à-vis literature and women's failures both as writers and as consumers of plays.[57] For example, Marilyn Atlas's 1982 essay on Gerstenberg praises Gerstenberg's early work but authoritatively announces that

"Chicago . . . was the perfect place for her to begin her dramatic career, but she should have left the city."[58] Stuart Hecht asserts that Gerstenberg's recognition is deserved but also "distorted." Hers was only a "transitional life," its subject remaining "entrenched in the values and biases of an earlier age," her work failing to meet the "more sophisticated standards" of years following the her "innovative" work during the experimental 1910s, her later comedies "not on par with the work of contemporaries such as Susan Glaspell or Floyd Dell."[59]

These retrospectively prescriptive assessments, which seem to say that Gerstenberg should have known better/grown up/moved on, may reveal less about Alice Gerstenberg than they do about ways of seeing theatre and writing theatre history that privilege some kinds of activism and challenge to a status quo while scorning or ignoring others. They also participate in the ongoing bias for cutting off the Little Theatre movement at its pre-1920 knees, refusing the work of the crucial years that made noncommercial theatre an accepted form of important art and valuable pedagogy in the United States. These received categories perpetuate familiar yardsticks of success for Little Theatre innovation, yardsticks dependent on national visibility, canonicity, professionalism, and careerism. Not only were there more roadblocks for women than for men on any of these paths, but such traditionally masculinist standards overlook the possibility that some women's relation to family and community made these trajectories less pressing and less interesting than other approaches to supporting anticommercial theatre and local participation. Gerstenberg managed some of both for longer than most.

To what extent is Gerstenberg "typical" of women in the Little Theatre movement? Her social privilege and college education make her fairly ordinary within this already–self-selected group, although her great wealth puts her in a smaller category, situating her with heiresses Alice and Irene Lewisohn as artists and with the upper echelon of Drama League members. Gerstenberg's Midwest origins and achievement in New York make her a compatriot of playwrights Zona Gale, Susan Glaspell, and Zoe Akins. Like Constance D'Arcy Mackay, another woman writer from the Midwest and active in New York in the Little Theatre movement, Gerstenberg wrote plays for children. Like Zona Gale, she preferred to live in the Midwest and was devoted to her parents. A keen sense of the particular community—geographic as well as social—for which she wrote and produced characterized her own work, as it did the work of Jane Winsor Gale at the Boston Toy Theatre, Ellen Van Volkenburg (Maurice Browne's wife) at the Chicago Little Theatre, and Geraldine Wilson Knight at the Dallas Little Theatre, not to mention the less-famous founders and workers in the myriad Little Theatres that emerged in the 1920s who sought to interact with and create support for theatre within their own communities.[60] Gerstenberg, like Irene Lewisohn, never married and never had children. Other playwrights of the era who bore no children include Sophie Treadwell and Rachel Crothers, Glaspell, Mackay, and Gale (who married at fifty-four and then adopted a three-year-old girl to whose support she had already contributed). Gerstenberg is arguably atypical, however, in that she continued her involvement with theatre and playwriting for most of her life; many women playwrights turned to other kinds of writing or even other work altogether. Akins left New York to be a screenwriter; Treadwell, author of the feminist and quasi-expressionistic *Machinal,* moved to Arizona and eventually switched to writing novels; even Glaspell produced only one widely known play, *Alison's House,* after her Provincetown years, when she focused on fiction.

Gerstenberg's two unpublished autobiographies[61] reveal four ongoing passions: the theatre, her family, Chicago, and her social world. The pleasure she takes in the material aspects of the latter sometimes threatens to overwhelm the other elements in the memoirs. Food, catering, hospitality, decor, and flowers loom large, as do lists of the people involved in the arts and social activities she describes. She relates in detail what she wore for many of the activities she recounts. In her youth, clothes were made by couturieres or dressmakers who came to the home. The twenty-seven-year-old Alice appeared in *Anatol* at the Chicago Little Theatre in a fashionable, fitted afternoon dress of gray mousseline de soie "which shimmered subtly under the lights," gray satin shoes embroidered with beads, and an ankle-length white rabbit fur coat with magenta satin lining. Her childhood underwear had lace and beading and required that the laundress, with each hand-washing, rethread "yards of baby blue or pink ribbon." Gerstenberg deplored the difficulties of getting live-in help after World War I, bemoaned the post-Depression cessation of white kid gloves being de rigueur at the opera, and reports without comment her mother's cluelessness when, following a talk by Emma Goldman, Julia Gerstenberg's response to a critique of her employing servants so that she herself could be relieved of physically laboring to maintain her household's material standards was "But . . . I pay for services rendered."[62]

There is no question that Alice Gerstenberg, an only child whose grandfather was a founding member of the Chicago Board of Trade and whose father inherited that position, enjoyed a life available only to the very wealthy. It may, however, be unclear to a present-day reader that, while her life differed in degree from the standards of the more ordinary middle class, differences in kind were not as radical as they might seem at first glance. Servants were a feature of home life for all but the poorest of working-class Victorian women; those who came of age in the 1910s were the first generation of urban, middle-class women to do most of their own housework and raise their children largely without help.[63] Dressmakers served the middle as well as the upper class, albeit not as couturiers and not necessarily for the construction of every garment. White gloves were still ordinary enough in the 1950s that they could be a June Cleaver joke not because the television mom of *Leave It to Beaver* had them in her wardrobe but because of the everyday circumstances in which she wore them. The excursions and indulgence Gerstenberg enjoyed, including the opera and symphony subscriptions, would become ordinary for many upwardly mobile baby boomers. She spent childhood summers at a lake in Wisconsin, took a single trip at age nine to California and Alaska with her mother, and later traveled as a teenager to Europe once, again with her mother. She drove through New England on a short vacation with her parents when she was in her early thirties. The only other exotic travel she describes in her memoirs is a trip to Mexico with her aunt and cousins following the death of her parents when she was in her fifties. She attended Bryn Mawr ('07) because her mother wanted Alice to have the education she herself did not. Julia Gerstenberg selected the college, so it is quite possible that the feminism of Bryn Mawr's president, M. Carey Thomas, was important to the mother's ambitions for her daughter.[64] Gerstenberg enjoyed parties, clothes, dancing, and—unlike many of the Greenwich Village bohemians—she also grew up loving commercial theatre, which she experienced frequently at Chicago's Garrick Theatre. She was perhaps most unusual among the well-known Little Theatre workers of the 1910s who left home and achieved recognition in New York in that she admired and was devoted to both her parents, who, in turn, supported her efforts and doted on her.

Gerstenberg began writing professionally within a year of graduating from college. Her first four plays, one-acts written for girls in a Chicago acting school, were published in 1908 as *A Little World* and reflected college life as she had known it. Her writing during the Little Theatre years and beyond cannot be divorced from her idea of a particular audience nor from a belief that the double standard had crippling consequences for women. Her dramatic métier was frequently farce with settings and language usually realist. She wanted to induce Chicagoans with money to support noncommercial theatre and new local playwrights. She also understood that many Little Theatre participants and audiences comprised educated women whose outlets for creative activity were limited by social constraints, both class based and culture-wide. Her strategies as a writer were generally two: unusual forms conveying familiar situations, as in "Overtones," and, more frequently, easier-to-recognize forms sometimes pushed to extremes. She used both as vehicles for feminist critique. She wrote several plays with all-female casts. Her mixed casts usually have an equal, if not a greater ratio of women to men. Gerstenberg's Little Theatre one-acts are her best-known works, with *Ten One-Act Plays* enjoying fifteen printings between 1921 and 1959.[65] These plays, however, are part of a nexus of writing and theatre work that mutually constitute an "ongoing reconstruction of experience" that is gendered and that takes seriously the value of amateur theatre.

Unquenched Fire (1912), the novel that was Gerstenberg's first published work to receive some national attention, tells the story of Jane Carrington, a Chicago society girl who goes to New York to be an actress. In this book, published a year before she wrote "Overtones," Gerstenberg was already exploring what would later be called the split subject. Jane is keenly aware of her ability to be in an emotional situation while simultaneously being able to watch and chart her own reactions and those of others. The character recognizes this as an artistic skill; Gerstenberg wrote in her memoirs of her own ability to exercise this paradoxical sensibility, self-consciously filing tense or funny moments away for future use in her work even as she was experiencing their unfolding. Jane also embodies the split between "woman" and "artist"; in the end she must choose between them. The decision even to seek paid work as an actress is hardly a simple one. Jane must concoct a reason to leave home. She gives up every comfort she has known, and not only do her family and friends cut her off financially and socially, but the press reports with glee on her every action. Sister Carrie has little to lose but her factory job; Jane Carrington gambles the very material luxury to which Carrie aspires. Both Gerstenberg and her mother had been interested in being actresses; Julia's plans were simply put aside under family pressure, while Alice acted at college and in amateur settings. *Unquenched Fire* fleshes out some of the anxieties and consequences Gerstenberg may have imagined for herself. The believability of the theatre world she describes reflects the time she spent in New York with

David Belasco in negotiations for a production of a play she wrote in 1912. The production never materialized because the actress for whom Belasco had intended it as a vehicle, Nance O'Neill, was not available.

What is unusual in the novel is that Jane has entered into an unconsummated, companionate marriage with a sympathetic playwright who offers her home, shelter, and the liberating position of being respectably wedded to a man who approves of and supports her work. In the end, though, it is the husband, whom Jane has long since come to love and who has always adored her, who coolly tells her to stick with the stage and give up her ideas of a cozy home. He is unwilling to forgive her the single transgression, described in the book as what might be called heavy petting, which she guiltily needs to confess. He further informs her that he knows her better than she knows herself. Jane, a New Woman, suffers under the scrutiny of the supposedly liberal husband, berating herself for "add[ing] the curse of Adam to the curse of Eve."[66] She emerges as a star, but she is punished as a woman. Gerstenberg recognized what social historians would later see as "the limitations of willed equality," in which freethinking career women were largely subject to compulsory—and in Christine Stansell's assessment, "compulsive"—heterosexuality in a "pattern of men's privileges and women's subordination."[67] Even companionate marriage was viable largely to the extent that the man tolerated his wife's freedom; his own was a given.[68] While most of Gerstenberg's characters would opt for marriage within social conventions, few would fail to experience its strictures.

A year later, Gerstenberg wrote "Overtones," inspired by a visit to a Chicago acquaintance who had moved to Manhattan. The acquaintance asked her husband twice within a few seconds whether, as he embarked for a neighborhood visit, he was going to take the car. "At this point, I heard a click at the top of my head, as if the shutter of a camera had closed and my mind said to me about her, 'I know you have an automobile, I heard you the first time.' . . . We are not two women sitting on this couch having tea. We are four women, each with an underlying self."[69] The resultant split subject device of "Overtones" is the most common reason for the attention the play received. It portrays a meeting over tea between two young women who have both loved the same man, John, a painter. Harriet gave him up because she feared he would never make enough money to keep her comfortable; Margaret married him and they are, indeed, very poor. Margaret visits Harriet in the hope that her friend will commission a portrait and thereby provide both money and contacts; Harriet commissions the painting so she can be in John's presence again and try to win him back. These women, however, are the socially well-behaved "overtones" of their "primitive" selves, Hetty and Maggie, who speak in strident voices and state directly what the social selves repress: desperation, compromise, helplessness within proscribed roles, and hunger, both physical and emotional. The play ends twice—once with the primitive selves at each others' throats, and then, after these have exited in a blackout, again with the overtones cordially bidding each other good afternoon.

It is easy to read the play as Victoria Sullivan and James Hatch do, noting that it presents "two women solely in their relationships to a man."[70] Another frequent reading focuses on the "invention of a separate onstage character representing ones' alter ego [that was] later used by Eugene O'Neill in . . . *Strange Interlude.*"[71] Neither interpretation suggests the feminist reading that Mary Denise Maddock offers when she calls Gerstenberg's interest in the inner psyche a "critique of a society that represses women so severely that they break apart," adding that, while O'Neill's characters transcend or reconcile their warring selves, Gerstenberg's do not.[72] The emphasis on technique and the dismissal of this aspect of the subject matter foreclose a response that says "attention must be paid" to ordinary women. While each overtone is conversant with her own primitive self, and while the primitives address each other, neither social self ever speaks to the other's primitive self. Neither, in other words, acknowledges that, just like herself, the other suffers from unhappiness and repressed secrets. The women are split off from each other's honest company and comfort as much as they are from having integrated public selves.

Maddock's invocation of "a" society rather than simply "society" repressing women in this play is apt with regard to Little Theatre drama. It was created by and for bourgeois interpretive communities, some more bohemian than others. Hecht is correct in suggesting that the "popularity of Gerstenberg's plays suggests a general acceptance of her world-view by the nation's amateur theatres."[73] Many of the one-acts she wrote in the 1910s and 1920s were widely produced. But the producing groups, including colleges and Little Theatres bearing the earmarks of "community" as well as "art," were hardly all made up of Lake Shore Drive matrons married to or descended from industrial barons. The worldview that appealed—because it was recognizable to many women—was one in which most well-off and many middle-class women usually had no careers—particularly not after marriage. Among other things, in that most middle-class of female professions, teaching, working after marriage was usually forbidden by school boards, whatever a woman might wish to "choose." It was a worldview that was cognizant that men controlled finances and enforced a double standard; that working women—usually domestics in the plays—were ignored or misunderstood by their employers, male and female; and, perhaps most damning of all, that women were socialized to eschew forming strong emotional bonds with each other. Such a worldview, whether comfortably inhabited or not, would have been, especially in the 1920s, the ordinary attitude assumed in advertising and even college education, both of which usually urged middle-class women to fulfill themselves through sex appeal, marriage, housekeeping, and consumerism.[74] Plays that allowed women to embody roles challenging this setup must have satisfied, at least for some, more than only an investment in reproducing upper-class mores.

Gerstenberg's 1915 novel *The Conscience of Sarah Platt* offers a matrix for reading her other work. The story of the forty-five-year-old "spinster" whose Victorian "conscience" is the result of misguided upbringing is virtually a feminist polemic, straddling the line between melodrama and realism. The text also presents a cross-class critique of women's options in American life. Sarah is a schoolteacher in New York who enjoys the children she teaches, but who, despite having a class of sixty pupils, barely earns enough to make ends meet in her residence hotel. She depends on small gifts from family and one male friend, a hypochondriac and the true old maid of the book. Sarah's psychic tragedy occurs when she is reunited with the man she once loved but lost because she was too repressed to respond to his overtures. Given a second chance, she repeats her mistake. This time, because he is married and wants a physical relationship with her, she not only says no but suffers a nervous breakdown and chooses suicide. Gerstenberg based the character on a childhood friend of her mother's, a woman who worked as a stenographer to support her family but who, like Sarah, was underpaid in a pink collar ghetto. The woman's reticence toward a man she loved was the effect of the era's enforced "shyness and cruel silence."[75] Gerstenberg spelled out her goals in a publicity interview: "Sarah Platt's history has only been recorded to show how necessary it is for a woman to be a human being first and a woman afterward, and to learn to express her individuality with the same freedom and confidence that men do."[76]

Sarah is one of five women in the book, each offering a perspective on the "woman question." Her older sister, Grace, who is married to a wealthy man, is negligible as an intellect but is exemplary as a mother;

she wants her daughter to marry for love, not convenience, and she wants her daughter to enjoy herself and take her time about choosing a spouse. The daughter, Corinne, is athletic, free-spirited, and adores her mother. In a scene that literally relegates stuffy convention to the cutting-room floor, Corinne refuses to wait while her Aunt Sarah mends the lace trim that has started to tear from the hem of Corinne's petticoat. Rather, Corinne rips off the entire decorative circle, steps out of it, and walks away from the stricture it symbolizes. Sarah's two friends from college are a housewife and an editor. The middle-class housewife, Agnes, anticipating by at least forty years the debunking of the feminine mystique, announces that "it isn't enough . . . I want to be more than a wife and a mother, I want to be an individual, too."[77] Agnes sees her home as a prison, although it is a comfort to her husband. She hates cooking and longs to return to teaching, but her husband—who trivializes her culinary and sewing efforts as well as her conversation, although not intentionally unkindly—will not hear of it. The editor, Keturah, sports the ring of a man to whom she was engaged in her youth. When he died, rather than mourn or try to marry someone else, she realized she had grown beyond that particular love and made other choices. She has delightful memories and no regrets; Sarah has neither. Again, society "breaks women apart," both from being integrated selves and from each other. No woman character in the book is both married and leading a rich intellectual life, the latter clearly important to Sarah, Keturah, and Agnes. Sarah impresses all who meet her with her erudition and lively conversation, and Gerstenberg contrasts her with the socialites at one of Grace's parties, where only Sarah understands the art and theatre the others treat as so many chic notches on their sophisticate belts. The concerns of *Sarah Platt* include the housewife, the underpaid teacher, the independent professional woman, and the intellectually shallow snobbery of the idle rich.

Familiar forms could allow audiences to focus on social critique, free from the novelty of expressionism—the general term for objectifying a character in the manner of "Overtones"—or cubism, the term Gerstenberg used to describe her "Illuminatti in Drama Libre" (1919), in which He and She banter in phrases of one, two, or three words, whose "meaning" must be supplied by actors and staging. In "The Buffer," (1916), which uses realism that borders on lecture, an unhappy couple stays together for the sake of their daughter. The set-up had already been used by Eleanor Gates in her 1913 fantasy, *Poor Little Rich Girl*. In Gates's play, the child falls ill, dreams of parental reconciliation, and awakens to find her dream come true. Gerstenberg refused this happy ending. "The Buffer" takes seriously the question of incompatibility as well as its somatic effects on children. The family doctor suggests "the clean cut wound of divorce" (in part because he is in love with the unhappy mother) as "better than an open sore," but the parents hesitate.[78] Besides the doctor, the housemaid is the only character who sees clearly that the parents' bickering is making the child ill and old before her time. Gerstenberg portrayed servants and working women outside the educated professions sketchily, but, they, too, are sometimes given rebellious voices. Of interest as well is the refusal of the widow whom the unhappy husband loves to continue an unconsummated affair when the means for making all four adults happy has been discussed outright. The "other woman" here, far from being a villainess, is a voice of honesty and reason.

In "Hearts" (1917), Gerstenberg used obvious metaphors of a card game—playing for hearts/love, trumping others, refusing to be the dummy—to create a scenario in which the real winner prizes cooperation, not competition. The beautiful new wife of a doctor is scorned by his socialite patients because they are jealous of her good looks and of the attention men pay to her. She fakes a suicide attempt to elicit the women's assistance, whereby she can see—and show them—that their true selves do "have hearts." It is easy to read this comedy as a vaudeville sketch in which the gossips get their comeuppance, but the heroine's goal is community. "All our lives depend upon one another," she says to the frantic card player who blurts out that "If I'd known your life depended upon us I'd have done a lot of nice things for you."[79] Twelve years later, Gerstenberg again assembled a quartet of women in a home setting in "Mere Man." Here, the women are high-powered, unmarried professionals—an advertising executive, a lawyer, a financial adviser, and a doctor—who try to dissuade their pianist friend from marrying because of all the ways in which her independence will be co-opted. The pianist's wish to "triumph over the bondage of marriage and make it serve my freedom," anticipated the myth of the 1980s "superwoman" by half a century.[80] Coral may or may not be making the "right" choice. Again, the possibility of independence within marriage is left open-ended, but the existence of a community of successful women who are not in competition with each other is clearly portrayed as a supportive structure.

Gerstenberg's rendering of successful men was less sanguine. In "At the Club" (1925), three men discuss marriage and love in the safe setting of their social club.[81] One cheats on his wife but expects her to be faithful.

A second was engaged to a women he admired but ditched when he realized she'd had other male friends. His obsessive concern for purity of mind and body led him to draw false conclusions about nonsexual friendships. The third man is in love with a married woman whose husband fails to see her humanity as he polices her chastity. The cheated wife, the jilted fiancée, and the lover are all the same woman. At the play's conclusion the husband leaves with a gun to shoot her; the lover telephones her to tell her to leave the house. The indictment of male privilege could not be clearer.

Male privilege also dominates "The Unseen" (1918), a play whose title refers to what now might be casually talked about as "fate." Gerstenberg had a longstanding interest in parapsychology; in this play the description is "uncanny influences helping or harming us."[82] As Jeffery, a visionary architect, and Lois, his wife, discuss his prospects and wait to hear about a crucial commission, they berate Hulda, the Swedish maid who can't do anything right. It is easy to read the play with an eye to how the privileged professional and his spoiled wife scorn and ridicule the clumsy maid who has no training for her job and no familiarity with the culture and manners she is expected to accommodate. But Lois shares Hulda's status as well as Jeffery's. Her well-being depends on his. She has not trained Hulda properly and can find neither the time nor the skill to get that part of her responsibility right. She herself has forgotten to call the bakery to order dessert, although Jeffery initially blames Hulda. Since Jeffery makes so little money, Hulda is the only maid they can afford, but he resituates his own inadequacy as Lois's. Lois has failed to turn someone who has advertised for "general housework" into a gourmet cook, parlor maid, and butler. Hulda misplaces a crucial telegram when she is distracted by the simultaneous ringing of the telephone and Lois's relentless offstage calling for her. (Lois has lost her thimble; Gerstenberg's choice of a traditional metaphor for smallness underscores the triviality of the wife's problems and concerns.) The lost telegram, located a week later, has meant a lost commission; Jeffery goes purple with rage, curses Hulda, and fires her on the spot. She is redeemed when the newspaper reveals that the second choice for the commission was killed in a train wreck at the job—a train wreck that would have claimed Jeffery's life, were it not for the intervention of the woman he now calls an "angel." Hulda may drop plates and smile "stupidly," but she stands up for herself. She demands the wages Jeffery would deny; she states clearly that she never pretended to know how to cook more than eggs and potatoes; and she practices improving her formal serving when her employers bother to tell her the rules. Lois and Hulda both depend on Jeffery and are subject to his financial status as well as his moods, but, as the play ends, it is Lois who seems happy to remain in the doll's house while Hulda has shown some moxie.

Gerstenberg revisited the trapped-housewife-in-familiar-dramaturgy recipe in her unpublished play *Got Your Number* (1942). The "farce on numerology" features the energetic and bored wife of a well-off but un-prepossessing businessman. Jean, a cross between Hedda Gabler and Dulcy, is tired of volunteer work, animal rescue, and reading. She wishes her husband would run for office so she could have adventures and social events to attend. Her life changes when Rama, an East Indian who hires on as a butler, introduces her to numerology. Jean remakes herself, her home, and her social circle as she herself seeks a career as a numerologist. Rama is exposed as part of a con team seeking a patent the husband holds, but not until the play has devolved into mayhem. Jean realizes at the end that if she refigures her numerology using her childhood nickname rather than her proper name, she is intended to be a homebody and "an old-fashioned slave." Gerstenberg calls to mind Plautus as much as she does Kaufman, or even Ibsen. The plot is impossibly convoluted, physical comedy and types loom large, and the servants are smarter than the masters here. The cook, Maggie, exposes Rama. Jean's overworked secretary finally quits when she is pushed beyond any reasonable employment limits. Even the silly Dodo, a girl who arrives for the numerology meeting and is put to work in the kitchen, meets a man with whom she is compatible and proceeds happily with work and courtship. Jean may be financially well-off, but her life is otherwise a joke. All of the working women are more independent and self-aware than either of the upper-middle-class wives in this play. Still, the possibility of being happily married as well as professionally employed and self-aware does not materialize. Jean's infantilization is underscored by the fact that she finds her "true" self by reverting to her childhood name. Gerstenberg's dramaturgy in this play is relatively old-fashioned and her character types are familiar, but the situation she portrays should not be lost in yet another focus on form.

Reading Gerstenberg's Little Theatre work only in terms of her playwriting ignores the ways in which she wanted to weave theatremaking, outlets for women, and support for original plays into the world of Chicago's arts supporters. Her plays are an intertext to her other activities on behalf of theatre and women. Her unwillingness to leave Chicago and her social set cannot simply be dismissed as the result of her being stuck in the past. Her own view was that Chicago's "climate itself stimulates the 'I will' spirit . . . . We kept on striving to build for a richer soil for the arts."[83] No aspect of the Little Theatre movement ignored the local; even the Manhattan practitioners were writing and producing to local standards. Moreover, Little Theatre depended on the financial support of the well-off; its most bohemian practitioners never pretended otherwise. Gerstenberg left the Chicago Little Theatre at the end of its first season because Maurice Browne scorned the financiers from whom he expected help and also because he refused the advice of company members who realized that his dismissive treatment of supporting members was hurting the venture. Gerstenberg applauded his effort to create an art theatre that would pay its own way; she understandably resented the "usual tone of the radical of the day to . . . think that goodness was only a quality special to the have-nots."[84] (Browne wrote in his autobiography, *Too Late to Lament,* about his penchant for alienating people upon whose support he depended.) It would become axiomatic later in the century for regional theatres to provide perks and services for donors and volunteers, whatever artists might privately believe about the sensibilities of some of their sponsoring individuals; Gerstenberg was aware that this was a requisite schema for wooing financial supporters.

The Washington Square Players' opening of "Overtones" in 1915 took place minus Gerstenberg's presence because she was rehearsing a production of "Overtones" for Arthur and Mary Aldis's Lake Forest Players, a private amateur theatre outside Chicago. The Aldises were patrons of the arts and the wife was a playwright. As early as 1909, Arthur Aldis had articulated a view of what needed to be addressed if theatre was to merit support and recognition. Unlike music or art, he noted, theatre was not part of the recognized schooling of the well-to-do and, therefore, was not in their minds as something to be "supported." Rather, it was seen "very differently—at its best as an amusement and at its worst as a vice." To try to better the amusement morally and aesthetically, he saw two routes. One was to establish a stock company of repertory theatre with a capable director and "superior" choice of plays. "The object of such a theatre would be to try to interest the large number of theatre goers of moderate means and to gradually lead them on toward better things." The other plan would be something smaller, "to begin upon the 'intellectual heights', hoping that their rarefied atmosphere would be gradually enjoyed by more and more people."[85] Gerstenberg participated in the latter but also realized there was a third strategy. She grasped that overcoming the view of theatre as trivial or faintly disreputable could have as much to do with who attended as with content. She perceived that social acceptability could be used as a means to support commercial ventures and thereby acclimate the elite to an art form that they then might be persuaded to support in more experimental undertakings. Recall that Gerstenberg had enjoyed star vehicles as a child. Theatregoing had been ordinary enough among arts supporters in the late nineteenth century. When she came of age as a playwright, however, well-mounted touring vehicles were on the way out, and bids to "elevate" drama were not uncommon.

In 1926, Gerstenberg was engaged by a wealthy member of vaudeville's Orpheum Circuit board of directors to provide personal attention and ticketbuying assistance to "the elite of the town" who might otherwise have stayed away. For two years, she watched every production, filed reports with the New York office, and "work[ed] up a clientele to be regulars every week."[86] Her goal was in part simply to get socialites to feel that theatre was desirable, but she used her position and the Palace Theatre itself to support the work of the amateur writers and actors in the Playwrights Theatre, an organization she founded in 1922 to produce the original work of Chicago playwrights. Between matinees and evening shows, she organized Twilight Play readings, inviting audience members with tickets to the earlier matinee to stay for the readings and those arriving for the Twilight play to return for the evening show, following a discussion of the original play over a quick dinner at a local eatery. The Palace provided the room for the readings. For a brief time beginning in 1936, the Players Theatre shared a building with a theatre school, but when the owners reclaimed the building for another use, the PT again became a movable feast of sorts. Among the playwrights whose work the PT presented was Michael Todd, the Hollywood director.

Gerstenberg used her position as a publicist for a commercial producer in the late 1920s to facilitate a professional reading of a play for a fledgling playwriting student at Northwestern. The student, Anne Frierson, had written *Quagmire* for an African American cast. Gerstenberg arranged for the visiting company of *In Abraham's Bosom,* Paul Green's Pulitzer Prize winner, to read the play, which was reviewed favorably in the *Daily News.* In the 1930s, she worked at Hubert Osborne's repertory company to make subscribers feel welcome. She used her membership in Chicago's Arts Club to arrange for Playwrights Theatre readings and productions that would have guaranteed audiences and interest. Local awareness of local work was her mission. "The Little Theatre must grow roots deep in its own area because that is where it functions to benefit the inhabitants." She also believed that local critics had a responsibility to help educate audiences, not by praising all things local but by providing the context for recognizing experiments either in dramaturgy or in organizational structure. Her 1936 talk at the joint meeting of the National Drama Council and National Theatre Conference reflected her concerns and addressed "Experimental productions of new scripts. Responsibility of the Community theatre for the experimental production of plays written by local playwrights. The organization of the audience for experimental productions."[87]

Average playgoers were not irrelevant to Gerstenberg, regardless of the contours of her personal social world. The preface she wrote for a 1934 anthology of one-act plays talks briefly about the one-act form but is also of interest for its ideas about how audiences might be better treated and given more for their money. She recognized that the usual 8:45 curtain suited the "fashionables" who liked to dine at leisure but that it created a problem for working people who hardly wished to race home between work and theatre but who, otherwise, were left with time to kill, even after dinner in an affordable restaurant. Gerstenberg suggested that theatres open at seven-thirty and make their smoking rooms available for a half hour of relaxing and reading the paper, followed by a one-act play as a curtain raiser. Like the "workshop annex" Sheldon Cheney advocated for the string of art theatres he envisioned across the nation, these curtain raisers would offer a take-it-or-leave-it opportunity for curious audiences to experiment with the new in the midst of safer offerings.[88] The productions would also, of course, offer opportunities for playwrights.

Much of the theatre work that Gerstenberg did challenges ideas about theatrical significance because she crossed the lines between "art" and "community" with seeming abandon and because the designation "experimental" is so often reserved for the former. Yet she enabled people who might otherwise not have chosen to do theatre or who might have done it with less guidance to turn their expressive and teamwork energies precisely to theatre, by willingly venturing into new territories. She founded the Junior League children's theatre in 1921 because she realized that the league president's request to start a theatre group would pose a rehearsal problem for an adult-focused venture. The young women members, most of whom were married, were expected to be home at night, and working men could not rehearse during the day. Gerstenberg proposed plays for children, since many of the then-popular fairy tales and stories about children lent themselves to all-female casts. Her idea was to give opportunities to more young women, but she was also aware of these particular amateur participants' need for assurance that cross-gender casting would not make them look ridiculous, as it might well have in a realist or classical endeavor. Also, plays for children were not being offered elsewhere in Chicago. Gerstenberg's experience with her adaptation of *Alice in Wonderland,* which had run briefly on Broadway in 1915, made her aware of the problems of mounting a production whose target audience was really only available for matinees.[89] In 1929, she was commissioned to write a stage adaptation of *The Water Babies,* a children's book, for the Repertory Theatre of Boston expressly for a run for children. Shortly thereafter the Junior League of New York offered her an office from which to set up a children's theatre for them.

The expectation that theatre for young audiences was appropriately the province of women has only recently begun to change. Concomitantly, creative drama, another branch of traditionally women-run theatre for young people, has only relatively recently been acknowledged as an activity that too often fosters the perpetuation of restrictive gender roles.[90] Gerstenberg accepted the opportunity to create plays for children because occasions arose and because she typically welcomed chances to involve people in theatre as a creative outlet. She paid more attention to creating opportunities for people to make and experience original, non-commercial theatre in Chicago than she did to maintaining a position within the professional theatre community. The idea that she failed to live up to some kind of potential or to leave the right legacy needs to be weighed against the paucity of opportunities for professional women playwrights in New York (and their virtual absence elsewhere). Moreover, many of the Little Theatre workers of the 1910s continued their involvement with theatre in the 1920s as teachers, lecturers, writers in other genres, or freelance directors, all roles that Gerstenberg herself played. The theatre work available to Gerstenberg as a Chicagoan, a woman, and a playwright allowed her to explore ideas and reach others for many years, within particular parameters of that combination.

As late as 1947, Gerstenberg was interviewed for the *Chicago Daily News,* where she objected to psychiatrist George W. Crane's assertion that "most bachelors and old maids are like turtles," since "persons who don't marry withdraw into a shell and lose interest in the world." Gerstenberg not only called Crane "fifty years behind the times," she also noted that unmarried women both avoid being "chained to a stove" and often show more "maternal interest in humanity than a lot of married women."[91] The implications of her shorthand reply would be unpacked in some detail a half century later by Shannon Jackson in a study of Hull-House and Jane Addams, another unmarried woman who worked for social change in Chicago. Jackson notes the anxiety and criticism that come into play in discussions of unmarried civic housekeepers and proposes "asking why biological connection always serves as the index of motherhood and whether 'childlessness' is experienced as an absolute condition."[92]

Gerstenberg's ideas about domesticity are complicated. She wrote that she believed most people needed marriage and children and that this was the bedrock of human society, yet she herself prized her independence and realized that marriage might well have interfered with the work she valued. She also noted that half her graduating class at Bryn Mawr did not marry and she referred to her books as her children.[93] This tangle of values and terminology (spinsters as maternal; books as children; the unmarried as turtles; biology as the index of motherhood) suggests some of the common assumptions with which Gerstenberg struggled in her own life. Yet she also believed in the social and artistic contribution that the woman not employed outside the home could make to her city and to her own family. For instance, it is easy to read her dismay over the "servant problem" as class privilege and resentment, but Gerstenberg's concerns were not for the impossibility of leading an idle life without household help; rather, she was dismayed at the intellectual poverty and the consumerist self-absorption of many of the financially comfortable housewives she saw. She believed that a well-off wife who was supported by her husband yet had time for nothing but the proverbial cooking and cleaning was little better than the lowest of wage-slaves. Such a wife might do better both for her own well-being and for the social order if she reevaluated her priorities. In a 1967 letter to the Bryn Mawr *Alumnae Bulletin,* Gerstenberg weighed in on a discussion about "the servant problem which can play such an integral part in curtailing, or expanding, intellectual pursuits for women." At age eighty-one, she might have been forgiven for taking a nostalgic tack, but this is not what she did. Rather she advocated allowing tax deductions for paying domestics, thereby offering incentive to expand the labor market. Moreover, she urged "upgrading" the social standing of domestic workers "to that of airline hostess, nurse, Peace Corps worker, etc." Finally, if educated women could not appreciate that they had the financial means to liberate themselves from at least part of the stultifying life that Betty Friedan exposed in such detail, Gerstenberg suggested they might rethink domestic help—the key to more time for intellectual or artistic enrichment—as being better than a mink for the kind of status that really counts.[94] The economic questions raised in the 1990s by Nannygate suggest that the cross-class, gender-related challenges Gerstenberg posed were far from resolved by the end of the century, ranking her among progressive rather than regressive thinkers.

The combination of Little Theatre ideals and the concerns of senior citizenship may seem like the forced marriage of an odd couple. Little Theatre of the 1910s is stereotyped as youthful rebellion staged via iconoclasm and self-expression; women's involvement in the 1920s community expansion of Little Theatre can be ridiculed as arising from a need for glamour or for compensatory attention-getting. Soul-searching in the face of aging gets almost no mention in either scheme, although the topic of Alice Brown's "Joint Owners in Spain"—a pair of querulous old women in a public home for the aged (a play in which Gerstenberg appeared in 1913)—is an exception. Gerstenberg wrote her own play about aging in 1922. "Ever Young" portrays four socialites in their late fifties and early sixties who gather every evening after dinner at their hotel in Palm Springs to lament their invisibility within a world that prizes youth. Each has a symbol of how she defines and defends herself. One carries a lorgnette with which to look down on others; a second hides behind the domestic safety of knitting; a third needs support and walks with a cane; the fourth wears a strand of pearls for every man who has been her spouse or lover. The women achieve self-awareness, tentative autonomy, and community by renouncing their received roles and crutches. The lorgnette gives way to generosity and truth telling. The pearl-wearing friend gives up her admirer since he is the fantasy lover who enables her friend to walk without the cane. She chooses generosity rather than continue the lifelong practice of competing for men and placing that activity ahead of maintaining loyalty with other women.

"Relational values," a concern of feminist playwrights through the middle of the 1910s, was replaced by this same segment of the American playwriting community in the late 1910s and early 1920s with a focus on individualism, only to yield later in the 1920s to a recognition that somehow women had been co-opted in a system that might make some women's immediate lives easier but that did so by insuring the continuance of the structures producing the problems of inequality in the first place.[95] Gerstenberg was certainly "traditional" in that she always recognized the value of female and family relations; she was nontraditional for always seeing the trap of giving up too much of one's identity within a marriage. She prized both individualism and family life. In her own case, she turned down a few marriage proposals and lamented the lack of others, but she did not eschew that most homely of duties—nursing both parents through their final months. Her first mention in her memoir of the wealth of drama that could be mined if playwrights considered the elderly is a conclusion to her description of her father's fear and disorientation shortly before his death.[96] Theatre by and about senior citizens would not gain public attention until the 1980s, but Gerstenberg began such work decades earlier. In the 1950s, dismayed by the death of a friend who had shut herself in and drunk herself to death after her husband's demise, Gerstenberg wrote a three-act play called *The Hourglass* as both a protest against the emptiness of the lives of older women and a bid to her cohort to attend to their inner resources. She also wrote *On the Beam,* a play about using spiritual resources to combat the loss of faith in oneself that forced retirement can induce. Gerstenberg would follow her own advice again by writing *Time for Living* in 1969.

Alice Gerstenberg's career is unthinkable outside the parameters and influence of the Little Theatre movement. She took seriously a belief in the local and in the value, for participants in all departments, of a supportive community of theatre workers. She lectured on, taught, or practiced playwriting for most of her life. She believed that playwrights deserved a forum for their work, whether or not it would all end up on Broadway or in anthologies, and she created opportunities for original plays to be heard. She wanted audiences to have the opportunity to experience new work and she wanted critics to create a climate in which that work would be legible and welcome. Many of her plays feature financially comfortable women in domestic environs, yet she used familiar settings to challenge received opinion and social strictures. As Janice Radway asserts in her study of romance novels and their readership, the fact that a genre fails to meet the formalist criteria of the theorists or scholars does not automatically mean that it is of no use in developing self-awareness and the ability to be assertive among members of its target audience. The difference between value to scholars and value to the users of literature is particularly important in theatre, where meaningful growth may occur as a result of participation in a production as much from the originality of the script that is the springboard for the production. Gerstenberg worked both sides of the art/community fence within Little Theatre, thereby inviting a consideration of the multiple uses of the word "experimental." At face value "experimental" is often used in discussions of art to refer to something untried or simply new. But another dictionary definition is "based on experience and practical evidence rather than on ideas."[97] Most readers would recognize this definition in relation to that familiar school experience, the science experiment, where an experiment is an exercise that is not about proving anything new, but rather about experiencing first-hand the already-known. Much experimentation in amateur or educational theatre is about the first-hand, and what is new in that for the novice participant. Moreover, "experimental" can become a catchall adjective for theatre that is "downtown" or anticommercial but that can still, within those designations, be derivative or predictable. It remains a challenge to audiences reading about Little Theatre or other experimental work of the past and to audiences encountering present-day work to consider the sorts of uses—obfuscating as well as challenging—to which "experimental" is applied or denied.

Alice Gerstenberg greeted changes with a willingness to go on writing, producing, and speaking about and on behalf of women and theatre. Her life was indeed transitional in the sense that she made rather than resisted changes. If she was unwilling or unable to play the role of tough rebel or to give up her financial status—something that few theatre artists who achieve success rarely do anyway—she accomplished for decades the feat that was often short-lived for female playwrights of the Progressive Era. Alice the artist and Alice the woman continued to face each other in the mirror. One can imagine they were often smiling.

Modeling a Future

The Dallas Little Theatre and "The No 'Count Boy"

Actors, like poets, are born; technicians are made; and audiences can be made—better.
—Florence Busby, "Making an Audience Alert"

In 1925, the Dallas Little Theatre won first place in New York City's Little Theatre Tournament with its production of Paul Green's one-act "The No 'Count Boy." The company made national news for this victory, in part because it was their second consecutive prize in the Broadway-based competition. The DLT would take first place yet again in 1926 and in 1927 would serve as the ideal Little Theatre for the *Encyclopedia Britannica's* entry on the subject. The 1924 and 1926 prize-winning plays were John William Rogers's "Judge Lynch" and Margaret Larkin's "El Cristo," treating, respectively, lynching and the *penitente* religious sect in New Mexico. Although neither of these playwrights achieved national recognition, Paul Green went on to win the Pulitzer Prize for *In Abraham's Bosom,* which opened on Broadway in 1926, and the leading actress from "The No 'Count Boy" left Dallas for a Broadway career. The ability of the Dallas company to mount winning productions with able actors, to bet on an unknown writer on the cusp of international fame, to hire up-and-coming young directors, and to find funding for two new buildings within a decade all made it a model in its day for existing companies around the country and an inspiration for the founding of dozens of Little Theatres in Texas.[1] By one account, it was "among Little Theaters in the United States . . . conceded to be second to none."[2] The DLT ceased operation in 1943, but four years later, when Margo Jones started Theatre 47, one of the first of the American regional theatres that would burgeon in the 1960s, she used lists left by the DLT as her membership basis. Accordingly, the DLT is the terminus of this book because it can be studied both as a capstone to the Little Theatre project begun around 1912 and as a springboard for the regional and community theatre networks that emerged in later decades.

The Dallas production of "The No 'Count Boy" accomplished what so much Little Theatre work had aimed for and what so much regional theatre work still aspires to—bringing to life an original play that challenges mainstream audiences without alienating them. Green's play is not a piece of abstract writing; rather, it fits a category of work that would remain a locus of progressivism and controversy right into the present. It represents ethnic "others" as "universal" yet with many details of cultural specificity, and its sympathetic portrayal of rural African American characters was crafted with the expectation that its audiences would be white. While the script was soon embraced by African American companies, the DLT production was offered by whites in blackface. Appreciating the success of the production requires an investigation of the terms of both liberalism and iconoclasm at the time of the production. Appreciating the ways in which it set the stage for much of the programming and dramaturgical controversies that would continue right into the twenty-first century requires not just an idea of how social activism and access to public representation have changed but also a look at the ways in which the very audience the Little Theatre movement successfully constructed problematizes activism and representation.

A Prize-Winning Company

Members of the Dallas Women's Forum launched the DLT in 1920. The small constituency that asked the larger forum membership of well-to-do women to endorse the theatre cited their desire to participate in "a civic and democratic movement fostered in the Eastern and Western cities, by the public schools and universities, in reply to the need for broader culture."[3] The theatre's charter, like the proposal, invokes ideas that had circulated in the previous decade, noting that the theatre's purpose "is the promotion of dramatic expression as a fine art, especially amateur dramatic expression, and for the support of the literary and scientific undertaking implied in the promotion thereof."[4] As what might be called a second wave Little Theatre, the DLT experimented less with new ideas per se than with transplanting these ideas to their home soil and making them take root locally. Although the founders themselves were not artists, the charter focused on the needs of participants ("expression") more than audiences or the community at large, who are implied as "support." From the start, the theatre served the needs of its participants, donors, and first-night audiences and struggled with how and how much to include a larger public.

Early choices in artistic leadership reveal familiar gender biases bundled with ideas of progress. The first director of the DLT was a local teacher of expression, Lena Budd Powers. Powers directed five of the seven productions of the 1920–21 season and all but one of the eleven offerings of 1921–22. Reviews of her productions were favorable, but the company wanted a "professional" director.[5] Powers was the last unpaid DLT director. In 1922, Alexander Dean, a graduate of Dartmouth and of George Pierce Baker's 47 Workshop, was appointed director of the DLT following two years on the faculty of the University of Montana. He left Dallas after one year to become an associate professor of dramatic arts at Northwestern University and was, in turn, replaced by Oliver Hinsdell, a graduate of Northwestern who had served for two years as director of New Orleans's Petit Théâtre du Vieux Carré. The shift in directorship is an index of how Little Theatre values retooled ideas of worthwhile amateurism and self-actualization in terms of university-acquired professionalism and imported leadership.

Both Dean and Hinsdell issued formal statements espousing egalitarianism. Dean declared his belief that "playgoers proper" could support the theatre and that "patronage" should be "dispensed with." He also claimed that since the Little Theatre was "for the people," there should be no class distinction in casting. "Anybody could try out," he wrote in a mission statement. "The best actor was to play the part." Hinsdell reiterated the open shop stance, inviting participation "regardless of . . . occupation or social standing."[6] He diplomatically insisted that the "little theatre must be for the masses and not the classes," while again, like Dean, stating that it must be "self-supporting." Unlike Dean, though, Hinsdell did not eschew patronage outright. DLT records reveal that a single patron, Louis Lipsitz, intended to donate most of the necessary capital for the theatre's second new building. When Lipsitz died and the money was not forthcoming from his estate, the theatre took out a large mortgage that it was unable to pay off. DLT historian Henry Edgar Hammack believes that overspending during Hinsdell's years at the helm put the theatre in a financial situation from which it was never able to recover[7]—an ironic situation in light of Hinsdell's how-to book *Making the Little Theatre Pay.*

Hinsdell also recognized that "the process of educating an audience is a slow one and requires infinite patience." For Hinsdell this educating was a gendered project. "To be sure," he noted, "there were a few women with great enough vision to see the real value. The men seemed to think it a fad" and regarded it as a place for women to "pass their time away . . . to indulge their vanities." Approaching men through their luncheon clubs was his answer.[8] The goal was for the men to write (or allow their wives to write) checks to the theatre as much as it was to earn their general goodwill. Hinsdell balanced statements about inclusiveness with practices that were exclusionary. At the gala formal opening of the DLT's new building in 1927, he delivered a speech that again stressed the theatre's formal desire for "everybody to be able to come here to live and to laugh and to play together . . . . We are all amateurs."[9] The price of opening night tickets, as well as the price of membership in general, however, guaranteed a well-off constituency. Tickets for the gala cost five or ten dollars depending on seat location; extra programs were sold for five dollars apiece.

It would be easy to say that the high-price gala and souvenir program were never intended for general audience members, but the elite audience colored the way some in Dallas viewed the theatre. Critics commented upon the self-absorbed behavior of the theatre's socialite audience and on the theatre's skittishness about venturing too far into the realms of seriousness or experimentation, the latter policy presumably adopted to accommodate the influential component of the audience. Levi Burgess, a one-time president of the Drama League of America, attended opening night of the DLT's *The Silver Cord* in February 1930 and later described the audience as "the rudest outside of Mayfair."[10] John William Rogers in his 1925 review of *The Tragedy of Nan* regretted "the tardy arrival of several dinner parties full of suppressed hilarity." Surely, he suggested, those who cared enough about the theatre to invite friends to suppers beforehand could "arrange to have guests at the theater some time before the middle or end of the first act."[11] The *Dallas Morning News* commented that opening night as "society night" at the theatre regularly included groups who arrived late and treated the performance as an interlude between dinner and postperformance sociability.[12]

Department store displays publicizing the theatre during its annual subscription drive further complicate an assessment of the company's public profile. The stores were downtown and probably included Neiman Marcus, which was founded in 1907 and both of whose namesakes were DLT subscribers. The store then, as now, was associated with the sort of excess and fantasy for which its catalogues are famous.[13] Creating an equation of Little Theatre with a glamorous outing helped minimize any sense that amateur work might be dreary or didactic. Of course, for those who could only afford to look and not to buy in Neiman Marcus, the equation could backfire. When the theatre fell on especially hard times in the 1930s, it sought new subscribers outside the usual ranks of the elite. The *Dallas Morning News* quoted one presumably non-elite new subscriber's surprise at being approached: "I didn't know the Little Theatre wanted me to come to its shows. I'll be glad to."[14]

Programming was also a source of compromise and criticism, and observers commented on the audience's conventional morality and its preference for light fare. In the 1924–25 season, Eugene O'Neill's *The Emperor Jones* was to be the second production if Anna Cora Mowatt's 1845 comedy of manners *Fashion,* the season opener, was a success. If not, something "less experimental" was to be substituted.[15] (*The Emperor Jones* was presented.) Howard Aronson complained in a 1929 letter to the *Daily Times Herald* that "Broadway 'successes' are not the bill of fare to serve up to a Little Theater audience, unless the mentality of the Little theater [*sic*] audience differs from what it used to be."[16] Rogers's review of the 1930 *Camille* damned leading actress Julia Hogan with faint praise, noting that "she never discarded a lady-like refinement which clung to her shoulders like a fragile, shimmering scarf. To put real flesh and blood into a character like Camille would have probably proved so alarming to Little Theater audiences that Miss Julia may have chosen the best way to trip along the primrose path."[17] The following year, Somerset Maugham's *The Constant Wife* opened following two bills of short plays originally presented by the Washington Square Players. Rogers pointedly commented that "after venturing twice into the less conventional paths of drama, the Dallas Little Theater has fled incontinently back to Broadway."[18] Even the classics were subject to revision along prim guidelines. The 1938 production of *Lysistrata* "employ[ed] a theme that may be objectionable to a good many citizens, but the text has been pruned, almost to the dry bone."[19]

One way to generate income regardless of audience skittishness about programming was to set up a school. The DLT's first "Laboratory School of the Theatre" was a summer project started in 1927 as a result of requests from participants at the Southwest Theatre Conference in April of that year.[20] In 1936, the DLT opened a school with a full-time program that featured some courses for college credit through Southern Methodist University, forging an alliance between two branches of Little Theatre. There were also individualized courses of training, and the school brochure hinted that students would be involved in Little Theatre productions. It also cited a connection between Hollywood motion picture casting and the DLT. The school was run by Charles H. Meredith, a one-time silent film star who replaced Hinsdell as artistic director in 1931. The path from Little Theatre and amateur status to commercial entertainment and mass-circulation success was established in the necessary interest of income, although under the rubric of education. The work of the school appealed to the students' own ambitions as well as depending on a certain managerial blind eye to audiences, who increasingly looked for Broadway standards and therefore had little interest in paying to see students perform.[21]

No single project or production made the DLT "second to none," but in the aggregate, the company was a standout, at least in the 1920s. Arguably, it was the acumen of a single woman that put the Dallas Little Theatre in the national limelight via her willingness to use her own money, her capacity for keeping her finger on the pulse of national developments in Little Theatre, and her interest in presenting challenging plays. Geraldine Wilson (Mrs. R. E. L.) Knight (1896–1949), a Dallas heiress who attended Wellesley College and graduated from the University of Texas, joined the theatre during the 1921–22 season and was elected president for the first of three consecutive seasons in the spring of 1923.[22] According to early members of the company, it was she who engaged Hinsdell, donated the land for the first theatre building on Olive Street, and arranged to form a stock company to finance that building.[23] It was also Knight who wanted the company to enter the Little Theatre Tournament in 1924 and who, despite others' doubts, funded the trip.[24] Later that year, it was she who read "The No 'Count Boy" in *Theatre Arts Monthly* and suggested it for the 1925 tournament. She would play the lead in the piece and shortly after the victory in New York would conceive and expedite the idea of presenting a play with participants from Little Theatres in Pasadena, New Orleans, Chicago, Evanston, Buffalo, Chapel Hill, Birmingham, Kansas City, Chicago, and Dallas, and hosting the production of *Outward Bound* in Dallas.[25] Entering her third term as president of the DLT, she cited a new building as one of her objectives and started a building campaign.[26] During the three years of her presidency, the mayor of Dallas declared Dallas Little Theatre Week each spring. Knight left Dallas upon her husband's death in the middle of her third term as president. She moved to Cincinnati and then New York, where she was to enjoy a two-decade career as an actress using the stage name Margaret Douglass. She married H. Ben Smith, her leading man from "The No 'Count Boy" and appeared on Broadway during the 1930s and 1940s in *Russet Mantle, The Fatal Weekend, The Women,* and *Bloomer Girl.*

Unquestionably, the victories in the Little Theatre Tournament helped publicize the artistry of the DLT. The tournament was sponsored by the New York branch of the Drama League, and its stated purpose was to enable Little Theatres in the metropolitan area to see each others' work.[27] The event's founder, Walter Hartwig, defended the first tournament against at least one accusation that it was intended to "point the finger of scorn at Broadway."[28] The tournament, he claimed, was strictly for the pleasure and interests of the Little Theatres, their members, and their audiences. But surely part of that pleasure had to do with venue, visibility, and prizes. The silver cup that was awarded annually was the gift of David Belasco, the Broadway producer who once ridiculed the efforts of Little Theatre workers, disparaging "the well-meaning innovator, with false theories of art to exploit," and the "faddist and crank who is chiefly intent upon seeking notoriety for himself" and comparing the New Stagecraft to a freak show display of a five-legged calf. Both may draw a crowd, said Belasco, but no one in the audience would say that "the one is good art or that the other is a good kind of calf."[29] Belasco also provided the theatre for the 1924 event. Later in the 1920s, awards for original scripts were made by publisher Samuel French. A dozen years after the earliest Little Theatre projects, the close embrace between Broadway and the tributary theatre was clear. Amateurs and rebels had always aspired to recognition; Broadway had no reason to refuse to look at experimenters whose work might make money. When the DLT first won the Belasco Cup in 1924, it was the only group from outside the New York metropolitan area to enter. In 1925, there were entrants from West Virginia, Ohio, Pennsylvania, and Michigan. In 1926, the companies over which the DLT triumphed included one from England. News coverage of the events in the New York dailies (*Times, Sun, Herald Tribune, World,* and *Post*) as well as brief announcements in several other American cities' newspapers, articles in the nationally distributed *Christian Science*

Monitor, Time, and *Life,* and coverage in the industry-focused *Billboard, Drama,* and *Theatre Arts Monthly* all contributed to the idea that the DLT was important and exemplary. Hinsdell's 1925 book and Alexander Dean's 1926 *Little Theatre Organization and Management*—both of which drew heavily on DLT work and experiences—as well as the 1927 *Encyclopedia Britannica* entry added to the creation in the mind of a nationally distributed imagined community of Little Theatre audiences a clear idea of this theatre's achievements and worth.

The tournament and the press coverage constructed parallel but different audiences. The event itself targeted insiders; newspapers and magazines also reached outsiders who may or may not have known about the winning company before. Nonetheless, by fixing the DLT within the "grid [imposed] on the distribution of events that will be recognized," newspapers did not so much tell the public exactly *what* to think regarding the DLT as they simply told them to think *about* it.[30] For a reader outside the Dallas or New York areas, or without an overriding interest in theatre, merely encountering the DLT within the limited number of column inches allotted to performing arts would make the company seem newsworthy and would render it a laudable model or product. As part of its service as what Michael Schudson calls "use-paper," the daily journal provided guidance in the ways of modern living for the upwardly mobile, the uncertain, and the merely curious.[31] Since Little Theatre, to recall the words of the DLT founders, was part of efforts at civic, democratic, and cultural improvement in major cities and in public schools and universities, it was a necessary component of enlightened, forward-looking, educated life. Therefore, it was entirely suitable for general news coverage.

The company's institutional visibility, financial growth, and victory in the artistic competition do much to explain why it was a model for peer troupes, but these do not account for how and why "The No 'Count Boy" struck an emotional and intellectual chord with audiences and critics. All three DLT tournament winners were read by New York reviewers as southern plays. Only "The No 'Count Boy" resonated with a "universalism" then understood to be the desideratum of excellent drama.

The Quest for Self in Others: Race, Authenticity, and "Folk Plays"

"The No 'Count Boy" captured the imagination of readers and spectators in part because they were prepared for its dramaturgy and saw it as a fine example of an emergent phenomenon: the folk play. From a present-day perspective, folk plays may simply look like regional or local color pieces that focus on poor rural characters who are often superstitious. In the 1920s, however, ideas about the folk and the folk play were being developed by a number of artists and intellectuals with an eye to social value and revised concepts of Americanism. The genre could, according to its proponents, be a tool in forging national identity via a recognition of universalism in the local, especially anything local connected with the land or sea. Little Theatre practitioners and audiences who embraced this work were, therefore, positioned as avatars of aesthetic and social progress.

The folk play in the United States has a complex genealogy. It was the focus of the work of Professor Frederick Koch (see fig. 6.1) at the University of North Carolina, whose students, beginning in 1918, specialized in writing plays with rural North Carolina subjects and characters. Koch was a tireless promoter; his work garnered statewide as well as national attention, and he later worked with students from other parts of North America who wrote folk plays about California, Mexico, and the Canadian prairies. Paul Green (1894–1981; see fig. 6.2) began his playwriting career in Koch's class and was one of a handful of students—none of whom were black—to write a species of folk play called "Negro plays." Green's work captured the attention of Alain Locke, one of the Harlem writers who were also defining and promoting folk literature and characters as a vital necessity for African American self-actualization. Since Green was white, the value of his work both to Locke and to later African American Little Theatre groups that presented his plays depended not on any simplistic equation of "author's bloodline=truthful insider art," but on its performativity. By this I mean not only how well it lent itself to persuasive rendition on the stage but also how it activated readings and responses that engendered respect and sympathy for African Americans as complex and worthwhile Americans. Both Locke and Koch also depended on (and frequently invoked, as did critics) a third source of folk play discourse, namely the work of Dublin's Abbey Theatre and John Millington Synge. The 1911, 1913, and 1914 tours of the Irish Players of the Abbey Theatre had given American Little Theatre theorists just enough experience of the company's work to believe in its international significance, but too little to understand the complicated politics of who spoke for and what passed for indigenous Irish folk.[32] Similar confusions would both trouble and benefit the life of "The No 'Count Boy."

All three sources—Koch's development and promotion of his students' folk plays, the Harlem Renaissance's grappling with "the folk" as sources of genuine negritude, and the Irish Players' work—trafficked in notions

Fig. 6.1. Frederick Henry Koch, ca. 1920. Courtesy of the North Carolina Collection, University of North Carolina Library at Chapel Hill.

Fig. 6.2. Frederick Henry Koch and Paul Green, ca. 1938. Courtesy of the North Carolina Collection, University of North Carolina Library at Chapel Hill.

of authenticity. This slippery concept produced writing that had as much to do with the eye of the anticipated beholder as it did with the authors' private definitional struggles or actual ethnographic accuracy, even though it was generally the latter that was touted. Consider just two responses to productions of plays about African Americans, one performed by southern white players in blackface in New York, the other by northern black Americans in Atlanta. A critic for the *New York World* praised the Dallas Little Theatre actors for their work in "The No 'Count Boy" because it "brought to life Negroes more real than any on 135th Street and Lenox Avenue."[33] Dubose Heyward attributed the failure of Nan Bagley Bishop's play *Roseanne* in Atlanta in large part to the fact that "it is as impossible for the southern black to be portrayed by the Harlem Negro as by a northern white, plus grease paint."[34] Here, each writer claimed to recognize authenticity in performance, but each also acknowledged that performativity, familiarity, legibility, and sympathy underlay believed-in authenticity more than did any putatively immanent feature of race. Southern whites made convincing southern blacks (more "real" than actual urban blacks) for northern white audiences; northern blacks could not pass muster as southern blacks before a southern white audience.

No matter who their target audience, folk works, if they were to succeed, needed to promote not only a recognition of otherness but a sense of self as well. Audiences drawn to plays with characters outside their own purview no doubt sought exoticism in the theatre, but everything in Western dramaturgy encourages identification with, as well as of, difference in drama. Recognition of the mimetic was crucial in folk work presented to an audience drawn from the region or population actually depicted, although this may have been less about accuracy than Koch and others said it was, for two reasons. First, some of the subjects were drawn from a long-gone or a mythical past, meaning that they were already mediated when their playwrights first took them up. Second, segregation and the price of a theatre ticket meant that many of the then-contemporary actual human subjects of plays were barred from attending. Identification was crucial to the success of work presented to audiences removed from the actual everyday existence of the characters depicted, especially when this existence represented a step "down" for spectators. To identify with a king or adventurer puts spectators or readers in an imaginary situation more prestigious or exciting than their own; to identify with a sharecropper, moonshiner, or fisherman, there must be features of the character's emotional or moral life that seem desirable or worthy. The concept of the worthiness of folk drama depended on the idea that through an appreciation of folk ways and folk narratives, those who did not think of themselves as "folk" (in other words, middle-class theatregoers) expanded their idea of Americanness and overcame the anomie of homogenized, consumer-driven existence, while those who did find a real-life connection with the characters depicted saw their self-worth and everyday assumptions validated in a stage representation.

Frederick Henry Koch (1877–1944) promulgated the folk play virtually from the moment he arrived at the University of North Carolina in 1918. The cadre of playwrights he trained included not only Green, but many who went on to become teachers and, in at least the case of Hubert Heffner, who founded the Wyoming Playmakers, to export Koch's model wholesale.[35] Koch was forty years old when he took up his duties in Chapel Hill, and he had spent at least sixteen years refining the ideas that would coalesce in his work with the Carolina Playmakers. The Playmakers began as an extracurricular group whose tours featured the plays written in Koch's English classes. Eventually Koch was rewarded not only with a new, full-fledged theatre program at the university, but also with a new building. The son of an accountant, Koch aspired to a career as an actor and studied at Boston's Emerson College after graduating from Illinois Wesleyan in 1900. Although he made money giving readings of Shakespeare, he honored his family's preference that he choose another career and earned a master's degree in English in 1909 at Harvard, where he studied with George Pierce Baker. Koch's first job was in the English department at the University of North Dakota, where he founded the amateur touring group, the Dakota Playmakers.

Koch began evolving his ideas about the social value of playmaking as early as 1902, when he published the first of a pair of articles called "Ethics of the Histrionic." Part 1 dealt with the ethical effect of impersonation upon actors and part 2 with the ethical significance of theatre for audiences. Koch argued that the effect on an actor of playing a role was strong, since the actor used his own soul and self in the creation, entering sympathetically into the embodying of the other. Sympathizing with ethical characters would, bit by bit, cause actors to realize a higher standard in their own lives. In the case of "degenerate" characters, though, Koch sidestepped what might seem like proto-Stanislavskianism to opt for Diderot's paradox: the actor might embody the unethical character to perfection, but this would in no way mean that the actor himself would thereby degenerate. Rather, his "ego" would actually reject outright identification with the bad and triumph via the "great law of dramatic contrast." The actor would still derive an ethical elevation from playing the role, as the effect of playing a part always accrues to the actor's "best self."[36] While Koch never published anything quite like this again, morality and betterment continued to be his stated goals with regard to playmaking.

In considering the value of impersonating "folk" characters, Koch's nascent philosophy of acting made it possible to attribute value to playing poor, uneducated, or Negro characters at worst because one's better self would purge the dross from the system and polish the gold, but at best because something intrinsic in the character's ethos would inspire the actor. Certainly in "The No 'Count Boy," the eponymous character's ability to dream and to value music and the imagination over hard labor and submission to cruel authority would have made him worthy of admiration for playgoers who believed in the importance of the arts and artmaking as an antidote to quotidian getting and spending. For audiences, Koch believed that theatre is an index of social progress. A late Victorian, he advocated "the soul's quest for truth, goodness, and beauty" over "mere material sense-gratification." In these schemas, vaudeville has "no hygienic effect" and, recalling Rousseau, Koch recommended pastoral as a better bet. The highest good theatre can do is to engender in its audience "a genuine *sympathy* for the human life presented" through "*truth idealized*" (emphasis in original). Theatre, then, is therapeutic because it generates sympathy for others by deploying their truth in a "universalized" form.[37]

Koch put his ideas into effect in North Dakota, where he specialized in encouraging the production of two genres: the pageant and the prairie play. Both were intended to encourage the generation of materials derived from the playwrights' own localized experience in order to validate, reflect, and unite the immediate community. In what may have been his first use of the term "folk," Koch in 1913 invoked the usual Little Theatre ideals of elevation, improved literary values, and an "emancipated society" to be had from a proper appreciation of theatre and the "abiding values" of drama. His model for good amateur theatre, which should have chthonic origins, was the "many generations of folk-players" that made the flowering of Shakespeare's genius possible.[38] The "folk consciousness" Koch attributed to the pageant makers in North Dakota was linked to Woodrow Wilson's "birth of a new day" as a contribution to a communal coming together via fresh "art-expression."[39] Koch did not need to sell these goals to the University of North Carolina. Not only did the university president, Edward Kidder Graham, recruit him to create a drama project akin to the Dakota Playmakers, but the university issued a leaflet extolling the virtues of the community pageant as a means of "expand[ing] . . . racial personalities by merging them into a new tradition, symbolic of the spirit that is to make all earth's children one folk."[40] The leaflet article stresses the essentially Elizabethan underpinnings of American literature and culture, and it does make a nod to the recent infusion of non-English-speaking immigrants. The goal, though, is "to fuse all these groups into one" especially via pageantry.[41]

Koch's touchstone was always Anglophone, and North Carolina was, he asserted after moving there, a good place in which to circulate his ideas because of the relative homogeneity of its white population's forebears. "The State is still regarded by the people as a family of 'folks,'" he said in 1922, "because the population is almost pure Anglo-Saxon, and still remarkably homogeneous."[42] The statement is shocking in its oblivion to African Americans as North Carolinians; at the same time, it suggests that Koch and his readers took for granted that African American North Carolinians were native, Christian, English speaking, and often living the same poor farm lives as their white neighbors. The wave of southern and eastern European immigration and the issue of adjusting to new Americans who spoke languages other than English or who were Catholic or Jewish was of little immediate concern in most of North Carolina in the 1910s and 1920s. Moreover, because black and white "folk" shared much similar lore and many similar habits of farming, medicine, and superstition, Koch was working in a milieu where similarities were as striking as differences, a milieu where the status quo was one of "fierce segregation and casual integration."[43] Accordingly, the possibilities of black-as-white or vice versa were not illegible or completely alien, so long as they were posed with care.

Koch's use of "folk" in describing the plays he encouraged his students to write remained remarkably consistent in two ways. First, it referred the local, the familiar, and the physical environment. Second, it was presented so that it could be—and was—variously interpreted by critics, audiences, and writers in different locales both with regard to authenticity and to efficacy. At his most general, Koch would say that "the term 'folk' with us applies to that form of drama which is earth-rooted in the life of our common humanity."[44] This enabled advocates of a conservative stripe to see folk work in "Plato and Aristophanes trying to knock some sense into the Athens of their day, Shakespeare peopling that same Athens with Elizabethan

mechanics and Warwickshire hunts, Ibsen photographing the local doctors and vestrymen of a Norwegian parish, Carpaccio painting the life of
St. Ursula exactly as if she were a lady living in the next street to him. . . ."[45]
Identification, then, might mean identifying with the best of the Western
canon in trying to come to grips with a folk play about a tenant farmer.

Articles about North Carolina folk plays that appeared in the New York
press or that quoted prominent New York theatre critics stressed how
forward-looking the genre was, not only because it was something new
but also because it was comparable to what the Irish Players did with
works of Synge and Lady Gregory.[46] For instance, Augustus Thomas, best
known as a playwright but writing in 1922 as executive chairman of the
New York–based Producing Managers' Association, waxed expansive
about plans for a national theatre and asserted that the whole future of
American drama depended on "spontaneous movements" such as those
in "Chapel Hill, Georgia," [sic] devoted to producing plays dealing with
local folklore, plays "fully equal to any of the Irish folk lore plays produced
by the Abbey company under Lady Gregory's direction."[47] Little matter
that Thomas's geography was wrong and that many folk plays treated
social issues and not folklore. His standard of worth was European and
contemporary, and, as he understood it, the Carolina folk play passed
muster. Audiences attuned to his New York stage standards might safely
embrace this material.

Koch hedged his bets in discussing the folk play, cannily recognizing
that various interpretive communities needed to forge identification
with the material in their own ways. In a lecture covered by at least one
New York reporter, Koch emphasized that, while the "true" drama of the
folk play lies in its depiction of struggle (the Aristotilean *agon*), it also
"mirror[s] the color and atmosphere of a circumscribed locale . . . and
present[s] people unaffected by the rapidly fusing civilization of the more
settled and prosperous sections of the country."[48] Such a description allowed New York theatregoers and critics—whose interest and validation
Koch sought—to appreciate the plays even while seeing their characters
as stereotypes such as "the fine old families of the first cavaliers, . . . the
'poor whites,' the shiftless Negro, and the toilers in the cotton mills." Poor
white, at least, was put in quotes by the writer for the *New York Evening
Post*.[49] "Shiftless Negro" was not, arguably because even punctuation was
a rhetorical strategy for negotiating identification and legibility.

One might question the extent to which Koch himself was able to distinguish between genuine ethnography and stageworthy story. In an

anecdote about a Chinese student, Koch recalled discouraging the young man from writing the play he proposed initially, a play about a mixed marriage between a Chinese-born boy and his young American wife. Koch told the student that he "can't do it" since he should write of his "own people" and "can't understand the mind of an American girl." The fledgling playwright had been in the United States for five years and had earned a degree at the University of Wisconsin, where he had surely met American girls of a marriageable age. Koch urged him to write a "real Chinese play" using folklore from "old China." In fact the student, Cheng-Chin Hsiung, wrote both plays. That the "charming play . . . in the manner of the Chinese stage—a play of romance, of comedy, of poetry" was picked up by *Theatre Arts* may say as much about Little Theatre audiences' interest in the exotic as it does about the value of personal experience in writing the folk play.[50]

The response of North Carolinians to Koch's students' folk plays problematizes issues of authenticity even as it underscores the distance that white, middle-class theatregoers kept from the very subject matter they claimed and recognized as folk. An anonymous reviewer in Burlington, North Carolina, admired the "real country boy and the country girl in courtship with the simplicity that has marked the life of these good folks," thereby simultaneously authenticating ("real") and othering ("these good folks") the representation in a single sentence.[51] A Raleigh columnist admired a playwright's "first-hand knowledge" and "honest self-expression," with no sense that a combination of the two might not yield accuracy.[52] In other words, the honest self-expression of a white, middle-class student in her late teens or early twenties (the profile of most of the Playmakers members) might reflect a highly selective, biased, or incomplete first-hand knowledge of impoverished, uneducated, superstitious referents underpinning her characters, even if these were based on neighbors. Another newspaper writer in Burlington claimed emphatically that the plays "are not representative of North Carolina. They are exceptions, violent exceptions, and are misleading. The day might have been when we were noted for our 'we-uns' and 'you-uns' . . . but they are extreme exceptions."[53] A reviewer in Montgomery noted that one student actor had an accent that was "too collegiate" for a business man, and that a "twentieth century college boy" had a nearly impossible task in trying to portray an old Confederate colonel. In the same evening of one-acts, another student actor was called "not best suited for a negro role," although he "came out strong as the tragedian in the second play."[54] Here,

ideas of credible representation slip back and forth between attempts at
mimesis that fail because the self bleeds through the attempt to portray
something recognizable from social experience and attempts that fail or
succeed because of how they measure up to stage conventions. Yet a
writer, such as, for example, Paul Green, who wrote black characters with
an eye to subverting "negro roles" and whose knowledge of poor black
Americans was far more intimate than his knowledge of stage tragedi-
ans, still ran into reviewers and spectators whose multiply calibrated
critical yardstick is evident here. A clear example of such critical conflation appears in a *New York Times* review of *Carolina Folk-Plays,* a five-
play anthology edited by Koch. The work "aims to mirror the lives of
those very men and women who take part in the performances and for
whose benefit the performances are designed," asserts the reviewer, unaware that those who take part in the performances and comprise the
audiences may enjoy the depiction of but do not live the lives of "pecu-
liar if highly typical . . . Carolina backwoodsmen."[55]

The negotiated relation between self and other is strikingly evident in
Elizabeth Lay's (later Mrs. Paul Green) prologue to her 1919 one-act
"When Witches Ride." Written in iambic pentameter, the lines betray
Lay's thrall to Anglosaxondom and its literary deities and also her inter-
est in timelessness:

> Yet we may catch the childlike wondering
> Of our old negroes and the country folk,
> And live again in simple times of faith
> And fear and wonder, if we stage their life.

"We" are white, in a position to stage the lives of "others" who are
simple and childlike yet who are "ours" as opposed to "others." Theatre
and movie audiences were strictly segregated in Chapel Hill into the
1960s, and the university itself did not admit black students until the
1950s, yet "our" Negroes and country folk presumably have something
to do with and to say to "us." Moreover, it is in the staging of the lives
that their values infuse us. Koch's ideas about the salutary effects of acting and identifying with the essence of a character and his ideas of finding common humanity in local color are both present here. Significantly,
white writers, actors, and audiences are being encouraged to see their
common humanity in and with "old negroes."

For Frederick Koch and most of his students, plays about rural African Americans were one species among many of the folk play. For Alain

Locke and other writers and activists in the Harlem Renaissance, specifically African American folk plays were one strand of an African American folk art that was to be the means to self-actualization for black citizens and to the recognition of a unique and respectable black aesthetic by whites as well. Locke was one of many who theorized about African American folk art in several genres; his particular attention to drama and theatre make his ideas central here. At the simplest level in Locke's writing, Negro "folk" were the actual poor, rural, African Americans that Koch's students depicted. This basic definition enabled Locke to praise "The No 'Count Boy" as well as *The Emperor Jones* and Ridgeley Torrence's *Three Plays for a Negro Theatre* for each being "a realistic study of Negro folk-life."[56] But there was tension within the African American world of arts and letters as to whether the folk experience and arts to which African Americans should turn were those of the African continent or the more recognizable but presumably contaminated products of the American diaspora. Even diaspora experience was subject to debate, as some writers questioned whether rural experience was useful, germane, or even current for the tremendous number of African Americans who had migrated in recent years to northern cities and who had little interest in returning to or identifying with a nonurban past. These questions were much in view the year of the DLT victory with "The No 'Count Boy," owing to the publication of Locke's anthology entitled *The New Negro.*

Locke's book was an expanded version of a special issue of *Survey Graphic* magazine that he had edited in March 1925. The issue was dedicated to the arts, and Arnold Rampersad, editor of a 1992 reprint of the book, states that its target audience was probably whites.[57] Locke was a professor of English and philosophy at Howard University and a product of Harvard and Oxford who had never lived in the American south. He stressed in his introduction to the volume that the "culture of the Negro is of a pattern integral with the times," and that a "darkened Ghetto of segregated race life" or "a mind and soul bizarre and alien as the mind of a savage, or even as naive and refreshing as the mind of the peasant or the child" were history at best.[58] What, exactly, comprised contemporary Negro culture was subject to debate. At one end of the spectrum, George Schuyler asserted that Negro art "made in America" was nonexistent in the early twentieth century; "the Aframerican is merely a lampblacked Anglo-Saxon" who, like any other immigrant, became like any other American after a few generations. Since Africans had been on the American continent longer than most other ethnic groups, Schuyler saw the idea of art that was "expressive of the Negro soul" as "hokum."[59] Langston Hughes responded to Schuyler by defending "the racial arts in America." Hughes refused "standardization" and the "Nordicized Negro" in favor of an art undergirded by "tom-tom cries and . . . tom-tom laughs"—the other end of the spectrum.[60]

Locke straddled the line on this issue. In noting that the South "has unconsciously absorbed the gift of [the Negro] folk-temperament," he asserted that there *was* a racial temperament unique to the Negro, something he would elsewhere claim as the defining characteristic black actors brought to their craft.[61] Locke argued that Africans had arrived on American shores bringing "as an emotional inheritance a deep-seated aesthetic endowment," which had survived but had been reshaped as a result of slavery to emerge reflecting "essentially the working of environmental forces rather than the outcropping of a race psychology." Therefore, poor, rural African Americans were "folk" not in that their arts and behavior were characteristically African but because their particular ethos was the result of the meeting of hard-wired temperament and socially situated "ordeals." Ideally, the New Negro would recuperate the legacy of the African continental arts, especially since these were defined by "discipline, style, technical control," and "originality of expression." Going back to African sources would bypass what might seem retrograde or embarrassing about his rural brothers' behavior ("naïve . . . as the mind of the peasant or the child").[62] Still, both the New and the less artistically sophisticated Negro could claim a heritage at the same fountainhead; both the pure and the slavery-inflected version of "folk" were, therefore, "authentic."

As with Koch's use of "folk" in advertising and describing his students' plays, Locke's strategies deployed definitional slippage to advantage. In his 1922 recommendations, "Steps Toward the Negro Theatre," he praised Koch's university model while also warning against the "superficially representative." He cited the contributions of black and white artists, extolling the "catholic appeal" of work by actor Charles Gilpin (black), playwrights Eugene O'Neill and Ridgeley Torrence (white), and the administrative efforts at (black) Howard University where the fledgling theatre department was aided by designer Cleon Throckmorton (white). But catholicity was tempered with the "ultimate" need for Negro theatre to be a theatre of self-expression.[63] David Krasner notes that Locke, trained in philosophy, worked with pragmatism and relativism as means of theorizing a folk art that would serve the Renaissance program of "interpret[ing] the folk to itself, to vitalize it from within." This art was to be universal as well as an individual expression of the artist while also serving "race loyalty," a three-way paradox with which Locke struggled in much of his writing.[64] Locke shared with Koch not only a flexible use of the term "folk," but also the belief that plays about African Americans furthered the project of "the dramatic exploration and working out of the native elements of American life."[65] In other words, black folk were American folk. Elizabeth Lay's focus on the childlike and the simple was retrograde by Locke's standards, but her desire to invigorate (white) American life by staging American blackness depended upon common ground and shared national stakes, an idea of "native elements" that meshed with his thinking.

The blackness that whites wanted to stage and the blackness that the New Negro project extolled were valued for "authenticity" but were not necessarily the same blackness. As J. Martin Favor argues, notions of racial purity and immutable traits ("authenticity") pose at least two problems. First, they reinscribe the very ideas of essentialism that their liberal champions often wish to overcome. Second, they offer no room either for development or for the inclusion of diverse constituents (rural, urban, educated, illiterate, etc.) unless they are in many respects performative.[66] Performative projects bring subjects into being through doing or writing, in essence creating authenticity as they go along. In racial terms, then, black is as black does, so long as this doing is accepted as authentic by an audience. In real life, the audience is the other people one encounters, often randomly or even at a distance. In the theatre, however, the audience is a select group who parse race (among other things) both by means of everyday strategies and by means of theatre discourse.

Part of the theatre discourse that defined authenticity in American plays' folk characters emerged as a result of the three visits of the Irish Players of Dublin's Abbey Theatre to the United States in the early 1910s. References to playwright J. M. Synge as a touchstone for folk authenticity and to the Irish Players as a model for performing same run throughout the American Little Theatre era's writing on what to emulate. The Abbey's work was a continuation of the project begun by the Irish Literary Theatre, opened in 1899 by Lady Augusta Gregory and W. B. Yeats, one of many theatre undertakings driven by a desire to assert artistic and political independence from England.[67] The Irish Players' first tour to the United States is remembered for two reasons. First, visible founding members of the American Little Theatre movement wrote about its influence on their work. Second, audiences disrupted performances as they objected to the representation of Irish peasantry, most particularly in J. M. Synge's *Playboy of the Western World*. Authenticity was the stated issue. Synge, a native of Ireland whose plays would shortly become the touchstone for Irish folk plays for at least two decades, had spent much of his early adulthood in Paris and was first greeted by the Irish press in 1903 with accusations of inauthenticity, with his work being labeled "artistically impure," and with one critic calling "In the Shadow of the Glen" "no more Irish than the *Decameron*."[68]

Recent scholarship on Irish theatre of the early twentieth century points out that Synge, Gregory, and Yeats manipulated ideas of authenticity just as their American counterparts in the Little Theatre movement did. John P. Harrington locates the Abbey project squarely within an international scene and sees its founders trying to carve out a niche for themselves within the already-lively performance world of Dublin. Yeats compared the company's work to that of Paris's Théâtre Libre and London's Independent Theatre. The project of offering indigenous art to an Irish audience (Locke's "interpret[ing] the folk to itself, to vitalize it from within") was aimed, however, almost from the outset, at elite theatregoers, and as early as 1903, the company, now called the Irish National Theatre Society, presented its work in London and sent some of Yeats's plays to New York. If the supposed goal was social activism, Harrington notes that the actual rhetoric was about aesthetics, particularly the sort of aesthetics that appealed to a kind of literary elite. "[E]lided from the prospectus . . . was the ambition to link a remote past ('ancient idealism') to a future ('to build up a Celtic and Irish school of dramatic literature'), without reference to an exploitable present."[69]

The present, of course, is where actual audience members live, so invocations of past and future needed to have some valence at the moment of reception. Both Synge and Lady Gregory made efforts to adapt to audience response in the interest of keeping their work visible and viable. After the 1907 opening of *The Playboy* in Dublin, Synge emphatically told a newspaper interviewer that the play, which had aroused audience ire, was not intended as a realistic representation of Irish life. The preface to the play, which was printed in the program, made the opposite statement. Synge had spent time on the Aran Islands, wrote a book about the Islanders, and presented himself as an authority on authentic peasant life.[70] Dubliners objected to a depiction of Irish life that foregrounded physical ills (lack of national health), young women preferring an outsider to one of their own, and mentions of female undergarments.

The audience members who raised these objections were not Aran Islanders or peasants from any part of Ireland, but "their urbanized descendants, whom Yeats, Synge, and Lady Gregory disliked."[71]

Irish American audiences objected not to depictions of the old country per se nor even to a precise distinction between the factual and the fictional, but to possible aspersions that the representations might cast on them. As Harrington observes, "[t]heir interest was in their future, not their past, and this required of immigrants a better pedigree than Synge's characters suggested. . . . The image was crucial . . . ." Irish writer Seamus MacManus proclaimed the American bill of sixteen plays "not Irish at all." The *New York Times* announced, before the tour, that the Abbey plays would be "poetical . . . mystical . . . subtly humorous [and] obscure." Yeats, whose essays about theatre favored exactly such an aesthetic, wrote to the *Times* to assure them that such a definition was a misunderstanding, and that the Abbey plays attracted clerks and shopgirls, denying an interest in appealing to a "few educated and leisured men and women." In fact, the tour appealed primarily to the latter sort of American spectator, which made it a critical failure of sorts, but which also made it possible to raise funds for the theatre among the select whose company Lady Gregory kept throughout the tour. Harrington points out that Abbey principles and the works of Irish playwrights were embraced throughout the 1910s and 1920s by New York's "big three" Little Theatres, the Provincetown and Washington Square Players and the Neighborhood Playhouse. By the time the Abbey company returned in 1931, *Playboy* was a staple of their repertory and a safe choice, offering Americans something both removed from their everyday life and a known quantity.[72] In short, the real, the authentic, the universal, the timeless, and the expedient were conflated, and the ingredients in the recipe for success were adjusted until they appealed to a certain Little Theatre audience: interested practitioners and their followers in cities with a market for European anticommercialism.

For an analogous play with African American characters to succeed in the United States, practitioners and publicists needed to build on certain assumptions even as they were resisting others. The members of the Dallas Little Theatre and the context of their city tell much about how ideas of race, theatre, universalism, and art worked together for this production. The elite who comprised the early membership in the DLT were all white, but they were neither all Protestant nor all local in origin. Dallas demographics and history contributed to determining who "passed";

the city achieved size and prominence only in the late nineteenth century, and it was not characterized by the sort of labor and residential crowding that had much to do with how hereditary Americans responded to newly arriving immigrant groups in other, older cities. A small but visible Jewish community was part of Dallas society, and several members were involved in DLT activities. These included department store owners Eli Sanger, Herbert Neiman, and Stanley Marcus, the first a board member and the latter two subscribers. When the DLT's second building's cornerstone was laid in 1927, Rabbi David Lefkowitz gave the benediction.[73] Another group to participate in the early years of the DLT were British expatriates who relocated in the city to participate in the cotton industry that boomed around 1920. Identifying Jews and Britons as comparably white was itself arguably taking a progressive stance for the early 1920s.

Whiteness is not merely self-evident in this context. Science and social science supported the idea of nationalities or ethnicities as races; in this context, much Little Theatre activity sought either to Americanize or to exoticize non-Anglophones or, conversely, to exclude them.[74] Matthew Frye Jacobson cites 1924 as a turning point in Anglo-Saxon supremacy and the start of a consolidated identity based upon "the notion of a reforged, consanguine Caucasian race."[75] The precipitating event for the nationalization of this inclusive idea of whiteness was the Johnson Act, the immigration restriction law that instituted a quota system based on 2 percent of each group's population according to the 1890 census. By basing the quotas on the contours of the population prior to the biggest waves of eastern and southern European immigration, the act worked to encourage immigration from the countries of earlier settlers (Nordic, Teutonic, Anglo-Saxon) and to stem the arrival of those from newer source countries. The result, in Jacobson's insightful analysis, was a "new, binary racial arrangement" in which a premium was placed on color—the feature that now enabled unity where there had previously been division. This premium both invited and arguably forced "all whites—Mediterraneans, Celts, and Hebrews included—[to be] responsible for the reified social category created by and for white privilege." Although the "consolidated whiteness of the new immigrants" was good for empire building and assimilation, it depended on "a syntax of simple whiteness and its others" and, accordingly, did not eliminate discrimination and difference so much as redistrict them. Indeed, as Jacobson notes, even with the midcentury revival of ethnic diversity to mark cultural differences while celebrating "universalism," the single anomaly remained "'the Negro.'"[76] Arguably, then, the production of "The No 'Count Boy" was very progressive in that it located the universal in the ultimate unmeltable "other."

At the same time it was regressive in its dependence on blackface, a practice that, when deployed by whites, both eliminates the actual character referent from the proceedings and reinforces whiteness rather than any ethnicity or other form of individuality under the burnt cork. Blackface enacted, in Eric Lott's trenchant analysis, "the dialectical flickering of racial insult and racial envy, moments of domination and moments of liberation, counterfeit and currency."[77] White actors played black roles in blackface from the earliest days of Anglo-American theatre; stars from Edwin Forrest to Ethel Barrymore blacked up for nonmusical plays.[78] Until the twentieth century, for the most part, white theatre supporters considered black performers simply incompetent as serious actors even as these supporters expected to see black characters onstage, thereby mobilizing Lott's dialectics. Blackface's best-known manifestation, minstrelsy, trafficked in shufflers, dandies, slaves, mammies, malapropism-prone bloviators, watermelon eaters, and other stereotypes that were served up in a popular entertainment context for a mixed-class audience. When black performers did begin to work on Broadway and on major circuits, they, too, were often in blackface and first appeared only in musicals, where they managed to work subtly within the stereotypes to subvert them. The first black actors to perform roles in serious plays intended for white or mixed audiences appeared during the Little Theatre movement and met with some enthusiastic and some wary responses. For instance, actor Charles Gilpin was praised for his performance in *The Emperor Jones* (1920), but he was unable to find enough other work to keep a career going and aroused controversy when Drama League members were uneasy about seating him at their theatre awards dinner. *All God's Chillun Got Wings* (1924) was almost shut down by the mayor prior to its Broadway opening in 1924 because of its mixed-race cast, topic of intermarriage, and onstage kiss. The kiss was altered because the white leading lady, Helen MacKellar, refused to kiss her black leading man on the mouth. As late as 1929, Kenneth Macgowan singled out the students at Hillsdale College because they "boldly introduced a Negro player for the Emperor Jones into a white cast."[79] Thus, blackface remained a noncontroversial choice for at least a few more years, particularly for a play that was not a fluffy comedy and that offered gentle social critique.

"The No 'Count Boy," like a few earlier works by O'Neill and Torrence, was serious drama that rejected Victorian values and, in Ann Douglas's analysis, provided "access to black America, to America as itself black-and-white."[80] These plays aspired to realism and were praised for just that. One sober assessment of Green's text claimed that the playwright "neither exaggerates nor reduces. He reports exactly. The result is extraordinary verisimilitude."[81] The value placed on this sort of realism is, in Douglas's reading, a form of antimodernism, as mimesis had been the province of the nineteenth century but was "inadequate in the wake of the Great War; even if it constitutes some kind of psychological health, it is regressive on the artistic level."[82] A kind of national psychological health was, however, much of what was on the minds of artists like Green, Koch, and many educators, who realized that middlebrow sympathies were not best gained via avant-garde art. To further the project of what Neil Harris has called "the nationalization of culture," these Little Theatre artists understood the value of balancing the ideologically new with the dramaturgically and theatrically comfortable.[83]

"The No 'Count Boy" served this balancing act well. The plot and characters are simple and meant to charm. The four-character piece features a romantically inclined girl, Pheelie (Ophelia); her steady but utterly pedestrian fiance, Enos; a captivating drifter (the title character) who arrives seemingly from nowhere and turns Pheelie's head with his wild tales, beautiful harmonica playing, and the proposal that they run off together; and the drifter's mother, who appears at the end of the play to deflate the boy's tall tales, excoriate him for his shiftlessness, and take him back to the farm, leaving Pheelie to contemplate a safe but impoverished, dreary life of sharecropping (see fig. 6.3). The setting is the front porch of a simple cabin in North Carolina, and the play is written in dialect. Since the situation depicted foregrounded personal dreams and disappointments rather than larger social systems that might produce these and since the black characters neither discussed nor encountered white antagonists, little in the text was particularly incendiary, although it was read as having thematic weight. Green saw the piece as a version of "the age-old and destructive conflict between beauty and the work of three meals a day" and the crucial need for a life of the mind and for dreams.[84]

The playwright's own upbringing and life made him an ideal candidate to write a "Negro play" that passed for realism and also passed Eurocentric muster as being reminiscent of Synge. The eponymous char-

Fig. 6.3. "The No 'Count Boy" presented by the Dallas Little Theatre, May 1925. *Left to right:* Jack Hyman, Geraldine Wilson (Mrs. R. E. L.) Knight, H. Ben Smith, Mrs. W. P. Bentley. From the collections of the Fine Arts Division, Dallas Public Library.

acter was, according to Green, based on an actual field hand with whom he had once worked. Green spent the first twenty-two years of his life in Harnett County, North Carolina, where, although his family owned their land, they farmed and lived much like their poor black neighbors, and where Green was once listed in the local paper as a champion cotton picker.[85] One magazine profile of the playwright anxiously assured readers that Green could serve to "immortalize" the "Nordic...type" and scoffed at the many uninformed northerners who believed he was "a colored gentleman."[86] Green would go on to take a degree in philosophy at the University of North Carolina and join the faculty in philosophy before switching to drama when a department was created. He pursued both a serious interest in folklore and an interest in making a name as a playwright, researching the former throughout the 1920s and earning a Guggenheim fellowship in the latter for a year of European study, writing, and theatregoing.[87] His 1967 story "Rassie" memorializes a black childhood friend who died of typhoid fever when both boys were ten. If "Rassie"'s narrative structure makes the most of an emotional story, its details also offer clear sources for Green's easy familiarity with everything from the games and food shared by black and white North Carolinians at the turn of the last century to his early understanding that washing a corpse and helping build a coffin were necessities shared across racial lines, even for the very young. He was a savvy careerist who also drew on a genuinely mixed-race experience of childhood.

Few audiences, however, and virtually no Little Theatre groups in the 1920s were mixed race.[88] White practitioners and viewers could use the DLT production as "a device for claiming and legitimating a certain kind of interpretive activity," W. B. Worthen's explanation of how theatre can enable exegesis predicated on "precisely the freedom *not* to see."[89] Little Theatre audiences comprised what Herbert Blau calls a "self-produced collectivity intent on remaining a mystified subject."[90] The meaning that this collection of mystified subjects produced in its own image was predicated on ideas of the real that reflected and protected their own sense of self. Whites needed, in Ann Douglas's assessment, for blacks to "be very black . . . to provide therapeutic healing for whites."[91] Therefore, the *New York World* critic's observation that the Negroes brought to life in the DLT performance were "more real than any on 135th Street and Lenox Avenue," carried no irony for the mystified (in perhaps both senses) white writer or his anticipated readership who, if they had been to Harlem at all, probably regarded the outing as a titillating excursion for entertainment or who, if they encountered blacks outside of Harlem, saw them as servants.[92] In an emperor's-new-clothes moment, one review reported a six-year-old boy who "wanted to know how Pheelie kept the black on her arms from frescoing her frilly white dress."[93] The child saw what the adults elided or danced around: an actual white body bringing blackness into being while keeping literal black embodiment at bay. Adults were less straightforward about this ventriloquism. In a review of the final round of the tournament, a Dallas reporter said of the hometown actors that "had they not come from Texas almost anybody would have sworn they were real Negroes," later pointing out how the company "discarded their natural good looks [and] blacked their faces."[94] Texas origins offered reassurance of whiteness. (Negro companies from New York City did compete in the tournament in the later 1920s, which makes the safety valve here look particularly provincial and racist.) Good looks in this schema inhere primarily in color, which can override facial structure, body build, carriage, or vitality as criteria for judging beauty. Makeup for "Negro roles" was typically quite dark, thus fulfilling the fantasy requirement that (stage) blacks be "very black," while also creating a color line so rigid that there was no danger of an unpainted white person possibly being mistaken for the real "real" thing.

"The No 'Count Boy" was a valuable cultural product, although one
that was handled with caution. The DLT's first performance of the play
was given at the tournament. Only after their victory did they return for
a brief, highly praised run in a large commercial theatre in Dallas and
then accept invitations to perform the piece in Buffalo and at the annual
convention of the Drama League of America in Cincinnati. The play was
published late in 1925 by Henry Holt and Company as part of a collection of one-acts by Green. Letters from Holt and Hinsdell reveal that
editor Roland Holt at first did not want to publish Green's "Darkey plays,"
as the company was already bringing out a collection of Green's "White
plays" (quotation marks in original) and feared glutting the market with
two volumes.[95] It did not seem to the editors to be an option at that
moment to select some from each and combine them. The publisher also
cited the limited market for Negro plays, calling them "pretty red meat
to offer, for example, to schools and young amateurs. Only the rather
sophisticated Little Theatre groups could touch them . . . ."[96] There was
talk of changing "The No 'Count Boy" to a whiteface play, although it is
unclear whether Green or Holt made the suggestion. Hinsdell opposed it.[97]
After the victory in the tournament, however, Roland Holt's tone and tune
changed. He and his wife Constance D'Arcy Mackay saw both performances of the play on Broadway and wired Green their congratulations
on the prize. The collection of plays Holt published included "The No
'Count Boy" and five others featuring white characters.[98] It was as tricky
to integrate a book as it was an array of characters in a performance, but
Green's work played a specific, if small, role in providing access to America
as black-and-white. In a final, ironic twist on the story of this play's
"universalism" and the similarities between black and white American life,
"The No 'Count Boy" was revived in 1954 in New York on a bill of three
short plays by Paul Green and was played by white actors as whites.[99]

Red meat was, however, a prized item for some, and "The No 'Count
Boy" worked to make this preference publicly acceptable. The play fit
Pierre Bourdieu's description of the cultural product as "a constituted
taste" that "functions as an authority which authorizes and reinforces
dispositions by giving them a collectively recognized expression."[100] With
the imprimatur of "success," achieved in part through good reviews and
production in an expensive, visible venue, the play and others like it went
from being risky to being cultural capital. Forty years before Bourdieu's
work on the class-based determination of tastes, Walter Lippmann observed that "we adjust the facts we see to [our] code. . . . Actually, our

canons determine greatly what we shall perceive and how." Lippmann's concern was not just the presence of codes or stereotypes as ways of making sense of the world. Nor was it primarily the fact that stereotypes are "not neutral," but "highly charged . . . . the fortress of our tradition . . . behind [whose] defenses we can continue to feel ourselves safe in the position we occupy."[101] His concern was the belief that the individual was qualified, by virtue of being free and American, to judge any and all situations based on personal experience, coupled with the American failure to see the limitations of that experience. Lippmann's pseudoqualified individuals interpreted theatre like Blau's mystified subjects, legitimating their interpretive activities via Worthen's freedom precisely not to see, linked with an interest in looking at that which visible and reputable channels of publicity put before them. As a collective, a cohort of such individuals constituted the imagined community of Little Theatre supporters who connected the dots of fun/intellectualism/authenticity/originality/Europeanism/popularity/self-worth/inclusivity/exclusivity to construct and circulate codes that would keep noncommercial theatre alive and in the public consciousness while maintaining boundaries around the "universal."

Well into the 1930s, the Carolina Playmakers would continue to present "Negro plays" and labor plays featuring middle-class whites as writers and performers. Nancy Pennington notes Frederick Koch's "unwillingness to adapt folk drama to a changed world beyond the footlights," resulting in "distortions in the portrayal of the very people Koch and his followers claimed to interpret accurately." The 1939 *Watermelon Time* offered blacks as "our happy people, the blessed irresponsibles whom 'civilization' has not yet 'uplifted.'" *The New Nigger* did resist stereotypes and showed black tenant farmers opposing the tyranny of their white overlord. In a 1936 performance at Hampton Institute, the title was changed to *Big John* in anticipation of audience sensitivities, but the word *nigger* remained throughout the body of the play, producing tension and hostility. "Secure in their ability to interpret the lives of all," writes Pennington, "the Playmakers saw no incongruity in a white troupe in blackface at a black college performing a play about black people written by a white person. They blamed the strained atmosphere on the audience's misunderstanding of the meaning of the play."[102]

All-black ensembles began in the 1910s to work in the Little Theatre mode. Perhaps the best known of these was Harlem's Lafayette Players, which was founded by Anita Bush in 1915, lasted until 1932, and had Charles Gilpin (of *Emperor Jones* fame) in its first production. The company offered black actors a chance to appear in mainstream Broadway plays and to prove that blacks could do more than sing and dance.[103] Loften Mitchell characterizes the company as a "me, too" organization— "one devoted to showing white folks that I, too, can play roles that you think are yours alone, that I, too, am human . . . in short, a defensive organization."[104] The Krigwa Players, an adjunct of the new National Association for the Advancement of Colored People, aimed to produce "plays *about* Negroes, *by* Negroes, *for* Negroes, and *near* Negroes" (emphasis in original).[105] The company integrated the Little Theatre Tournament, winning a Samuel French award for best original script with Eulalie Spence's 1927 comedy "Fool's Errand." The "for and near" part of the formula did not preclude white attention or participation in a national movement, although plays presented and published by Krigwa for black audiences tackled far more controversial social questions than the "who's having the baby?" of Spence's play.

It is easy from a present-day vantage to see the shortcomings of American theatre's romance with presenting African American plays and characters to white audiences. As William Sonnega points out, such productions too often serve "to display virtue [rather] than to solve social problems" and function, at best, as "compensatory deference."[106] "Separate but equal" rarely spells parity and, in any case, does not further the black-*and*-white project. For the DLT in 1925, that project was sympathetic projection via impersonation in terms palatable to liberal theatre practitioners accustomed but not totally blind to class and race privilege. "The No 'Count Boy" was mounted one year after the Johnson Act and two years after Dallas had turned out seventy-five thousand strong to greet the Imperial Wizard of the National Ku Klux Klan on "Klan Day" at the state fair.[107] Surely the play took a different tack from either of the earlier actions. Questions of identification, inclusion, mimesis, and ventriloquism have become only more fraught in the decades since the production. This should not erase the possibilities that it opened and encouraged regarding the uses of identification and performativity to improve the lives of Americans—arguably the overall goal of the entire Little Theatre movement and the reason for its concern with audience construction.

Coda

Half a continent from Dallas, another theatre enjoyed its own version of a "No 'Count Boy" success story. Arlington (Massachusetts) Friends of the Drama, founded in 1923 by members of the Arlington Woman's Club, presented a play about a mixed-race affair in which one of the lovers is married. Members of AFD worried that the drama about othering and self-deception would not sell, and some opposed presenting it altogether. The controversial play was part of a season of mostly Broadway revivals, and scheduling was handled so that it was preceded by a crowd-pleasing musical. The director of the play held a master's degree in directing from Emerson College's well-known drama program. AFD suffered, as did DLT, from a public perception that it was only for the elite, although its members were willing to man a publicity booth on the street at Town Day in Arlington and the governor had declared an Arlington Friends of the Drama Day in the Commonwealth of Massachusetts the previous season. AFD owned its own building and, under the leadership of its woman president, made the commitment to take out a large mortgage in order to pay for major renovations. The controversial production went on to garner outstanding reviews and to take the lion's share of awards at the Eastern Massachusetts Association of Community Theatres festival, winning for best production, makeup, costumes, lights, set design, and direction, as well as garnering a special prize for the Greek chorus–like ensemble devised by the director.

The AFD production opened in 1998; it was David Henry Hwang's *M. Butterfly*. Much had changed in the seventy-four years since the DLT victory. *M. Butterfly*'s playwright is Asian American, the lovers in the piece are both men, the Asian lead was played by an Asian American, and both leading actors were out gay men in their offstage lives. The director was a woman who made a living as an executive for Hewlett-Packard. Yet the largely white company was still fascinated by both explorations of exotic "others" and by Broadway successes. In this case the challenging play and the Broadway success were one and the same, but this was not a new phenomenon. Eugene O'Neill had instituted that combination as early as *The Emperor Jones*.

Leah Hager Cohen's book about the AFD production points to how Little Theatre values forged in the 1910s and 1920s remain remarkably consistent even as the terms of their realization are subject to constant negotiation. Cohen herself could be seen as an heir to the Little Theatre movement. At age ten, she was taken out of school by her mother so that both could work with the socially conscious Bread and Puppet Theatre for a month. She finished high school early to enroll in New York University as a theatre major. From childhood, she was fascinated by the exposure, vulnerability, and participation that theatre facilitated for playmakers and audiences. But even before the end of her first semester at NYU, she began to feel that there was something "gross" about the "insiderly" culture of professional theatre into which students were being initiated, a culture that would brook no irreverent challenge and whose actor training was so inwardly focused that even the sixteen-year-old freshman felt she was missing her chance to study something of the very cultures, worlds, histories, and problems that she had hoped one day to portray onstage. She elected to switch schools and majors in order to become a writer, but this did not end her fascination with theatre. Her book is an exploration of "what it is about amateur theater that makes people not just desire but need it," even as both theatre and amateur are words that conjure condescending smiles in most adults.[108] As her title, *The Stuff of Dreams,* suggests, what people find in theatre is the license to give free play to freedom from emotional boundaries.

Not surprisingly, since one person's dream is another's nightmare, there is friction about what to produce and how AFD produces it. And there is tension about who speaks for whom, as whom, and to whom. In the "to whom" realm, Cohen unearths no surprises. AFD members are generally willing to support productions even when they don't "like" the choice of play. Cast members sell tickets to their friends. The local senior citizen center provides the audience for dress rehearsal, and on that night, audience behavior is predictably unpredictable. Seniors bring food, they unwrap it noisily, and they leave if they want to without waiting for intermission or the end of the play. Audiences are almost exclusively white. Rhetoric about civic value butts up against indifference or lack of awareness: a civic council that didn't seem to know about the existence of AFD urged the development of an entertainment district in Arlington with a community theatre, which "would not only attract local residents seeking edifying activities for their leisure time, but has the potential to draw people from neighboring communities."[109] "Edifying leisure" is vintage Little Theatre language; the council's not knowing that Arlington *had* a community theatre suggests a disconnect between what actually exists "on the street" and the ideals of (insular?) civic reformers. Sometimes just such disconnects characterized some of the original Little Theatre idealists.

AFD reflects all the major revisionist strands set in motion by the Little Theatre movement. Many AFD members have studied theatre, and several have degrees. If they have other "day jobs," it is partially because not only Broadway but now even educational theatre cannot accommodate all the graduates who would like paid work in their area of expertise.

Despite decades of audience study and surveys, American theatre audiences for amateur and professional theatre alike remain predominantly white, middle-aged, upper middle class, and college educated. Studies conducted with an eye to finding ways to increase audience interest generally focus on the responses of exactly such audiences; those that conclude with the need to branch out rarely consider the entrenched elements that keep audiences segregated and the alteration of which would not necessarily draw in others.[110] These elements include everything from the location of theatre buildings in particular city districts to the price of tickets, the class expectations attached to theatregoing, professional artists' impatience with the public and how that affects both programming and public perceptions, and even methods of teaching theatre in schools and universities.

Present-day concerns across amateur and professional lines suggest how well the Little Theatre movement did its job regarding making theatre a valued part of the country's culture. Even commercial theatre supporters learned to use Little Theatre rhetoric in thinking about theatre. A 1949 study conducted by Edward Bernays, the so-called "father of public relations," surveyed audiences in twenty-seven cities for the League of New York Theatres. While respondents predictably favored musicals over all other kinds of plays and clamored for more New York hits and cheaper tickets, the vast majority of those interviewed considered commercial theatre "an important factor in the cultural life of their city. They said it provides a better type of entertainment, has educational and cultural values, helps community betterment, broadens life experience, stimulates the mind, furthers aesthetic appreciation, is more effective than the movies, and has good social implications."[111]

Among the "good social implications," if one reads the phrase as suggesting more than snobbery, is the possibility of public assembly and discussion surrounding challenging theatre work. Cohen speaks of theatre helping participants "question the obvious," as the very act of embodying another (or "other") results in the birth of something new—something that is neither the objectified character referent nor merely the unquestioningly rooted actor, but rather "a presence that did not enter through any door; . . . [that] was born here, onstage, in a collaboration of bodies, ideas, music, movement, images."[112]

Anna Deavere Smith sought to include audiences in the project of questioning the obvious in a 1998–2000 undertaking called the Institute on the Arts and Civic Dialogue. With funding from the Ford Foundation, she wanted to "enhance aesthetic excellence and enrich public discourse at a time when many institutions tend to be further and further away from the public will. . . . What does the artist gain by moving from the safety of his or her studio into the midst of things, and what is lost? What does the public gain or lose by entrusting the consideration of social issues to art?"[113] Smith's efforts to handpick an audience and require their responses as a condition of participation in a dialogue about evolving works of art may sound familiar. Like George Pierce Baker eighty years earlier, Smith worked under the auspices of Harvard University. At the end of the century, the project founder and director was an African American woman, and most of the artists were members of the avant garde and were not white. Artists on the 1999 roster, for example, included African American choreographer Donald Byrd, Asian American choreographer/director Ping Chong, Latino director Robert Castro, Albanian playwright Arben Kumbaro, and the African American legal scholar/social theorist Patricia Williams, who was collaborating on a jazz piece. Cornel West was the keynote speaker for opening dinner of the artist/scholar community. The audience, however, was still upper middle class, white, and mostly from Cambridge or Boston.

Theatre audiences and artists continue to struggle with authenticity, with fulfillment, with "cultural values," and with America as black-and-white. In 1997, Smith moderated a debate between August Wilson and Robert Brustein about the merits of black-and-white theatre. Wilson, probably the twentieth century's foremost African American playwright, argued for a version of plays "*about* Negroes, *by* Negroes, *for* Negroes, and *near* Negroes," going so far as to refuse the idea that cross-racial casting was a beneficial idea at all. One response to his segregationist stance was Henry Lewis Gates Jr.'s discussion of an already-existing all-black theatre known as the Chitlin Circuit that offers melodramas with immediate resonance for their mostly blue and pink collar audiences. Since "the people behind the shows tend not to vaporize about the 'emancipatory potentialities' of their work or about 'forging organic links to the community,'" this theatre exists below the radar of the "serious" theatre community—the latter community built solidly on Little Theatre rhetoric but one now embraced by blacks and whites.[114] Opposing Wilson was Brustein, then the artistic director of the American Repertory Theatre in Cambridge (a coparticipant in Smith's Institute) and the one-time dean of the Yale Drama School, who argued for a color-blind theatre. Yet theatres that seriously attempt to cultivate audiences "that reflect the state

... and the diversity of its cities as well as its rural and suburban areas" and that aspire to "vigorous classics" can easily run afoul of their mainly white, upper-middle-class spectators when they work with other community members. A 2000 reworking of *The Good Person of Szechuan* called *The Good Person of New Haven* featured black, Latino, and Asian American actors from New Haven in a version of Brecht's parable that invoked recent events in their own city. Subscribers at the Long Wharf Theatre resented what they saw as "pageantry" that was "not about us," in a few instances expressing offense at being offered a show about people of color. In a venue committed to serious theatre, audiences see (white, European-influenced) "theatre for theatre's sake" as "real theatre," perpetuating a tenacious bourgeois optic in the name of art and failing to persuade local citizens that such work is not just "more shows 'about a bunch of white people.'"[115] In 2002, music critic Anthony Tommasini suggested that it may be time to challenge the Gershwin estate's stipulation that *Porgy and Bess* be performed by an all-black cast (except for the few minor white roles). Lest it look as though white liberals favor color-blind casting while minorities insist on "authenticity" in characters depicting people of color, African American bass-baritone Simon Estes weighed in on the question in complete favor of color-blind casting across the board in opera. "People of color can sing 'Porgy' magnificently," he said. "People who are not of color can sing it magnificently."[116] In a similar vein, Doris Chu, director of the Chinese Culture Institute of Boston, responded to a question about the necessity for casting an actor of Asian descent in the role of Song in *M. Butterfly* by saying, "Any actor can play any role. . . . Art should have no barrier."[117]

Descent is itself a troubled idea, and Werner Sollors argues persuasively that even traits considered hereditary are subject to negotiation, slippage, change, and reconstitution. While the opposite of descent relations (those of blood or nature) are consent relations (those of law, marriage, or other voluntary affiliation), Sollors's thesis is that neither is untouched by the other. In the case of American identity, he points out that it is only "because Americans take so much for granted among themselves that they can dramatize their differences comfortably."[118] Could any phrase point better to the very processes undertaken by the Little Theatre movement and continued by its heirs than "dramatize their differences comfortably?" Surely this is reformance at work in the bid for a creative audience at the vanguard of an inadvertent revolution. Is any site more rife with the contradictions and tensions of this dramatization than a theatre presenting a controversial play? If the assembled few at such a site continue to be the minority who seek an alternative image of society, they still value theatres as places to experience alterity precisely because of the safety afforded in an arena where emotions and misbehavior are sanctioned.

What better place to negotiate and ponder the grafting of consent onto descent than in an American Little Theatre? Sollors's study locates that negotiation in literature; theatre ups the stakes by including shared time, place, and actual bodies. If the "composing" in my title refers to a history of self-actualization and institutionalization, it is also a bid to see the present tense in realizing our ongoing possibilities as theatre audiences. For those for whom there is no substitute for being enmeshed in the stuff of dreams—Little Theatre legatees spanning a spectrum that includes Leah Hager Cohen, the Arlington amateurs, August Wilson, Robert Brustein, Anna Deavere Smith, myriad educators, and their students aspiring to a life in the theatre—it is an obligation.

Notes
Bibliography
Index

Notes

1. Little Theatre and Audience Construction: A Modern(ist) Project

1. On the evolution of American spectatorship see Butsch.

2. See Levine, chap. 1; and Taylor, especially chap. 5.

3. DiMaggio, "Cultural Boundaries and Structural Change," 29.

4. McDermott, 14–15.

5. Filene, 21, 27.

6. Filene, 27.

7. "Euphemistic realism" was the term used by the curators of the 1994–95 American Impressionism and Realism painting exhibit, organized by the Metropolitan Museum of Art, New York, and the Amon Carter Museum, Fort Worth.

8. For descriptions and discussions of pre–Little Theatre productions and practices, see McNamara; Brockett and Findlay, 87–91; Bernheim, 30–109; Poggi, 3–99; Glenn Hughes, 326–54; Norman Hapgood, 6–37; and Dreiser.

9. Constance D'Arcy Mackay.

10. Quoted in Bernheim, 102.

11. Bailey.

12. Stansell, 161.

13. See Brockett, 495–96; Brockett and Findlay, 228–29; Wickham, 239–40; Glenn Hughes, 355–379. Mark Fearnow questions the sharp divide when he points out that "theatre histories have tended to consider the Washington Square Players and the Theatre Guild as two distinct organizations, but there are good reasons to see them as one continuous theatre that underwent a reconfiguration and renaming during a hiatus that lasted less than a year" in 1918 (356).

14. Heacock (unpaginated). Louise Burleigh argued effectively for the use of "community theatre," which she defined in 1917 as "a house of play in which events offer to every member of a body politic active participation in a common interest" (xxxii). The use of "a" rather than "the" body politic seems to offer

an escape clause for groups who see themselves as artists but are defined other-wise by outsiders.

15. Heap quoted in Watson, 348. J. Ellen Gainor suggests that Heap's con-ventional ideas about drama and her interest in formalism rather than social problems made it hard for her to grasp subtle innovations. See Gainor, 108–11.

16. "Drama: Little Theatres," 702, 703. John Frick suggests the dual purposes (encouragement and laboratory) possible within a single movement in its vari-ous branches in his discussion of alternative American theatres of the teens and twenties. Oddly, while the body of Frick's text situates the work of "small, out-of-the-mainstream theatres" in those two decades, the boldfaced heading of the chapter section in which this assessment appears is called "Alternative Theatre During the Teens." The section immediately following is called "Alternative Theatre During the Thirties," as though the 1920s were a blank slate or hiatus rather than part of a continuum (Frick, 223).

17. Dickinson, *The Insurgent Theatre*, 227–43.

18. Lawren, 300–343.

19. Wainscott, 104.

20. Cheney, *The Art Theatre*, 213.

21. Worthen, 3.

22. Dickinson, *The Insurgent Theatre*, 56.

23. This was also the solution proposed by Danny Newman in the 1977 *Sub-scribe Now! Building Arts Audiences Through Dynamic Subscription Promotion,* which became a popular resource in American regional theatres. Constance D'Arcy Mackay's 1917 *Little Theatre in the United States,* a report from the field, revealed many Little Theatres depending on subscriptions (25, 30, 81, 104, 135, 170). Some experimented with giving tickets away in the interest of being demo-cratic (96). Several had a membership system in some of which only members could purchase tickets, although members might buy tickets for guests as well as for themselves (47, 111, 140, 150, 160). This "private club" arrangement helped circumvent fire and building codes, especially in New York City.

24. Cheney, *The Art Theatre*, 216.

25. Eaton, "Audiences," 27.

26. Dickinson quoted in Gard et al., *Grassroots Theater,* 86.

27. Garrison, 100.

28. See London, 46–47.

29. Hutchins Hapgood, one of the original members of the Provincetown Players, notes of the founding group, "no one of them had been identified with the theatre, and only one had written plays. . . . They didn't even go to the the-atre, for the theatre didn't express life to them. Their own intimacies, they knew, were not expressed in the theatre. . . . It seemed to them that, if a simple begin-ning of an answer to these questions was made, a step might be taken in the solution of our bigger social problems, in our deeper self-consciousness" (*A*

Victorian in the Modern World, 393). Not only is a fleeting commitment to theatre unsurprising based on the backgrounds of the participants, but the confusion of "bigger social problems" with "deeper self-consciousness" suggests the probability of jumping ship with the realization that the two are not the same thing and that, if either or both is of primary concern, theatre is at best only part of an answer.

30. Jackson, 8.

31. Carter and Ogden, 11–12.

32. Jackson, 90.

33. Anderson, 30.

34. Roach, 45, 42.

35. Glenn Hughes, 1. Hughes "forgets" in the space of less than a page that Spain is part of Europe.

36. Hodin, 212.

37. The study was undertaken to "discover what sort of entertainment is presented to citizens of an American city in the middle of a forty-week season." (Twentieth Century Club, 6, 3.)

38. Butsch, 77, 115.

39. Hodin, 212.

40. Smith, 14, 18.

41. Mabie, "Opportunities for Service in Departments of Speech," 3, 2.

42. Jackson, 241. Embedded quote is from Hull-House drama and dance teacher Edith de Nancrede.

43. Gainor, 7.

44. Ehrenreich, 6, 12. The "fear of falling" Ehrenreich describes is one not only of losing the financial comforts of class status ("falling" below a certain income and consumption level), but also of falling into "inner weakness, of growing soft, of failing to strive" (15), hence the appropriateness of including upper-middle-class volunteers' work (see my chap. 4) as, in part, a product of the class outlook toward achieving. See also DeMott.

45. See Mickel; and McConachie and Friedman.

46. Sinclair Lewis, *Main Street,* 204–11.

47. See Berger.

48. Jackson, 51.

49. Dickinson, *The Case of American Drama,* 206.

50. Dickinson, *The Case of American Drama,,* 207.

51. See Leonard.

52. Browne, "The Temple of a Living Art," 10, 13.

53. Richard Hofstadter persuasively argues for reformism into the 1930s. Paula S. Fass parses the difference between Progressivism and progressivism, using the latter for the 1920s as "an angle of vision . . . an optimistic approach to social problems" (30).

54. See Ewen and Ewen; Ewen; Lears, *No Place of Grace;* and Douglas, *Terrible Honesty.*

55. See Painter; Wiebe; May; Miller; Stevenson; Lynd and Lynd; and Allen.

56. See Lears, "From Salvation to Self-Realization"; and Susman.

57. Garrison, 53.

58. Hofstadter, 133.

59. May, 245.

60. Cited in Sarlós, 38.

61. Kinne, 278.

62. An analogous event, organized in 1974 by Broadway producer Alexander Cohen to bring together commercial and not-for-profit (regional) producers, caused so much "divisiveness" that the experiment was not tried again until 2000. Stuart W. Little's study of the 1974 conference cited a similar gathering on Broadway during the Depression but said the 1930s meeting lacked such a "comprehensive structure" (23). No mention was made of the 1927 meeting, although the 1974 concerns—how commercial and not-for-profit theatre could work together to solve problems of funding, government support, and attracting new audiences—resemble those of the Little Theatre era. "Divisiveness" is from Michael Janeway's observations of the ACT II Conference (32).

63. Beckerman, 340.

64. "The Great World Theatre," 840. The New Theatre's building was too large for intimate playing, and it had the horseshoe shape of European opera houses, notorious for poor sightlines. It was located in the west 60s of Manhattan—far from both the theatre district and even from the theatre-loving immigrants its managers claimed to want to attract. It failed after two seasons, in no small part because the stars it engaged were both expensive and old-fashioned.

65. Cheney, *The Art Theatre,* 1925 edition, 2–3.

66. Elam, 55.

67. Strychacz, 43, 27.

68. For a discussion of the intense focus on progress and cultural leadership in the Midwest, see May, 90–106.

69. See Heller and Rudnick; Black; and Sarlós.

70. Christine Stansell notes that "by the early 1900s, middle-class versions of bohemia existed across the country," comprising everything from actual artists' colonies to groups of clubwomen and young marrieds "assembled under the bohemian rubric" (45).

71. Grana, 88, 73.

72. Williams, 61, 56.

73. Dell, 663.

74. Glaspell, 235–36.

75. See Humphrey; and Fishbein.

76. Stansell, 87, 18. Stansell also points out that not only latter-day critics but

even pacifist social critic Randolph Bourne grasped that participatory democracy on the Greenwich Village model "might come to serve as a substitute for that democracy" (221).

77. Stansell, 18

78. Brooks is looking at the educated elite of the 1990s who seek to embrace the anti-establishmentariansm of the 1960s in combination with the financial conquests of the 1980s. In using the notion of "proto" Bobos, I am borrowing his concept although not wholly sticking with his periodization of it.

79. Brooks, 46; Fishbein, 188.

80. Such contributions in the main affect the "imperial middle," the people whose idea of "America" travels unmarked but is the product of class interest. DeMott criticizes this class blindness because "it produces a culture in which men and women of intellectual and artistic talent are persuaded that the highest cause such talent can serve is that of its own independence" (9). Stansell concludes her study of the Greenwich Village bohemians of the 1910s with the observation that post-war *embourgeoisement* of bohemianism was welcomed by a consumerist, leisured society looking to spend its war profits, thus reinforcing the links between rebellion and consumerism (335).

81. Williams, 33, 15.

82. Stansell, 160.

83. Lears locates a decided antimodernist strain squarely at the center of many modernist projects, particularly those that sought regeneration in Oriental, premodern, pastoral, and preindustrial religions and crafts. He notes that questing, usually privileged (anti)modernists, "[u]nable to transcend bourgeois values, . . . often ended by revitalizing them" (*No Place of Grace,* 57.)

84. Perloff quoted in Knight, 206.

85. Singal, 8.

86. Fishbein, 207.

87. See Hamar.

88. Strychacz, 27–28.

89. Strychacz, 36.

90. Browne, "The Temple of a Living Art," 10.

91. Dewey, *Democracy and Education,* 72; and Michaels, 53.

92. Constance D'Arcy Mackay, 144, 105–6, 138, 90.

93. Bryant, 42.

94. See Mester.

95. Bryant, 23. The 1915 one-act "Enemies," also a Provincetown production, by Neith Boyce and Hutchins Hapgood, featured characters named "He" and "She." If Bryant's methods seem quaint and dated, consider Edward Albee's 2001 play *The Play About the Baby,* which also features four characters, two of whom are Boy and Girl, with the older couple now Man and Woman, and which was described by Ben Brantley in the *New York Times* as taking place "in an allegorical

ether" (February 2, 2001, B4.) Albee also continues the Little Theatre tradition of audience construction and edification in Man's act 2 speech excoriating lazy, anti-intellectual audiences.

96. For a comprehensive description and analysis of this production, see Blood, "Neighborhood Playhouse," 281–321.

97. Kallen, 104.

98. Blood, 318–19.

99. Bourdieu, *Distinction*, 239, 232.

100. Bourdieu, *Distinction*, 241.

101. The society, founded in 1912 and modeled on the London Stage Society, arranged for the 1914 New Stagecraft exhibition to travel from Cambridge, Massachusetts, to New York. The group also engaged Harley Granville Barker to direct three plays on Broadway in 1915, as well as doing its "regular" work of producing dramas it wanted to support.

102. Sarlós, 68.

103. Hutchins Hapgood, *A Victorian in the Modern World*, 147.

104. Sarlós, 82, 76.

105. Constance D'Arcy Mackay, 35.

2. Imagining the Little Theatre Audience: Precedents and Prejudices

1. The Boston Museum of Fine Arts was incorporated in 1870 and opened to the public in 1876; New York City's Metropolitan Museum of Art was started in 1870, followed by the Philadelphia Museum of Art in 1876 and the Art Institute of Chicago in 1879. Boston's symphony orchestra was established in 1881 and New York's in 1845; by World War I, symphony orchestras were fixtures in St. Louis, Cincinnati, Minneapolis, Pittsburgh, Chicago, and San Francisco.

2. See Ohmann. Barbara Ehrenreich's "professional middle class" is defined in shorthand as the "class [that] uses consumption to establish its status" and that most fears "losing control" (14, 247).

3. Ohmann, 155, 158–59, 163, 171.

4. Moses.

5. Metcalfe.

6. Esteve; Eaton, "What's the Matter with the Road?"; and Eaton, "The Menace of the Movies."

7. Deland; and Palmer.

8. Gerould.

9. Calder.

10. Frohman; and Eaton, "The Real Revolt in Our Theatre."

11. Strachey.

12. Andrews.

13. Aristotle, 73; also see Barish, 86–87, 133–34, and passim.

14. Barish, 406–7.

15. Barish, 156–57.

16. Glenn Hughes, 92–93.

17. Quoted in Bernheim, 15.

18. For descriptions of early audience behavior see Butsch, chaps. 1–4; and Henneke.

19. Levine, 203, 207, 184.

20. Esteve.

21. May, 30.

22. The American Academy of Dramatic Art, among the first schools devoted exclusively to the training of actors, opened in 1884. The first university theatre training program to offer a degree was that of the Carnegie Institute of Technology (now Carnegie Mellon University), begun in 1913. Benjamin McArthur's study *Actors and American Culture, 1880–1920* highlights the privileged origins of the actors in his sample but acknowledges that they comprised a minority among the overall actor population (31).

23. Palmer.

24. Strachey, 224.

25. Deland, 497.

26. See Hogan, et al.

27. Meyer, 91.

28. See Carlson, 13–14.

29. Bourne, "Our Cultural Humility," 504.

30. Bourne, "Our Cultural Humility," 505.

31. Bourne, "The Cult of the Best," 276.

32. Greek ideals also influenced emerging trends in dance. Isadora Duncan as a performer and Margaret H'Doubler as a dance educator predicated their ideas of "natural" movement and the cultural utility of dance on their understanding of ancient Greek movement and society. See Ross.

33. Wiley, 59–65.

34. Macgowan, *The Theatre of Tomorrow*, 283.

35. Wiley points out that Browne's thinking about Greek art and drama was directly influenced by Pater's argument that "success is defined not by moral conduct but by the intensity of one's aesthetic experience" (29).

36. Wiley, 128.

37. Maurice Browne, *Too Late to Lament: An Autobiography*, 118–19.

38. Wiley, 170.

39. Sarlós, 35, 36.

40. On Cook, see Sarlós, 50–51.

41. "Oligarchy" is in Browne, "The Temple of a Living Art," 8. Tingley calls Browne a "Lothario" (132). Also see Kramer's chapter "Now a Grecian Temple" in his *Chicago Renaissance.* Lock suggests that Browne's real commitment was to the ninety-plus hours a week he and the company toiled together and that

the experience of performing before an audience (where Browne was not literally in moment-to-moment control as he was in rehearsal) was of secondary interest.

42. See Erenberg, especially chap. 2, "After the Ball: Hotels and Lobster Palaces, 1893–1912."

43. Halttunen, 184.

44. "Sophocles' Antigone." Although the clipping is undated, the production was offered four times in March 1890, and the review refers to "the performance . . . yesterday afternoon," making it likely from March.

45. Banta, 659.

46. "Sophocles' 'Antigone.'"

47. Wiebe, 295.

48. Wiebe, 165.

49. Quoted in Sarlós, 32.

50. Goldman, 303.

51. Constance D'Arcy Mackay noted that "[m]any Little Theatres in cities avoid paying the theatre tax and the fireman's salary by doing away with the box office and depending on subscription" (218). Membership was, I would argue, less a way of "doing away with box office" than a transitional way to segue from outright amateurism to a version of professionalism. Mackay's text is slippery about the terms "professional" and "semi-professional" and resists "amateur," although the companies she discusses did not pay a living wage, when they paid anything at all. It is clear that for some, especially the Provincetowners, "the plays they produce are as frankly 'for sale' as the pictures in an art store's gallery" (49). The agreed-upon enemy was not "professionalism," it was "commercialism," but even this is problematic with regard to producing a product that was "frankly for sale."

52. Goldman, 61–62, 102, 137.

53. Constance D'Arcy Mackay, 243.

54. Quoted in Bullard, 84.

55. See Lears, "The Figure of the Artisan: Arts and Crafts Ideology" in *No Place of Grace* 60–96.

56. Gillpatrick, 5.

57. Crosby.

58. Dan H. Laurence, editor of Shaw's letters, notes that Jay was "oblivious to the fact that vast quantities of mail were being delivered to the bottom of the Atlantic with an average of three million tons of commercial shipping a year being destroyed by enemy action on the seas" (140).

59. George Bernard Shaw to Beulah Jay, 17 November 1917, in Laurence, 140–42.

60. See Sollors, "A Critique of Pure Pluralism," 258, 263, 269.

61. Higham's *Strangers in the Land: Patterns of American Nativism 1860–1925* remains a central study of the era and its nativist anxieties.

62. Kadlec, 136.

63. Dewey quoted in Kallen, 132.

64. For a brief and cogent discussion of the paradoxes of racialism, see Erdman, 121–27.

65. Higham, 122–23; Dewey, "Americanism and Localism," 684–88.

66. Higham, 139, 147, 151, 172, 155–56, 271, and 318.

67. For a superb study of how this shift occurred, see Jacobson.

68. In 1912, 90 percent of African Americans lived in the south, where most were tenant farmers or servants.

69. See Seller.

70. Lipscomb.

71. Matthews, 141.

72. Matthews, 145.

73. Erdman, 131–32.

74. Corbin, 30, 32, 35.

75. On textbooks see FitzGerald, 50–105. Although WASPS may not have intended this, Catholics—a recurring target of nativist prejudice—who were English-speakers benefited somewhat from the emergent concern about new immigrants, as, for example, during the 1890s, when vaudeville comics "shifted from the 'two Irishmen' joke to newer routines involving 'two Jews'" (Lears, *No Place of Grace*, 108).

76. Corbin, 47.

77. Corbin, 41, 43. See also Hutchins Hapgood, *The Spirit of the Ghetto: Studies of the Jewish Quarter of New York.*

78. Corbin, 31. For a less romanticized, more populist thumbnail sketch of Italian audiences and performances, see Butsch, *The Making of American Audiences*, 131–32.

79. Corbin, 32.

80. Corbin, 37, 38. Erdman points out that Jews were routinely seen "as a species of oriental exotic" in late-nineteenth-century United States (25, 26, 31).

81. Corbin, 43.

82. See Seller; and Dormon.

83. Corbin, 48.

84. "Soiled" is quoted in Rich, 197; Addams, 387.

85. Addams, 384.

86. Hecht, "Social and Artistic," 175.

87. See, for example, Heniger. Heniger's goals, expressed in fairly commonplace Progressive vocabulary, included character development (13), "civic duty" (61), "true spiritual growth" (37), "moral and artistic uplift" (15), and "kind-

ness and humanity toward animals" (18). Her first production was *The Tempest*. Her discussion of her second Shakespeare production, *As You Like It*, in 1904, reveals not only her do-good motives, but also her sense of the inadequacies of the neighborhood residents. The play was selected because of "its power to represent a suitable ideal to the neighborhood" who "deserved all the comfort and strength which come from spiritual fellowship with a higher type of human being" (24). By working with Shakespeare, youngsters were to become clean, well-comported, articulate, and spiritually superior.

88. Hecht, "Social and Artistic," 176–77.
89. Rich, 202–3. Pelham's article is "The Story of the Hull-House Players."
90. Addams, 391.
91. Shapiro.
92. Hecht, "Social and Artistic," 178–79.
93. Jackson, 233.
94. Jackson, 209.
95. Jackson, 234–47.
96. See Bourdieu, "The Forms of Capital."
97. Cheney, *The Art Theater*, 224.
98. Cheney, *The Art Theater*, 67.
99. See Blood, "Neighborhood Playhouse"; and Crowley.
100. Lears, *No Place of Grace*, 10.
101. Crowley, 160, 161, 17–18.
102. As amateur attempts at comparative religions, Lewisohn's observations are neither uninformed or naive, but they capture little of what made the described practices distinctive for the people who performed them. I am grateful to J. Ellen Gainor for suggesting a view of the Lewisohns as amateur anthropologists.
103. The usual reason given for German-Jewish fear of the "Ost Juden" is that outbreaks of anti-Semitism against the newly arrived rural, Yiddish-speaking, often unwashed, unsophisticated, poor, superstitious, and politically radical Eastern European Jews would be turned against the wealthier, better-educated, already-assimilated German Jews. Blood points out, quoting research by Selma Berrol, that the origins of these fears were actually economic, as German Jews owned 97 percent of the New York garment trade in 1885 as well as most tenements on the Lower East Side, and their most pressing worries were about unionism and radical rhetoric being turned on them not by natives but by the new arrivals themselves (243).
104. Blood, "Neighborhood Playhouse," 202, 203.
105. Crowley 82, 167, 75, 181, chaps. 20–24, and p. 34.
106. DiMaggio, "Social Structure, Institutions, and Cultural Goods," 38. DiMaggio is cofounder of the Center for Arts and Cultural Policy Studies at Princeton University.

107. Arvold, "Little Country Theater," 91, 89. Undated pamphlet. The date is probably 1912 or 1913, as the article refers to the Little Country Theater as "scarcely a year old." In his book a decade later, Arvold rephrased the observation to note that "moral degeneracy in the country, like the city, is usually due to lack of proper social recreation" (*The Little Country Theater*, 24, also 22). An appendix to Arvold's book included not only lists of plays and books about costuming, make-up, production, and publicity; it also listed twenty-seven books under the heading "Country Life." See also Cremin, 82–84.

108. Arvold, "The Little Country Theater," 93.

109. For a discussion of the "Anglocentric and hierarchical vision of society and culture" promulgated by pageant leaders in the 1910s and early 1920s often in the name of inclusiveness, see Glassberg. Quote is from p. 52. A number of people who wrote scripts for municipal and historical pageants were also prominent playwrights and educators in Little Theatre, including George Pierce Baker and Constance D'Arcy Mackay.

110. Arvold, *The Little Country Theater*, 159.

111. Norman Hapgood, 144, 233.

112. Dickinson, *The Insurgent Theatre*, 35, 36.

113. "Editorial comment."

114. DiMaggio, "Social Structure," 39.

115. The Johnson Act of 1924 is discussed at greater length in chap. 6.

116. Blood, "Neighborhood Playhouse," 85.

117. Larrabee, 135.

118. The latter combination would appear in the writing of some educators in the 1920s and is discussed in chap. 5.

3. Producing the Audience

1. See Arvold, *The Little Country Theatre;* Dickinson, *Chief Contemporary Dramatists;* and Hubbell and Beaty. Macgowan and Cheney both conclude their books discussed here with lists of suggested reading in essay form.

2. Janice Radway points out that, until the corporate takeovers that began in the 1960s, American publishing was seen as a "seat-of-the-pants" industry by critics and supporters alike (35 and n. 3 on 243–44). The spate of theatre books that appeared during the Little Theatre movement followed by the demise during the 1920s of publishers that specialized in theatre books reflects an era in the industry when personal taste governed publishing choices in the absence of marketing sophistication.

3. Moderwell, 18, 122.

4. Moderwell, 257, 262, 267, 268.

5. Moderwell, 261, 264, 265, 281, 267, 266, 258, 282. "Minorities" is Moderwell's word, and he uses it twice.

6. Dickinson, *The Insurgent Theatre*, 129, 63, 15–16, 81.

7. Gerstenberg, "Come Back With Me," 64.

8. Dickinson, *The Insurgent Theatre,* 218–19, 148–49. See chap. 2 for Browne's belief in a rhythmic ideal.

9. Although much of his own work focused on literature and playwriting, his university was an aggressive proponent of practical studies. For example, Wisconsin's Madison campus was the first American university to offer modern dance with an eye to training citizens and spectators, not professional artists. That program got its start the same year that Dickinson published *The Insurgent Theatre.* Ross.

10. The American spelling of "theater" in his title (he also uses this spelling in referring to other books, regardless of the latters' own editorial choices) puts a certain American stamp on his position, although it is unclear whether the orthographic choice was made by him or by his publisher, Knopf, an "insurgent" itself as one of a group of new publishers specializing in modernist, theatre, and classic texts. For a brief discussion of upstart publishers interested in modernist literature and new theories, see Stansell, 156–57.

11. Shipp.

12. Cheney, *The Art Theater,* 87.

13. Dickinson, *The Insurgent Theatre,* 110.

14. Cheney, *The Art Theater,* 96, 164.

15. Cheney, *The Art Theater,* 226.

16. Cheney, *The Art Theater,* 226, 216, 222. Cheney discusses endowment on 228 and 249–52.

17. See Bloom. Jones, who studied with Max Reinhardt in Europe immediately after graduating from Harvard, introduced the New Stagecraft to New York audiences with his 1915 design for Harley Granville Barker's production of *The Man Who Married a Dumb Wife.* He designed O'Neill's earliest Broadway successes and later designed for the Theatre Guild.

18. Macgowan, *The Theatre of Tomorrow,* 242.

19. In the 1880s, August Strindberg had suggested that the workings of human minds in "real life" are "irregular" and reflect a "hodge-podge" of influences. This articulation of the real as irregular is different from Realism's concern for causality in character and in plot construction. (See Strindberg, 423, 422.)

20. Macgowan, *Theatre of Tomorrow,* 152, 151–52, 268–71, 273.

21. Hinsdell, *Making the Little Theater Pay,* 53, 78, 45.

22. Hinsdell, *Making the Little Theater Pay,* 22.

23. See Postlewait's discussion of these two strains of performance, 124–25.

24. The publication was *Theatre Arts Magazine* from 1916–1923, then *Theatre Arts Monthly* until 1939, and *Theatre Arts* thereafter. I use *Theatre Arts* for all references, since this catalogue listing provides access to all volumes.

25. Gilder, et al., xiv, xv.

26. She served as editor until 1945 and remained as publisher until 1948. See Katter.

27. The WorldCat database shows 970 libraries holding *Theatre Arts* and 232 holding *Drama*. "Principal organ" is from Keith Newlin, ed., *American Plays of the New Woman*, 19.

28. Publishing plays was part of the agenda of other sophisticated magazines of culture and commentary, such as *Smart Set, Drama, Seven Arts,* and *Forum;* in this respect *Theatre Arts* was important but not original.

29. Gilder, et al., xiv.

30. See Stratman; and Mott, vol. 1, 165–66 and vol. 4, 255–261. For an in-depth portrait of one short-lived journal, see Kaynor.

31. See Ohmann.

32. Wilson.

33. Smith, 135.

34. The publication's gendered identity is discussed in the next chapter.

35. Katter, 65–66.

36. Unless otherwise noted, my references to *Theatre Arts* cover the years 1916–1925.

37. Charles U. Larson, 18.

38. Katter, 65.

39. Morrisson, 9.

40. "What We Stand For."

41. Katter outlines five overriding characteristics of *Theatre Arts,* the first of which is "a desire to correlate in the theatre all of the arts" and the last of which is to encourage the non-commercial theatre movement throughout the country (74).

42. Cheney, "Foreword."

43. Katter reports that writers were paid for all published articles but that pieces about Little Theatres were construed as publicity and paid at half the regular rate (65).

44. Cheney, "New York's Best Season."

45. Gale, "The Wisconsin Players," 128.

46. Cheney, "The Most Important Thing in the Theatre."

47. Head and Gavin, 60.

48. *Theatre Arts* 9, no. 11 (November 1925): 760.

49. Katter, 65.

50. Cheney was a native of Berkeley and a graduate of the University of California, where his mother worked as a placement director.

51. "Editorial comment."

52. Zolotow. *Drama* printed 27,000 copies in 1917 (Brino-Dean, 159 n. 89) compared to the few hundred of *Theatre Arts,* but the intended sphere of influence ultimately differed.

53. Mumford, 67, 74, 67, 71–73.

54. Tony Schwartz calls this phenomenon "evoked recall" (69). Operating on the idea that it is better to "get a message out of receivers than to put one into them," persuaders who want to enable the sense of spontaneous feeling or recognition plant experiences and then summon them (21–22, 24–25, 55, 65, 67).

55. Peters, 127.

56. Pavis, 16.

57. St. Denis, 75–77

58. Duncan, 21.

59. Levinson.

60. In August, 1933, the entire issue of *Theatre Arts* was devoted to Dramatic Arts of the American Indian.

61. For an extended discussion of this production, see Curtis.

62. Gale, "The Colored Players and Their Plays," 139.

63. "Oriental and Western Acting," 177.

64. Coomaraswamy and Block, 113–22.

65. Coomaraswamy and Block, 122.

66. Eaton, *The American Stage of To-Day*, 330–31. Eaton may have had in mind some of Strindberg's interest in the irregular and erratic workings of the psyche as referents for realism. See n. 19. Recall, too, Annie Nathan Meyer's impatience with photorealism as already old-fashioned in 1915.

67. Eaton, "Crowds and Mr. Hamilton." Hamilton's complaint about spectators going to the theatre merely to be part of a theatre audience need not necessarily be totally damning, as it presumes an interest in the social event and the public convocation that differentiate seeing a play from reading one. Certainly attention to this phenomenon anticipated (albeit negatively) Susan Bennett's much later observation that a theatre ticket always promises two things: the experience of an individual play and the experience of being in a theatre, regardless of the particular play. (*Theatre Audiences*, 126.)

68. Eaton, "The American Theatre and Reconstruction," 8.

69. Eaton, "The American Theatre and Reconstruction," 10. Here, Eaton's characterizing the difference between New York and the nation as "unfortunate" is particularly ironic. If the disjuncture is regrettable, why would playwrights not aim for "the best?" If the rest of the nation was a buried treasure, why the word "unfortunate?" Again, the editors made no comment. Hindsight suggests that the national network works to recuperate Broadway appeal, as nonprofit regional theatres become the venues for newly franchised Broadway or off-Broadway successes often eager to copy rather than reinterpret these plays.

70. Eaton, "The American Theatre and Reconstruction," 11.

71. Mark Fearnow asserts that there are good reasons to see the two organi-

zations as a continuum rather than following common theatre history precedent that regards them as separate entities.

72. Fearnow, 353–54.
73. Helburn, 272.
74. Helburn, 270.
75. Eaton, "Audiences," 28, 26, 28.
76. Editorial, *Theatre Arts* 4.
77. Orville K. Larson, 46.
78. Helen Louise Cohen, 689.
79. Marquis, 98, 240.
80. "The Great World Theatre," 761–62.
81. See Wainscott. While he does not foreground the Little Theatre movement per se as the source of the innovations he sees on Broadway and nationally, many of the innovators he cites began their careers and honed their skills in early Little Theatres.
82. McBane, 3.
83. McCandless.
84. Kinne, 67.
85. G. P.
86. Cited in Kinne, 136.
87. George Pierce Baker, "The Theatre and the University," 101.
88. See Baker's introduction to *Harvard Plays: The 47 Workshop.*
89. Kinne, 134.
90. Workshop programs are available at the Harvard Theatre Collection.
91. George Pierce Baker papers, Harvard Theatre Collection. Statement is from a folder labeled II GPB's The 47 Workshop. A similar description occurs in the introduction to *Harvard Plays,* but the punitive actions are not included.
92. Letter from J. M. Lindley, 10 November 1923 in the George Pierce Baker papers, Harvard Theatre Collection.
93. By the 1920s, universities offering ongoing course work in drama and theatre and, in increasing numbers, practicum-based degrees included the Universities of Michigan, Wisconsin, North Carolina, Iowa, and North Dakota, as well as Columbia, Cornell, and the Carnegie Institute of Technology. Among the smaller colleges that offered innovative courses in theatre early in the century were Grinnell, Vassar, and Smith.
94. See letters from Kathleen Middleton, Mrs. Frank (Florence Ramsay) Huckins, F. W. D. Hersy, Frederic C. Day, A. G. Pirrot, Mrs. William H. (Lora Standish) Weston Jr., Alice Spaulding, Amy Morrison, Perle Mary Hopson, and Sybil Holbrook. Letters are in the George Pierce Baker papers, Harvard Theatre Collection.
95. For a discussion of Harvard's attitudes on exclusion, see Weber.

96. DiMaggio, "Social Structure," 39.

97. Executive Committee Minutes and Reports (21 October 1918), Harvard Theatre Collection.

98. Baker, "The New Mexican of Today."

99. Baker, *Dramatic Technique,* 509–10, 514.

100. Baker, *Dramatic Technique,* 511–12.

101. Kinne, 56–57.

102. Baker, *Dramatic Technique,* 68.

103. Baker, *Dramatic Technique,* 517.

104. Richard Wightman Fox points out that forward-looking sociologists in the 1920s recognized that even small-town America was hardly uniformly white and Protestant. In "Epitaph for Middletown: Robert S. Lynd and the Analysis of Consumer Culture," Fox presents critiques of the Lynds' choice of Muncie, Indiana, as "typical," charging the Lynds with inaccuracy and nostalgia in their rendering of the actual United States of their day. Among major theatre cities, Boston had a large Irish population as early as 1846 and significant Italian and Jewish populations in place by 1900. Overall in the country, by 1903 it ranked fifteenth among the 161 principal cities in terms of foreign-born populations (Bushee, 1–2).

105. See, for example, Helvenston; Mabie, "The Responses of Theatre Audiences, Experimental Studies"; and Hansen and Bormann.

106. See chap. 2 for a discussion of experimental productions with immigrant participants in which exactly such "distraction" was part of the point for well-heeled audience members.

107. *The Trap* was not published and there is no extant manuscript either in the Harvard Theatre collection or at the New York Public Library for the Performing Arts, Billy Rose Collection. The letters are part of the George Pierce Baker Papers in the Harvard Theatre Collection.

108. Bourdieu, *Distinction,* 58, 31.

4. "Fall Girls of Modernism": Women and/as Audiences

1. Clayton Hamilton, "Organizing an Audience," 164.

2. Dickinson, *The Insurgent Theatre,* 128. Charles and Daniel Frohman were brothers who controlled theatres in Boston and New York. They had run a minstrel company in the 1880s and Daniel was a partner in the Famous Players Film Company. Perhaps most significantly, with regard to assessing and having an effect on theatre audiences nationally, Charles was a member of the powerful Theatrical Syndicate, which was founded in 1896 and dominated theatre booking for two decades.

3. Burton, 180.

4. See Bank.

5. See McConachie, *Melodramatic Formations,* chaps. 6, 7, and 8.

6. For connections between department store shopping and theatre see Leach, especially 80–81, 127, and 143–45.

7. Butsch, 122; see, too, my discussion of Hodin in chap. 1.

8. Butsch, 78; on audiences becoming increasingly quiet, see Henneke; and McConachie, "Pacifying American Theatrical Audiences, 1820–1900"; on other commercial producers' practices to attract women, see Dudden, especially chaps. 5 and 6; on the segmenting of theatrical entertainments to separate venues, see Levine, especially chap. 1.

9. Veblen applied his theory even to the not-so-leisured, who also achieved a sense of belonging by having the wife spend her husband's income so as to assure his, and thereby their, status.

10. See Douglas, *The Feminization of American Culture;* and Welter.

11. Coontz, 11.

12. Blair, *Clubwoman,* 8.

13. Stansell, 89.

14. Chinoy, 57–59.

15. Chinoy, 6. Crothers was the only woman playwright of the Progressive Era to make a good, ongoing living at playwriting, enjoying a string of Broadway productions over several decades.

16. See Pasquier.

17. McConachie, *Melodramatic Formations,* 235.

18. As Little Theatre emerged in the 1910s, an increasing, although still small, number of women were self-supporting and paid for their own theatre tickets.

19. Ann Douglas, conversation with the author, 23 October 1996.

20. Levine, 196–97.

21. Warfield.

22. Warfield.

23. Douglas, *Terrible Honesty,* 380. Lewisohn, a drama critic for the *Nation* and a novelist, was married to Provincetown playwright Mary Bosworth Crocker. The couple separated in 1924, and Lewisohn cited his wife's age (she was nineteen years his senior) as an indication of her "moral obliquity" in choosing a husband only three years older than her eldest child. Two years later, he wrote an autobiographical novel in which the protagonist sees himself as Hamlet, Oedipus, and Orestes and murders his older wife by bludgeoning her with a poker. He then calmly calls the police and prepares to go to jail (126, 244).

24. Clayton Hamilton, "The Psychology of Theatre Audiences," 236, 235, 237, 245.

25. See Blair, *Clubwoman* and *Torchbearers;* Radway; and Lisker.

26. Although she is talking about novelists and playwrights, Kornelia Tancheva's observation also serves with regard to critics and essayists when she notes "[t]he repression of women writers in both the construction of the dominant modernist paradigm and in the textual practices of the canonized modernists."

Implied (if not outright) antifeminism signaled "modernism" and sophistication in one's critical work (153–54). J. Ellen Gainor suggests that even the sophisticated Jane Heap and Margaret Anderson of the *Little Review* developed a sympathy for modernist aesthetics that foreclosed their ability to recognize, especially in Susan Glaspell's play *Bernice,* the concerns and doings of ordinary women characters who subtly subverted the strictures of traditionally expected behavior for women. In other words, women with modernist sympathies were themselves perpetrators of certain kinds of assertions of independence and blind to others (108–11).

27. Ella Costillo Bennett, 241. One male fiction writer concocted a tale of a touring stock company in which no other feature of being on the road was so grueling as meeting with matinee girls after a show (Jenks, 48).

28. Nichols, 30.

29. Macadams, 77.

30. Bell, 244.

31. Rauh, 24.

32. Hobart, 244.

33. Ten Broeck, 372.

34. A. P., "A Woman Who Financed and Built a Little Theatre," 113, 114.

35. A. P.,"Acting Helps a Woman to Live," 14.

36. Patterson, 168.

37. Beckley.

38. Pierce, 92–93.

39. Savage.

40. Stengel.

41. Plummer, 11. For a discussion of the Theatre Guild and its audiences see chap. 3.

42. Hokinson, "The Boxers: The Exclusive in Their Mad Pursuit of Pleasure," 25; and Plummer.

43. Hokinson, "Matinee Girls of 1924," 25.

44. Hokinson, "Other Aisle, Please," 29.

45. Stengel.

46. Malcolm Cowley provides a glimpse of how body image changed in as little as two years. In his 1934 memoir, he discussed Greenwich Village bohemians and recalled two groups in the Village in the late 1910s and early 1920s: those who had lived there before 1917 and those who arrived after the war. Cowley, born in 1898, was in the latter group (tellingly called "we," as the others are "they"). He characterized the stereotypical female radicals of the earlier vintage as wearing "funny clothes" and having "heels set firmly on the ground and abdomens protruding a little—since they wore no corsets and dieting hadn't become popular—they had a look of unexampled solidity; it was terrifying to

be advanced upon by six of them in close formation." The generation of intellectuals and writers Cowley depicted was almost exclusively male (70).

47. Miles, 22, 70.

48. Lewis, *Main Street*, 341.

49. Bucco, 13; Conroy, 197.

50. Bucco, 15.

51. Smiley, 10.

52. Crowe, 86.

53. Lea, 188.

54. No less than Sam Hume, artistic director of the Detroit Arts and Crafts Theatre, which supported the founding of *Theatre Arts,* turned down one of Alice Gerstenberg's one-acts as "too experimental." The play, "Attuned," a one-character piece in which a young wife intuits that her husband has been killed overseas during the war, now seems like a heartfelt, realistic character study, or even a sentimental love story. To Hume, the idea of two souls communicating telepathically was simply not within the realm of what he wanted to risk producing. Hume's letter is in the Alice Gerstenberg papers at Chicago's Newberry Library.

55. Lewis, preface to *Main Street.*

56. Hofstadter, 281; see also Miller.

57. Douglas, *Terrible Honesty,* 3–9 and 217–53. Quote is from 381.

58. See Lynn D. Gordon, who chronicles the racism that characterized most colleges and their students, including students in all-female colleges. Black and Jewish students—usually high achievers, or else they wouldn't have risked applying at all—were discouraged by admissions officers and snubbed or ignored by fellow students. Professors sometimes didn't bother to learn how to pronounce their names, white students refused to eat with blacks, and Jews were denied admission to Phi Beta Kappa because their legitimate hard work made them prey to being characterized as "greasy grinds," whose presence would alter the "character" of the society (42, 47–51).

59. Best, "The Drama League of America, 1914," 149.

60. "The Drama League of America," the *Evanston News-Index,* March 28, 1910, quoted in Bogard, 8.

61. "The Drama League of America," the *Evanston News-Index,* March 28, 1910, quoted in Bogard, 20, 58, 20.

62. Figures on membership, details of finances and specific projects, and copies of various internal memos and correspondence are available in Bogard. An overview of the projects and publications of the league in its first fifteen years is Best's pamphlet, "Drama League of America: Its Inception, Growth, Accomplishment and Promise."

63. Blair, *The Torchbearers,* chap. 6.

64. Bogard, 79.

65. Best, "The Drama League of America, 1914," 136.

66. Worm.

67. William B. Guthrie, "The New Drama League," the *Chicago Record* (7 May 1910) quoted in Bogard, 13.

68. Broun, the *New York World*, 11 April 1923, quoted in Bogard, 76. Terry Brino-Dean points out in his study of Drama League aesthetics that the league never precisely defined "good" drama, thereby making it possible "to unite people of the organization around a common cause" (200), arguably a cause as coded—or chimerical—as Broun's.

69. Best in the General Federation of Women's Clubs *Report Tenth Biennial Proceedings* (1910), quoted in Blair, *Torchbearers*, 151.

70. "The Drama League of America," (1911) 116.

71. "Drama League Junior Dept. in Chicago," the *Chicago Record*, 30 August 1912, quoted in Bogard, 39.

72. Zilboorg, 276.

73. Best, "Drama League of America: Its Inception, Growth, Accomplishment and Promise," 4.

74. Edward B. Gordon, 29.

75. *Variety* report quoted in Bernheim, 102.

76. Bogard, 30, 33, 75, 40–43.

77. Best, "The Drama League of America: Its Inception, Growth, Accomplishment and Promise" 7.

78. See Chansky.

79. Ehrensperger, "A National Drama Celebration," 150.

80. Dolan, 5.

81. Bogard, 71–72.

82. Bogard, 59–60, 83–86, 128–29.

83. Blair, *Torchbearers*, 159; Bogard, 121–22.

84. Like *Theatre Arts, Drama* had different names over the course of its existence. I use *Drama* as this was always the primary word in the title, whether it was a quarterly or a monthly.

85. "Editorial," *Drama*, 1.

86. "Drama League of America to Lose New York Center."

87. Katter, 43–72.

88. Ehrensperger, "Women and the Little Theatre."

89. As we shall see in the next chapter, university programs also perpetuated—in the name of progress and inclusion—a gender-divided theatre landscape that included lower salaries in its pink-collar ghettos. Nonetheless, universities did offer women access to professional theatre training at the hand of innovators.

90. Blair, *The Clubwoman as Feminist*, 108.

91. Lemons, 54.

92. Freedman, 35.

93. Quoted in Rapp and Ross, 59.

94. The *New York Times* review of a Broadway revival in 2001 calls the play a "glorified cat show" featuring "grotesques that only a female impersonator could love" (Brantley).

95. Black, 5.

96. See Cole.

97. See, for instance, Freeman; and Leah Hager Cohen.

98. Cowan, "Two Washes in the Morning." See, too, Jensen and Scharf, introduction; Freedman; and Rapp and Ross.

99. For a discussion of generational differences between feminist activists, see Smith-Rosenberg's final chapter.

100. Allen, 86.

101. Cheney, letter to Nafe Katter.

102. Katter, 143–44.

103. Katter, 143; Giddins, 97.

104. For a discussion of this feminist split in politics and labor, see Cott.

105. Jonas and Bennett. Quoted participant is Lisa Kron, 3. Observations about universalism and gender are on pp. 2–3. The statistic about Broadway ticketbuyers does not appear in the final report; it was in the draft circulated in August 2001 at the Women and Theatre conference in Chicago.

5. Textbook Cases: Learning to Be and See Little Theatre Women

1. McDermott, 14–15.

2. Cowley, 6, 295.

3. Cowley, 60–61.

4. Macgowan's work on several fronts is discussed in chap. 3.

5. Macgowan, *Footlights Across America,* 129–30.

6. Macgowan, *Footlights Across America,* 99, 140–41, 153, 247. In 1930, Sue Ann Wilson, the executive secretary of the woman-focused Drama League of America, replied to a female correspondent who was hesitating about accepting an appointment at a Little Theatre in Texas, hoping for something further east. Wilson wrote: "If there is a possibility for you to secure a directorship in Paris, Texas, I would advise you to grab the offer. It is almost impossible to place a woman as a little theatre director. All inquiries we receive are for men, and no matter how good a woman may be, I have never been able to place one in a good little theatre position" (Brino-Dean, 305).

7. The history of the Dallas Little Theatre, discussed in chap. 6, reveals just such a pattern.

8. For a detailed consideration of how this nexus of official input worked in American schools from the primary grades through graduate school as recently as the early 1970s, see Frazier and Sadker.

9. Many colleges and universities offered some courses in dramatic litera-ture, but a full-fledged major with an emphasis on practicum was less wide-spread. See Hamar, 572–594.

10. Macgowan, *Footlights Across America,* 153.

11. Tyack, 172.

12. Macgowan, *Footlights Across America,* 153.

13. See Perlmann and Margo.

14. See Nasaw.

15. Katz, 99.

16. McClellan and Reese, 161.

17. See Rury. "Professional-managerial" class is Richard Ohmann's term; see chap. 2

18. Dudden, 180.

19. Dreiser, 383.

20. It is beyond the scope of this study to investigate the "real life" causes of this desire for fulfillment and for display in depth. More than a half century after the height of the Little Theatre movement, a spate of writing in the area of psy-choanalytic feminism would posit that femaleness itself is, by definition, an "act." Femininity in this scheme both accommodates and is a warped version of the male psyche. The symptoms and some particular characteristics of feminine behavior morph, but, in this line of thinking, they always exist in opposition to and in the service of male norms. These norms are learned so early and they so thoroughly saturate the culture that they feel inevitable and are misrecognized as products of nature and not culture.

21. See Pasquier.

22. Lynn D. Gordon, 2.

23. Smith-Rosenberg, 253.

24. Gordon, passim.

25. See also Hamar.

26. Macgowan, *Footlights Across America,* 129–30.

27. Female impersonator Julian Eltinge, despite his popularity, is not the influence I am thinking of here so much as, say, actresses such as Edith Wynne-Matheson and Margaret Anglim, both of whom appeared as the title character in Philip Ben Greet's touring production of *Everyman.* Women themselves were among those who resisted innovative casting, as is clear in Sarah Barnwell Elliott's "Whose Fault Is It?" (1911), which discusses how cross-dressing in the-atre is a violation of "truth and beauty." The appearance of this article in *Drama* is a reminder of the recuperative strategies of some women within the Little Theatre movement.

28. Cremin, 93.

29. Kozelka, 595–97; Cremin, passim.

30. Helen Louise Cohen, 689.

31. See Susman; Lears, "From Salvation to Self-Realization"; Ewen; Goodrum and Dalrymple, 35–39; and Allen, chap. 5.

32. See Rury.

33. Kozelka, 612.

34. Kozelka, 601–2 and 608–9.

35. "Her Ph.D. No Bar to Role in Play."

36. Tyack, 24.

37. Smith-Rosenberg, 281.

38. Joseph, 144–47.

39. F. R. Donovan quoted in Joseph, 144.

40. R. Pulliam cited in Joseph, 146.

41. Evans, 49.

42. Evans, 75.

43. Evans, 183, 175.

44. Evans, xi, 163, 20, 34, 80.

45. See Filene.

46. Locke, "Steps Toward the Negro Theatre," 67.

47. Gillespie, 103–5.

48. Dewey, "The Act of Expression," 61–63, 65, 75.

49. See Eunice Mackay.

50. J. Ellen Gainor's study of the work of playwright Susan Glaspell and its contemporaneous as well as its recent reception demonstrates how even informed scholars and critics throughout the twentieth century have missed (or dismissed) the playwright's feminism and innovation, either measuring her against (masculine, modernist) "universal" standards or collapsing her feminism into essentialism and failing to grasp the materialist negotiations in her work at both a formal and a content level.

51. "Innovative nostalgia" is Robert M. Crunden's phrase for the pulling-in-two-directions agenda of many Progressive Era artists.

52. See Hubbell and Beaty.

53. "Overtones" is in *Plays By and About Women*, eds. Sullivan and Hatch; "Trifles" is in *Plays by American Women 1900–1930*, ed. Judith Barlow (New York: Applause, 1985), and in three editions of *The Harcourt Brace Anthology of Drama*, ed. W. B. Worthen. Both plays are included in *The Oxford Book of Women's Writing in the United States* and are the only examples of drama from the first half of the twentieth century.

54. See Newlin. Susan Bennett notes the irony and problem of a "homogeneity of selection" even in anthologies seeking to recuperate the previously ignored or excluded. New works by women gain admission to the canon because of some performance of "a filial relation either by the play, the playwright, or the editor" that guarantees a reinforcement of old standards via a historiographic method that inevitably pulls women's history "back into the trajectory

of what has always already been known" ("Theatre History and Women's Dramatic Writing," 52–53).

55. Gerstenberg, letters to Nancy Cox-McCormack Cushman, 1.20.

56. Some were rewritten with new titles, and "Overtones" was reworked as a three-act play in 1922.

57. See, for instance, Aimone; Suzanne Clark; Bonnie Kime Scott; Mersand; Pasquier; and Jaudon and Kozloff.

58. Atlas, 63.

59. Hecht, "The Plays of Alice Gerstenberg, 1, 13.

60. For a detailed description of women's work to support the Pasadena Community Playhouse in the 1910s and 1920s, see Blair, *The Torchbearers*, 160–77.

61. Gerstenberg, letters to Nancy Cox-McCormack Cushman and "Come Back With Me."

62. Gerstenberg, "Come Back With Me," 8, 90, 360.

63. Stansell, 259; Cowan, *More work for Mother*, 174–81.

64. See Newcomer, 56, 118, 189, 225.

65. The plays are "He Said and She Said," "Overtones," "The Unseen," "The Buffer," "Attuned," "The Pot Boiler," "Hearts," "Beyond," "Fourteen," and "The Illuminatti in Drama Libre." References to these plays are from the 1921 edition.

66. Gerstenberg, *Unquenched Fire*, 404.

67. Stansell, 262.

68. See Stansell chaps. 7 and 8; and Rudnick.

69. "Come Back With Me," 246, 247.

70. Sullivan and Hatch, viii.

71. Hecht, "The Plays of Alice Gerstenberg," 4.

72. Maddock, 41, 42.

73. Hecht, "The Plays of Alice Gerstenberg," 13.

74. See Rapp and Ross; and Fass.

75. "Come Back With Me," 86.

76. Beckley.

77. Gerstenberg, *The Conscience of Sarah Platt*, 128.

78. "The Buffer," 112.

79. "Hearts," 206.

80. See Lisker, 76.

81. Gerstenberg, "At the Club," 147–72.

82. "The Unseen," 78.

83. Letter to Nancy Cox-McCormack Cushman, 2.7, 2.9.

84. "Come Back With Me," 17.

85. Gerstenberg, "Come Back With Me," 227.

86. Gerstenberg, "Come Back With Me," 505.

87. Gerstenberg, "Come Back With Me," 548, 524.

88. Cheney, *The Art Theater,* 87.

89. "Come Back With Me," 426.

90. See Wright.

91. "Spinster Takes Issue with Dr. Crane."

92. Jackson, 164.

93. Gerstenberg, "Come Back With Me," 77, 124.

94. Gerstenberg, letter to the editor.

95. This is Carole L. Cole's thesis in her analysis of twenty-four plays by American women in the decades immediately before and after the passage of suffrage.

96. Gerstenberg, "Come Back With Me," 578.

97. *Encarta World English Dictionary* (New York: St. Martin's Press, 1999), 627.

6. Modeling a Future: The Dallas Little Theatre and "The No 'Count Boy"

1. See Hervey.

2. "Hinsdell's Departure from Little Theater Is Reported."

3. Quoted in Hammack, 35.

4. Dallas Little Theatre charter (4 January 1921).

5. Hammack, 53.

6. *Daily Times Herald* (Dallas), 10 September 1922, quoted in Hammack, 56; Temple, 8; Hinsdell quoted in Hammack, 67.

7. Hammack, 301.

8. Temple, 28, 27. Appealing to men may be read as pragmatic, since many privileged women still needed the permission of husbands or fathers for direct access to money. A later remark, though, suggests that Hinsdell believed stage-struck women should properly be disciplined by their husbands and that having control of their own money led to folly, even when this money was spent on performing endeavors. After he became an acting coach at RKO in Hollywood, Hinsdell stated, "Doting mothers . . . are responsible for 10,000 heartaches a year in this town . . . . If fathers were to take a firmer hand in these situations, by the simple expedient of cutting off the funds, a lot of time, expense and sorrow would be saved" (Heffernan).

9. Hinsdell quoted in Hammack, 133.

10. Quoted in Potts, 60.

11. Rogers, review of *The Tragedy of Nan.*

12. Potts, 60.

13. See Hendrickson, 180–87.

14. *Dallas Morning News,* 7 November 1934.

15. Hammack, 81.

16. Aronson.

17. Rogers, review of *Camille.*

18. Rogers, review of *The Constant Wife.*

19. Potts, 72.

20. "The Dallas Laboratory School of the Theatre," 48.

21. Hammack, 305.

22. See Davis and Broge, entry for Robert E. Lee Knight, 605.

23. True Thompson, quoted in Hammack, 65.

24. Rogers, "Looking Backward."

25. See Potts, 41; and "The Amateur's Green Room," 43.

26. True Thompson, quoted in Hammack, 65.

27. Primary materials about this event are in three scrapbooks titled "Belasco Cup," New York Public Library.

28. Letter from Walter Hartwig.

29. Belasco, 228–29.

30. Rock, 68.

31. Schudson, 102.

32. For a discussion of the international intentions of the Irish National Theatre, see Harrington, "The Founding Years and the Irish National Theatre That Was Not."

33. "Players of Texas Come Back Strong."

34. Heyward, 154–55.

35. "Native Theatre Dream of Professor at University: Carolina Playmaker Idea Rapidly Expanding to Other States."

36. Koch, "Ethics of the Histrionic: In Actor and Audience. I—Actor."

37. Koch, "Ethics of the Histrionic: In Actor and Audience. II—Audience."

38. "Drama and the People."

39. "The Dakota Playmakers," 21.

40. Greenlaw, 14.

41. For an extended consideration of how pageantry reinforced white, Protestant hegemony, often in the name of inclusiveness, see Glassberg. A number of people who wrote scripts for municipal and historical pageants were also prominent playwrights and educators in Little Theatre.

42. "The Carolina Playmakers."

43. McGovern.

44. Koch, "Drama in the South: The Carolina Playmakers Coming of Age," 11.

45. Henderson, "Scholium Scribendi," 25.

46. Bost; Ida Hamilton, "The Carolina Playmakers."

47. Colgate Baker.

48. "Producer of New York May Give Folk Plays."

49. Sawyer.

50. Koch, "Drama in the South," 16.

51. "The Folk Plays Last Night at the Municipal."

52. Nell Battle Lewis.

53. "For the Lord's Sake, Call It Off."

54. J. A.

55. "Sock and Buskin on Rural Stages."

56. Locke, "The Drama of Negro Life," 702.

57. Rampersad, ed. Introduction, *The New Negro,* xvi.

58. Locke, *The New Negro,* xxvi.

59. Schuyler, 662–63.

60. Langston Hughes, 692–94.

61. Locke, *The New Negro,* 15; Locke, "The Negro and the American Stage," 112, 116.

62. Locke, "The Legacy of the Ancestral Arts," 255 and 256.

63. Locke, "Steps Toward the Negro Theatre," 67, 68.

64. Krasner.

65. Locke,"The Drama of Negro Life," 702.

66. Favor, 20, 12.

67. See Trotter.

68. Harrington, "The Founding Years and the Irish National Theatre That Was Not," 10.

69. Harrington, "The Founding Years," 5.

70. Susan Cannon Harris, 90, 91.

71. Conor Cruise O'Brien quoted in Harrington, *The Irish Play on the New York Stage 1874–1966,* 56.

72. Harrington, *The Irish Play on the New York Stage,* 60, 55, 65, 72, 73.

73. See Ornish; and Winegarten and Schechter. Photographs in the Dallas Little Theatre general files at the Dallas Public Library include one of Lefkowitz at the cornerstone ceremony (1927) and an undated one of Stanley Marcus with the DLT's fourth director, Charles Meredith.

74. See chap. 2.

75. Jacobson, 93, 96.

76. Jacobson, 98, 94, 272, 156, 110.

77. Lott, 18.

78. See Mitchell, 16, 26, 38, 96.

79. Macgowan, *Footlights Across America,* 152.

80. Douglas, *Terrible Honesty,* 295. See also Curtis, who makes several references to Synge and the Irish Players in discussing Ridgely Torrence's project of writing serious plays with nonminstrel type black characters. She cites both the playwright's own stated goals and critical responses (10, 60, 67, 77, 80, and 222 n. 8).

81. "Prize Play to Be Given This Week."

82. Douglas, *Terrible Honesty,* 214.

83. See Neil Harris, 28; and Jameson, 136, 141, 144.

84. "Prize Play to Be Given This Week."

85. Barrett H. Clark, 4.

86. Howard Mumford Jones, 2.

87. See Pearce; and Paul Eliot Green Papers.

88. Some white Little Theatre workers and social workers started and served as directors of groups for African American participants. One of these was the DLT's Louis Hexter, who started a Negro Little Theatre in Dallas in the late 1920s and presented "The No 'Count Boy." Another, Rowena Jelliffe, put theatre at the center of her settlement work at Cleveland's Karamu House, where she was director of theatre activities from 1919 to 1946. Her group (and audience) were integrated but largely African American, and she foregrounded work with African American content.

89. Worthen, 53.

90. Blau, 280.

91. Douglas, *Terrible Honesty,* 282–83.

92. Carl Van Vechten, a white intellectual who was knowledgeable about Harlem and many of its artists and writers, tantalized and scandalized readers with his 1926 novel *Nigger Heaven.* The book exposed how racism affected every class of blacks and how even the most well-meaning whites naively saw blacks as happy-go-lucky. The male protagonist is a college-educated writer who is unable to find gainful employment outside Harlem except as an elevator operator. One of Van Vechten's themes is the color hierarchy that prevailed among blacks, in which lighter skin was more desirable.

93. "Home Folks See Belasco Cup Winner."

94. "Dallas Little Theatre Is Paid High Tribute for Prize Winning Performance in New York Meet."

95. Holt, letter to Paul Green, 19 September 1924.

96. Bayly.

97. Holt, letter to Paul Green, 11 May 1925; and Hinsdell, letter to Paul Green, undated, but the second week of May 1925 from content.

98. Other plays in the collection, entitled *The Lord's Will,* are "Old Wash Lucas," "The Old Man of Edenton," "The Lord's Will," "Blackbeard" (written with Elizabeth Lay), and "The Last of the Lowries."

99. Material about this production, which was presented at the Theatre de Lys under the direction of C. W. Christenberry, is in a folder titled "Salvation on a String" (the name give to the evening's bill) in the New York Public Library for the Performing Arts Billy Rose Collection. Critics compared "The No 'Count Boy" both to the work of Synge and William Saroyan. Most of the reviews were negative or mixed, with one critic calling the plays "intrinsically lugubrious and of scant entertainment value" (*Newark Evening News,* 7 July 1954) and Walter Kerr backhandedly acknowledging Paul Green's status as "the ablest of the cornpone poets" (*New York Herald Tribune,* 7 July 1954). "The No 'Count Boy" was the best liked of the three and was played and received as a comedy.

100. Bourdieu, *Distinction,* 231.

101. Lippmann, 79, 64.

102. Pennington, 53, 55–56.

103. See Thompson.

104. Mitchell, 70.

105. Hatch, 773. The quote summarizes a call for a new black theatre issued in 1926 by W. E. B. DuBois in the magazine *Crisis.*

106. Sonnega, 84.

107. Payne, 166.

108. Leah Hager Cohen, 142, 141, xix.

109. Leah Hager Cohen, 82.

110. See Helvenston; Touton; Mabie, "The Responses of Theatre Audiences, Experimental Studies"; Baumol and Bowen; Hansen and Bormann; Gard, et al.;. Andreasen; and Marquis.

111. Bernays, 20, 21.

112. Leah Hager Cohen, 123.

113. The Institute on the Arts and Civic Dialogue.

114. Gates, 140.

115. Kuftinec, 206, 220, 217, 220.

116. Tommasini.

117. Leah Hager Cohen, 53.

118. Sollors, *Beyond Ethnicity,* 14.

Bibliography

Addams, Jane. *Twenty Years at Hull-House.* 1910. Reprint, New York: Macmillan, 1973.

Aimone, Joseph. "Millay's Big Book, or the Feminist Formalist as Modern." In *Unmanning Modernism: Gendered Re-Readings,* edited by Elizabeth Jane Harrison and Shirley Peterson, 1–13. Knoxville: University of Tennessee Press, 1997.

Allen, Frederick Lewis. *Only Yesterday: An Informal History of the 1920's.* New York: Harper and Row, 1931; New York: Perennial Library, 1964.

"The Amateur's Green Room." *Theatre* 42, no. 292 (July 1925): 43.

Anderson, Benedict. *Imagined Communities.* London: Verso, 1993.

Andreasen, Alan R. *Expanding the Audience for the Performing Arts.* Washington, D.C.: Seven Locks, 1991.

Andrews, Charlton. "Elevating the Audience." *Theatre* 25, no. 192 (February 1917): 102, 120.

Antoine, André. "Recollections of the Théâtre Libre," *Theatre Arts* 9, no. 3 (March 1925): 178–198.

A. P. "Acting Helps a Woman to Live," *Theatre* 20, no. 161 (July 1914): 14.

———. "A Woman Who Financed and Built a Little Theatre." *Theatre* 20, no. 163 (September 1914): 113–14.

Aristotle. *Poetics.* Translated by Gerald Else. Ann Arbor: University of Michigan Press, 1967.

Aronson, Howard. Letter. *(Dallas) Daily Times Herald,* 22 January 1929, 8.

Arvold, Alfred. *The Little Country Theater.* New York: Macmillan, 1923.

———. "The Little Country Theater." Undated Pamphlet. New York Public Library, Lincoln Center, Billy Rose Collection.

Atlas, Marilyn. "Innovation in Chicago: Alice Gerstenberg's Psychological Drama." *Midwestern Miscellany* 10 (1982): 59–68.

Bailey, Beth. "From *Sex in the Heartland* to the All-Volunteer Military." Talk given at The College of William and Mary, 23 April 2001.

Baird, George M. P. "Mirage." In *Contemporary One-Act Plays of 1921*, edited by Frank Shay, 9–40. Cincinnati: Steward Kidd, 1922.

Baker, Colgate. "Augustus Thomas on the National Theatre." *The New York Review*, 23 December 1922.

Baker, George Pierce. *Dramatic Technique.* 1918. Reprint, Westport, CT: Greenwood, 1970.

———. Introduction to *Harvard Plays: The 47 Workshop.* New York, 1918.

———. "The New Mexican of Today," *The Providence Journal*, 6 February 1888.

———. Papers. The Harvard Theatre Collection.

———. "The Theatre and the University," *Theatre Arts* 9, no. 2 (February 1925): 99–105.

Bank, Rosemarie. "Hustlers in the House: The Bowery Theatre as a Mode of Historical Information." In *The American Stage: Social and Economic Issues from the Colonial Period to the Present,* edited by Ron Engle and Tice L. Miller, 47–64. Cambridge: Cambridge University Press, 1993.

Banta, Martha. *Imaging American Women: Ideas and Ideals in Cultural History.* New York: Columbia University Press, 1987.

Barish, Jonas. *The Antitheatrical Prejudice.* Berkeley: University of California Press, 1981.

Baumol, William J., and William G. Bowen. *Performing Arts: The Economic Dilemma: A study of Problems Common to Theater, Opera, Music, and Dance.* New York: Twentieth Century Fund, 1966.

Bayly, Charles, Jr. Letter to Paul Green, 24 March 1925. Paul Eliot Green Papers, Manuscripts Department, Southern Historical Collection, Wilson Library of the University of North Carolina at Chapel Hill.

Beckerman, Bernard. "The University Accepts the Theatre: 1800–1925." In *The American Theatre: A Sum of Its Parts*, 339–55. New York: Samuel French, 1971.

Beckley, Zoe. "Girl Author's Best Seller Based on Story Mother Told of Loveless Spinster." *New York Evening Mail*, 21 November 1915.

Belasco, David. *The Theatre Through Its Stage Door.* New York: Harper, 1919.

"Belasco Cup" Scrapbooks. New York Public Library for the Performing Arts Billy Rose Collection. Call numbers MWEZ+n.c. 10,594–10,596.

Bell, Lisle. "When Milady Shops for Seats." *Theatre* 35, no. 253 (April 1922): 244.

Bennett, Ella Costillo. "The Matinee Girl." *Theatre* 19, no. 159 (May 1914): 241.

Bennett, Susan. *Theatre Audiences: A Theory of Production and Reception.* New York: Routledge, 1990.

———. "Theatre History and Women's Dramatic Writing." In *Women, Theatre, and Performance: New Histories, New Historiographies,* edited by Maggie B. Gale and Viv Gardner, 46–59. Manchester: Manchester University Press, 2000.

Bernheim, Alfred. *The Business of the Theatre: An Economic History of the American Theatre, 1750–1932.* 1932. Reprint, New York: Benjamin Blom: 1964.

Berger, Maurice. *White Lies: Race and the Myths of Whiteness.* New York: Farrar Straus Giroux, 1999.

Bernays, Edward L. "Theatre Survey." *Theatre Arts* 33, no. 11 (December 1949): 17+.

Best, Mrs. A. Starr. "Drama League of America: It's [*sic*] Inception, Growth, Accomplishment and Promise." Pamphlet published through *Drama*, Chicago, 1925.

———. "The Drama League of America, 1914," *Drama* 4, no. 13 (February 1914): 135–50.

Black, Cheryl. *The Women of Provincetown, 1915–1922.* Tuscaloosa: University of Alabama Press, 2002.

Blair, Karen. *The Clubwoman as Feminist: True Womanhood Redefined, 1868–1914.* New York: Holmes and Meier, 1980.

———. *The Torchbearers: Women and Their Amateur Arts Associations in America, 1890–1930.* Bloomington: Indiana University Press, 1994.

Blau, Herbert. *The Audience.* Baltimore: Johns Hopkins University Press, 1990.

Blood, Melanie N. "The Neighborhood Playhouse 1915–1927: A History and Analysis." PhD diss., Northwestern University, 1994.

———. "Theatre in Settlement Houses: Hull-House Players, Neighborhood Playhouse, and Karamu Theatre." *Theatre History Studies* 16 (June 1996): 45–69.

Bloom, Thomas Alan. *New Studies in Aesthetics.* Vol. 20, *Kenneth Macgowan and the Aesthetic Paradigm for the New Stagecraft in America.* New York: Peter Lang, 1996.

Bogard, Morris Ray. "The Drama League of America: A History and Critical Analysis of Its Activities and Achievements." PhD diss., University of Illinois, 1962.

Bost, Mrs. W. T. "Activities of Tar Heels." *Greensboro Daily News,* 15 May 1921.

Bourdieu, Pierre. *Distinction: A Social Critique of the Judgement of Taste.* Translated by Richard Nice. Cambridge: Harvard University Press, 1984.

———. "The Forms of Capital." In *Handbook of Theory and Research for the Sociology of Education,"* edited by John G. Richardson, 241–58. Westport, CT: Greenwood, 1986.

Bourne, Randolph. "The Cult of the Best." *The New Republic* 5 (15 January 1916): 275–77.

———. "Our Cultural Humility." *Atlantic* 14 (October 1914): 503–7.

Brantley, Ben. "Ow! Watch Those Claws." Review of *The Women. New York Times,* 9 November 2001, weekend A:1

Brino-Dean, Terry. "Aesthetic Revisioning in the Efforts of the Drama League of America, 1910–1931." PhD diss., Indiana University, 2002.

Brockett, Oscar G. *History of the Theatre.* 7th ed. Boston: Allyn and Bacon, 1995.

Brockett, Oscar G., and Robert R. Findlay. *History of European and American Theatre and Drama since 1870.* Englewood Cliffs, NJ: Prentice-Hall, 1991.

Brooks, David. *Bobos in Paradise: The New Upper Class and How They Got There.* New York: Simon and Schuster, 2000.

Browne, Maurice. "The Temple of a Living Art." Chicago Little Theatre, 1914.

———. *Too Late to Lament: An Autobiography.* London: Gollanez, 1955.

Bryant, Louise. *The Game.* In *The Provincetown Plays, First Series.* New York: Frank Shay, 1916.

Bucco, Martin. *Main Street: The Revolt of Carol Kennicott.* New York: Twayne, 1993.

Bullard, F. Lauriston. "Boston's Toy Theatre." *Theatre Magazine* 15, no. 133 (March 1912): 84–86.

Burleigh, Louise. *The Community Theatre in Theory and Practice.* Boston: Little, Brown, 1917.

Burton, Richard. "The Drama as Education." *Drama* 3, no. 10 (May 1913): 180.

Busby, Florence. "Making an Audience Alert." *The Carolina Stage* 5, no. 2 (February 1940): 12–13.

Bushee, Frederick A. *Ethnic Factors in the Population of Boston.* New York, 1903.

Butsch, Richard. *The Making of American Audiences: From Stage to Television, 1750–1990.* London: Cambridge University Press, 2000.

Calder, Chester T. "What's Wrong with the American Stage?" *Theatre* 17, no. 145 (March 1913): 74–80, xi.

Carlson, Marvin. "Theatre Audiences and the Reading of Performance." In *Theatre Semiotics: Signs of Life,* 13–14. Bloomington, Indiana University Press, 1990.

"The Carolina Playmakers." *New York Times Magazine,* 31 December 1922.

Carter, Jean, and Jess Ogden. *Everyman's Drama: A Study of the Noncommercial Theatre in the United States.* New York: American Assoc for Adult Education, 1938.

Chadwick, F. E. "The Woman Peril in American Education." *Educational Review,* February 1914: 109–19.

Chansky, Dorothy. "Good Reading: New York's Premier Theatre Bookstores." *Dramatics* 69 (March 1998): 5–8.

Cheney, Sheldon. *The Art Theater: Its Character as Differentiated from the Commercial Theater; Its Ideals and Organization; and a Record of Certain European and American Examples.* New York: Knopf, 1917, 1925.

———. "Editorial Comment." *Theatre Arts* 1, no. 4 (August 1917): 185–86.

———. "Foreword." *Theatre Arts* 1, no. 1 (November 1916): 1.

———. Letter to Nafe Katter (New Hope, PA, 20 December 1953), Edith J. Isaacs Papers, State Historical Society of Wisconsin, Box 1, Folder 14.

———. "The Most Important Thing in the Theatre." *Theatre Arts* 1, no. 4 (August 1917): 167–71.

———. "New York's Best Season." *Theatre Arts* 1, no. 2 (February 1917): 67–70.

———. *The Theatre: Three Thousand Years of Drama, Acting and Stage Craft.* New York: Tudor, 1935.

Chinoy, Helen Krich, and Linda Walsh Jenkins, eds. *Women in American Theatre: Careers, Images, Movements.* New York: Crown, 1981.

Clark, Barrett H. *Paul Green.* New York: Robert M. McBride, 1928.

Clark, Suzanne. *Sentimental Modernism: Women Writers and the Revolution of the Word.* Bloomington: Indiana University Press, 1991.

Cohen, Helen Louise. "Education in the Theatre Arts." *Theatre Arts* 8, no. 10 (October 1924): 688–92.

Cohen, Leah Hager. *The Stuff of Dreams: Behind the Scenes of an American Community Theatre.* New York: Viking Penguin, 2001.

Cole, Carole L. "The Search for Power: Drama by American Women, 1909–1929." PhD diss., Purdue University, 1991.

Conroy, Stephen S. "Popular Artists and Elite Standards: The Case of Sinclair Lewis." In *Critical Essays on Sinclair Lewis,* edited by Martin Bucco, 197–204. Boston: G. K. Hall, 1986.

Coomaraswamy, Ananda, and Stella Block. "The Chinese Theatre in Boston." *Theatre Arts* 9, no. 2 (February 1925): 113–22.

Coontz, Stephanie. *The Way We Never Were: American Families and the Nostalgia Trap.* New York: Basic Books, 1992.

Corbin, John. "How the Other Half Laughs." *Harper's New Monthly Magazine* 98 (December 1898): 30–46.

Cott, Nancy. *The Grounding of Modern Feminism.* New Haven: Yale University Press, 1987.

Cowan, Ruth Schwartz. "Two Washes in the Morning and a Bridge Party at Night: The American Housewife Between the Wars." In *Decades of Discontent: The Women's Movement, 1920–1940,* edited by Lois Scharf and Joan M. Jensen, 177–96. Westport, CT: Greenwood, 1983.

———. *More Work for Mother: The Ironies of Household Technology from the Open Hearth to the Microwave.* New York: Basic, 1983.

Cowley, Malcolm. *Exile's Return: A Literary Odyssey of the 1920's.* New York: Viking, 1951.

Cremin, Lawrence A. *The Transformation of the School: Progressivism in American Education, 1876–1957.* New York: Knopf, 1968.

Crosby, Edward H. "Toy Theatre Is Formally Opened." *Boston Sunday Post,* 27 December 1914.

Crowe, David. "Illustration as Interpretation: Grant Wood's 'New Deal' Reading of Sinclair Lewis's *Main Street.*" In *Sinclair Lewis at 100: Papers Presented at a Centennial Conference,* 95–112. St. Cloud, MN: St. Cloud State University, 1985.

Crowley, Alice Lewisohn. *The Neighborhood Playhouse*. New York: Theatre Arts Books, 1959.

Crunden, Robert M. *Ministers of Reform: The Progressives' Achievement in American Civilization 1889–1920*. New York: Basic Books, 1982.

Curtis, Susan. *The First Black Actors on the Great White Way*. Columbia: University of Missouri Press, 1998.

"The Dallas Laboratory School of the Theatre." *Drama*, November 1927: 48.

Dallas Little Theatre charter. 4 January 1921. Dallas Little Theatre papers, Dallas Public Library, Fine Arts Division.

"Dallas Little Theatre Is Paid High Tribute for Prize Winning Performance in New York Meet." *Dallas Times Herald*, 24 May 1925, sec. 8.

Davis, Ellis A., and Edwin H. Broge, eds. *The Encyclopedia of Texas*. Dallas, n.d.

Deland, Lorin F. "A Plea for the Theatrical Manager." *Atlantic* 102, no. 4 (October 1908): 492–500.

Dell, Floyd. "Rents Were Low in Greenwich Village." *American Mercury* 65 (December 1947): 662–68.

DeMott, Benjamin. *The Imperial Middle: Why Americans Can't Think Straight about Class*. New Haven: Yale University Press, 1990.

Dewey, John. "The Act of Expression." In *Art as Experience*, 1934. Reprint, New York: Penguin Putnam, 1980, 58–81.

———. "Americanism and Localism." *The Dial* 68, no. 6 (June 1920): 684–88.

———. *Democracy and Education: An Introduction to the Philosophy of Education*. New York: Macmillan, 1916. Reprint, New York: Free Press, 1966.

Dickinson, Thomas H. *The Case of American Drama*. Boston: Houghton Mifflin, 1915.

———, ed. *Chief Contemporary Dramatists: Twenty Plays from the Recent Drama of England, Ireland, America, Germany, France, Belgium, Norway, Sweden, and Russia*. Boston: Houghton Mifflin, 1915.

———. *The Insurgent Theatre*. 1917. Reprint, New York: Benjamin Blom, 1972.

DiMaggio, Paul. "Cultural Boundaries and Structural Change: The Extension of the High Culture Model to Theater, Opera, and the Dance, 1900–1940." In *Cultivating Differences: Symbolic Boundaries and the Making of Inequality*, edited by Michele Lamont and Marcel Fournier, 21–57. Chicago: University of Chicago Press, 1992.

———. "Social Structure, Institutions, and Cultural Goods: The Case of the United States." In *The Politics of Culture: Policy Perspectives for Individuals, Institutions, and Communities*, edited by Gigi Bradford, Michael Gary, and Glenn Wallach, 38–62. New York: New Press, 2000.

Dolan, Jill. "Rehearsing Democracy: Advocacy, Public Intellectuals, and Civic Engagement in Theatre and Performance Studies." *Theatre Topics* 11, no. 1 (March 2001): 1–17.

Dormon, James H. "The Varieties of American Ethnic Theater: A Review Essay." *Journal of American Ethnic History* 4 (Spring 1985): 85–91.

Douglas, Ann. Conversation with the author. 23 October 1996.

———. *The Feminization of American Culture.* New York: Knopf, 1977.

———. *Terrible Honesty: Mongrel Manhattan in the 1920s.* New York: Farrar, Straus and Giroux, 1995.

"Drama and the People." *The Student* (University of North Dakota), 29 May 1913.

"The Drama League of America." *The Drama* 1, no. 1 (1911): 116.

"Drama League of America to Lose New York Center." *New York Times,* 18 May 1927.

"Drama: Little Theatres." *The Nation* 108, no. 2809 (3 May 1919): 702–3.

Dreiser, Theodore. *Sister Carrie.* 1900. Reprint, with an introduction by E. L. Doctorow, New York: Bantam Doubleday Dell, 1982.

Drucker, Rebecca. "The Jewish Art Theatre." *Theatre Arts* 4, no. 3 (July 1920): 220–24.

Dudden, Faye E. *Women in the American Theatre: Actresses and Audiences 1790–1870.* New Haven: Yale University Press, 1994.

Duncan, Isadora. "The Dance." *Theatre Arts* 2, no. 1 (December 1917): 21.

Eaton, Walter Prichard. *The American Stage of To-Day.* Boston: Small, Maynard, 1908.

———. "The American Theatre and Reconstruction," *Theatre Arts* 3, no. 1 (January 1919): 8–14.

———. "Audiences." *Theatre Arts* 7, no. 1 (January 1923): 21–28.

———. "Crowds and Mr. Hamilton." In *The American Stage of To-Day,* 282–90. Boston: Small, Maynard, 1908.

———. "The Menace of the Movies." *American Magazine* 76 (13 September 1913): 55–60.

———. "The Real Revolt in Our Theatre." *Scribner's* 72 (July–December 1922): 596–605.

———. "What's the Matter with the Road?" *American Magazine* 74 (July 1912): 359–68.

Editorial. *Drama* 10 (October 1919): 1.

Editorial. *Theatre Arts* 4, no. 1 (January 1920): 69.

Editorial comment. *Theatre Arts* 2, no. 1 (December 1917): 49–50.

Ehrenreich, Barbara. *Fear of Falling: The Inner Life of the Middle Class.* New York: Pantheon, 1989.

Ehrensperger, Harold. "A National Drama Celebration." *Drama* 13 (January 1923): 150.

———. "Women and the Little Theatre: A Rambling Diagnosis with Notes on Certain Characteristics," *Little Theatre Monthly* 4, no. 1 (October 1927): 19+.

Elam, Keir. *The Semiotics of Theatre and Drama.* London: Routledge, 1980.

Elliott, Sarah Barnwell. "Whose Fault Is It?" *Drama* 1, no. 3 (August 1911): 105–10.

Erdman, Harley. *Staging the Jew: The Performance of an American Ethnicity, 1860–1920.* New Brunswick, NJ: Rutgers University Press, 1997.

Erenberg, Louis A. *Steppin' Out: New York Nightlife and the Transformation of American Culture, 1890–1930.* Westport, CT: Greenwood, 1981.

Esteve, M. "What the Stage Should Be." *Theatre* 7, no. 1 (July 1890): n. pag.

Evans, Dina Rees. "A Preliminary Study of Play Production in the Secondary Schools." MA thesis, University of Iowa, 1929.

Ewen, Stuart. *Captains of Consciousness: Advertising and the Social Roots of the Consumer Culture.* New York: McGraw Hill, 1976.

Ewen, Stuart, and Elizabeth Ewen. *Channels of Desire: Mass Images and the Shaping of American Consciousness.* Minneapolis: University of Minnesota Press, 1992.

Fass, Paula S. *The Damned and the Beautiful: American Youth in the 1920s.* New York: Oxford University Press, 1977.

Favor, J. Martin. *Authentic Blackness: The Folk in the New Negro Renaissance.* Durham: Duke University Press, 1999.

Fearnow, Mark. "Theatre Groups and Their Playwrights." In *The Cambridge History of American Theatre.* Vol. 2, *1879–1945,* edited by Don B. Wilmeth and Christopher Bigsby, 343–77. New York: Cambridge University Press, 1999.

Filene, Peter G. "An Obituary for 'The Progressive Movement.'" *American Quarterly* 22, no. 1 (Spring 1970): 20–34.

Fishbein, Leslie. *Rebels in Bohemia: The Radicals of* The Masses, *1911–1917.* Chapel Hill, University of North Carolina Press, 1982.

FitzGerald, Frances. *America Revised.* New York: Vintage, 1980.

"The Folk Plays Last Night at the Municipal." *Burlington (North Carolina) Daily News,* 2 May 1922.

"For the Lord's Sake, Call It Off." Editorial comment, *Burlington Daily News,* 2 May 1922.

"Four Years of Its Colorful History Told." *Dallas Times Herald,* extra edition, 29 April 1924.

Fox, Richard Wightman. "Epitaph for Middletown: Robert S. Lynd and the Analysis of Consumer Culture." In *The Culture of Consumption,* edited by Richard Wightman Fox and T. J. Jackson Lears, 101–41. New York: Pantheon, 1983.

Frazier, Nancy, and Myra Sadker. *Sexism in School and Society.* New York: Harper and Row, 1973.

Freedman, Estelle B. "The New Woman: Changing Views of Women in the 1920s." In *Decades of Discontent: The Women's Movement, 1920–1940,* edited by Lois Scharf and Joan M. Jensen, 21–42. Westport, CT: Greenwood, 1983.

Freeman, Norine. "Our Own 'Greenwich Village': Little Theatre Is Being Revived Behind Doors of Music Hall." *The Cincinnati Post,* 7 December 1936: 11.

Frick, John. "A Changing Theatre: New York and Beyond." In *The Cambridge History of American Theatre.* Vol. 2, *1879–1945,* edited by Don B. Wilmeth and Christopher Bigsby, 196–232. New York: Cambridge University Press, 1999.

Frohman, Daniel. "The Audiences of Yesterday." *Theatre* 30, no. 225 (November 1919): 294–95.

Gainor, J. Ellen. *Susan Glaspell in Context: American Theater, Culture, and Politics 1915–48.* Ann Arbor: University of Michigan Press, 2001.

Gale, Zona. "The Colored Players and Their Plays." *Theatre Arts* 1, no. 3 (May 1917): 139–40.

———. "The Wisconsin Players," *Theatre Arts* 1, no. 2 (February 1917): 128–30.

Gard, Robert, Marston Balch, and Pauline Temkin. *Grassroots Theater: A Search for Regional Arts in America.* Madison: University of Wisconsin Press, 1999.

———. *Theater in America: Appraisal and Challenge for the National Theatre Conference.* Madison, WI: Dembar Educational Research Services, 1968.

Garrison, Dee. *Mary Heaton Vorse: The Life of an American Insurgent.* Philadelphia: Temple University Press, 1989.

Gates, Henry Lewis, Jr. "The Chitlin Circuit." In *African American Performance and Theater History: A Critical Reader,* edited by Harry J. Elam Jr. and David Krasner, 132–38. New York: Oxford University Press, 2001.

Gerould, Katharine Fullerton. "The Extirpation of Culture." *Atlantic* 116 (October 1915): 445–55.

Gerstenberg, Alice. "At the Club." In *Comedies All.* London: Longmans, 1930.

———. "Come Back with Me." Unpublished autobiography (1959–1962). Alice Gerstenberg Papers, Chicago Historical Society.

———. *The Conscience of Sarah Platt.* Chicago: A. C. McClurg, 1915.

———. *Got Your Number.* Unpublished manuscript, New York Public Library for the Performing Arts Billy Rose Collection, 1942.

———. Letters to Nancy Cox-McCormack Cushman, 13 June 1950 (1) and 30 January, 1951 (2). Alice Gerstenberg papers, Newberry Library, Chicago.

———. Letter to David Sievers, 22 July, 1955. Alice Gerstenberg papers, Newberry Library, Chicago.

———. Letter to the editor, *Bryn Mawr Alumnae Bulletin* 3 (1966–67).

———. "Mere Man." In *Comedies All.* London: Longmans, 1930.

———. Preface to *One-Act Plays for Stage and Study,* vii–x. New York: Samuel French, 1934.

———. *Ten One-Act Plays.* New York: Brentano's, 1921.

———. *Unquenched Fire.* Boston: Small, Maynard, 1912.

Giddins, Gary. "Laughing Man: Moss Hart and the Broadway He Co-Created." *The New Yorker,* 21 May 2001.

Gilder, Rosamond, Hermine Rich Isaacs, Robert M. MacGregor, and Edward Reed, eds. *Theatre Arts Anthology.* New York: Theatre Arts Books, 1950.

Gillespie, Patti. "Feminist Theory of Theatre: Revolution or Revival?" In *Theatre and Feminist Aesthetics,* edited by Karen Laughlin and Catherine Schuler, 100–130. Madison, NJ: Fairleigh Dickinson University Press, 1995.

Gillpatrick, Wallace. "Boston's Toy Theater: What It Stands for and What It Has Accomplished." *The New York Dramatic Mirror,* 11 December 1912.

Glaspell, Susan. *The Road to the Temple.* New York: Frederick A. Stokes, 1927.

Glassberg, David. *American Historical Pageantry: The Uses of Tradition in the Early Twentieth Century.* Chapel Hill: University of North Carolina Press, 1990.

Goldman, Arnold. "The Culture of the Provincetown Players." *The Journal of American Studies* 12, no. 3 (1978): 291–310.

Goodrum, Charles, and Helen Dalrymple. *Advertising in America: The First 200 Years.* New York: Harry N. Abrams, 1990.

Gordon, Edward B. "A Community Drama Program." *Drama* 9 (October 1919): 163.

Gordon, Lynn D. *Gender and Higher Education in the Progressive Era.* New Haven: Yale University Press, 1990.

G. P. Editorial. *New York Times,* 8 January 1935.

Grana, Cesar. *Bohemian Versus Bourgeois: French Society and the French Man of Letters in the Nineteenth Century.* New York: Basic Books, 1964.

"The Great World Theatre." *Theatre Arts* 9, no. 11 (November 1925): 761–62.

"The Great World Theatre." *Theatre Arts* 9, no. 12 (December 1925): 836–42.

Green, Paul Eliot. *The Lord's Will.* New York: Henry Holt, 1925.

———. "The No 'Count Boy." In *The Lord's Will and Other Carolina Plays,* 143–93. New York: Henry Holt, 1925.

———. Papers, Manuscripts Department, Southern Historical Collection, Wilson Library of the University of North Carolina at Chapel Hill.

———. "Rassie." Self-published. 1967. Folders 3900–3901, Paul Eliot Green Papers.

Greenlaw, Edwin. "The Community Pageant: An Agency for the Promotion of Democracy." University of North Carolina Extension Leaflets, War Information Series, no. 16. Chapel Hill: University of North Carolina, 1918.

Halttunen, Karen. *Confidence Men and Painted Women: A Study of Middle-Class Culture in America, 1830–1870.* New Haven: Yale University Press, 1982.

Hamar, Clifford Eugene. "College and University Theatre Instruction in the Early Twentieth Century." In *History of Speech Education in America,* edited by Karl Wallace, 572–94. New York: Appleton-Century-Crofts, 1954.

Hamilton, Clayton. "Organizing an Audience." *Bookman* 34 (October 1911): 161–66.

———. "The Psychology of Theatre Audiences." *Forum* 39, no. 2 (October 1907): 234–38.

Hamilton, Ida. "The Carolina Playmakers." In *Diversion: A Tourist Magazine of the South,* undated clipping probably 1924. Manuscripts Division, Wilson Library, University of North Carolina, Chapel Hill.

Hammack, Henry Edgar. "A History of the Dallas Little Theatre, 1920–1943." PhD diss., Tulane University, 1967.

Hansen, Brian, and Ernest K. Bormann. "A New Look at a Semantic Differential for the Theatre." *Speech Monographs* (1967).

Hapgood, Hutchins. *The Spirit of the Ghetto: Studies of the Jewish Quarter of New York.* 1902. Reprinted with a preface by Harry Golden, New York: Schocken Books, 1965.

———. *A Victorian in the Modern World.* New York: Harcourt, Brace, 1939.

Hapgood, Norman. *The Stage in America, 1897–1901.* New York: Macmillan, 1901.

Harrington, John P. "The Founding Years and the Irish National Theatre That Was Not." In *A Century of Irish Drama: Widening the Stage,* edited by Stephen Watt, Eileen Morgan, and Shakir Mustafa, 3–16. Bloomington: Indiana University Press, 2000.

———. *The Irish Play on the New York Stage 1874–1966.* Lexington: The University Press of Kentucky, 1997.

Harris, Neil. *Cultural Excursions: Marketing Appetites and Cultural Tastes in Modern America.* Chicago: University of Chicago Press, 1990.

Harris, Susan Cannon. "More Than a Morbid, Unhealthy Mind: Public Health and the *Playboy* Riots." In *A Century of Irish Drama: Widening the Stage,* edited by Stephen Watt, Eileen Morgan, and Shakir Mustafa, 72–94. Bloomington: Indiana University Press, 2000.

Hartwig, Walter. Letter to the editor. *(Columbus, Ohio) State Journal,* 25 May 1923.

Hatch, James V., ed. *Black Theater, U.S.A.* New York: Macmillan, 1974.

Heacock, Lee F. "Community *or* Little Theatre—Which?" *The Little Theatre Monthly* (published in conjunction with *Drama*) 3, no. 3 (December 1926).

Head, Cloyd, and Mary Gavin. "The Unity of Production." *Theatre Arts* 5, no. 1 (1921): 60–68.

Hecht, Stuart J. "The Plays of Alice Gerstenberg: Cultural Hegemony in the American Little Theatre." *Journal of Popular Culture* 26 (Summer 1992): 1–16.

———. "Social and Artistic Integration: The Emergence of Hull-House Theatre." *Theatre Journal* 34, no. 2 (May 1982): 172–82.

Heffernan, Harold. "Movie Mad Mothers Are Serious Problem." *Dallas Morning News,* 6 May 1946.

Helburn, Theresa. "Art and Business: A Record of the Theatre Guild, Inc." *Theatre Arts* 5, no. 4 (October 1921): 268–74.

Heller, Adele, and Lois Rudnick. *1915, the Cultural Moment: The New Politics, the New Woman, the New Psychology, the New Art and the New Theatre in America.* New Brunswick: Rutgers University Press, 1991.

Helvenston, Harold. "West Coast Audiences: Their Tastes and Standards." *Theatre Arts* 17 (July 1923): 557–64.

Henderson, Archibald. "The Evolution of Dramatic Technique." *The North American Review* 189 (March 1909): 428–44.

———. "Scholium Scribendi." In *Pioneering a People's Theatre*, edited by Archibald Henderson, 20–27. Chapel Hill: University of North Carolina Press, 1945.

Hendrickson, Robert. *The Grand Emporiums: The Illustrated History of America's Great Department Stores*. New York: Stein and Day, 1979.

Heniger, Alice Minnie Herts. *The Children's Educational Theatre*. New York: Harper, 1911.

Henneke, Ben Graf. "The Playgoer in America 1752–1952." PhD diss., University of Illinois, 1956.

"Her Ph.D. No Bar to Role in Play." *(Cleveland) Plain Dealer,* 28 January 1933.

Hervey, Hubert C. "A History of the Community Little Theater of Texas: Emphasizing the Dallas Little Theater as Representative." MA thesis, Texas Technological College, 1930.

Heyward, DuBose. "The New Note in Southern Literature." *Bookman* 49 (April 1925): 154–55.

Higham, John. *Strangers in the Land: Patterns of American Nativism 1860–1925,* 2d ed. New Brunswick: Rutgers University Press, 1988.

Hinsdell, Oliver. Letter to Paul Green, 1925. Paul Eliot Green Papers, Manuscripts Department, Southern Historical Collection, Wilson Library of the University of North Carolina at Chapel Hill.

———. *Making the Little Theatre Pay: A Practical Handbook*. New York: Samuel French, 1925.

"Hinsdell's Departure from Little Theater Is Reported." *Dallas Morning News,* 31 March 1931.

Hobart, George V. "Mrs. Blabb Goes to the Matinee." *Theatre* 35, no. 253 (April 1922): 244.

Hodin, Mark. "The Disavowal of Ethnicity: Legitimate Theatre and the Social Construction of Literary Value in Turn-of-the-Century America." *Theatre Journal* 52, no. 2 (May, 2000): 211–26.

Hofstadter, Richard. *The Age of Reform: From Bryan to F.D.R.* New York: Vintage, 1955.

Hogan, Robert, Richard Burnham, and Daniel Poteet. "The Abbey Company in America, 1911–1912" (appendix 1). In *The Rise of the Realists, 1910–1915*. Dublin: Dolman, 1979.

Hokinson, Helen. "The Boxers: The Exclusive in Their Mad Pursuit of Pleasure." *Theatre* 39, no. 274 (January 1924): 25.

———. "Matinee Girls of 1924." *Theatre* 39, no. 279 (June 1924): 25.

———. "Other Aisle, Please." *Theatre* 40, no. 282 (September 1924): 29.

Holt, Roland. Letters to Paul Green, 19 September 1924 and 11 May 1925. Paul Eliot Green Papers, Manuscripts Department, Southern Historical Collection, Wilson Library of the University of North Carolina at Chapel Hill.

"Home Folks See Belasco Cup Winner." *Dallas Times Herald,* 26 May 1925: 13.

Hubbell, Jay B., and John O. Beaty, eds. *An Introduction to Drama.* New York: Macmillan, 1927.

Hughes, Glenn. *A History of the American Theatre 1700–1950.* New York: Samuel French, 1951.

Hughes, Langston. "The Negro Artist: A Defense of Racial Art in America." *The Nation* 121, no. 3181 (23 June 1926): 692–94.

Humphrey, Robert E. *Children of Fantasy: The First Rebels of Greenwich Village.* New York: John Wiley, 1978.

Institute on the Arts and Civic Dialogue. Press release. Cambridge, MA: W. E. B. DuBois Institute at Harvard University, 16 June 1999.

J. A. "Folk Plays Much Better Than Before." *(Morganton NC) News-Herald,* 26 April 1923.

Jackson, Shannon. *Lines of Activity: Performance, Historiography, Hull-House Domesticity.* Ann Arbor: University of Michigan Press, 2000.

Jacobson, Matthew Frye. *Whiteness of a Different Color: European Immigrants and the Alchemy of Race.* Cambridge: Harvard University Press, 1998.

Jameson, Frederic. "Reification and Utopia in Mass Culture." *Social Text* 1 (Winter 1979): 130–48.

Janeway, Michael. "Who's Teaming Up in the Tug-of-War among the Two Theatre Sectors, Pop Culture and the Press?" *American Theatre* 18, no. 10 (December 2000): 32+.

Jaudon, Valerie, and Joyce Kozloff. "'Art Hysterical Notions' of Progress and Culture." *Heresies* 1, no. 4 (Winter 1978): 38–42.

Jenks, George C. "When Mabel Meets the Actors," *Theatre* 18 (August 1913): 48, viii.

Jensen, Joan M., and Lois Scharf, eds. *Decades of Discontent: The Women's Movement, 1920–1940.* Westport, CT: Greenwood, 1983.

Jonas, Susan, and Suzanne Bennett. "New York State Council on the Arts Theatre Program Report on the Status of Women: A Limited Engagement?" January 2002. www.womensproject.org/image/Wit.pdf.

Jones, Howard Mumford. "Paul Green." *Southwest Review* 14, no. 1 (Autumn 1928): 1–8.

Joseph, Pamela Bolotin. "'The Ideal Teacher': Images in Early Twentieth-Century Teacher Education Textbooks." In *Images of Schoolteachers in America,* edited by Pamela Bolotin Joseph and Gail E. Burnaford, 135–57. Mahwah, NJ: Lawrence Erlbaum, 2001.

Kadlec, David. *Mosaic Modernism: Anachism, Pragmatism, Culture.* Baltimore: Johns Hopkins University Press, 2000.

Kallen, Horace. "Democracy *versus* the Melting Pot." In *Culture and Democracy in the United States: Studies in the Group Psychology of the American Peoples.* New York: Boni and Liveright, 1924.

Katter, Nafe Edmund. "'Theatre Arts' under the Editorship of Edith J. R. Isaacs." PhD diss., University of Michigan, 1963.

Katz, Michael B. "The Origins of Public Education: A Reassessment." In *The Social History of American Education,* edited by B. Edward McClellan and William J. Reese, 91–117. Urbana: University of Illinois Press, 1988.

Kaynor, Fay Campbell. "The Dramatic Magazine (May 1880–August 1882)." *The Journal of American Drama and Theatre* 11, no. 3 (Fall 1999): 46–62.

Kinne, Wisner Payne. *George Pierce Baker and the American Theatre.* 1954. Reprint, New York: Greenwood, 1968.

Knight, Christopher. *The Patient Particulars: American Modernism and the Technique of Originality.* Lewisburg: Bucknell University Press, 1995.

Koch, Frederick Henry. "The Dakota Playmakers: An Historical Sketch." *Quarterly Journal of the University of North Dakota* 9, no. 1 (October 1918): 13–21.

———. "Drama in the South: The Carolina Playmakers Coming of Age." An address delivered on 5 April 1940, for the Southern Regional Theatre Festival. Reprinted from *The Carolina Playbook* 1939–40 in *Pioneering a People's Theatre,* edited by Archibald Henderson, 7–19. Chapel Hill: University of North Carolina Press, 1945.

———. "Ethics of the Histrionic: In Actor and Audience. I—Actor." *Emerson College Magazine* 11, no. 1 (November 1902): 10–13.

———. "Ethics of the Histrionic: In Actor and Audience. II—Audience." *Emerson College Magazine* 11, no. 4 (February 1903): 110–15.

———. Papers. Southern Historical Collection, Manuscripts Department, Library of the University of North Carolina at Chapel Hill.

———. "Toward the Municipal Theater." *Quarterly Journal of the University of North Dakota* 6, no. 2 (January 1916): n. pag.

Kozelka, Paul. "Dramatics in the High Schools, 1900–1925." In *History of Speech Education in America,* edited by Karl Wallace, 595–616. New York: Appleton-Century-Crofts, 1954.

Kramer, Dale. *Chicago Renaissance: The Literary Life in the Midwest 1900–1930.* New York: Appleton-Century, 1966.

Krasner, David. "The Real and the Folk: Alain Locke and African American Dramatic Theory." Talk given at the American Society for Theatre Research, San Diego, November 2001.

Kuftinec, Sonia. "Staging the City with the Good People of New Haven." *Theatre Journal* 53, no. 2 (May 2001): 197–222.

Larrabee, Ann. "'The Drama of Transformation': Settlement House Idealism and the Neighborhood Playhouse." In *Performing America: Cultural Nationalism in American Theater,* edited by Jeffrey D. Mason and J. Ellen Gainor, 123–36. Ann Arbor: University of Michigan Press, 1999.

Larson, Charles U. *Persuasion: Reception and Responsibility.* Belmont, CA: Wadworth, 1995.

Larson, Orville K. *Scene Design in the American Theatre from 1915 to 1960.* Fayetteville: University of Arkansas Press, 1989.

Laurence, Dan H., ed. *Bernard Shaw Theatrics.* Toronto: University of Toronto Press, 1995.

Lawren, Joseph, ed. *The Drama Year Book 1924.* New York: Joseph Lawren, 1924.

Lawrence, D. H. "The Dance of the Sprouting Corn." *Theatre Arts* 8, no. 7 (July 1924): 447–57.

———. "The Hopi Snake Dance," *Theatre Arts* 8, no. 12 (December 1924): 836–60.

Lay, Elizabeth. "When Witches Ride." In *Carolina Folk Plays,* edited by Fredrick Henry Koch, 3–23. New York: Henry Holt, 1922.

Lea, James. "Sinclair Lewis and the Implied America." In *Critical Essays on Sinclair Lewis,* edited by Martin Bucco, 184–96. Boston: G. K. Hall, 1986.

Leach, William. *Land of Desire: Merchants, Power, and the Rise of a New American Culture.* New York: Vintage, 1994.

Lears, T. J. Jackson. "From Salvation to Self-Realization: Advertising and the Therapeutic Roots of the Consumer Culture, 1880–1930." In *The Culture of Consumption,* edited by Richard Wightman Fox and T. J. Jackson Lears, 1–38. New York: Pantheon, 1983.

———. *No Place of Grace: Antimodernism and the Transformation of American Culture, 1880–1920.* 1983. Reprint, Chicago: University of Chicago Press, 1994.

Lemons, J. Stanley. *The Woman Citizen: Social Feminism in the 1920s.* Urbana: University of Illinois Press, 1973.

Leonard, William Ellery. "Glory of the Morning." In *Wisconsin Plays,* edited by Thomas H. Dickinson. New York: B. W. Huebsch, 1920.

Levine, Lawrence W. *Highbrow/Lowbrow: The Emergence of Cultural Hierarchy in America.* Cambridge: Harvard University Press, 1988.

Levinson, Andre. "The Spirit of the Classic Dance." *Theatre Arts* 9, no. 3 (March 1925): 165–77.

Lewis, Nell Battle. "Carolina Playmakers Form an Oasis in Our Artistic Desert." *Raleigh News and Observer,* 11 February 1923.

Lewis, Sinclair. *Main Street.* 1920. Reprinted with an afterword by Mark Schorer, New York: New American Library, 1961.

———. "Main Street's Been Paved." *The Nation* 119 (10 September 1924): 255–60. Reprinted in *The Plastic Age (1917–1930),* edited by Robert Sklar. New York: G. Braziller, 1970.

Lippmann, Walter. *Public Opinion.* 1922. Reprinted with a foreword by Ronald Steel, New York: Simon and Schuster, 1997.

Lipscomb, A. A. "Uses of Shakespeare Off the Stage." *Harper's New Monthly Magazine* 65 (June–November 1882): 431–38.

Lisker, Donna Eileen. "Realist Feminisms, Feminist Realisms: Six Twentieth-Century American Playwrights. PhD diss., University of Wisconsin-Madison, 1996.

Little, Stuart W. *After the Fact: Conflict and Consensus: A Report on the First American Congress of Theatre.* New York: ARNO, 1975.

Lock, Charles. "Maurice Browne and the Chicago Little Theatre." *Modern Drama* 31, no. 1 (March 1988): 106–16.

Locke, Alain. "The Drama of Negro Life." *Theatre Arts* 10, no. 10 (October 1926): 701–6.

———. "The Legacy of the Ancestral Arts." In *The New Negro,* edited by Alain Locke, 254–67. 1925. Reprinted with an introduction by Arnold Rampersad, New York: Macmillan, 1992.

———. "The Negro and the American Stage." *Theatre Arts* 10, no. 2 (February 1926): 112–20.

———, ed. *The New Negro.* 1925. Reprinted with an introduction by Arnold Rampersad, New York: Macmillan, 1992.

———. "Steps Toward the Negro Theatre." *Crisis* 25, no. 2 (December 1922): 66–68.

London, Todd. *The Artistic Home: Discussions with Artistic Directors of America's Institutional Theatres.* New York: Theatre Communications Group, 1988.

Lott, Eric. *Love and Theft: Blackface Minstrelsy and the American Working Class.* New York: Oxford University Press, 1993.

Lynd, Robert S., and Helen Merrell Lynd. *Middletown: A Study in Modern American Culture.* 1929. Reprint, New York: Harcourt Brace Jovanovich, 1956.

Mabie, E. C. "Opportunities for Service in Departments of Speech." *The Quarterly Journal of Speech Education* 6, no. 1 (February 1920): 1–7.

———. "The Responses of Theatre Audiences, Experimental Studies." *Speech Monographs* 19, no. 4 (November 1952): 235–43.

Macadams, William. *Ben Hecht, A Biography.* New York: Scribner's 1988.

Macgowan, Kenneth. *Footlights Across America: Towards a National Theatre.* New York: Harcourt, Brace, 1929.

———. *The Theatre of Tomorrow.* New York: Boni and Liveright, 1921.

Mackay, Constance D'Arcy. *The Little Theatre in the United States.* New York: Henry Holt, 1917.

Mackay, Eunice. "The Drama in the High School." In *The English Forum* (The Official Organ of the North Carolina Council of Teachers of English) 2, nos. 1–4 (May 1925): n. pag.

Maddock, Mary Denise. "Private Scripts, Public Roles: American Women's Drama, 1900–1937." PhD diss., Indiana University.

Marquis, Alice Goldfarb. *Art Lessons: Learning from the Rise and Fall of Public Arts Funding.* New York: Basic Books, 1995.

Matthews, Brander. "The English Language: Its Debt to King Alfred." *Harper's Monthly Magazine* 103 (June 1901): 141–45.

May, Henry. *The End of American Innocence: A Study of the First Years of Our Own Time 1912–1917.* 1959. Reprint, New York: Columbia University Press, 1992.

McArthur, Benjamin. *Actors and American Culture, 1880–1920.* Philadelphia: Temple University Press, 1994.

McBane, Ralph. "Establishing the Endowed Theatre." *Players Magazine* 5, no. 2 (January 1929): 3.

McCandless, Stanley Russell. "The Baker Map." *Theatre Arts* 9, no. 2 (February 1925): 106.

McClellan, B. Edward, and William J. Reese, eds. *The Social History of American Education.* Urbana: University of Illinois Press, 1988.

McConachie, Bruce. *Melodramatic Formations: American Theatre and Society, 1820–1870.* Iowa City: University of Iowa Press, 1992.

———. "Pacifying American Theatrical Audiences, 1820–1900." In *For Fun and Profit: The Transformation of Leisure into Consumption,* edited by Richard Butsch, 47–70. Philadelphia: Temple University Press, 1990.

McConachie, Bruce, and Daniel Friedman, eds. *Theatre for Working Class Audiences in the United States, 1830–1980.* Westport, CT: Greenwood, 1985.

McDermott, Douglas. "The Theatre and Its Audience." In *The American Stage: Social and Economic Issues from the Colonial Period to the Present,* edited by Ron Engle and Tice L. Miller, 6–17. New York: Cambridge University Press, 1993.

McGovern, Charles. "Only in America: Race, Ethnicity, and the Making of Popular American Music." Talk given at the College of William and Mary, 6 February 2002.

McNamara, Brooks. *The Shuberts of Broadway.* New York: Oxford University Press, 1990.

Mersand, Joseph. "The Woman in the Audience Grows Up: A Study of the Contribution of Female Audiences to American Drama." Unpaginated manuscript. New York Public Library for the Performing Arts Billy Rose Collection, 1937.

Mester, Terri A. *Movement and Modernism: Yeats, Eliot, Lawrence, Williams, and Early Twentieth-Century Dance.* Fayetteville, University of Arkansas Press, 1997.

Metcalfe, James S. "Is the Theatre Worth While?" *Atlantic* 96 (December 1905): 728–34.

Meyer, Annie Nathan. "The Vanishing Actor and After." *Atlantic* 113 (January 1914): 87–96.

Michaels, Walter Benn. "American Modernism and the Poetics of Identity." *Modernism/Modernity* 1, no. 1 (1994): 38–56.

Mickel, Jere. *Footlights on the Prairie: The Story of the Repertory Tent Players in the Midwest*. St. Cloud, MN: North Star, 1974.

Miles, Carlton. "Main Street Comes to Broadway: The People Who Keep New York's Theatres Going—What They Want and What They Get." *Theatre* 37, no. 267 (June 1923): 22, 70.

Miller, William D. *Pretty Bubbles in the Air: America in 1919*. Urbana: University of Illinois Press, 1991.

Mitchell, Loften. *Black Drama: The Story of the American Negro in the Theatre*. New York: Hawthorn, 1967.

Moderwell, Hiram Kelly. *The Theatre of To-Day*. New York: John Lane, 1914.

Morrisson, Mark S. *The Public Face of Modernism: Little Magazines, Audiences, and Reception 1905–1920*. Madison: University of Wisconsin Press, 2001.

Moses, Montrose J. "The Disintegration of the Theatre." *Forum* 45 (April 1911): 465–71.

Mott, Frank Luther. *A History of American Magazines*. Cambridge: Harvard University Press, 1957.

Mumford, Claire Dana. "A New Master and the Audience." *Theatre Arts* 2, no. 2 (February 1918): 67–74.

Nasaw, David. *Schooled to Order: A Social History of Public Schooling in the United States*. New York: Oxford University Press, 1979.

National Endowment for the Arts. *The Arts in America*. Washington, DC, 1988.

"Native Theatre Dream of Professor at University: Carolina Playmaker Idea Rapidly Expanding to Other States." *Raleigh News and Observer*, 11 August 1924.

Newcomer, Mabel. *A Century of Higher Education for American Women*. Washington, D.C.: Zenger, 1959.

Newlin, Keith, ed. *American Plays of the New Woman*. Chicago: Ivan R. Dee, 2000.

Newman, Danny. *Subscribe Now! Building Arts Audiences Through Dynamic Subscription Promotion*. New York: Theatre Communications Group, 1977.

Nichols, Dorothy E. "The Playgoers' Paradise: Theatre of the Future as Visioned by a Broadway Theatregoer." *Theatre* 44, no. 308 (November 1926): 30.

Ohmann, Richard. *Selling Culture: Magazines, Markets, and Class at the Turn of the Century*. London: Verso, 1996.

"Oriental and Western Acting." *Theatre Arts* 1, no. 4 (August 1917): 177.

Ornish, Natalie. *Pioneer Jewish Texans: Their Impact on Texas and American History for Four Hundred Years 1590–1990*. Dallas: Texas Heritage Press, 1989.

Painter, Nell Irvin. *Standing at Armageddon: The United States 1877–1919*. New York: Norton, 1987.

Palmer, A. M. "Why Theatrical Managers Reject Plays." *Forum*, July 1893: 614–20.

Pasquier, Marie-Claire. "Women in the Theatre of Men: What Price Freedom?" In *Women in Culture and Politics: A Century of Change*, edited by Judith Friedlander, Blanche Wiesen Cook, Alice Kessler-Harris, and Carroll Smith-Rosenberg, 194–206. Bloomington: Indiana University Press, 1986.

Patterson, Ada. "A Toy Theatre to Be Managed by Two Girls." *Theatre* 17, no. 148 (June 1913): 168.

Pavis, Patrice. Introduction to *The Intercultural Performance Reader*. New York: Routledge, 1996.

Payne, Darwin. *Dallas: An Illustrated History*. Woodland Hills, CA: Windsor, 1982.

Peacock, Ann. "The Critic and the Public." *Theatre* 14, no. 125 (July 1911): 8–10.

Pearce, Howard D. "Transcending the Folk: Paul Green's Utilization of Folk Materials." *Mosaic* 5 (Summer 1971): 91–106.

Pelham, Laura Dainty. "The Story of the Hull-House Players," *Drama Magazine*, May 1916, 250.

Pennington, Nancy. "A People's Theater? Folk-Playmaking at the University of North Carolina, Chapel Hill, 1918–1944." MA thesis, University of North Carolina at Chapel Hill, 1992.

Perlmann, Joel, and Robert A. Margo. *Women's Work? American Schoolteachers, 1650–1920*. Chicago: University of Chicago Press, 2001.

Perry, Clarence Arthur. *The Work of the Little Theatres: The Troups They Include, the Plays They Produce, Their Tournaments, and the Handbooks They Use*. New York: Russell Sage Foundation, 1933.

Peters, Rollo. "The Newest Art." *Theatre Arts* 2, no. 3 (Summer 1918): 119–30.

Pierce, L. France. "Big Metropolitan Theatre Directed by a Woman." *Theatre* 7, no. 74 (April 1907): 92–93.

"Players of Texas Come Back Strong." Review of "The No 'Count Boy" as performed by the Dallas Little Theatre. *New York World*, 7 May 1925.

Plummer, Ethel. "All Sorts and Conditions in New York Audiences." *Theatre* 42, no. 294 (September 1925): 11.

Poggi, Jack. *Theater in America: The Impact of Economic Forces 1870–1967*. Ithaca: Cornell University Press, 1968.

Postlewait, Thomas. "The Hieroglyphic Stage: American Theatre and Society, Post–Civil War to 1945." In *The Cambridge History of American Theatre*. Vol. 2, *1870–1945*, edited by Don B. Wilmeth and Christopher Bigsby, 107–95. New York: Cambridge University Press, 1999.

Potts, Helen Jo. "A Study of the Little Theatre of Dallas: 1920–1943." MA thesis, Southern Methodist University, 1968.

"Prize Play to Be Given This Week." *Dallas Morning News*, 24 May 1925, 7.

"Producer of New York May Give Folk Plays." *New York Daily News*, 30 December 1922.

Radway, Janice. *Reading the Romance: Women, Patriarchy, and Popular Literature*. Chapel Hill: University of North Carolina Press, 1984.

Ranck, Edwin Carty. "What Is a Good Play?" *Theatre* 30, no. 221 (July 1919): 24–25.

Rapp, Rayna, and Ellen Ross. "The 1920s: Feminism, Consumerism, and Political Backlash in the United States." In *Women in Culture and Politics: A Century of Change,* edited by Judith Friedlander, Blanche Wiesen Cook, Alice Kessler-Harris, and Carroll Smith-Rosenberg, 52–61. Bloomington: Indiana University Press, 1988.

Rauh, Stanley. "Diary of a Ticket Speculator," *Theatre* 42, no. 292 (July 1925): 24.

Rich, J. Dennis. "Art Theatre in Hull-House." In *Women in American Theatre,* edited by Helen Crich Chinoy and Linda Walsh Jenkins, 197–203. New York: Crown, 1981.

Riis, Jacob A. *How the Other Half Lives: Studies Among the Tenements of New York.* 1890. Edited by Sam Bass Warner Jr. Cambridge: Harvard University Press, 1970.

Roach, Joseph. "Imagined Communities: Nature, Culture, and Audience Restaged." *Nineteenth Century Theatre* 21, no. 1 (Summer 1993): 41–49.

Rock, Paul. "News as Eternal Recurrence." In *The Manufacture of News,* edited by Stanley Cohen and Jock Youngs, 73–80. Beverly Hills: Sage, 1981.

Rogers, John William. "Looking Backward 1941 [*sic*]." In program for *The Torchbearers,* presented by the Dallas Little Theatre, May 1931.

———. *The Lusty Texans of Dallas.* New York: E. P. Dutton, 1951.

———. Review of *Camille.* Dallas Little Theatre. *Daily Times Herald,* 25 November 1930.

———. Review of *The Constant Wife.* Dallas Little Theatre. *Daily Times Herald,* 19 February 1931.

———. Review of *The Tragedy of Nan.* Dallas Little Theatre. *Daily Times Herald,* 20 January 1925, sec. 2: 12.

Ross, Janice. *Margaret H'Doubler and the Beginning of Dance in American Education.* Madison: University of Wisconsin Press, 2000.

Rudnick, Lois. "The New Woman." In *1915, the Cultural Moment: The New Politics, the New Woman, the New Psychology, the New Art, and the New Theatre in America,* edited by Adele Heller and Lois Rudnick, 69–81. New Brunswick: Rutgers University Press, 1991.

Rury, John L. "Vocationalism for Home and Work: Women's Education in the United States, 1880–1930." In *The Social History of American Education,* edited by B. Edward McClellan and William J. Reese, 233–56. Urbana: University of Illinois Press, 1988.

Sarlós, Robert Károly. *Jig Cook and the Provincetown Players: Theatre in Ferment.* Amherst: University of Massachusetts Press, 1982.

Savage, Courtenay. "A Woman of No Imagination." *Theatre* 30, no. 224 (October 1919): 226+.

Sawyer, Charles Pike. "The Mirror." *New York Evening Post,* 17 May 1923.

Schudson, Michael. *Discovering the News: A Social History of American Newspapers.* New York: Basic Books: 1978.

Schuyler, George S. "The Negro-Art Hokum." *The Nation* 121, no. 3180 (16 June 1926): 662–63.

Schwartz, Tony. *The Responsive Chord.* New York: Anchor/Doubleday, 1974.

Scott, Anne Firor. *Natural Allies: Women's Associations in American History.* Urbana: University of Illinois Press, 1991.

Scott, Bonnie Kime. Introduction to *The Gender of Modernism: A Critical Anthology.* Bloomington: Indiana University Press, 1990.

Seller, Maxine Schwartz, ed. *Ethnic Theatre in the United States.* Westport, CT: Greenwood, 1983.

Shapiro, James. *Oberammergau: The Troubling Story of the World's Most Famous Passion Play.* New York: Pantheon, 2000.

Shaw, George Bernard. Letter to Beulah Jay, 17 November 1917. In *Bernard Shaw Theatrics,* edited by Dan H. Laurence. Toronto: University of Toronto Press, 1995.

Shipp, E. R. Obituary of Sheldon Cheney. *New York Times,* 14 October 1980, B23.

Simonson, Harold P. *Zona Gale.* New York: Twayne, 1962.

Singal, Daniel Joseph. "Towards a Definition of American Modernism." *American Quarterly* 39, no. 1 (Spring 1987): 7–26.

Smiley, Jane. "All-American Iconoclast." Review of *Sinclair Lewis: Rebel from Main Street* by Richard Lingeman. In *The New York Times Book Review,* 20 January 2002, 10.

Smith, Susan Harris. *American Drama: The Bastard Art.* New York: Cambridge University Press, 1997.

Smith-Rosenberg, Carroll. *Disorderly Conduct: Visions of Gender in Victorian America.* New York: Knopf, 1985.

"Sock and Buskin on Rural Stages." *New York Times Book Review,* 4 February 1923.

Sollors, Werner. *Beyond Ethnicity: Consent and Descent in American Culture.* New York: Oxford University Press, 1986.

———. "A Critique of Pure Pluralism." In *Reconstructing American Literary History,* edited by Sacvan Bercovitch, 250–79. Cambridge: Harvard University Press, 1986.

Sonnega, William. "Beyond a Liberal Audience." In *African American Performance and Theater History,* edited by Harry J. Elam Jr. and David Krasner, 81–98. New York: Oxford University Press, 2001.

"Sophocles' Antigone." *Boston Advertiser,* 1890. Clipping Files, Harvard Theatre Collection. Undated.

"Sophocles' 'Antigone,'" *Boston Transcript,* 13 March 1890.

"Spinster Takes Issue with Dr. Crane, Says It Is Wives Who Are Turtles." *Chicago Daily News,* 14 January 1947.

Stansell, Christine. *American Moderns: Bohemian New York and the Creation of a New Century.* New York: Henry Holt, 2000.

St. Denis, Ruth. "The Dance as an Art Form." *Theatre Arts* 1, no. 1 (November 1916): 75–77.

Stengel, Hans. "The Box Office Angle: What the Public Wants Revealed by Hans Stengel, Who Went to the Play to Review the Audience." *Theatre* 39, no. 275 (February 1924): 13.

Stevenson, Elizabeth. *Babbitts and Bohemians: The American 1920s.* New York: Macmillan, 1967.

Strachey, Lionel. "Theatricitis." *Theatre* 4, no. 142 (1904): 224.

Stratman, Carl. *American Theatrical Periodicals, 1798–1967—A Bibliographic Guide.* Durham: Duke University Press, 1970.

Strindberg, August. Preface to *Miss Julie*. In *The Modern Theatre*, edited by Robert W. Corrigan, 420–26. New York: Macmillan, 1964.

Strychacz, Thomas. *Modernism, Mass Culture, and Professionalism.* New York: Cambridge University Press, 1993.

Sullivan, Victoria, and James Hatch, eds. *Plays by and about Women.* New York: Random House, 1974.

Susman, Warren I. "Culture and Civilization: The Nineteen-Twenties." In *Culture as History: The Transformation of American Society in the Twentieth Century,* 105–21. New York: Pantheon Books, 1984.

Tancheva, Kornelia. "'I Do Not Participate in Liberations': Female Dramatic and Theatrical Modernism in the 1910s and 1920s." In *Unmanning Modernism: Gendered Re-Readings,* edited by Elizabeth Jane Harrison and Shirley Peterson, 153–67. Knoxville: University of Tennessee Press, 1997.

Taylor, Gary. *Reinventing Shakespeare.* New York: Weidenfeld and Nicolson, 1989.

Tebbel, John, and Mary Ellen Zuckerman. *The Magazine in America 1741–1990.* New York: Oxford University Press, 1991.

Temple, Lura. "The Dallas Little Theatre: A History (1920–1927)." MA thesis, Southern Methodist University, 1927.

Ten Broeck, Helen. "Motherhood and Art." *Theatre* 24, no. 190 (December 1916): 372.

Thompson, Sister M. Francesca. "The Lafayette Players, 1915–1932." In *The Theatre of Black Americans,* edited by Errol Hill, 211–30. New York: Applause Theatre Books, 1987.

Tickner, Lisa. "Men's Work? Masculinity and Modernism." *Differences* 4, no. 3 (1992): 1–37.

Tingley, Donald F. "Ellen Van Volkenburg, Maurice Browne and the Chicago Little Theatre." *Illinois Historical Journal* 80 (Autumn 1987): 132.

Tommasini, Anthony. "All-Black Casts for 'Porgy'? That Ain't Necessarily So." *New York Times,* 20 March 2002, sec. B: 1, 2.

Touton, Harriet Louise. "The Theatre Audience." *Sociology and Social Research* 19, no. 4 (July–August 1934): 554–64.

Trachtenberg, Alan. *The Incorporation of America: Culture and Society in the Gilded Age.* New York: Hill and Wang, 1982.

Trotter, Mary. *Ireland's National Theaters: Political Performance and the Origins of the Irish Dramatic Movement.* Syracuse: Syracuse University Press, 2001.

Twentieth Century Club. Drama Committee. "The Amusement Situation in the City of Boston. Based on a Study of Theatres for Ten Weeks from November 28, 1909, to February 5, 1910." Boston, 1910. New York Public Library, Lincoln Center.

Tyack, David B. "Pilgrim's Progress: Toward a Social History of the School Superintendency, 1860–1960." In *The Social History of American Education,* edited by B. Edward McClellan and William J. Reese, 165–208. Urbana: University of Illinois Press, 1988.

Van Vechten, Carl. *Nigger Heaven.* 1926. Reprinted with an introduction by Kathleen Pfeiffer, Urbana: University of Illinois Press, 2000.

Veblen, Thorstein. *The Theory of the Leisure Class: An Economic Study of Institutions.* New York: Macmillan, 1912.

Wagner-Martin, Linda, and Cathy N. Davidson, eds. *The Oxford Book of Women's Writing in the United States.* New York: Oxford University Press, 1995.

Wainscott, Ronald H. *The Emergence of the Modern American Theater 1914–1929.* New Haven, Yale University Press, 1997.

Warfield, David. "The Theatre Nuisance." Unsourced clipping (probably 1913). Robinson Locke scrapbook #478. New York Public Library for the Performing Arts Billy Rose Collection.

Washington Square Plays. New York: Doubleday, Page, 1916.

Watson, Steven. *Strange Bedfellows: The First American Avant-Garde.* New York: Abbeville, 1991.

Weber, Bruce. "The Harvard Class of '00." *New York Times Magazine,* 28 April 1996, 44+.

Welter, Barbara. "The Cult of True Womanhood: 1820–1860," *American Quarterly* 18 (Summer 1966): 151–74.

"What We Stand For," *Theatre Arts* 1, no. 4 (August 1917): unpaginated page following inside cover.

Wickham, Glynne. *A History of the Theatre,* 2d ed. London: Phaidon, 1994.

Wiebe, Robert. *The Search for Order 1877–1920.* New York: Hill and Wang, 1967.

Wiley, Eric. "Hellenism and the Independent Theatre Movement in America." PhD diss., Louisiana State University, 1999.

Williams, Raymond. *The Politics of Modernism.* London: Verso, 1989.

Wilson, Christopher. "The Rhetoric of Consumption: Mass-Market Magazines and the Demise of the Gentle Reader, 1880–1920." In *The Culture of Consumption,* edited by Richard Wightman Fox and T. J. Jackson Lears, 39–64. New York, Pantheon, 1983.

Winegarten, Ruthe, and Kathy Schechter. *Deep in the Heart: The Lives and Legends of Texas Jews, a Photographic History.* Austin: Eakin, 1990.

Worm, A. Toxen. "Good Ladies Drama League the New Menace to American Stage." *New York Review,* 28 May 1910.

Worthen, W. B. *Modern Drama and the Rhetoric of Theater.* Berkeley: University of California Press, 1992.

Wright, Lin. "Creative Drama: Sex Role Stereotyping?" In *Women in American Theatre,* edited by Helen Krich Chinoy and Linda Walsh Jenkins, 266–73. New York: Crown, 1981.

Zilboorg, Gregory. "The Intelligentia [*sic*] and the Street." *Drama* 11 (May 1921): 276, 295.

Zolotow, Sam. "Publication Ends for Theater [*sic*] Arts." *New York Times,* 2 June 1964.

Index

Abbey Theatre, 39–40, 60, 194, 205–7
Abbott, George, 98
abstraction, 26, 28
actors: African American, 52, 90, 179, 204, 214–15; American Indian, 90–91; ethical effect on, 197–98; training, 112
Actors and American Culture, 1880–1920 (McArthur), 231n22
actresses, 111–12, 117–18, 152, 154–55, 192
Addams, Jane, 5, 56–59, 182
Adding Machine, The (Rice), 11, 94
African Americans, 51–52, 187, 233n68; actors, 90, 179, 204, 214–15; as assimilated Americans, 203–5; Little Theatre groups, 52, 194, 252n88; plays, 202–3
Agassiz Theatre, 99
Age of Innocence (Wharton), 126
"Aims and Methods of Dramatic Work in Secondary Schools" (Robb), 161
Akins, Zoe, 167, 168
Albee, Edward, 229–30n95
Aldis, Arthur, 178–79
Aldis, Mary, 178
Allen, Maud, 26
amateur ideal, 43–46
American Academy of Dramatic Art, 231n22
American Educational Theatre Association (A.E.T.A.), 157, 163, 166

American Impressionism and Realism, 225n7
American Indians, 15–16, 28, 66, 90–91
American Laboratory Theatre, 87
American Plays of the New Woman, 164–65
American Playwright, 83
American Repertory Theatre, 219
American Theatre, 12
American Theatre, 83
Ames, Winthrop, 98
Anderson, Benedict, 10
Anderson, Margaret, 18, 242n26
Anglim, Margaret, 246n27
Anglosaxondom, 48, 50–52
Antigone, 44, 232n44
antimodernism, 22, 210, 229n83
Appia, Adolphe, 4, 72, 75, 77
Aristotle, 36
Arlington (MA) Friends of the Drama (AFD), 215–18, 221
Arlington Woman's Club, 215
Armory Show, 18, 20
Arnold, Matthew, 38
Aronson, Howard, 190
"Art and Business" (Helburn), 93
art museums, 35, 230n1
Arts and Crafts movement, 47
Arts Club (Chicago), 179–80
Arvold, Alfred, 11, 64–66, 139, 235n107

279

French, Samuel, 192
Frick, John, 226n16
Friedan, Betty, 183
Frierson, Anne, 179
Frohman, Charles, 107, 240n2
Frohman, Daniel, 107, 240n2
Frohman office, 107, 240n2

Gainor, J. Ellen, 13–14, 226n15, 234n102, 242n26, 247n50
Gale, Jane Winsor (Mrs. Lyman), 46–47, 167
Gale, Zona, 6, 23, 35, 86, 90, 167, 168
Galsworthy, John, 41, 62
"Game, The" (Bryant), 26–27
Garrick Theatre, 169
Garrison, Lydia, 103–6
Gates, Eleanor, 174–75
Gates, Henry Lewis, Jr., 219
Geddes, Norman-Bel, 87
General Federation of Women's Clubs, 142
German Jewish immigrants, 62
Germans, 66–67
German theatre, 33–34, 72–73
Gerstenberg, Alice, 74–75, 117, 151, 164–85; art/community divide and, 180, 184–85; audience and, 169, 177–80; Chicago arts supporters and, 177–78; children's theatre and, 167, 169, 180–81; critiques of, 166–67, 172; feminist critique in plays of, 165–66, 170, 173–74, 183–84; ideas about domesticity, 181–83; novels, 154, 164, 170, 173; one-act plays, 164, 170, 180, 243n54; personal characteristics of, 167–68; portrayal of men, 175–77; and realism, 174–75; social privileges of, 167–69; split subject in works of, 170–72, 174; views on aging, 183–84; Works: Alice in Wonderland, 117, 181; "At the Club," 175–76; "Attuned," 243n54; "The Buffer," 174–75; The Conscience of Sarah Platt, 173–74; "Ever Young," 183; Got Your Number, 177; "Hearts," 175; The Hourglass, 184; "Illuminatti in Drama Libre," 174; A Little World, 169; "Mere

Man," 175; "Overtones," 117, 164, 170, 171–72, 174; Ten One-Act Plays, 170; Time for Living, 184; Unquenched Fire, 154, 164, 170–71; "The Unseen," 176–77; The Water Babies, 181
Gerstenberg, Julia, 169, 170
Gillmore, Inez Haynes, 21
Gilpin, Charles, 204, 214
Glaspell, Susan, 7, 13–14, 21–22, 35, 62, 167, 242n26, 247n50; Alison's House, 168; "Suppressed Desires," 23; "Trifles," 6, 164
Glassberg, David, 235n109
"Glory of the Morning," 16
Goldman, Emma, 168
Good Gracious Annabelle, 86
Good Person of New Haven, The, 220
Good Person of Szechuan, The, 220
Goose Hangs High, The (Beach), 160
Gordon, Lynn D., 243n58
Gorelik, Mordecai, 87
Gorky, Maxim, 92
Graham, Edward Kidder, 198–99
Grana, Cesar, 20–21
Grant, Madison, 51
Greek theatre, 41–42, 44, 87, 231n32, 231n35
Green, Paul, 7, 252n99; background, 210–12; In Abraham's Bosom, 11, 179, 186; "Rassie," 211. See also "No 'Count Boy, The"
Greenwich Village, 20, 22, 26–27, 93, 111, 169, 229n80, 242–43n46
Greet, Philip Ben, 79, 246n27
Gregory, Lady Augusta, 28–29, 200, 206–7
Group Theatre, 94

Hackett, Walter, 160
Halttunen, Karen, 43
Hamilton, Clayton, 91, 107, 114, 238n67
Hammack, Henry Edgar, 189
Hampton Institute, 214
Hapgood, Emilie, 31, 46
Hapgood, Hutchins, 31, 35, 98, 226n29
Hapgood, Norman, 31, 66, 98

Dorothy Chansky is an assistant professor of theatre at the College of William and Mary, where she teaches theatre history, theory, criticism, and feminist theatre. She has served as the book review editor of *Theatre Journal* and the education editor of *InTheater* magazine. She was the 1999 winner of the Amy and Eric Burger Theater Essay Prize for "Memory, Manhood, Management, and 'Mentalities': *The C.C.C. Murder Mystery* and Its Audience."

Theater in the Americas

The goal of the series is to publish a wide range of scholarship on theater and performance, defining theater in its broadest terms and including subjects that encompass all of the Americas.

The series focuses on the performance and production of theater and theater artists and practitioners but welcomes studies of dramatic literature as well. Meant to be inclusive, the series invites studies of traditional, experimental, and ethnic forms of theater; celebrations, festivals, and rituals that perform culture; and acts of civil disobedience that are performative in nature. We publish studies of theater and performance activities of all cultural groups within the Americas, including biographies of individuals, histories of theater companies, studies of cultural traditions, and collections of plays.